ROCK SOLID

A Novel By

Paul Slatter

TNCS - Publishing Edition

Copyright – 2017 by Paul Slatter – 1103027 B.C. Ltd.

ISBN: 978-1973866299

First Trade Edition:

1103027 B.C. Ltd.

Also by Paul Slatter

Burn

Trust Me

For

SunSun

Amicus meus

The Vancouver Series

Book Two:

Rock Solid

Chapter One

Paawan Gill woke to the early morning sun on his face, looked up through the camouflaged netting, and saw its first rays high in the morning sky lining the clouds with gold. He breathed in the fresh morning air blowing in untouched from the vast sea that lay before him as he floated. And as the unmistakeable smell of rubber hit his face from the small holes in the inner tube wrapped firmly around his chest, he stretched his lips, pulling at the tape that silenced his screams as the dark waters of the riptide swept him towards the beautiful inlets at the southern end of the Strait of Georgia.

Paawan held out his hands, fighting the current, and desperately trying to steer his body towards the security of land as a torrent of water pulled him further away from the sanctuary of the tree-lined shore and out towards the open ocean.

How he had ended up here, fighting for his life inside a rubber tire hidden away from any thin chance at salvation by cheap netting better used for hunting ducks, he didn't know. But here he was, frantically clinging to life, his turban gone, his black hair out in the open, the water splashing his face, its salt stinging his eyes, his feet wrapped in chains.

Only hours before, he'd been kissing her, her soft lips against his as she writhed beneath him, their tongues entwined—their silence beautiful after as they'd rested. He'd stroked her. Marvelled at the softness of her skin. As he'd laid in the dark, he'd wondered how many years he'd been away, as though feeling all at once the time that had gone before'—time he'd wasted and lost without her touch, time he could have spent loving her instead of living life on a razor's edge. Instead, he'd flown, he'd lived for the rushing air beneath his arms, swooping like a bird, fuelled only by courage as

1

he tempted fate with the strange madness only a few men have it in them to do. But as he'd laid there with her in the darkness, listening to her breath, feeling her clasped hands wrapping his body, he'd known that those wasted years would soon be forgotten. She'd missed him as he'd missed her. She was his again, and this time, without a word, they both knew it was to be forever.

******

Charles Chuck Chendrill sat on the train and thought back to the Russian he'd found earlier in the day and wondered if he could find a new matching plate set for the aging Englishman who liked to employ his services and paid well.

The Russian was gone, but he could still feel the burn on his stomach and the jarring of the train in his broken ribs as it pulled and pushed its way along the tracks, driven by binary code. *What a week it had been.* Now he just needed the plate set and he could go relax until someone else called worrying about something that would probably mean nothing in the grand scheme of things.

He leaned back and watched a group of Asian girls, who, from what Chendrill could tell by their shape, could only be dancers. The girls standing there giggling at the sight of a guy on a poster posing in his silver underpants. He smiled. He was getting to know that kid in the poster well now—and his mother even better. As crazy as he was, the kid was alright, a real character at least. He was the kind of guy who could steal your car and make you feel guilty for not asking him if he wanted to borrow it.

But that shit wouldn't last long with Chendrill. Once yeah, it had happened, but the second time the kid wouldn't just be back on the bus, which Chendrill had been making him take to preserve his normality, despite his unexpected fame. After all, he had been employed on full rate plus a Ferrari to keep an eye on the wonder kid, this up-and-coming international sensation who lived in the basement room at his mother's house. And so far, it had been well worth it.

Chendrill was a private investigator who once had been a cop and worked in the city he grew up in and loved. A guy with his own style who could make it happen, solve your problem, or simply tell you to go fuck yourself in his own Machiavellian way, should you be so deserving.

Pulling out his phone, he called Williams, the kid who showed promise as a police detective, but needed the years to fall behind him before anyone would take him seriously. Ditcon was there, Williams said, and so was the Russian, laying on the floor, and so were the press—outside on the sidewalk with Ditcon as he gave interviews and took the credit for having solved a case he never would have gotten close to had Chendrill not stepped away from his paid job babysitting the kid—who, once again, stood before him in a poster wearing silver undies that were certain to get these Asian dancing girls' minds whirling come bedtime—and put the puzzle together.

He got off the train at Granville Street and took a cab back to his apartment that overlooked the park and the people who frequented it. *Jesus my ribs hurt*, he thought. . . the guy with the baseball bat sneaking up on him like that just because Chendrill had been fucking his girl—even if she wasn't his girl any longer.

How long was this pain going to rip through him? From experience, it was at least five to six weeks of no sleep and staying away from people who made him laugh, but how was that possible when he worked for the most eccentric gay guys in town and was paid to look after a guy who had stolen their underpants?

It was going to be tough.

Tough, but not as tough as the last week had been when he'd nearly been burned alive for trying to fix something he knew the people in charge would let slip through the cracks. But as he lay down on his soft comfy bed and closed his eyes for a moment, knowing he still had to go find a matching plate set, little did he know that what had just occurred was nothing compared to what was coming.

******

About an hour later, he was woken up by the guy who kept food on the table and, at least for the moment, a Ferrari in the garage, and Chendrill told him straight, "If it's about the plate, then you need to give me time."

And as he lay there in pain, he heard Sebastian's worry nearly break the phone in his hand, "It's an emergency, Chuck. If it's not here at seven, I'll look like a fool."

And he would, there was no doubt about it, Chendrill thought, as he began to try and ease himself off the bed, having people over for dinner and someone having to sit there with an odd plate in front of them—my God!

Chendrill sat back up and walked to the bathroom—his abdomen still sore. Was it worth it, he thought, sticking his nose in like he had, chasing the Russian down and nearly being burned to death in the process? He had done it for the sake of his old friend Daltrey, so it had been—this was certain.

Chapter Two

Rann Singh stood in the bright and clean washrooms at the Surrey Center Mall, staring at himself while he fixed his purple turban in the long mirror above the sinks.

A purple turban, pink top, and brown shoes with no socks were the way to go. He'd got the call from the girl who worked as a cleaner and told her he'd pay her the $500 she wanted for the photos, as long as they were the only ones.

"They are—I promise," she'd said. They'd agreed to meet and Rann had wondered who this girl with his phone number was.

He walked out into the mall and waited next to the coffee stall and looked around. *She could be anywhere*, he thought. Then he saw her through the crowd, looking at him, her body long and skinny, her hair bleached white showing her brown roots that, undoubtedly, some of the $500 would go into repairing.

They sat down and sipped the coffees Rann had bought as she took the brown envelope from her bag and slipped it across the table to him. Opening it up, he sneaked a look inside, stared a moment, then said, "I know this guy."

"Yeah—he's rich, he sells condos downtown."

"Who's the girl?" Rann asked.

The girl with the bleached hair and white skin like an albino bunny shrugged and said, "She lived in this place I used to clean, I used to see her there sometimes. We all thought she was his mistress or something, but she's gone now."

Rann opened the package for a second look, then closed it again. The girl was beautiful, really hot, like some kind of supermodel. Then he said in his London accent, "What a fucking darling!"

"So, you going to pay me?"

Rann looked at the girl in the picture and then at what she was doing, and felt himself rising below. Looking up, he stared at the girl sitting before him. She wasn't too bad really—she had the pure white skin he liked, and she'd been looking at his turban quite a bit. Giving it a shot, he said, "Only if you let me see you again."

The girl with the skinny frame and the bleached hair shot him a look and smiled. She got asked out a lot, but this was the first time she had been asked out by an East Indian with a turban who spoke with a funny English accent.

"What makes you think you're my type?"

"Because you keep looking at my turban."

"I was wondering if my hair's longer than yours, that's all."

And cocking his head to the side, Rann Singh, from London, on the run from the Metropolitan Police, opened his wallet, peeled off the $500 in cash, and handing it over with a cheeky smile said, "Well if you sleep with me, maybe you'll find out."

******

He took the envelope and let the contents fall out onto the kitchen table of his rented apartment on the outskirts of Whalley and took a better look at them. They were a little perverse, but he'd seen and dealt with worse—in the world of a blackmailer, one saw many things. He remembered the guy for sure now, the realtor who plasters his face on the back of almost every bus ploughing its way through town.

This could be a good one, he thought, *real good*. Anyone spending that much on self-promotion would do whatever it took not to have his reputation damaged in any way. Maybe he'd even thank him in the process—after all, almost everyone had a secret, especially this guy.

Rann Singh was a blackmailer through and through. It was almost all he'd ever done for the last ten of the twenty-eight years this world had been blessed with his presence. Born on the outskirts of London near Heathrow, the only son of Sikh parents, who as children in the seventies had been asked to leave Uganda by Idi Amin after the dictator woke one morning from a dream sent to him by God, or so he claimed, and had given all the Indians, who kept the country's economy stable, ninety days to leave.

With the money they'd smuggled out in magazines and books and inside their turbans, Rann's grandparents and his father—then twelve years old—resettled in Hounslow in the suburbs west of London, buying a small three bedroom home close to Heathrow Airport and sending Rann's father off with his hair wrapped up in a hanky on the top of his head to the local primary school to be teased and mocked and called a *Paki cunt* and *wog* along with all the other Indians from Uganda who'd arrived and were not Pakistani and had never been to India.

The days turned into weeks, then months, and the kids threw stones at his grandmother dressed in her sari as she waited patiently by the school's gate. Rann's grandfather took a job as a diesel mechanic at a Ford dealership as big as the one he'd owned in Entebbe less than a year before when Amin had stolen it from him along with his home.

By the time Rann was born, his grandfather, sick of suffering chronic racism for the second time in his life, said goodbye to his son and grandchild along with the rain and the grey skies of London, packed his bags for Uganda's more stable neighbor Kenya, and returned to the Africa he loved.

Settling into an unoccupied homestead ranch he'd found

nestled securely at the foot of the Aberdare Mountains two hours north of Nairobi, he took to living alongside the arrogant and condescending white colonials residing in a country they claimed was their own, but who called him *choot* for wanting to do exactly the same.

And as the busy years passed in Hounslow on the outskirts of London with the same frequency as the lodgers who came and went from the small upstairs room Rann's father let out in the home under the flight path that Rann's grandfather had paid for with money he'd smuggled out from under a dictator's nose, Rann's father met his mother and, each with a doctorate in medicine, set up practice nearby.

Five years after Rann was born, he too headed off to school, as his father had, in his spotless blue crested blazer and shiny shoes to be called a *Paki cunt* for the first time in his life while his hanky covered hair, all neatly wrapped up in a bun, was pulled from the top of his head by the children of the men who had done the same to his parents—men who now lived on welfare with their ugly wives on the council housing estate nearby, who worked low-income jobs, and who would sometimes sit before Rann's parents in their new surgery, in their dirty shoes, on National Health Service coin, telling Rann's father their woes—usually depression, fuelled by self-inflicted obesity or alcoholism. These were men living in denial that they'd gone nowhere with their lives, struggling to face these dim facts as Rann's parents listened patiently, while their own kids, destined for the same, bullied their doctor's son at school. Spitting on him in the playground, bashing his bun, just as they had done themselves to the decent man they now came to seeking solace—though they didn't know it. "Go black home," their children had shouted to Rann, adding the 'L' to 'back' in an ignorant attempt to validate their argument—even though he had been born in the same hospital as them, and was at home. These vile, dirty, feral children without guidance, with open sores and football boots for shoes, who would still smile and say hello when Rann would see them at his father's surgery when they were sick—when they were away from the gangs that were gradually becoming smaller as the neighborhood's ratios changed.

And then one day at the tender age of twelve, as Rann sat at the front of the class listening to every word, his mother and father headed to a hospital along the Great West Road and never came home. Rann waiting at the school gate at the end of the day and later in a neighbor's home as he watched them cry, wondering why he was being kept away from school until his grandfather and grandmother arrived from Africa to tell him the bad news of how they and his Sikh god Guru Nanak would be looking after him from now on, as his parents, sadly, were never coming back.

Within a year of his mother and father's death, Rann knew every inch of the ranch his grandfather had left to come and raise his grandson. "My ranch," he'd say, unconsciously stroking his long grey beard as his turban wobbled, sitting there with his feet in sparkling, curly toed slippers up on a stool next to the blocked off fireplace.

"My ranch, I gave it up for you, Rann. Its roof was made of straw, and had a village for the help around the side. To the front was a view of the Aberdare Mountains, which rose up from the earth and pierced the blue of the heavens as the forest tried to climb its slopes, a forest deep and dense, full of wild animals. Its enormous trees started at the fields we owned, endless fields reaching all the way from the mountains to our ranch and the gardens where the women from the village bend over sweeping the grass clean with brooms made from fallen branches and strong twigs held together by twine." Rann listened daily, wondering if the smell of his grandmother's spices would ever leave his clothes and skin, and how he could get out of helping his grandfather paint the house a different shade of purple, feeling guilty, as if it was his own fault his parents were gone and his grandfather had sold his ranch and left Kenya, letting the home he loved with its view of the mountains and its women who swept the lawn go, under value, to a South African whose name, Malcolm Blou, was now a curse word in the small three bedroomed, strangely painted house under the flight path to Heathrow.

By the time he'd left school, Rann had blacked out with rage four times and blackmailed three people. The first was at the age of eleven, when he and a friend hit up his brother for smoking. Then, a year after his parents' car crash, the pair had followed their religious education teacher into the school's carpark and asked the man if he could help them, as they'd found porn stashed away in amongst the Bibles in the teacher's cupboard and were both in need of a new bicycle. After six months had passed, Rann's grandfather began to wonder why he had not returned the new bicycle he had said he'd borrowed from a friend, and asked him about it. As Rann sat crying, confessing all, and worrying he'd lose his Raleigh 10 speed, he'd heard his grandfather say, "It is okay Rann—you were helping this man, you were sent on a course from God to save him."

And the truth was, he had saved him—saved his job, saved his marriage, saved his life.

"You have saved him because the man has changed his ways," Rann's grandfather had carried on saying, "and he has paid you for this, just as the priest himself would be paid for helping and saving a man's soul."

The third came just as he was about to set foot out into the wide world looking to put his life and soul into something to gain some sense of fulfilment from his own hard work, and what he found came easily to him. It was simple—for every ten hardworking family men doing what they could in life to better themselves within the ever growing Indian and Pakistani communities, where benefit fraud was already rife, there was always one who was really trying to beat the system.

He'd answered the door one morning to a slightly officious government employee who was looking for the whereabouts of the man who rented the spare room upstairs, but never slept there. The strange man only ever showed up once a week, usually on Fridays, wearing what Rann thought looked like pajamas. And, waiting for the occasional plane to pass, Rann answered the government employee's questions as honestly as possible.

Yes, he knew this man. Yes, he lived here. Yes, he rented the small room upstairs. "No, you can't see the room, it's not my place to show you, sorry sir. No, the gentleman is not working, but I know he is looking for work every day. He is a good man, a God-fearing man."

And on and on he went.

On the following Friday when the man's check arrived, popping through the door all the way from the department of social services, Rann opened it to see he was receiving 200 pounds a week and a quick calculation told him the gentleman had pulled in over 10,000 from this address alone. When the man arrived that afternoon to get his post and pretended to pray, he'd found the check in the envelope gone and the benefit fraud officer's card in its place along with a note, which simply read,

> *God has called upon me to help you. He fears you will end up in prison. Please send me 2000 pounds upfront and then 100 a week from then on so as I can continue to carry out work for Him within our community.*

All proceeds were to be delivered to a Post office account.

And the man had paid, but not with the 2000 pounds or the 100 a week thereafter. He'd paid by giving the details of ten other fraud players working the system—with a one-thousand-pound sweetener on top.

Of these, two paid, two disappeared, and a fifth had a visit from the government fraud officer as a warning to the other five who were dragging their heels.

And that's how it all started for Rann Singh, the kid destined to follow in his parents' footsteps and become a doctor, until one fateful day his life was changed by a man asleep at the wheel, waking from a dream—just as his Ugandan-Indian parents' lives had been changed when their destiny was turned upside down by a ruthless dictator who, asleep at the wheel of his nation, woke up from a dream.

Taking his beloved grandfather's misguided advice, Rann found his own path in this world and set out upon it, slowly learning a trade which fed off people's fears and indiscretions, with little care for the hurt and suffering his actions caused the people caught in his web—and who, usually, were no worse than him—because in his grandfather's eyes, and so his too, he was helping them on their path to salvation.

Chapter Three

Patrick De'Sendro, voted the most reliable realtor in Vancouver for the fifth year running by a committee he owned and operated himself, slipped his cock back into his pants and put down the telescope, listening to the man with the London accent speaking quietly into the phone. He had been waiting with baited breath all day for a call to come in from Hong Kong about the decision on a penthouse condo. He'd also been waiting all day for the blonde across the way to come home and strip down like she did every evening before she took a shower. And when she had and he'd pulled it out, the phone had rung—typical. The call hadn't been from overseas, but the guy on the other end clearly was, though he hadn't said the words Patrick had been expecting.

"Patrick? I'm sorry to disturb you, but are you the guy on the back of the bus, the realtor?"

Still holding his crotch, Patrick answered, "Yes, I'm here to make your dreams come true, thanks for calling—how can I help?"

Then there was silence, long and embarrassing, and as Patrick was about to ask if the man with the London accent was still there, he heard him say, "I'm glad it's you, you see, because I've just discovered something that someone was going to do to you that I think may have hurt you and your business."

And hearing these words, Patrick's heart skipped a beat as he felt the sudden rise in temperature envelope his body, sending instantaneous beads of sweat to the crown of his head. He stayed silent, his brain whirling away as a host of unscrupulous real estate deals came back to life in his head. Then the man said, "There is a girl who has found photos of you and I've managed to stop her handing them over to a friend who's in your line of work. You see, for some reason, and I don't know why, she doesn't like you."

Oh my God, Patrick thought, it had to be the photos Alla had of him, the ones she used to like to tease him with after he'd been watching her making love to some stranger through his telescope, the ones she used to let him see, holding them in her hand as she stood dressed in sexy underwear in front of the full-length window of her luxury condo opposite his.

What was going to happen if any of the people he knew found out? What would he do? How could he sit down again in a corporate boardroom and broker a deal for a condo complex again? The silence he would receive as he walked into a room or an open house full of piranhas would be deafening, so he said, "We don't need that."

'We'—he was bringing the guy into it now, he thought, making it like they both had a problem. The guy with the London accent replied, "No, *we* don't. It's the reason I'm calling. I've heard through the grapevine that you're a great guy. You sold a property to one of my friends some time back and did 'im' a right favor on the deal. This is why I'm calling; I think I know a way I can stop her."

A right favor? Patrick thought, looking to the window of the apartment across the way, the girl there again, faint in the distance with her blonde hair, but the erection Patrick had had in his pants now completely gone and forgotten.

There was a couple of Brits he'd sold a place to some while back and saved them a fortune in the deal—or so they'd thought—they spoke like this guy, clipping their sentences and throwing in words he couldn't comprehend. He hadn't liked them, the way they'd treated him like a parasite, acting as though he should be giving them the commission and working for free. So, he said, "Yes, I remember Michael and his lovely wife. They're a fantastic couple—special people. Please give them my best and tell them to give me a call."

And knowing there was no chance he'd ever meet them, Rann said, "I will, you're right, they're a great couple. But sadly the girl who's got the photos, she's not so nice. It's why I'm calling."

Patrick took a deep breath. He had to get Chendrill on this quickly, he thought, knowing the photos were out there now that Daltrey was sadly no longer around to keep them safe. Then he said, "I have a private investigator looking for them—I'm glad you called, I'll get him to pop over and see you."

Then there was silence. And the Brit said, "Yeah—but it's best we don't involve a third party or the girl. . . . she'll get pissed and give those photos of you to her mate, just like that, she won't give a shit, she'll just do it. See, she said to me, she don't like you for some reason, said your teeth are too big—that's how nasty she can be. I said, no he's alright, he saved Michael and his missus a fortune."

Then Patrick said the words Rann had been waiting to hear, "Just tell her I'll make it worth her while if she just gives them back."

And Rann knew he had him right where he wanted him to be.

******

Chendrill watched Patrick cut his lemon poppy loaf into sections and pop them into his mouth. His ribs were still hurting, sending unexpected electric shocks through his torso every time he moved or tried not to laugh, but Patrick was funny, especially now as he attempted to appear coy and innocent as he said to him a second time, "Why can't people just be nice and honest?"

Because they aren't, Chendrill thought. If the world were like that he'd be out of a job, and he wondered how nice and honest Patrick was when he was selling a property. So, he said, "Everyone wants a little bit more than they can get—you know this. You've pushed the odd deal to keep commissions high I'm sure."

Patrick placed another piece of cake in his mouth and looked outside to the forty-foot poster of some naked kid stuck in an elevator with a broken nose, and, completely lying, said, "Trust me, I never have—and besides, I never actually said I'd pay this guy anything."

Chendrill stayed quiet on that one. From what he could tell, he had in a roundabout way, but getting into it with him was not worth the effort. As he looked again at Dan in the poster, Patrick said, "Strange thing was it sounded to me as if the guy was trying to do me a favor."

They always did, thought Chendrill—blackmailers were like that, never actually admitting they were doing anything wrong at all, just trying to help out.

"Yeah, they're good at that, these types of people. But don't be fooled—this fuck, whoever he is, he's still trying to put one over on you—even if he seems as though he's on your side."

"Maybe he is though; he said I'd helped his friend Michael."

Chendrill frowned and took a swig of his coffee, then laughed, and held his side. "Fuck me Patrick, you need to let it go that this guy is a saint and knows your friends—he doesn't, he just adlibbed it all once you started talking. That's what these shitheads do. Has he mentioned a dollar figure?"

Patrick shook his head.

"Well he will and as you're a rich man, you can expect it to be big."

"How big?"

"Bigger than the cost of one of your ads on the back of a bus big."

Then Patrick took a deep breath and said, "Fuck me, I don't care how much. I just want this mess gone."

And hearing this, Chendrill leaned in and said, "And the moment you start paying, it's never going to be."

Patrick took a deep breath and let it out and stared at a group of Asian girls sitting together taking up space with their computers, then he said, "What is it with these girls in this town? Why do they have to go fucking with me?"

Chendrill didn't answer, couldn't be bothered. The chances were slim to none that there was even a girl involved, though one had definitely instigated it all by taking the photos—but she wasn't likely to be doing that again anytime soon.

Then Patrick looked up at him and asked, "I read in the paper that some guy was found dead downtown. Was that the guy I saw?"

Chendrill nodded, it was exactly the same guy Patrick had seen stalking his friend and Chendrill's old flame from way back just before he'd gone all medieval on her.

"And were you involved, Chuck?"

Chendrill sat there, staring at the table as he remembered seeing the man on the floor. "No, someone got there before me. "

Chendrill left Patrick to worry about his reputation in the coffee shop and walked back through Yaletown. He turned another corner in the old warehouse shipping area turned chic and trendy with yuppie boutiques and loaded with fast cars and restaurants. He stepped through the doorway of the offices for Slave Media nestled in amongst it all. The pretty girl at reception smiled, telling him he looked good today and that Sebastian was waiting in the boardroom.

"Where have you been?" asked Sebastian as Chendrill opened the door and stepped inside. "I've been trying to reach Dan, but he's not answering his phone."

Chendrill sat down at the table opposite and smiled.

"Maybe he doesn't want to talk to you?"

Sebastian looked back at him shocked; that was the last thing he was expecting to hear.

"Why would you say that?"

"Because you've plastered photos of him naked in a pair of some gay guy's silver undies all across town and now he can't go out."

"No one knows they're Mazzi's."

"He does."

"Well he was all cool when he was wearing them at the time."

And Dan had been cool—cool enough to steal the keys to Mazzi's apartment, cool enough to wear his clothes, cool enough to drive his Ferrari, but not cool any longer since Mazzi had caught him and broken his nose with his man purse then taken photos, paying him handsomely for it instead of having him thrown in jail.

Sebastian said, "He'll come around, but you need to keep an eye on him."

"I am, he's at home."

"Please tell him he's getting some great press."

"I don't think he gives a shit, Sebastian."

Confused now, Sebastian looked back at him and picked up

the dog Chendrill had once saved for a cool $10,000 by simply going to the pound.

"He's not mad at us?"

Chendrill shook his head, "No, I'm just playing with you. Like I said he couldn't care less. All he wants to do is sit in his room."

"And do what?"

"You can work that one out."

Then Sebastian said thinking, "Oh? Well can you go around and tell him from me that he's just terrific, please?"

"That's it? You called me in to ask me that?"

"Yes, and to ask what's happened to Mazzi's Ferrari?"

This one threw Chendrill. He wasn't expecting them to know that the company car they gave him had been towed and was sitting in a tow company's lot, with Chendrill refusing to pay the fee. So, he said, "Some fat prick who uses his neck as a pillow has it."

"I know. They called here and asked me to come down. Told me I'd stolen it the last time they had it and now they want double. They said if I don't come down and pay, they're going to send it off to their friend's place on the river at Annacis Island to get it crushed."

Chendrill smiled. The cheeky fuckers had towed the Ferrari Sebastian let him use before and Chendrill had gone straight over to the yard and stolen it back. Now they had it again and were flexing some muscle with empty threats. Still smiling, he said, "They're going to crush a Ferrari—same as they would a twenty-year-old piece of shit Chevy?"

"That's what they're saying, Chuck!"

"Don't worry, it's bullshit; they haven't got the guts," Chendrill said, but he knew different. These guys wanted to be Hells Angels, but didn't have the smarts to become one—or the guts to chance getting themselves killed if they were. But they could crush a Ferrari and get away with it. All they had to do was crush it, take photos, then report it stolen—it was the way they were and the kind of thing they'd do so they could brag about it to their friends whilst they drank beer and mouthed off about their wives. He needed to get it back, Chendrill thought, but they could go fuck themselves if they thought he was going to be paying anything, let alone double.

Chapter Four

Rann Singh adjusted his turban as he sat in the booth of a franchise restaurant where wannabe supermodels worked as waitresses. Today's was blue—blue like the ocean, he'd been told when he'd bought it from the store in Southall on the outskirts of London. Buying it there in the store that smelled like his grandfather's home the day before he'd been chased out of town by the cops for killing the guy with the big mouth. Rann losing his temper and blacking out like he did, just as he had the first time it had happened, when the shithead kids at his school had smacked his bun as they sang out a little rhyme that referenced his parents, who wouldn't be coming home, 'Two down—fifty thousand to go. You'll be next, you Paki cunt Joe.'

But that time he hadn't won and had woken up on the floor with knuckles bleeding and his blazer ripped, his head covered in lumps from their fists and feet.

The food was not bad for a franchise place. The girl was in the toilet, no doubt preening her bleached white hair that he liked so much on tall skinny white women. She was feeling horny she'd told him, as she giggled down the phone, and said she'd been thinking about what he'd said about letting her see his hair—then admitted it was because she'd kept seeing these pictures of a really hot guy naked all-around town. She needed to make her mind up, not that it mattered.

What he'd do, he thought, was have the meal and take her straight back to his place, tell her he had to get up early for an appointment or something. Then he'd take her to his bed and go into the bathroom and pull his turban off, let his hair down so it would fall in her face as he was fucking her, let her swim in it. Girls loved that.

Then he'd kick her out and call Patrick again, let him know he was going to have to pay big to keep his secret safe, or there were going to be a different set of photos of him displayed on the back of every other bus in town.

But the girl had been a while, and knowing girls who were about to get laid generally did take awhile, he pulled out the untraceable phone he kept in his inside pocket and dialed. And as soon as Patrick answered in his usual joyous tone, Rann simply said, "I've managed to sort it all out Patrick, don't worry. The girl said you could have the photos back and she's going to forget about everything. All she wants is the commission you got from the penthouse suite you sold last month; that's it, problem solved."

Rann waited for a moment and cut into his peppercorn steak, which was a little overdone, and looked up at the TV to the ice hockey—the Canadian guys at the bar staring at it as though it was Rann's Sikh god Guru Nanak himself. Then he heard Patrick say, "You know how much that is? Does she know she could go to prison? Besides I know you think I'm rich, but I really can't afford that kind of money!"

Cool as a cucumber, Rann quoted straight off one of Patrick's ads he'd seen on the way in, saying, "You can't afford not to," and sat there listening to the silence on the end of the phone. Then Rann continued saying, "I don't think she's thought it through Patrick, you know, about her getting prison time. But you should consider if things were to go too far and she starts handing out the photos, then everything comes out in the wash. And even if we can keep a lid on it and no one ever sees the photos, then rumours can start and rumours as you know tend to be worse than the real thing—but anyway, if you're not interested, I'll tell her. Like I said, I'm just doing you a favor because you helped Michael out."

He looked around the skinny white chick coming now from the toilet looking good, the guys at the bar giving her the stare, her hair preened, the layered black roots all gone.

Then he said, "Don't worry then, I'll let her know you're not interested—I'll pass your message on. Thanks."

And for once in his life, before Patrick could get the last word in, Rann hung up.

******

It wasn't until the next day that he called again—the girl with the bleached hair gone now from his bed. She had bathed in his long thick locks as he let his hair drop down onto her face and breasts whilst he fucked her hard, and she'd screamed noisily and held onto the sheets with her right hand, not letting go as he'd thrown her around the bed. And when he'd finished, all she wanted to know was which type of shampoo and conditioner he was using, and as she opened the door to leave, he said, "Come back again when you're ready and I'll tell you."

He gave it until four in the afternoon and with his feet up on a stool, he called Patrick again. "Patrick, it's me, you got me in trouble—I told the girl I'd been talking to you and you wanted to make a deal and she flipped. She's really upset."

Patrick stayed silent on the other end of the phone and then, trying to sound cool, he said, "Is this supposed to make me feel bad for her? After all, she is trying to blackmail me, let's be honest here—how do I know if there is even 'a girl'? You're probably the only one involved and you haven't even told me your name. All I know is that you're from London, so that narrows it down a bit if I decided to go to the police."

"I think you've got it wrong with me, Patrick my old mate, you see. The only thing I want out of this whole thing is the name and phone number of the girl doing that stuff to you in the photos."

It wasn't that he personally wanted to be sodomised by her, as pretty as she was, but he'd definitely like to fuck her, that was for certain, get her sweet lips wrapped around his dick and see if she could take it all the way down. The thing was, the girl was a true pro. He could see that, the way she was working this realtor's ass and staring into the camera at the same time, and the question was how many other people did she have photos of, others who also had their little secrets, others who's lives he could turn around and save. That was the key.

"I don't know who she is," lied Patrick, as he thought about how, in fact, he knew who she was and where she was right now, laid up in a hospital with a spinal injury. He heard Rann say straight back to him, "You telling me you let a stranger do that to you?"

Patrick stayed silent now on the other end of the phone. He'd done worse. He said, "What I do in my private life has nothing to do with you."

"You're right," Rann answered straight back down the phone, "I don't care, you could have a camel in the room with you. The thing is, you need to start caring, caring about the photos being out there and getting into the hands of the people who do care and also love and trust you."

Then having enough of it all and without taking into consideration any of the advice he'd paid Charles Chuck Chendrill for, Patrick said it again, "Why don't you just tell this girl—person, I'll make it worth their while to give me all the photos, but I think $250,000 is a little steep."

Chapter Five

They settled at $100,000 for the photos and Rann was happy with that.

Well worth it, he thought, as he took the sky train the next day, riding it for a while until he knew everyone on board with him as it completed its circuit over and over, then just as it was getting busy, he placed his white headphones under his black turban and made the call.

His instructions for Patrick had been simple, all the realtor had to do was wait at the bottom of the Main Street station with the money in a black sports bag and not get mugged, then Rann would let him know what the girl wanted him to do.

And now all Patrick had to do was get on a train.

"Well which train?" Patrick had asked in a fluster, "and what about my car?"

"Leave the car, let it get towed," Rann had replied, his voice not giving any chance of an alternative. Then he said carrying on, "Go up to platform two and get onto the next train heading east right now."

And as the train pulled into the station, Rann saw him standing there looking like a million dollars groomed and manicured in his Italian loafers.

******

Patrick stepped onto the train and took a seat. *Where the fuck was this idiot?* Wasting his day with all the cloak and dagger shit when they could have just as easily met in a coffee shop, he thought. He looked around the carriage which was full, Chinese students, two punks, old, young, a guy in a black turban at the other end probably listening to some Bollywood music like they liked to, and that guy in his underpants again, staring back at him like he wanted to fight. *BlueBoy condoms,* Patrick thought, it had been a while since he'd used one. His old girlfriend, the Russian, the one he was in love with still, used to let him ride bareback; said she liked the feel of him inside her, said she liked to feel him come then feel it seep out throughout the day, letting her know a part of him was still with her, because she loved him.

The train carried on, heading out to Surrey into the suburbs, people coming, people going. *Fuck me*, Patrick thought, staring at his watch, he could have sold a condo in the time this was taking up, not that he would have, but he could.

He stared out the window, the place now getting industrial, suburban, passing town houses and gardens and people who weren't rich like him and could never afford to pay this kind of cash to keep some loser's mouth shut.

Then his phone rang and heard the guy from London say, "Go stand by the end door. At the next stop, step off the train, place the bag on the bench that has your picture on it, and then step back onto the train and go home."

Patrick was startled. What was this guy going on about? He didn't know he had an advert running out this far on the sky train. No wonder this idiot knew who he was—fuck me, he was going to get it taken down first thing tomorrow.

The blackmailer was on here with him in amongst the rest, ready to get off in a mass exodus, the only station on the line where you could switch trains. This guy was good, Patrick thought, he'd give him that, choosing this station when he could have used any one of them along the way to make the switch.

He made his way to the end door and stood there waiting, the Indian in the turban there with him along the way staring at the guy in the poster along with a group of students.

Then as the train came into the station, he saw himself in the distance, smiling back on the bench, looking like a fool with his teeth all shiny, and wearing a sweater shaped with triangles that had absolutely zero attitude or sex appeal—not like the kid in the poster had in his shiny underpants, selling condoms.

On cue, the train stopped right opposite the bench as the guy from London said it would, and the doors opened, the Indian stepping off first and walking away towards the exit, the girls still giggling, staying on the train, pointing and laughing now at Patrick's picture. Patrick stepped off, took a deep breath, and placed the bag calmly next to the photo of himself and walked back, stepping onto the train just as the doors closed.

******

Rann Singh kept walking and did not stop until the train was safely out of sight and around the corner heading east.

Stopping, he turned, heading back towards the bag, cutting his way through the other passengers like a knife. Reaching it, he picked it up and headed quickly along the platform and down the stairs. He walked under the tracks and, following a big guy in a black camo-like Hawaiian shirt and jeans, climbed up the stairs to the platform on the other side.

The train heading west would be there soon; having studied the system he knew it was impossible for Patrick to switch trains at the next stop and come back. He reached the middle of the platform and waited, the bag heavy on his shoulder, the money in used tens and twenties like he always asked for. He looked to the rails below him as they began to sing as the metal shifted with the weight of the approaching train. Then he looked up, Patrick's photo there on the bench across the tracks, smiling back at him with his slogan right below saying, '*You can't afford not to.*'

And then the train pulled into the station, cutting the connection. The doors slammed open, Rann stepped onto the train and sat down, placing the bag on his knees and looking discreetly to the train's occupants around him, just as they did with him and his big turban.

Slowly, he looked back to the bag, opened it, and snuck a look inside—the bills all wrapped in cloth as he had asked, bound with string and a note sitting on top. Reaching in, he pulled it out, opened it, and read 'Now I know who you are and you've got problems—Charles Chuck Chendrill.'

Chapter Six

Charles Chuck Chendrill watched from the corner of his eye as the guy with the turban looked about the train to see who was watching him. He'd not been easy to spot the first time around as Chendrill had kept an eye on Patrick through the center doorway that linked the train's carriages. It was a good job the East Indian had put together. The drop could have been anywhere and having Patrick drop it off to himself on the station's bench had been an especially nice touch.

The guy was shitting himself now as he dug further into the bag, finding the money was just photocopied cut paper. Lifting his head again, the East Indian in the turban looked around as though he didn't care, Chendrill wanting to go over and sit next to him and say, 'Looks like you're the one taking it from behind now,' then arrest him. But he was no longer a cop, so he just watched and waited until the guy in the turban got off still carrying the bag slung across his shoulder, standing there outside the train looking back and forth along the empty platform as the doors shut behind him, and watching as the train pulled away. Chendrill sitting there lost in his own world, staring out the other window as the carriage moved past the Sikh in his turban carrying $100,000 dollars worth of nothing and a note that told him he was in trouble. And he was.

******

Patrick was pissed. As soon as he could, he was off the train and sitting in the rear of a taxi heading back into Vancouver.

He'd seen Chendrill disappearing down the steps only at the last second as the train pulled out of the station and wondered how he'd managed to hide himself so well in the first place. The guy from London who had a bag full of nothing was Chendrill's problem now, that was his job, that's what he did. He sorted stuff like this out and Patrick was paying him enough to trust Chuck when he said, 'don't worry!' So, he wasn't going to. He sold property and Chendrill sorted out parasitic idiots like this guy who had just entered his life.

The problem now was that he'd just seen himself, Patrick De'Sendro, for who he really was, grinning back at himself like some kind of moron in a triangle patterned cashmere sweater and shiny teeth. *For fuck's sake*, he'd just been sitting there for twenty minutes staring up at a guy in his underpants oozing more attitude and sex appeal in his little finger. No wonder the girls were going giddy, but then they'd seen him, and it was no wonder they were laughing—laughing like the guy Patrick had paid handsomely to put the campaign together in the first place, snapping shots off in his pathetic little studio, making Patrick feel like a king with all the sad little lighting strobes popping off, flattening out his wrinkles and making his teeth shine.

But that guy in his silver underpants covered in sweat, looking as though he wanted to move but couldn't—wow! It was another league. The girls weren't laughing at that guy; no, they were almost coming in their panties over the him. *Fuck, I am getting old,* Patrick thought, wearing a cashmere sweater like that with his white shirt sticking out the top, his hair all gelled, combed back in lines. Why didn't the guy tell him he looked like a prick, why? Because the man was a prick himself, that's why, and he'd suckered him in and made him feel special.

It's time for a change, he thought. He was a realtor, he looked like a realtor, everything about him screamed out that he'd sell your home and hit you with a fancy commission to pay for the 'Beama and big meals out at Caderos. A new advertising campaign was in order. He was pretty certain the city was sick to death of seeing his face on the back of buses and now benches at train stations. He needed to go big and needed to do it in style and he knew just the guy to take him there.

******

Sebastian had just taken a call from an old friend in London and had spent twenty minutes explaining that Dan, Slave's new hot signing was, as far as he could tell, not gay, so he should give up any hope of popping on a jet from London on the off chance he could take him out and get him drunk, when his phone rang again.

This time, though, it was Patrick and he said, "Sebastian, make me look as good as that kid does and I'll sell your next place for free."

Sebastian stared at the phone, which was still on speaker, and smiled. He liked Patrick, having bought his penthouse from him when he'd decided to move from the outskirts of London and settle down in Vancouver some years back.

"But I'm not looking to sell, Patrick."

"But if you do?"

"I'm not wanting to move, Patrick, I've just organized all my books."

And he had, every one of them across the shelves in such an order that they looked good and were alphabetized—or kind of. Then he asked, "But if you want to come for dinner, Patrick, then you're welcome."

That was something Patrick could do without. He'd been before and sat the night away talking about curtains with a bunch of gay men, especially the Swedish guy who worked with Sebastian, who carried his ego around in a suitcase. So, he said, "Sebastian, I'd love to, but before I get there, just for old times' sake, I would love you to give me a bit of your time and think about how you can make me look good."

After all, how else was he going to get himself a new advertising campaign and not have to pay corporate?

******

Rann Singh took the bag into the handicap toilet at Starbucks, locked the door, placed it on the sink, and began pulling out the contents which Patrick had spent the evening before filling, laughing out loud as he worked off his new, expensive color laser printer. Chendrill had said just fill the bag with paper, but going a step further, Patrick hadn't and instead replaced the Queen's face with his own and ran off $100,000 worth of 10's and 20's just like the guy from London had asked.

Fuck him.

Rann held one of the notes to the light above the sink and smiled, seeing Patrick's face looking back at him. *The cheeky fucker*, but he'd pay more now just for wasting his time, and Rann would start by leaving a copy of one of the photos in the elevator of Patrick's apartment block, and stick one of these bills right underneath.

That'll teach him for being a clown.

But who was this Chendrill, he thought, maybe a hired thug, or a PI of some sort, but they could be bought. Sitting down on the toilet, he pulled out his phone and stuck Chendrill's name into a search engine, smiling as the result came back—*Chuck Chendrill, Private Investigations*—phone number and address included.

That'll do, Rann thought as he stood and adjusted his turban in the mirror. I'll go looking, find some dirt on you, and you can either fuck off or start paying some cash like Patrick's going to have to. But he didn't have to look very far because as soon as he opened the toilet door, Chendrill was waiting on the other side. And the first words Chendrill said were, "You'd better hand over those photos or I'm going to strangle you with a bit of that cloth you've got wrapped around your head."

"That's racist," Rann replied, "I thought you Canadians didn't go in for that sort of thing."

And as quick as lightning, Chendrill snapped his head forward, smashing Rann on the bridge of his nose and sending him flying back and hitting the floor of the handicapped toilets.

Chendrill stepped forward and closed the door, locking it behind him and picking up the bag, emptied it on top of Rann's head.

"Give me the photos now and this'll end today. If you don't, it'll get worse."

Rann looked up at the big guy in the camo Hawaiian shirt and remembered him nipping past him at the station. Fuck, his nose hurt. He hadn't taken a hit like that since he was at school in Hounslow.

He reached down to his sock and began to pull the blade he kept there for such occasions and thought about burying it into Chendrill's leg—but where would that leave them.

So, he said, "How much do you want?"

"I don't want anything—just the photos."

Rann tried again, "I'll give you half of what the realtor pays me."

Chendrill stared down at the East Indian with blood running from his nose and leaking onto his nice silk shirt. The guy was holding his ankle, deciding whether to pull whatever he had hidden in his sock.

Then Chendrill said, "We can sort it out now. You take me to where the photos are and hand them over and we put this behind us or I take whatever you've got hidden in your sock away then I start to kick the shit out of you until I leave you for dead. If you die, you die and if you live, you live. But if you survive, you'll still owe me the photos, so we'll be back to square one when you get out of the hospital. So, what'll it be?"

Rann stared up at the big guy whose ribs were hurting and said, "I'm connected."

"Not now you're not. Right now, you're connected to the shit house floor."

Chendrill stared at the guy with the turban and the accent that didn't fit. Chances are he had connections in one of the Asian gangs that ran out of Surrey on the border with the U.S. They dealt in drugs and sold guns and occasionally got themselves shot. But he'd been threatened with worse. So, he said, "So it's make your mind up time, either you can give me the photos today or you can start thinking about not playing cricket on the weekend. "

"Okay!" the East Indian suddenly said and began to get up. "I have them here, you win."

And then as he reached his feet, he came at Chendrill. Quickly batting Rann's fist away to his side, Chendrill swung out with his free hand, catching the East Indian with his fist in the side of his head, sending Rann hard against the wall and a searing pain ripping through Chendrill's ribs.

They both stood there staring at each other—the East Indian with his turban wonky on his head, his eyes smiling, pointing right in Chendrill's direction. The East Indian now speaking in a voice which sounded like he was enjoying himself and just getting started, whispering back to Chendrill in his coarse London accent as he lifted his leg and pulled the knife out from his sock.

"I'm the ones who's gunna leave you for dead now, you cunt."

Fuck me, what a way to go, Chendrill thought, *dead on the floor of the shitter in Starbucks.* He could think of better ways— like having a massive heart attack in the middle of the night pounding some beautiful woman after a night out eating too much food in a restaurant someplace.

He stared at the knife, long and curved, almost ornamental. It was the second time he'd seen one like it in the past week, this one smaller.

Then he said, "What is it with you guys and these fucking knives?"

And the East Indian answered, "Tell the realtor he's got a week and if I see you, this'll be sticking in the stomach of you or anyone else who comes near me in a stupid shirt like that."

Chapter Seven

What was wrong with my camo Hawaiian? Chendrill thought about the shirt he liked to use for surveillance work as he sat himself down in the coffee shop and he held his ribs, wondering also how strange it was to have had two fights in one week. Fuck, his ribs hurt.

Reaching into his pocket, he pulled out the wallet he'd lifted from the East Indian just as he'd head butted him and sent him flying back into the toilet stall.

Rann Singh

17a – 199, 2022st

Surrey, BC

Well that was pretty easy, he thought. He had his licence now and the hole the East Indian Londoner was digging himself was getting bigger. It wouldn't be long before the guy would be calling to get it back.

Patrick drove through the busy streets of Vancouver cringing every time he saw his face on the back of a bus. Shit, what an idiot he looked. If ever there was time for change, it was now. Yes, he'd still sell places, but only up until he didn't need to do it any longer, which was in reality right now with the amount of money he had stashed away after selling real estate for the last thirty years, hedging his bets and winning as the highs and lows came and went.

He reached the outside of Sebastian's place and parked the Beamer, rode the elevator all the way to the 22nd floor, stepping out with a *bing* onto a door mat that said welcome and looked odd sitting so high up, parked on the most beautiful parqueted flooring he'd ever seen. The first one to greet him when the door opened was the dog, then looking up he heard Sebastian.

"Patrick, oh darling what have you been up to?"

Patrick thought about it. Well, he was being blackmailed and he'd been sent on a train ride along with all the little people and handed over a bag with exactly $100,000 of money that was only good in a mystical country where Patrick was king. On top of that, on the way back, he'd had an identity crisis. Then he'd gone and seen a whore, one he'd started to get to know since his last one had been attacked and couldn't walk anymore and this new one, she'd done to him exactly the same things that he was being blackmailed about in the first place. So, he answered, "Not much really, you?" as Sebastian came towards him holding out one hand and grabbing his.

"Oh well, Patrick where do I start?

******

They sat down to dinner at a table by the window which looked out across the bay, the room larger than was necessary but still cozy with its hardwood floors stylishly covered in places by handmade Moroccan rugs, their intricately woven work barely visible in the dim light. Sebastian at the foot of the table, Sebastian's business partner Mazzi Hegan at the other end with his tightly cut blonde hair with highlights, and Patrick in the middle.

"I called Chuck, but he said he was busy. I called Marsha and her assistant Buffy. She was in L.A., but said she would take a jet up anyway, then she called to cancel when she found out Dan wasn't going to show," Sebastian said, as he brought in a plate of freshly seared Bluefin Tuna and started putting it on the other two's matching plates.

"I'm glad on all counts, I can do without the drama from that slut," said Mazzi. "And tell me why oh why would I want to sit here with Chendrill and risk getting a seizure looking at his shirt?"

Sebastian took a deep breath.

"Because he's a friend of mine and Patrick's told me he's hiring him himself to look into a little personal matter he's got going on."

Good luck to them both, Mazzi Hegan thought as he discreetly moved the pieces of parsley from the Tuna with his fork. *They both don't know how to dress, so they should both get along great. They could hang out downtown and make anyone with a bit of style puke.* Then he said, "I thought that guy who's driving my car works for us."

"Me," Sebastian answered, "I pay him out of my own money. He works for me and if Patrick needs a hand with something, then he's going to get nothing less than the best."

Best what? Best guy who finds dogs? Hegan thought as he heard his business partner continue, "After all, you needed to find Dan after you'd broken his nose and he found him."

He had done that indeed, Hegan thought; he'd found the guy who was about to make him world famous after he'd snapped the shots that were being shown worldwide when Hegan had come home late one night and found Dan sleeping in his bed like Goldilocks in silver ginch. But nonetheless, he still said, "Well don't give him that much credit. I'm sure it wasn't that difficult."

Then he heard Sebastian say, "And he found Fluffy."

Hegan closed his eyes, *fuck me, here we go again about the dog.*

"Patrick, I lost Fluffy and called Chuck straight up, cold-called him right out of the phone book and an hour later, he was back."

Patrick nodded saying, "Yes, Chuck's the best."

Fuck me, Hegan thought, looking to the clock. He could be at some club now down on Davie hitting on young guy ass like he liked to, giving a guy a line, like 'you look good—but you'd look better sucking my dick...' He stared at Patrick, the realtor, thinking, this guy's probably never done a kinky thing in his life. Straight guys were like that, just stuck it in the slippery fish pie and pumped. He's probably never had anything except some prostate-obsessed doctor's finger up there in his life and I bet when he did, he moaned about it for weeks to his wife. Fuck, the guy was a walking advertisement for a realtor if he'd ever seen one—with his loafers and nicely pressed shirt and cufflinks. And Jesus, he was sick of seeing the guy's face on the back of buses, let alone having to stare and talk about him now over dinner—especially when all Mazzi wanted to do was talk about himself and how good his photos were. The next thing Sebastian was going to say to him no doubt was that the creep needed a makeover and he was the guy to do it.

Any minute now, they'd say it, he knew it, he could feel it coming closer with every mouthful of overcooked Tuna he took.

Then Sebastian said, "Patrick's looking for a new look, Mazzi. Have you got any suggestions?"

Yeah why don't you go fuck off and shoot yourself and do us all a favor, Mazzi Hegan thought as he stared at Patrick and said, "Well, you can lose the sweater for a start. Then we can talk."

"I think he looks cool in it, Mazzi, don't you think?"

Sebastian was a nice man, Hegan thought. As much as he hated his partner sometimes, the guy was good, better than himself, and he knew it. The man could see shit for what it was, but would never ever say so. So, taking his partner's lead, he said, "I don't mean it's not cool, because it's cool, realtor cool. If you're looking for a new look, then bring in a stylist first. Dee will do it, she's got an eye; she'll get you looking sharp."

Sebastian smiled, then said, "Patrick's already sharp—he just thinks it's time for a change. I was thinking the same thing, but I'd like you to help. You know, take some photos, Mazzi."

Fuck—Mazzi thought, he knew it, there he was on the verge of being an international sensation and wham he was back making idiots look good, which was basically his job, he knew that. But this idiot, the guy with the teeth, he was something different. He stared at him now, this realtor who sold condos all over town and made sure everyone knew his face. Once, years back, he'd fucked a guy and found a picture of Patrick taken from the paper under the bed. The fucking weirdo, whacking off to him no doubt. Mazzi couldn't imagine it, he'd rather puke gagging on a horse. He gave Sebastian a look, then smiled at Patrick. It was going to be a challenge—the multi-colored cashmere sweater with diamonds across the chest really had to go.

Chapter Eight

Rann Singh stood in front of his bathroom mirror and looked at the bruise on the bridge of his nose. An inch lower and the prick would have broken it. Why can't people just let him get on with his business? He and the realtor had an agreement and as far as he was concerned, the deal was done. Now he had to deal with this prick.

He still had the bag, which he'd have to burn somehow. If they were found, the notes with Patrick's stupid grin on the front instead of the Queen's would find their way to the cops, and then they would find their way to Patrick, who would explain why and then, ultimately, Rann would have more on his plate than a guy with a bad shirt.

He looked at his own, leaning his chin down, feeling the weight of his turban pulling his head forward. It wasn't ruined, but it would need to be dry cleaned now—and the fucker had nicked his wallet.

Things were not going smoothly.

He straightened himself up, pulled off his shirt, and stood there looking at himself in the mirror, then he walked to the living room and picked up the phone.

Thirty seconds later, Chendrill answered and Rann heard himself say, "I need my wallet."

"I need the photos."

"Maybe I'll call the police and have you charged with assault."

"Maybe I'll call the police and have you thrown out of the

country."

Rann stayed silent for a second, thinking, the realtor owed him $100,000 and that was that. This guy was getting irritating. Then he heard Chendrill say, "I don't want to have to come out to Surrey—drop the photos off for me downtown and if I never hear of you again, you'll be a better man for it."

"Maybe I'll start looking at what Charles Chuck Chendrill does in his personal life and see then if you're still such a cocky cunt."

"Do as you will."

"I know you work for Slave International."

Fuck me, Chendrill thought as he sat on the other end of the line, *how the hell did he know that?*

"Maybe I'll go digging around there as well, tell them you sent me."

"Maybe I'll come over there and get on with what I should have finished in that washroom."

Then Rann said, "Listen Mr. PI, we both know you're full of shit. I need my wallet, you need the photos. The realtor agreed to pay money for the photos. I'm doing him a favor by not letting them circulate and I can get another licence within a week. It's just easier if you give it back. If you don't want to, then go fuck yourself, I'll start circulating the photos."

And with that, he did. He sent the first one straight to Chendrill's email, the second he sent to the receptionist at Slave, and then sent another note to Chendrill that said, '*Don't fuck with me.*'

The guy with the turban was becoming troublesome.

******

About an hour later, Chendrill received an emergency call from Sebastian who said, "Chuck, I'm really shocked. I think I need you to come over and see something."

And half an hour later, he was there, sitting in the boardroom staring at the projector screen with Sebastian and Sebastian's dog and Mazzi Hegan grinning, saying, "Well it's not quite the makeover I was expecting, but at least things are improving."

Then Sebastian turned off the screen and, still sitting in the darkness, looked to Chendrill and said, "Is this the problem you're dealing with?"

Chendrill stayed silent and switched on the lights as Sebastian followed him with his eyes.

"The poor man, he must be so embarrassed."

Chendrill just shrugged and said, "I'm sure he will be if they keep coming out."

"He's commissioned us for his new campaign."

"Why, what's wrong with the one he's running?"

Mazzi Hegan looked at Chendrill, thinking, *What's wrong with your shirt?* Mr. Big, standing there all tall and toned wearing a Hawaiian like he always did. Mazzi almost said, 'If you don't know the answer to your own question, start looking in the mirror.' He was tough, though, in a butch kind of way, which was sexy in itself—but for fuck's sake, get rid of the shirts. But who was he to judge, he thought, only last night he'd felt the same about Patrick, pulling him apart in his mind as he'd pretended to like the food at Sebastian's, and now look at him, this square realtor, taking it like a man, even if it was some slut delivering the goods. He said, "Same as the guy's clothes—it's out of date."

Chendrill looked to the Swede with the frosted tips in his hair and silver pants.

"Really?"

Mazzi Hegan stared right at him, saying, "Yeah—really." They didn't get along and never would, not as long as Sebastian was letting him use his car, which in fact he hadn't seen for a few days. Then picking up on what Mazzi was really pissed about, Sebastian interrupted, "Chuck looks good in the Ferrari, Mazzi; besides you can't park."

Mazzi took a deep breath and knowing it was useless to carry on, gave up. Sebastian was right; he'd been having parking issues for some time now and his calling out the company chauffer at all hours to do it for him had caught up with him.

Then Sebastian asked, "Has this creepy guy you're dealing with got anything like this on anyone else?"

Chendrill looked automatically to Hegan, who answered, "Who hasn't got shit like that on me, I mean come on? I'm hot!"

Chendrill closed his eyes, the skinny prick looking like something out of ABBA, then opening them again said, "I don't think so."

"What about Dan?"

"No, this is nothing to do with anyone but Patrick and for some reason it's spilled over onto you guys because somehow it's leaked out that I'm contracted here."

To which Sebastian replied, "Oh it's not leaked anywhere Chuck, I've added you to our website."

******

Charles Chuck Chendrill sat in the back of a taxi as it cruised around the dirty back roads of Vancouver's East Side. He needed the Ferrari back if he was going to have to drive down to Surrey to sort out this fucker with the turban and the accent that didn't fit.

Sebastian was right, Chendrill was there in the center of things on Slave Media's website—directly under the heading 'Security' for fuck's sake—but for a grand a day plus expenses and a retainer, he'd deal with it—even if it had only been there a few days and it was already causing issues.

The taxi turned a corner again and came out onto the main road off McGill St.

A tow truck would be along pretty soon, he knew it. Their yard was just up the road and just after three o'clock, the traffic constrictions changed downtown and all the vultures would be flying back and forth feeding off the people with real jobs.

They carried along as Chendrill adjusted himself in his seat. It had been at least ten days since he'd taken one in the ribs from the guy from the bakery and although it was now half as bad as it was, they still hurt.

He needed to go see Dan, he thought, most of all he needed to see Dan's mother—sexy with her blonde hair and tight little frame. Dan had been quiet, too quiet really for a guy who'd hit the world stage running. Everywhere he looked now he saw him, posters, magazines with him standing next to the supermodel Marsha crying and looking a mess. It was a funny world.

Then he saw him in the distance driving the tow truck, dragging behind some poor mother's family van with blackened out windows behind, the alarm still going, his arm out the window with its tattoos all faded and stretched as his body gained weight. His big sovereign rings now permanently attached to his porky fingers like a young tree moving onwards and up, passing through and smothering its support with its bark.

Quickly Chendrill signalled the driver to pull up behind him and follow, pulling a slim jim from his inside jacket, Chendrill leaned over and paid the driver twenty and slipped out behind the tow truck in traffic, opening the van's rear door and climbing in.

Chendrill climbed over the shopping in the back of the van spread across the rear nestled in between the kid's seats. *The fucking prick*, Chendrill thought, envisioning the mother stuck there downtown with all the kids and whatever else she'd bought for the day. He couldn't have not seen it for what it was—the mother just grabbing something she needed and not leaving the kids in the car, getting out for a few minutes just so this prick could come along and fuck up her day.

The tow truck carried on, Chendrill sitting in the back now could see the driver's fat neck bulging as he twisted his sweaty head, nearly giving himself a heart attack every time he turned the steering wheel. They reached the yard and Chendrill felt the van shake and bang as the prick hit the potholes.

Mazzi Hegan's Ferrari sat there now across the lot, nose into the fence. Opening the rear door, Chendrill slipped out and moved along, hiding behind the other cars as he made his way to the red Ferrari and, opening the door with the key, slipped in. The tow truck driver stood there now stretching, his gut hanging over his jeans that hung from his ass. Across the way was another truck on its way in, waiting outside the gate with a Ford hanging from the back. Chendrill watched in the rearview mirror as the gate opened and as it did, he started the Ferrari, slammed it in reverse, and tore out across the yard backwards, past the tow truck driver staring there with his mouth open, and through the open gate out onto the road.

Fuck them.

He headed back up McGill Street until he hit the highway and joined the traffic heading out of town towards Surrey. Dennis would be there now, he thought, sitting in his basement suite, no longer lonely, waiting for the love of his life to get well enough to come home and begin to destroy his life again.

He hit the bridge, the Ferrari feeling good, its engine purring right behind him. He took a right just as he reached the other side, heading towards the address on the East Indian's licence. After scaling the area for five minutes he reached it and sat outside for a bit looking up at the tower block. It was nice, positioned and built in a part of town that was still a shit hole, the local authorities trying to clean it up one development at a time.

He'd called a friend, checking the guy out—Rann Singh, landed immigrant, twenty-eight, arrived in Toronto three years ago, and now here, blackmailing good honest citizens like Patrick.

He got out of the car and looked around as trucks passed blowing out smoke from their stacks and moving up through the gears. The Indian community here was big, bigger now in fact than he remembered, the street signs new and gleaming, mixing English with Urdu—the country's second language, French, left by the wayside as the world slowly changed.

An hour later, Chendrill saw him, walking towards him along the road, heading back from the sky train station in the distance, his turban now bright red matching his shirt. He wasn't hiding.

Rann reached the Ferrari and, slowing down to take in its majesty, noticed Chendrill standing there leaning against the wall of the building and said without missing a beat, "This yours?"

Chendrill nodded. Then the East Indian said, "I'm in the wrong business."

Feeling his rib tweak as he shrugged himself off the wall, Chendrill said, "You need a brain to do what I do." And just as Rann said, "Yeah right," Chendrill hit him again, this time right in the throat, dropping him to the ground. Reaching down quickly,

47

he pulled the knife from the guy's sock and threw it over a fence. Then reaching down and pulling out a set of cuffs, he had the East Indian's hands behind his back before the man could gather up his first full breath.

Pulling him to his feet, he placed his hands into the man's pockets and, finding his keys, began to march him across the road.

They reached the front of the apartment block and stepped inside, Rann breathing hard, still trying to get his breath, moving in front of him with ease, his feet light on the ground, his hands twisted up, almost breaking both wrists with every step.

Chendrill opened the door to Rann's home and stepped inside, lifted the man's arms up and away from his back and, forcing him to the floor, dragged the guy along the corridor by the scruff of his neck before bringing out another set of cuffs and securing him to the side of the fridge door. Then, as he stood watching Rann breathing hard, he said, "Don't pull too hard or you'll open the door and spoil the milk."

Chendrill walked away, looking around the place, stepping outside and putting his foot up on the balcony lounge chair as he looked down below at the Ferrari sitting there in the street looking out of place. He moved into the bedroom and came back with Rann's laptop in his hand and, opening it, said, "What's the password."

Rann replied, "You know I'm connected?"

Chendrill stared down at the man sitting there with his arm up against the door handle to the fridge. He said, "Yeah I can see— what's the password."

"It's fuck you."

Not fucking around, Chendrill lifted the computer and cracked it down hard across Rann's head, knocking his turban off onto the kitchen floor, then waiting for him to come around again asked, "What's the password?"

Rann stared up at the man now, the big fuck in his loud shirt standing in his home, giving out the orders. His turban gone, his hair now half out of the hanky and band hanging down the other side of his head. He said, "I'm not joking, it's 'fuckyou'."

Chendrill put the computer back on the dining table next to the kitchen, and typed in 'fuckyou'. He wasn't lying, it was.

"I'd say that's not the best choice of passwords."

He opened it up, quickly found all the photos of Patrick saved on the desktop, and deleted them. Then picked up the computer and bringing it down hard on the corner of the table three times, destroyed the machine completely, exposing the hard drive. He pulled a pair of pliers from his pocket, ripped out the hard drive, and threw it onto the table. Then said, "Where's the photos?"

Rann took another deep breath. He was fucked. It was obvious this guy was big, strong, methodical, and no dummy. Nodding to a dresser, he said, "In the drawer, there."

Chendrill walked over and opening the second one, pulled out the envelope. Letting the contents spill onto the table, he asked, "Is this it?"

Rann nodded as Chendrill kneeled beside him and said quietly, "If it's not—I'll come back and throw you out that window."

And Rann replied, "Maybe next time I'll throw you out that window."

From the look in the man's eyes, Chendrill could see he meant it and had every confidence in himself that he could. But still, he said, "Good luck with that."

Chendrill searched the rest of the apartment and found nothing. Picking up the hard drive, he popped it into the envelope, leaned down, releasing the East Indian and dropping the guy's wallet into his lap, and left.

He felt a bit guilty. He'd hit the man a little too hard across his head, and knew it was sacrilege to remove the guy's turban—but fuck him, that can happen when you blackmail people.

Riding the elevator down, Chendrill reached the Ferrari, opened the door, and threw the envelope onto the passenger seat as he climbed in and sat down behind the wheel. He only saw the lounge chair flying through the air from above briefly before it crashed down hard on the Ferrari's hood, barely missing the windshield.

This guy was irritating.

Chapter Nine

It took two days to fix the car, and in those two days Chendrill had been over to see Dan's mother four times, each time kissing her with a passion he'd never felt before with another woman. Dan, though, he'd only heard and not seen the whole time. And just as the car arrived, looking like new and paid for by Patrick, Sebastian called with another emergency.

As soon as he sat in Sebastian's office, Sebastian was on him, "He's been calling here again Chuck, this time he went for Mazzi telling him he's going to let the world know he's gay."

Chendrill was silent for the moment, taking it in, "And what did Mazzi say about it?"

"He just put the phone on speaker to make sure the guy knew the whole office could hear. Then announced to everyone he was homosexual and invited the guy over so they could get naked and have the guy fuck him on the boardroom table so there was absolutely no mistake about the fact."

Chendrill laughed, it was funny—but not funny at the same time. The guy wasn't giving up and the whole stunt was obviously aimed at winding Chendrill up so as he would run straight over there into whatever the guy with the turban had planned for him. Then Sebastian asked, "Have you seen Dan?"

He hadn't, but he'd certainly heard him making his presence known with the broom he kept by his bed and the disappearance of food from the fridge, which seemed to get emptied at all times of the day or night—and which, after giving his first money advance straight to his mother, was now always full. So, he said, "Don't worry about Dan."

"You know we've been getting calls and letters from all over the place about him; marriage proposals—the works, and that girl Marsha keeps calling wanting to speak with him."

"What's she want?"

"What do you think?"

"Oh! Well that goes without saying, I suppose."

"That's right, like we used to say back in London, she wants a bit of hickory, Chuck—hickory stick, rhymes with…"

Chendrill got it. Then he asked, "Have you told Dan?"

"I left messages yes. But he doesn't answer. I can only think that he doesn't care." Then Sebastian took a deep breath and said, "I thought this pesky guy was history, Chuck?"

So did Chendrill, who'd let the lounge chair incident go, hoping it would be enough to placate the man's ego after he'd knocked his turban off—but obviously not. He'd have to go talk to him again. So, he said, "Sebastian, there are some crazy people out there and sadly one of them has decided to pester us. I don't want you to worry about a thing—that's why you pay me."

******

He walked away from Slave's offices and headed towards the Ferrari he'd left parked along the way. He saw the tow truck first and then the driver with the fat neck and tattoos standing next to the car which, so far, had embarrassed him twice, and as he reached him, the tow truck driver said, "You're lucky; I was about to tow it."

"Then you're lucky you've still got a job, because you're too fat to be a doorman around here."

Chendrill knew the rules. The cars had to be parked illegally for these shitheads to tow them—otherwise it's theft. He moved past the tow truck driver and hit the key, giving it the *beep-beep-bop* and got inside. Then as he started the engine, wound the window down, and said to the guy as he began to pull away, "Go get a real job."

He pulled out of the space and drove along the road, passing the plethora of beautiful women who always seemed to hang around the area in the summertime and thought back to the blackmailing Indian, who was still causing trouble and who said he was connected. To whom? His own kind, he thought—most people usually were.

There were a few gangs in town, the Hells Angels—most of whom never rode bikes anymore—the Asians doing their thing with the whores in the massage parlors and with heroin, the white-trash guys paid by the mile, who drove oversized trucks and delivered drugs across Canada, and the East Indians.

He pulled out his phone and called the one he did know. Rasheed answered straight away, saying, "Was that your car that got hit by the lawn chair?"

"That's why I'm calling."

Rasheed was a good guy, to Chendrill at least. They'd gotten to know each other during the days when Chendrill had been on the police force, back when gangsters were being killed for no real reason other than pride. Seeing the writing on the wall, Rasheed had called Chendrill, taking himself out the way for a while with Chendrill happily arresting him on a bullshit charge and sticking him in a government holiday camp until the stupidity stopped—but not without a barrel full of info in exchange of course, and Chendrill had taken down the lot.

Now Rasheed ran things, East Indian things at least. As they sat down out of the way in a bar on the outskirts of Maple Ridge and watched as a drunken slob in a cowboy hat showed everyone he couldn't ride a mechanical bull, Chendrill asked, "Who's he?"

Rasheed looked around, realizing Chendrill was referring to his driver sitting there on his own, three tables down, with a diamond in his front tooth trying to look cool. Rasheed said, "Oh, that's Archall, calls himself Diamond. He's one of these wanna be rappers, he's been driving me for a while. I like him because he's not too sharp, so I don't have to watch my back, and he's good with tools."

Then changing the subject as he watched a guy hanging on to the saddle with all his might, Rasheed said, "There's a guy I want you to meet, he's supposed to be here tonight. I knew him from school, was crazy, used to dive under freight trains and roll out the other side. Now he flies those squirrel suits off mountains and out of planes. He's here this week—you'll see him if you go to the fireworks; he's going to fly in and then drop onto the beach. Told me on the phone he'll drop out real high, about 5 miles off, then come in like James Bond uninvited and scare the shit out of the crowd."

Chendrill listened, looking up at the bull then back to Rasheed. The crowd whooped it up as the bull spun around and around. The driver, Archall Diamond, sat showing off his tooth. Then Chendrill said, "What's this daredevil want with me, does he need a lift to the airport?"

Rasheed shook his head. "No, he's not wanting anything; he's in town and he's looking forward to showing off. Said he's back now for good and wants the city to know his name. The fireworks are going to be his swansong. A lot of the guys can't stand him, though; say he's a flash Paki, but they're just jealous. He's cool, thought you might like to meet him, that's all. Then if you're there you can say to whoever you're with you know him."

Chendrill would, he thought, as cheesy as it was he'd still throw it out there. He'd seen those guys, swooping down off the side of mountains in a documentary and wondered how they could do it and not worry about dying. Or maybe that was just it—they didn't.

He said, "Yeah, I'd like to," then laughing to himself followed up, "he can do all that but could he ride this thing?"

And Rasheed replied, "The truth is if he set his mind to it, he probably could, but he'd have them grease it up first so as it was more of a challenge."

Then Chendrill asked, "So, who's this Rann Singh?"

"He's not a real Indian, he's a Londoner. The guy's never been to the Punjab. In fact, I think, truth is, he's not even from England; he's an African Indian, lives here now though and mostly just blackmails people."

Chendrill smiled and thought, *'just'*, the prick saying it as though the guy were a waiter.

"Yeah, he's harmless, but he has a temper."

Then Chendrill thought back to the lounge chair flying through the air from the tenth floor of the apartment block and wondered if the guy had waited till he got in the car before he threw it.

"Have you spoken to him?"

Rasheed nodded. He had, Rann had called.

"Yeah, he was complaining. Said some PI with a loud shirt was getting in the way of business and had fucked up a big money score with a realtor. Said soon he was going to lose his temper with the man and end up breaking his legs."

Chendrill smiled, the prick, as if that was the big issue between them.

"Really?"

"Yeah he also said you knocked his turban off and a couple of other things concerning $100,000."

Chendrill shook his head and watched a woman climbing onto the mechanical bull, letting her big tits show from her low-cut top so the operator would give her an easy ride for the crowd to watch them wobble.

"There was never any $100,000. I gave that figure out to flush the prick out into the open as he was getting on my nerves."

"And he went for it?"

"Wouldn't you?"

Rasheed shook his head. He wouldn't, no. $100,000 was too much for a blackmail scam. They both knew it, he'd be the one getting scammed, as Rann Singh had been. Then he said, "The guy usually gets around $5,000 to $10,000 if he's lucky, sometimes just a grand. He's been away recently, in Asia I'd heard, but normally though when he's here, he's preying on guys who fuck those skanky crack whores down on the East Side, taking photos with his phone and getting the names and addresses from someone he knows at the insurance office from the plate numbers, then fucking with the married ones, says he's like an evangelical Bible thumper and is waking these people up—doing them a favor, saving their souls before they go too far and pick up some sexual disease. But it looks like now he's fucking with you."

Chendrill asked, "Why's he been in Asia?"

Rasheed replied, "Could be fucking pussy, he likes that they say—more than most guys if that's possible. But since he's got back, he's been asking about Sildenafil, stuff that makes your cock hard."

"He needs it?"

"No, wants to sell it." And then Rasheed said, "You want me to talk with him, tell him to lay off?"

Chendrill smiled, it would be an easy option, but he could sort the fucker out himself. So he said, "Thanks, but I'm a big boy. You don't need to."

But Rasheed did anyway. And the next day he was dead.

Chapter Ten

Rann and Rasheed had met at the side of a busy main road that headed south connecting the same road to the highway which led down to the border that crossed into the United States. Rann got there by bus as he liked to and Rasheed pulled up in his $75,000 Mercedes with low profiles and black windows as he liked to. Rasheed had called him a cunt and told him he wasn't even a real Sikh, just a plastic one—that he needed to start seeing real women, Sikh women, if he wanted to fit in and stop fucking these skinny white sluts like he was. After all, he'd never been to India and didn't even speak Punjabi. Same shit as he'd heard back home growing up outcast from the English and his fellow Indians. He was an African Indian, he spoke Swahili, which, like his mother and father, had mixed with English, but he was still a Sikh. Why did he have to put up with this shit all his life?

Then Rasheed said beneath the roar of the traffic as it passed by, "And you need to give me sixty percent of whatever you're getting from the hard-on pills you've got coming in."

Rann stood there watching as the trucks passed and wondered if he'd heard the man right. So, he said, "Tell me that again?"

"Sixty percent of what you make from your pills goes to me."

He had heard right, so he said, "You've picked a strange spot to start negotiations."

And waiting for a truck to pass, Rasheed said, "I did it because I knew no one else would be here."

It was an odd notion Rann thought, standing at the side of the road with hundreds of cars passing by every minute or so and thinking he was alone. He said, pointing to the cars, "I don't get it, if no one's here, who the fuck are they then?"

Rasheed said, "You and I are alone, we can talk and neither of us can cause trouble because hundreds of people are watching and they don't even know it."

Rann looked to the passing traffic packed together but moving quickly. It was an odd notion, but kind of right. He said, "Why should I pay you money for my pills when they get here, when it's got sweet fuck all to do with you."

Rasheed smiled and said straight back, "Because there's a middle man with everything in life, and you need distribution and I control things around here, my friend. If you want to sell your pills, you need to go through me—the same as if a movie producer wants to show his film, he has to go through the theatres because they're the guys with the means to get it out there and I'm the means to get your little pills out there. So you need to start realizing this and come to an arrangement or you can try peddling them in some other town."

Rann shook his head and looked out to the traffic as it flowed past and took a deep breath, tasting the fuel in the air. This was bullshit, more nonsense, another prick trying it on, and he'd come all the way here on the bus to hear it. Then he heard the guy say, "And as you're going for the big stakes now, hitting up millionaire realtors and shit, you need to start weighing me in on the blackmail funds as well and keep away from the big guy in the loud shirts."

"I would have thought a big prick like that could look after himself," Rann snapped back.

"He can. So, I'm telling you, you are best to stay clear of the fucker. It's advice, nothing less."

They stared at each other. Rasheed continued, "So how many of these pills you got to sell and how much you looking for them?" Keeping it light now, saying it like he was buying baseball cards.

"I've got 180,000 tablets coming in, 30,000 packets of six,

and I want eight bucks a tablet."

Rasheed did the math. Then said, "I'll give you three dollars a packet as long as they work, and they'll need testing first. That's it—ninety grand, that's what they're worth to me. If you don't like it, go sell them yourself, but I don't advise it as you'll be doing it for the next ten years trying. And you'll be treading on my toes, which isn't healthy because I'll fucking kill you and then maybe after if I fancy it, I'll kill your family also—just for kicks.

And that's when Rann felt the rage come from somewhere deep inside his soul, blacking him out as it had so many times before.

******

Chendrill read about Rasheed's demise the next morning as he'd left Dan's mother's house and drove the Ferrari back into town and saw it on the front page of the newspaper he no longer bought or read, but did this time.

'Local Gang Member Found Dead'

Below it was a picture of Rasheed in a turban, sporting two big knives crossing blades at the front.

An hour later, he called Ditcon at the Vancouver Police Department. It's not that he wanted to hand a murder on a plate to the one man who liked to step in and take credit for all the other police officers' work within the homicide section, but enough was enough with this guy who liked to throw things off his balcony. And he'd simply said, "It's Chendrill, the guy you found dead at the side of the road last night was killed by another Sikh by the name of Rann Singh."

And after just enough time had passed for Ditcon to write

Rann Singh's name on a piece of paper, Ditcon had said, "We know, we're already on it."

Hearing the conceited prick's tone, Chendrill wished he'd kept his mouth shut. Then he heard Ditcon say, "We're all over Mr. Singh. Do you have an address?"

"If you're all over him, why do you need an address?" Chendrill asked as he looked down at the floor and waited for the reply that never came.

Ditcon didn't have a clue and chances are if he'd have taken the guy there himself this morning, he'd already have let the guy go by now. Ditcon was too stupid to realize a good thing when he got it and was more interested in his own ego than in some gang banging East Indian, so he said, "I'll take that as a no then."

To which Ditcon replied, "We're not at liberty to make any statements at the moment."

God, the man annoyed him.

No, but you'll be calling me asking for my information the moment you realize you've got nowhere, won't you, you prick, Chendrill thought as he considered hanging up the phone but instead said, "Now I've given you a suspect. When you bring him in, ask him what he does for a living. He's a blackmailer and when he denies that, check out where he's just been in Asia and ask him about the drug Sildenafil. It's the drug that makes your dick hard, but I'm sure you're already aware of that. See what he says—the guy killed Rasheed—I know it and now so do you."

And Ditcon replied, "I'm already aware of the Asian trip and the blackmail. Thank you for your information."

Fuck, 'I'm already aware.' The man was an asshole, how was he aware? Had the guy told him? No—Chendrill had right there and then. He'd given Ditcon the case right there on a plate, and true to form, he'd still managed to steal it.

That's why everyone hated him.

But Rasheed was still dead and Chendrill had only been drinking with him the night before, both of them sitting there, Rasheed in his turban and Chendrill looking like a parrot in a bright red Hawaiian, watching girls ride the bull with their tits bouncing about. But there you go, the man was a gangster not a postman, and gangsters get killed. It came with the territory. Live by the sword, die by the sword.

******

Rann Singh left the storage locker facility and was still trying to work out exactly what had happened as he rode the train back to his apartment out in Surrey. The cops had been nice. They'd asked what happened and all he'd said was they were talking and when he'd looked away, a truck had passed and when he looked back, Rasheed was on the ground and he'd called the ambulance.

"Did you see the licence plate? What type? Color? Make?"

It was busy, he couldn't remember. But what he really couldn't remember was whether he'd pushed the gang leader into the truck's mirror or if Rasheed had stepped back himself. The rage inside him taking over and him blacking out for that split second after he'd been calling him a plastic Indian, calling him a Paki like they used to when he was a kid and then telling him to leave the big guy who wears the shirts be and forget the money because it was just bullshit anyway, and he was going to have to shell out almost all of what he'd make from the Sildenafil he was bringing in.

Why should he? he thought. Let him drive his fucked up Merc with the low tires and smoked out windows down to the airport and stick it in long stay and get on a plane to Thailand, source it all, and risk the death penalty or the rest of your life looking over your shoulder or behind bars sending it back over the border. Then having a Canadian customs guy already there in place—some guy scared of losing his family—and waiting for it on the other side so as he can check it through, giving it the all clear when it hits the post office downtown.

Let him do all that and then give away all the money to some fuckhead who thinks he's king shit just cause he speaks Punjabi and has a couple of Indian princesses as girlfriends. No, the rage that ran through him was strong. He couldn't remember if he pushed him or if the guy had stepped back into the truck's wing mirror that buried itself in his head and crushed his skull.

Chapter Eleven

Samuel Meeken was happy. The local telephone company was keeping the last remaining public phone box going on Denman Street in downtown Vancouver operating at his request, and as long as no one spent the afternoon using it to call their granny, he was going to put on his new cowboy boots and hat and go fishing.

He was in good shape now coming into his fiftieth year. The 500 sit-up and push-up routine he adhered to after each day at the post office was paying off—his stomach tight and chest muscles bulging under the layer of carpeted chest hair that he liked to comb before bed each night.

Samuel Meeken wasn't straight, he wasn't gay, he wasn't Bi, he wasn't A, B or even C sexual—he was multi-sexual, and that's what he'd say when he was asked in the post office canteen.

"I'm multi—I like to have sex with all living things, except children." And that's when the other postmen and postwomen stopped talking to him.

And now he was going fishing.

Standing by the window, he pulled back the curtains and stood there dressed just in his cowboy hat, boots, and chest hair, looking down from the 5th floor at the crowds passing the public phone. He dialed its number into his cordless, listened to it ring, and watched, waiting as the river of people passed below, some looking, but most ignoring the public phone's electronic chime. Seconds passed as maybe a hundred fish came through, then out of the crowd a lady stopped, taking a breather from the weight of the basket of groceries wedged firmly in the trolley she tugged along behind her.

Cautiously the old lady moved towards the phone taking a

look, then, pulling her trolley closer, she looked around at the shops and the others passing by paying no attention. Then on instinct like a hungry fish striking a baited hook, she reached out and picked up the phone to hear Samuel Meeken say, "Don't be frightened."

The old lady looked around and said, "Sorry?"

Samuel Meeken carried on, "Look up to my window and don't be frightened."

The old lady looked up, her eyes not as sharp as her younger self had once been, "I'm sorry?"

"Look at me I'm up here, above you."

The old lady looked up to the sea of windows above. Then she saw him on the 5th floor and said, "I see you, are you the cowboy?"

"Yes, I'm the cowboy, don't be frightened, I know you want me."

And she answered, "What do I want?"

"You want me."

"Do I?"

"Yes, come up to my apartment."

"Sorry?"

"We can make love."

The old lady stood there for the moment as the realization of what the man who was naked in the window above her dressed as a cowboy was saying. But she'd grown up in Calgary, so she knew what cowboys could be like and it wasn't the first time she'd been hit on by one—even if the last had been in 1964. So, she said, "I've just bought some milk. I need to get it into the fridge or it'll spoil and I've got a chicken in the oven."

And so, it went on throughout the day, Samuel Meeken standing waiting, with his fishing rod in his hand trying to reel in anyone he could—except children. It was about three hours later when the police came.

It wasn't the first time he'd been in a police car, and in fact it was usually the best part of the whole fishing trip itself; unless, of course, he actually caught a big one on the line and they were stupid enough to come up.

Now he sat there still in his cowboy hat and boots with a towel wrapped around his waist as the young cop Williams drove him to the station. Samuel called out with his hands cuffed behind him, looking to the sexy cop in the front seat ignoring the whole thing as though it was just another day in the park, which was exactly where Samuel, sitting there with his erection playing tents with the towel, wanted Williams to take him.

******

Marsha was equally excited, and having just received $20,000 for doing nothing but pout, was about to leave the sound stage in L.A. when she got the call from her agent Gill Banton who was having a barbecue at her home in Venice Beach and wondered if she would like to come. Not sure what to do, she said, "Totally." To which Gill replied, "Is that a yes or a no?"

"Oh totally, I was just going to meet this guy I met at the shoot, he's from Guatemala."

"What does he do?"

"Things"

"Which things?"

"Things with the lights, cables, you know."

Gill did, the guy was a lighting guy and she said back down the phone, "That's great, come here, but don't bring the Guatemalan—besides I thought you were still in love with this Dan guy?"

She was, they'd met in Vancouver after she'd gone there for a shoot just so she could do just that, but it hadn't quite worked out that way. Now she'd told the world press they were in love. It was quite a mess. Then Gill said, "There'll be someone here for you to meet. He wants to do a shoot with you, he'll pay well—but you'll need to meet him first."

And when she arrived, she met Patrick.

Patrick stood by the pool in his new linen shirt, trousers, and haircut, smiling at all the people around him. He was here now in amongst the beautiful people, the door well and truly opened for him by Sebastian and Mazzi Hegan—who for the moment were on fire—and he'd stepped right in.

Real estate was old news and celebrity management was the way forward he'd decided. The only way to get anywhere in his eyes was to start at the top and Marsha was just that.

He'd been out for the day shopping with Dee. She was weird in the way she dressed—purple boots and leggings with bright red hair—but she was cute for a woman of 40 and somehow, they got along. Gone were the cashmeres and in came the style—silks and cottons and trousers, alligator skin shoes and shirts that fell together with strange ties which he was sure would never work but they did and for just under $30,000 and a quick donation trip with his old loafers and shirts to the local realtor college, he was set—plus her fee of course.

And now he had Marsha in his sights, coming through the door with her little chubby assistant following behind making her look all the more skinny than she was, and gliding up to him she said, "I'm looking for Gill, she lives here."

The reality was that she hadn't seen her in such a long time she'd forgotten what she looked like. Patrick said, "Gill, your agent?"

"Ya, she lives here."

Patrick stared at this woman who was possibly as beautiful as his old girlfriend whom he used to let play with him and said, "I'm Patrick."

Marsha looked back at him, taking herself away from the rest of the crowd who were discretely looking at her and held out her hand, in the limp fashion people do when they don't really want to touch and said, "Marshaa."

Patrick took her hand and said, "Marshaar?"

And Marsha nodded saying, "That's right, with an A, Marshaa. Like Marshal, but without the Le."

'Le' as in the 'Le' when you first learn the alphabet in kindergarten—*Fuck this woman was dumb*, he thought, incredibly beautiful, incredibly rich, and incredibly dumb. This new line of work he was interested in was going to be easy. Then he said, "I'm from Vancouver. I hear you were just up there on a shoot." Marsha nodded and closed her eyes giving her answer more impact.

"Yeah," then she was silent for a second and opening her eyes, asked, "Do you know Dan?"

Patrick didn't, but he knew who she meant. He, like most of Vancouver, had seen the posters of him and the odd one of her licking the sweat off his chest. So he said, "Hey yeah Dan, great guy. We were just out."

And she asked, "Did he say anything about me?"

And Patrick carried on, "Of course, he's all for you. Says he can't wait to meet up again. We were talking about management and letting me take the stress off things—you know, letting you be who you are, and letting him be the guy he is. Let the agents fight it out and let the guys like me keep the wolves at bay."

"Yeah right, keep the wolves in the forest, yeah."

Then he said, "You want me to get him to call?"

And Marsha, the girl voted the sexiest woman in the world, who had just decided to change the pronunciation of her name, looked at him and, like a little girl blushing in the school yard, bit her lip and nodding her head said, "Yes."

Then he saw Gill coming towards him, her sling-backed $2,000 shoes clicking below her long legs flowing free in a sheer red skirt. Reaching them she smiled and said, "Oh—great, so the two of you have already met."

And Marsha replied, "Hi, I'm Marshaa. I'm looking for Gill."

Gill stared at her for a moment and as the moment passed, realized the girl wasn't kidding. She said, "Marsha, I'm Gill, love."

Fuck me, Patrick thought, *this is going to be easy.*

Chapter Twelve

Dan sat in his room staring at two hugely intricate electronic circuit maps side by side and listened to Chendrill talking with his mother in her bedroom, his big voice booming through the ceiling. They'd just been at it again, the two of them, and now even Chendrill had started to groan.

Looking up as he heard his mother laugh, he stood and looked through the window at the Ferrari outside. *Fuck*, he thought, the car had been gone for a bit and for awhile he'd thought maybe Mazzi Hegan had gotten his way—but now it was back. He should just steal it again like he had that other time when Chendrill was fucking his mum. But for some reason, Chendrill wasn't lasting as long as he had when they'd first met. So if he did, it wasn't going to be easy.

And what was the point of asking to borrow it when Chendrill, the goof, was just going to tell him to get the bus.

He sat back down again and turned on the computer, typed in 'D - A – N', and looked at the photos of himself come flooding back at him.

That's me, he thought—*Dan*. A legend now, a legend who still hadn't even gotten laid—apart from the blind chick in the park, before her guide dog had gotten nasty and bitten him. But in retrospect it may have just been the girl's purse he had his dick in by mistake.

He needed to go out again—get hold of Mel, and go dancing—but he couldn't show up on the bus or walk in off the street. He needed a ride, needed to arrive, then walk in—after all he was Dan, and Dan didn't do buses, even if his big thug minder/bodyguard had told him he should.

He stood up again and noticed the sock still stuck around his dick and pulled it off, tried to think back to how it had gotten there, and then remembered tugging one out to the pictures of Marsha— as she'd called herself after she'd invited him back to her suite, and licked the sweat from his chest. She looked good, but Mel was definitely more fun—and she worked at McDonalds.

He got dressed, walked up stairs and, reaching the fridge, opened it, grabbed a handful of cheese, then turned to see Chendrill standing there in a bright red Hawaiian and said, "Every time I see you, you make me want to eat a pizza."

"Very funny," Chendrill answered.

Then he asked, "Where's the car been?" And right on cue Chendrill answered, "Get the bus."

Dan closed the fridge door, the bottles inside clanging as it hit home.

"I'm an international superstar. I should be in the Ferrari; how can I sit on the bus and stare up at myself in the poster ads?"

"Close your eyes."

"People will see me."

"So, people saw you before."

"I thought you were supposed to be looking after me?"

"That's what I'm doing."

Yeah by fucking my mother, Dan thought, but said instead, "You want to go eat?"

******

They sat in McDonalds with the Ferrari parked up diagonally out front, Chendrill getting out around the block and letting Dan pull in under the golden arches and park it that way as he liked to do. Dan saying now, "You like my mum then do you?" Chendrill smiled—he did—listening as Dan carried on, "Worth taking one in the ribs for, was she?"

Chendrill nodded and said, "You know that, she's a good woman." Then Dan leaned back, taking a big bite of the triple decker burger and chowing down. Mel was not there now, but if he was lucky, she'd be in soon and he could apologize for sticking his head up her skirt and embarrassing her. Then he could see if she wanted to go out dancing again and let her sit on his lap in the front of the car whilst Chendrill dropped them off, tell her he's letting Chendrill drive it tonight because it's his birthday. Then he said, "You need to give her a bit more loving so she don't go looking around."

"And you're the expert?"

"Just an observation."

Then Chendrill said, "I need to give her more loving to give you enough time to steal the car again, is that the kind of loving you're referring to?"

Fuck, he was sharp this guy.

"No, the other guy bought her stuff."

The other guy, Chendrill thought. *The prick.* And he said, "Well I'm not him, and I can't cook pastry for shit, so don't get your hopes up. Besides, you're rich now. You can buy them."

Dan ignored that one about being rich, and said nothing—the look he gave to Chendrill over the burger he was still stuffing into his face was enough. But, pulling it out, he couldn't help it, "What, buy them from him? Yeah good move, I'll ask him to deliver, maybe he can bring his bat."

Chendrill moved at the memory of the baseball bat slamming into his side like it had, felt the pain in his ribs send an electrical pulse through his body, and thought, *yeah and fuck you too Dan, you smart ass.*

Chapter Thirteen

Rann Singh stood on his balcony wishing he'd thrown something else down at Chendrill instead of the lounge chair. He'd liked that one, the way he just had to push back and the whole thing reclined with the little pillow he could use for his head or his lower back if it was aching like it did sometimes after he'd been letting his hair down.

But now the chair was gone and so were two of the weights from each end of one of his dumbbells that he'd been dropping as he'd tried to hit those two cars full of East Indians as they cruised by with their blacked-out windows and Bollywood music blaring. Their tires so low, making them a perfect target as they slowed to crawl over the speed bump at the front of the building.

Obviously, they were all part of the group who hung with the big boy Rasheed and were upset about him and his collision with an oncoming truck's wing mirror. But fuck me, the guy should've been more aware of his surroundings instead of worrying about stealing his hard-earned cash.

Leaning down, he twisted the screws at the end of the second dumbbell and pulled off the two small weights positioned at either end. It was better; they were too heavy like that anyway and he only had them on there to impress chicks when they'd come over to see how long his hair was.

Leaning out, he took aim and gently threw out the third weight and watched it sail through the air, plummeting down towards the road, and saw as it just missed the souped up Mercedes and crashed hard into the tarmac just behind.

Fuck.

He had one left. With Chendrill he'd been on target the first time and the guy had gotten the message, disappearing quickly along with the $100,000 the kinky realtor promised. But he'd been in a rage then and you could do stuff like that when you were angry. Now though, he was just having fun, kind of, like playing darts, but with gravity. He picked up the fourth weight and sent it out there, this time a little to the left and with a bit of twist thrown in for good measure and watched it fall, spinning through the air like a discus thrown by one of those hairy Russian women he used to see in the Olympics.

Down it went sailing towards the Mercedes, on target this time, and hitting it with an almighty bam! Right dead center, making a fish pond out of the roof.

"Yes—Bullseye!" Rann said to himself, as he watched all the doors open and six East Indians pile out of the back and two out the front, the driver picking up the weight in disbelief.

Six in the back, Rann thought, it reminded him of his early days growing up in London when you'd see that many squeezed into an old Nissan going off in the morning to work at the airport. Now over here, they were driving Mercedes that got stuck on speed bumps. The other car pulled back, reversing up to the car. The driver got out and the rest unloaded out the back, all of them walking over to the driver of the dented car trying to look cool, seeing the dent, then the weight, then looking up at Rann. The driver not looking cool and quickly getting back in again and moving his ride out of range.

Rann looked at them all scurrying about picking up the other three weights he'd missed with, one of them down there without a turban, going native, pulling a pistol and aiming it towards him. Rann laughed to himself, saying, "You think you're going to hit me from there, you dopey cunt? You'll probably not even hit the building."

He remembered the man from when he'd first gotten into

town—Archall Diamond was his name. He called himself that because he'd drilled out a perfectly good tooth and stuck a diamond in its center. The man hung out with Rasheed pretending like he was the big guy and Rasheed worked for him, when in reality it was the other way around and Archall Diamond just drove his Mercedes, with its neon lights rigged underneath and a 40,000-amp booster in the back blaring out Bollywood bullshit, making him feel stupid as they'd cruised around Surrey. Archall speaking Punjabi to Rann even after he'd told him twice he didn't understand because he'd grown up speaking Swahili as his mother and father liked to do. The guy ignoring him and carrying on anyway, trying to show off and make an impression, letting him see the gun he was packing and would never use. Then showing him pictures of his girl with long legs who looked like she'd never once been fucked properly.

What a bunch of idiots.

Walking back inside, he grabbed a bucket and quickly filled the thing from the bath with both taps blasting out hot and cold. He came back and looked at them all still there staring back at him and swung the bucket out, saying out loud, "Ave some of that you fucking pricks!"

As he dumped the lot over the side at them, accidently letting the bucket slip at the last second on the recoil and watched the water splay out in front of him then drop down to the road, the bucket following behind landing next to where Archall was crouched with his gun. *Fuck*—he needed that, he thought as he saw the bucket hit the ground and smash into two. He had a girl coming over later and wanted to clean the bathroom.

Walking back inside, he closed the balcony door and turned on the TV. Hockey was on and he liked it; it was way better to watch than the football he'd grown up with, which everyone here called 'soccer' because they had their own football, which he just couldn't begin to understand. Hockey though was great, nice and fast with no fucking around, no diving or any of that kind of shit and no fancy hair, just tough fucks with broken noses and no teeth. And they liked to fight, get it sorted there and then, like he did.

He sat down and wondered how he was going to do the bathroom now. There was a big saucepan in the cupboard he never used that had been left accidently by the previous tenant—he'd use that. That would do it. Get the place all sparkling so when the skinny white girl he'd been chasing came over, she'd feel good and clean. Girls like it like that; it makes them feel safe.

******

Patrick was doing well down south in the land of the beautiful people, feeling good in his new look, getting comfortable with himself. Marsha was with him now as he listened to her every word, understanding her, as she talked about herself and how everyone around her were the stupid ones because it must have been one of them who'd leaked it to the gossip magazines about how she didn't know the price of a pint of milk. Telling her what she wanted to hear, he said, "Why should you need to know how much milk costs? That's what the little people are for."

Marsha nodded and looked towards her assistant Buffy eating cheesecake and told Patrick, "And that one, she can't even remember to pack my things when I have to go to England, which is just outside Europe. Told me after, she had to get a private little thingy so I could have my clothes there in London in the morning."

Patrick shook his head, feeling her pain, saying, "Chartered a jet?"

Marsha nodded, flicking her hair, "Yeah she rented one of them little ones, with the bed, and I bet she slept in it instead of putting my clothes on it and sitting in the small seat like she's supposed to."

Patrick shook his head, closing his eyes. *Unbelievable*, he thought, *unbelievable*. It had been a long time since he'd met anyone this stupid with this much money.

He looked over to Buffy, doing nothing and seeing everything, sharp as a tack, wasting away the day on the payroll watching all the people standing around the pool trying to look cool and no one going in—except her, when earlier she had and caused havoc in her flowery costume. All her phone calls were made, hotels and limos, beauty parlors booked, engagements arranged, and now just waiting and watching.

He asked, "Do you pay her?"

Marsha looked at Buffy, saying, "Someone has to; it's the way it is. How else would she be able to buy her DVD movies?"

"She likes films, does she?"

Marsha replied, shaking her head with her eyes half closed, "Yeah, she waits till there's a deal on any DVD's and gets them. She's got a whole suitcase full and just expects me to pay the extra baggage at the airport. Even today I saw she's just bought another three. 'I said why do you need another three Tom Cruise movies when you've already got loads,' and do you know what she said?"

Patrick stared at her, waiting for the answer to come.

"She said, 'Not all films are the same Marshaa,' she said it just like that, then she said it was worth it 'cos it was a three for the price of two deal at the supermarket where I sent her to get my stuff. Said she couldn't resist. You know, and I sent her there for me—you know what I'm talking about."

He did, he understood completely, the girl had no concept that other people had lives. Then Patrick smiled at her, saying to her in a tone that could melt butter straight from the fridge, "You don't need to worry anymore. I'm retired now see and need something to do. Why don't you just leave everything to me and get on with enjoying your life, that's all you need to do."

Then taking Marsha by the hand, he led her over to Buffy and, still smiling, leaned in and quietly said to her, "I have no doubts at all that you are a very sharp and intelligent woman. I'd like you to come and work with me and if you do, I'll pay you twice what you're earning now with full benefits."

Buffy stared at this man with the golden smile and white linen shirt who'd she'd never met before and had been spending the afternoon trying to work out where she recognized him from. He seemed sincere and was offering her a job and smiled nicely. So, she said, "But I work for Marsha."

And Marsha said back, "It's all good. Patrick's looking after me so I can do what I need to do."

Buffy stared at them both now, smiling, taking it all in. Marsha beautiful, but dumb as a post, this guy she'd never heard of before but whose face she now recalled seeing only two weeks before many times on the back of buses in Vancouver—here now looking different, doing the impossible, holding Marsha's attention for more than two hours and offering her a job with twice the money to boot. What was his angle, what was the catch? Then before she could ask, he said, "There's no catch, Buffy. You come and work for me and we both look after Marsha, I'll get someone else to do the work you do now and then I'd like you to assist me once Marsha begins to introduce me to all of her friends."

Knowing only too well Marsha didn't have any friends, Buffy waited for the 'but' to come and when it didn't, just said, "I thought you sold houses?"

Patrick carried on, ignoring her question as though he hadn't heard it, saying "I'll tell you what, if you've time, I'll arrange a jet

Paul Slatter

to take us all back up to Vancouver sometime soon and we could maybe get together with Sebastian and Dan, and there's this great crab house I know, you'll love it."

Buffy looked up, her eyes swiftly connecting with Patrick's and saying enough to tell him he's on the wrong track, and quickly taking over the conversation said, "Marsha's not eating shellfish at the moment Patrick, but Vancouver sounds great, I'll check the schedule with Gill."

Patrick moved on from Marsha, kissing her hand, treating her like a princess and knowing she wasn't. Buffy was great, he liked her, stopping him right there in a middle of a blunder with the crab comment before he could destroy a whole afternoon's work; yes, she was good, looking after him now and not even on the payroll.

He reached a crowd of people all standing around the pool, looking tanned and beautiful, their teeth capped and flawless, the women's tits and hair perfect, the guys looking younger and more perfect than when they were young for real. Then with charm a mile long, Patrick walked right in, put his hands around them all and said, "You guys look as good and happy as I've ever seen anyone. What's the secret?"

And their secret was pure bullshit and Patrick had more than anyone there—after all, he was the guy who'd just spent the afternoon chatting with Marshaa and she'd never dream of speaking to them, let alone smiling.

He was the man, and his balls were huge.

Chapter Fourteen

Rann Singh walked back to the window and looked down to the road; it was getting on and they were still there below waiting. *Why don't they just come up*, he thought, worried he'd have to karate their asses—after all they knew that's what he did and had done for some time now. After taking a second beating from the skinheads at school, it was all he'd done since. He was a black belt six times over and still couldn't believe the big guy with the loud shirt had managed to get the better of him sucker punching him twice—he must be getting soft.

Since losing his bucket, he'd sent a whole tin of peanuts down on to the posse that was forming and made good use of a china tea set he'd been given but didn't like, and seeing it smash all over the idiots below and their cars was special. *Fuck 'em.*

Soon though, he'd go down and take them on one at a time, put to use all the training he'd done in the past but didn't do as much now as he should. He'd take down the Punjabi warrior with his gun, break his fancy teeth with it first then bring it down on his head hard, so as every time he felt the lump on his head over the next few days he'd wished he'd kept his hair and wore his turban like a good Sikh should—the fucking cocksucker. It was nine in the evening. He'd give them till ten and go down and put the cat amongst the pigeons.

At ten he did just that, and as he came out the door taking them all by surprise, two began to run.

Feeling his china from the tea set crunching under his feet, Rann walked straight over to Archall Diamond in his silk suit and pointy shoes and went at him. Taking his gun from his hand before he could lift it, he smacked him on the head, knocking him out, and threw the gun over the wall into the same area Chendrill had thrown his knife when he'd disarmed him so easily. It felt good to be back. Then he said as the guy hit the ground, "You all need to have a whip round to pay for that tea set you made me smash on your heads—and my bucket."

The rest of the Indians stared back at him, not knowing now what to do since their spokesman was unconscious. Then he said to them all, "If you've come about Rasheed, then tell his mum and dad I'm sorry. He got hit by some truck that was going too fast."

Then one of the Indians said to him, "Diamond was there—he says you killed him."

"Well you can tell Diamond when he wakes up that he's a cunt, and if he keeps bothering me, I'll start getting really pissed. So, unless one of you have some sort of gun or knife and are wanting to use it on me, I suggest you go fuck off because I want to clean my bathroom and after I don't want to be thinking about you lot down here getting all cold and hungry whilst I'm in my bedroom chowing down on this hot little piece of white skinned perfection I've got coming over."

And that was that.

******

Chendrill kissed Dan's mother hard on the lips and felt her body move and heard her gasp as his dick pushed right up inside her, hitting the top.

He'd brought Dan back despite the young man's protests, but it was hard to concentrate on making love to the kid's mum when he knew somehow Dan was more than capable of beating the Ferrari's security system. *How was he doing it though?* he thought, as he kept one ear out for the door and the other on his new woman—who he was getting to like more and more as the days passed, the way she looked at him, the way she made him smile.

He moved his head away from her lips and began to kiss her neck just as he had earlier when he'd started chasing her around the room with that look in his eye. Slowly he moved his mouth up and gently kissed her ear as he slid in and out of her, her hands moving along his spine, unconsciously digging her nails into his back and ass as he began to pound. It was quiet downstairs. Dan, full of food, would probably also be full of sleep. If not, the broom would have been hitting the ceiling now.

Chendrill moved his mouth back to hers and began to kiss her passionately, feeling her small toned legs wrapping themselves around his back as she pushed herself back onto him as he began to fuck her hard. Her breathing heavy through her nose, him hearing the groan she always made when she was about to feel herself begin to come, her legs tight around him now, lifting herself up to meet him, feeling her wetness as he pounded and ground himself into her, kissing her, feeling himself filling her, reaching her top and her squeezing his cock with her muscles making Chendrill want to come himself, feeling it build more and more as he became thicker inside her. And as Chendrill pushed himself deep inside Dan's mother, Dan pushed the Ferrari away from the curb, one hand on the door seal and the other on the steering wheel, the car door open without the alarm sounding— the shoe box full of infrared electronic circuitry all soldered up and held together by tape sitting on the passenger seat. He reached the end of the road and got in at exactly the same time as his mother came, calling out without control and making Chendrill feel like a man who was big and strong and could do anything he wanted right there and then, anything he wanted now—except use his car.

Dan turned the steering wheel and felt its leather as it spun back through his hands as he pulled away along the main road that headed into town. *Yeahhhh*, he was back driving the machine again, hot rod motherfucking Ferrari, with no loud shirt wearing big fucking minder in tow giving him daddy lectures just because he was screwing his mother.

Putting his foot to the floor, he screamed the car through the gears and stared up at a poster of himself looking good. He said to himself, 'Hello handsome,' as he felt his nose, still broken and giving him breathing difficulties. Thinking of Mazzi Hegan standing there, having a shit fit about his stuff being all messed up, then pulling out his camera like one of those crazy war correspondent types. Except Mazzi wasn't crazy, he was talented.

He pulled the Ferrari up on the road just outside McDonalds and Mel got in. She was talking to him again now, the business of him putting his head up her skirt sorted. She'd shown up at the last minute as he was about to leave, then stayed whilst Dan had knocked back another cheeseburger and said, "I'm very sorry I acted inappropriately towards you in that club and would like to ask your forgiveness."

Just as Chendrill had told him to.

Now she was back and the night was young. They hit Robson Street like he used to and cruised it a dozen times, revving up the engine like an idiot in the process. Then he did the same around Yaletown, spinning the wheels hard outside Slave's offices for good measure. Then they hit a club.

The Tip Top Club was good, owned by an East Indian by the name of Rasheed, who'd just recently been killed in a bizarre fashion out on some road that led out of town. The club manager posing for a photograph with the hottest model in town at the moment, said, "It's a shame he's no longer around, he'd have been very happy to have had you here at his club."

As he let Dan and his girl in for free and sorted out the best VIP table there, the manager told him drinks and food were on the house.

Fuck me, Dan thought, this was good—all the girls staring at him now, giving him the look. *Fuck me*, and some were hot, not Marsha hot, but hot. Mel, though, was hotter and tonight the chances were high that, one way or the other, he was going all the way.

He picked up his drink, knocked it back and ordered another four, two each, and some fries and wings.

Then he started dancing, playing at first with Mel as she watched him from the table moving the way his mother had as a child, fluid, seamless as if the music was tailored just for her— and now him, moving through the crowd as though she was the only one there, not looking at another as they flirted and stared. Mel was his and no other; he would grab her by the hand soon and make her feel special, take her out there on the dance floor and hold her, dance slowly in time regardless of the music, love her and make her love him just as Chendrill had told him to earlier, as Dan had sat there listening for once with his mouth full of fries.

"You two are the only ones in the room, dance and play, but ignore the rest—no one else matters—then kiss her softly and in the end when she wants to she'll take you to her bed, not the other way around."

And Dan did, holding her and dancing the night away with no thought for any other, no girl who stared or caught his hand as he went to the washroom or waited for him as he'd returned, offering him herself with her tight skirt and big tits.

"This is what you do, Dan," Chendrill had said as they drove back from McDonalds, not knowing it was going to be quite as soon as he'd expected or that, as he was speaking, Dan was planning to leave the broom and let him get right into it with his mum so he could make the night-time rendezvous in style.

And when the time came, as they began to leave the club, the manager had offered the club's suite upstairs to them both so they could unwind and come back. Once up there, Mel had led him to the bed, slowly undressing herself, laying herself down for him to take her like the man he now was. This time with no guide dog biting him, or supermodel ego or crazy murals on the ceiling to contend with, everything was all laid out for him. This sexy young blond who worked at McDonalds, who used to smile and serve him fries, was his, holding out her hands, beckoning him towards the bed touching his shoulders gently, pulling him towards her, smelling her scent as his face grew close to hers, feeling her lips touch his, her hands on his neck, on his back; and then, feeling the panic rise up in him as she reached down lower, touching him as his body began to shake at the realization that he was there and was about to make love, as an unstoppable flow came across him, the release of uncontrollable, unstoppable muscles tightening as the ejaculation process that was the curse of so many young men started too soon somewhere deep in his loins and hit home with a bang.

Then as he gave out the tiniest of a whimper he heard Mel say, "It's okay, it's okay."

Then Mel's phone rang and it was Chendrill telling her it wasn't okay. He said, "Tell him please to bring the car back now or I'm going to come over there and kill him."

Chapter Fifteen

The next day, the papers said it all. Front page was another picture of Dan with his girl, holding her on the dance floor and next to it another of the world's most beautiful woman crying. Underneath read the line:

'Love conquers beauty'

"There's nothing I can do," said Sebastian through the phone to Marsha's agent as she lay in bed with another sexy model guy, this time from someplace she couldn't remember in Argentina.

"Well could you try? She's very upset—she's on the phone to me as we speak."

Sebastian was in a fluster. Gill had control of some of the best, but what could he do? If it was true and the guy was in love—and from the pictures it certainly looked that way—it was out of his hands. So, he said, "You can't stop the world from turning Gill; we both know that."

He heard her moan slightly and reply, "Come on Sebastian. We both know the only people these types truly love are themselves, so please be a sweetheart and do what you can with him—if you don't, I'll let it slip he's into guys and that'll shake it up a bit."

Goodness me, Sebastian thought, that was all he needed, the bitch threatening him with that, no better than that guy who'd been chasing down Patrick—the poor love.

He put down the phone and then picking it up again, called Chendrill and said into his answering service, "Chuck darling it's Sebastian, call me quick it's an emergency—we've got another one of those blackmailer type people on to us."

87

Fuck me not again, Chendrill thought as he listened to the message, all tired from not sleeping trying to track down Dan, the prick. Sitting down on his sofa, he called him back and straight away asked, "Who is it this time and what do they want?"

Sebastian took a deep breath, saying, "Gill Banton, Marsha's agent."

"Sorry—she's blackmailing us?" Chendrill stayed silent for the moment, thinking, then continued, "Why?"

Chendrill's stomach turned as Sebastian said, "It's all over the papers Chuck, this morning, with that girl in another club."

"Doing what?"

"In love with that girl he was with before, the one from McDonalds."

Thank God.

"So, he's young."

"Yes, but it's hurting her client, so Marsha's agent said she's going to put it out there that he's gay."

"I thought you guys loved outing people?"

"That's Mazzi's thing, not mine. He used to say you were. Especially after I gave you his car."

"Really?"

"Oh yes! And there's pictures of Dan driving it again in the papers."

"Don't worry—he won't be doing it again."

"How do you know?"

"Because I thumped him in the eye."

Sebastian was silent for a second. The guy was being paid to stop that kind of thing happening, not do that kind of thing, so he said, "I don't think your idea of looking after someone is quite the same as mine, Chuck. Is it bad?"

It was.

Dan had hit the end of their road, turned off the engine, and coasted. He parked the car, quietly opened the front door and snuck in, crept down the staircase in the darkness, opened the door to his basement room as slowly as possible to stop it creaking, got inside, closed the door and slid on the dead bolt he used to keep his mother out when she was in a rage or when he was knocking one out into one of her fluffy socks. He turned around to see Chendrill standing there in the darkness, his Hawaiian shirt blending in perfectly with Dan's Metallica poster on the wall. Then a fist came down from the man's solid frame, delivering a well-deserved love tap to the cheek, just enough to let him know Chendrill wouldn't have the piss taken out of him twice by Dan or anyone. Sometimes words were not enough.

******

There was silence for the moment, then Sebastian took a deep breath and said, "Well Mazzi won't like it."

"Mazzi broke his nose, that's why we're talking now."

And Sebastian said, "Dan's a human being, Chuck; hitting him is not a sport."

"If he keeps stealing the Ferrari, Sebastian, and he's not listening, he's going to get a thump, Sebastian, or would you prefer next time I just call the police?"

"No don't do that please—has he got a shiner?"

He did, a big one. "I've seen worse."

"Much worse?"

"Not really."

Shit, Sebastian thought. Then Chendrill said, "So what are we going to do about this agent who's got you in her sights now?"

******

Dan sat in his basement room feeling sorry for himself. Every time he got with this chick from McDonalds, something went wrong; but when he broke it all down, every time he managed to get with any chick he had problems, and the common denominator was him. *There you go, we can't all be perfect*, he thought. He was still on his way to richness and stardom, even if it was fleeting.

He got up and looked in the mirror at his eye. It was bruised, Fuck, that big ass prick ape of a man had a hard punch, saying out loud as he turned around looking to the ceiling on the way back to bed, "You were lucky."

And Chendrill was, Dan could have hit back and broke both his hands on Chendrill's skull—then where would they be? Dan not able to work, get up there on stage and look good because he had a bad sperm build up problem now that he was unable to masturbate.

Then his phone rang. It was Marsha and she was crying.

"Dan?"

"Who is this?"

"Marshaaa."

Dan stayed silent for a moment.

"What's up?"

"I can't sleep."

Dan looked at the clock. It was a quarter after midday. He knew the problem.

"Yeah."

"I saw the pictures with you and that slut again, in the club last night, you were kissing her."

Fuck me, how, Dan thought. He hadn't seen anyone taking photos in the club. Marsha carried on, "And of you looking cool with her in your Ferrari."

Dan felt his eye and said, "And?"

"And I thought we were in love?"

Dan stayed quiet, giving this one some thought, then said, "Sorry?"

Marsha continued, "We're in love Dan, I told the press."

Then he simply said, "The last thing I remember you telling me was that I was an asshole."

"Girls say that, but they don't mean it."

"Oh."

"So, I'm coming up soon, Patrick's putting it together. He told me you couldn't wait to see me."

"Who?"

"Patrick, he's taken control of me, you know not as an agent, you know with personal things because Buffy's an idiot. He's so cool, you should meet him." Dan was confused now.

"You just said I already know him."

"Yeah."

"I already know him, but I should meet him because he's cool?"

"Yeah."

Fuck me, Dan thought, this girl was hot but not in the brain. Then she said, "Buffy thinks he's cool too."

"Buffy?" Dan said, "Is she hot too?"

"No, she likes cheesecake, and she's stupid. She went swimming in a blue bikini that didn't fit at this party on the weekend and embarrassed the shit out of me, and she paid for a private jet for my luggage to be sent from your place to that place where the Queen lives just because she forgot to pack it."

"Oh."

"Yeah, she likes him too, but she's stupid, that's why Patrick's helping out now."

"Oh."

"And we're coming up and going for a meal at the fish restaurant with you and Sebastian, he's so cool. I love his little dog."

"We are?"

"Yeah, Patrick says you and him love it there."

"We do?"

"Yeah you like it—maybe you and I could go out after, go dancing, you know like you were yesterday with that bitch."

Dan stayed quiet for the moment, thinking. He was sitting in his basement room of his mother's house with a shiner from her new boyfriend, finding it impossible to get laid for some reason, and for the second time in his life the girl who was recently voted the most beautiful woman on the planet was coming on to him; not only that, she was jealous of the chick he'd been out with who worked at McDonalds. Then still feeling the soreness around his eye with his fingers, he said, "Sure, the club's really great, the manager there lets me use the presidential suite upstairs, it's really cool you know, to go up there after and wind down."

"Wow, cool, maybe we should go and hang out, dance a bit and then go play some more alone upstairs," said Marsha, as she oozed sex down the phone to Dan, who was now looking down at his dick getting hard in his pants.

Then he said, "The person who owns it just died though, got hit in the head by a truck, but they say he was a really nice guy."

"Cool, I can't wait to meet him."

"Really?"

"Yeah."

"The guy's dead, Marsha."

And Marsha said back. "Yeah but maybe we can see him when he gets out of the hospital—you know people can get better."

Chapter Sixteen

Gill Banton didn't want to do it, but there was little left in her arsenal. All it would take was an anonymous call to a reporter friend to tell him Dan was in the closet. But if she did, it could all backfire that her client was dating a gay guy. Sebastian was a good man, she knew that, and how he lasted being such a good man in the world she lived in she could never understand. He did good work—sometimes great work—and if she pissed him off, then he may never book up a client she represented again, even if they were right for the spot. He'd do that.

She picked up the phone and called Sebastian back and said, "Seb, darling, I'm sorry about this morning. I got out of the wrong side of the bed."

Whose bed? Sebastian thought. He knew of this agent's penchant for sleeping with her clients—some of which, it had even been said, were girls. But that was none of his business. Now, he thought, she was worrying, thinking he'd leave her on the sidelines come the next big campaign. So, he said, "Darling, don't be worrying about the future. I don't hold grudges." And he didn't, but he also never forgot.

"Are you sure we're all good then, precious?" Then she said to him, letting him know how she'd just done him a favor, "And I love Patrick, he's such a nice guy. He's organising a shoot with Marshaaa."

Sebastian smiled, thinking, *a shoot for who?* Patrick moved quickly, you didn't become the hottest real estate salesman in town without being able to hustle—and not let anyone know you were doing it for that matter. Soon he'd be getting the call from Patrick telling him how he was going to make Sebastian and his company look better than they already did—like he was doing him a favor when it was really Sebastian making it all happen, putting Patrick out there, redesigning him like he'd asked him to. Gill needed to watch it, he thought—pay more attention to what was going on outside the bedroom; or before she knew it, Patrick would have all her clients in the new stable he was building without even knowing he was doing it himself. With Sebastian pulling the strings, Patrick would be there sooner than he thought, holding the talent and sitting at his table on the weekends with his name on the back of one of Sebastian's expensive china plates.

The first thing he did after Gill Banton put down the phone was call Chendrill.

"Marsha's agent, the blackmailer. She's just called and apologized."

"Good," Chendrill said, and meant it. The last thing he needed was more bullshit.

"Patrick's been down in L.A. with her at her place."

"He has?"

"Yes, it's his new thing, models and actors."

My God, Chendrill thought, he'd be down there getting into all sorts of stuff, he could just imagine it. Then he asked, "Nothing more from the guy in the turban?"

There wasn't.

"I think all the blackmailing is done for the day around here," Sebastian said.

But it wasn't, Rann Singh was a tenacious fucker; and although Mazzi Hegan may have waved a banner flag running all the colors of the rainbows around the office, there was always another way to skin a cat—and he wouldn't be waving the same come fuck me flag at the tax man.

******

Malcolm Strong felt as though he'd once been a tight rope walker who, years before, had wowed the stage, dropping his pole to do cartwheels and handstands with ease across the tightly pulled rope with no net below, as the crowds held their breath waiting for him to fall and plummet the forty feet to meet his end on the stage below. But now, he was barely hanging on, the crowds waiting in silence as the tips of his finger clasped the rope, his nails slowly coming lose, prying away, peeling from his skin, ready to let him slip away into the darkness.

Malcolm was a customs inspector and was very close to having a nervous breakdown. He was a man who, at the proud age of forty-five, had a wife and a career that both looked healthy on the outside, but as with most things in life there were issues. Issues at work where he couldn't deliver the services and things they needed. Issues in the bedroom where his wife didn't deliver the things he needed. And after the sixth time he'd looked elsewhere for his satisfaction, he'd met Rann—and that's where his whole life really began to unravel.

Rann had photos you see. He had photos of Malcolm in his car cruising around for the crack whores of Vancouver's East Side. He had photos of him picking them up and dropping them off. And he had photos of the bit in between when he would close his eyes and think about the wife he loved doing the same to him—as she used to do all those years ago when she was younger, when she would rub her tongue up and down his dick and swallow when he came. But not now. Now she barely kissed his mouth, or sometimes stuck her ass out for him to fuck whilst she laid still. And he would bang into her from behind and feel her tits—very much like Rann had banged into him as he had pulled away after dropping off the whore on a corner, watching her get out without a word, off to buy crack with the thirty bucks she'd earned swallowing his come.

Rann had got out, felt the rain on his neck, apologized, then handed Malcolm the small dossier of his activities over the last little while attached to a little card with his phone number on it, and his wife's photo, and her phone number also.

"We should talk—I think I know a way I can help you," he had said.

And they had talked, in the corner of a small café, Rann with a hot chocolate, Malcolm shitting himself with nothing. Rann going through the motions, laying it on thick about how he was trying to help. Rann explaining that 'this guy' he'd come across, 'a real Christian bible thumper' was angry at the world, and was even angrier at Malcolm Strong because, it turned out, what Malcolm had been doing went against God's will, and it didn't help either that he'd been fucking the man's run-away daughter. This God-fearing man, said Rann, wanted retribution in cash for Malcolm's sins of the flesh.

And he'd paid—with money he didn't have and couldn't afford; and then, just as Malcolm thought the nightmare was over, Rann made a suggestion. He knew by now where the man worked, stationed at the post office in downtown Vancouver, checking and x-raying every parcel and document that came through from overseas and entered the country. Looking for contraband on a daily basis came with the territory, as did knowing what to look for, and finding it.

"What if you were told ahead of time what was coming through, and when it was going to be there?" he'd said, "And if you're good then maybe this nightmare you've created for yourself could just end the moment it slipped through."

Drugs, Malcolm thought, and he was right—but not in the sense of drugs as the general public knew them. It wasn't Heroin, Cocaine, Crack, or those other chemicals like Crystal Meth that monsters dreamed up and that the girls fucked and sucked their days and nights away on until eventually they died from starvation.

Rann had been thinking, doing the maths for a while now, on something some idiot named Padu had told him about one night as they sat together looking at white chicks in a bar in the Whaley area of Surrey.

As he watched Rann stare at a girl in tight jeans and high heels, the guy had said, "You like that? Well, you'd better have some of this," and he'd pulled out a pack of four hard-on pills marked with a V across the top.

"I don't need it, my Hampton works fine," and the guy had said, "I'm sure it does, but these'll make it super hard, whenever you wanted day or night, super hard."

And they had, and not even a whole one either, just a quarter; and as one of the skinny white chicks he liked to fuck held his hair that was falling into her face and came for the third time in the hour, he knew it was different. He was bigger, thicker, and way harder than normal—and he liked how it felt.

Then one night Padu, drunk in the bar with his pocket full of pills, told him the lot.

"I used to go over there to Bangkok, get laid, get my dick sucked by two chicks at a time if I wanted, buy couple of pockets full, bring them back in and make ten bucks on a tablet that's cost me a dollar."

"How many were you bringing in?"

"Ten to twenty packs every time, ten tablets in a pack. Paid for the trip. And the stuff's real, same stuff they charge double for at the doctors. Except there they don't have the same patenting laws we have here. It's the same shit, but even stronger. See those

Asians guys have just got those little dicks, so they keep trying to get them bigger, pump more shit in, stretch it out a bit."

"How much you bringing in now?" Rann had asked.

"A carry-on bag full every time, and they sell."

Then he'd heard the guy had gone down, doing a five stretch out in Abbotsford for drug trafficking, and it was him doing the dick sucking now.

But it had got him thinking. He'd sold the lot each time really fast just on his own, mostly to horny kids wanting to keep it up, trying to keep the party going after they'd blown too early, and the doctors here wouldn't let them have any. Ten dollars a tab now, but if they were fifteen or even twenty a tab, they'd still sell, and if he brought in a shitload, and set up distribution, he'd be able to forget being a prick with all this scurrying around in the dark and start thinking about moving forward with his life and get away from it all with his family.

As he sat there, not drinking the coffee he'd ordered, Rann said to Malcolm, "Don't worry, we're not talking junk, not heroin or any of that shit they sell around town. No one's going to die from what you'll let slip through the system, unless they have a heart attack from all the fun they have fucking, and tell me what's wrong with that?"

******

A week later, Rann Singh started sending word out that there was going to be shit coming in, tablets that would rip out the front of your trousers just as soon as you saw something you liked—and would stay that way till you said, 'down boy.'

Then he took a trip to the jail in Abbottsford. The guy had sat there like an idiot telling him the lot— where, when, and how. He bought them over the counter from a brother Indian working in a small pharmacy in Patpong. He sold them to the tourists and paid off the cops for the privilege. There was an Irish guy there he said, lived there working the bars, "a loud drunk, sells the same shit cheaper, but makes a living." That's who he'd been going to when he bought the shit in bulk.

"What's his name?" Rann had asked.

"Paddy," Padu had said straight back, "And he's bald or just likes to shave it cause he's missing half, one of those guys, you know."

"He's an Irishman who's bald and goes by the name of 'Paddy'?"

"Yeah."

Well that narrows it down some, thought Rann.

******

A week later Rann was on his way to Thailand, flying business class on the cash he'd earned creeping around in the darkness taking photos of filth. The place was different from what he'd imagined. The heat made his head itch under his turban. He wondered how his father had managed all those years living in Uganda before the regime moved him from his home.

Taking a beer, he sat down watching the activities. Here there was no skulking around in the alleyways like in Vancouver. It was out there for the world to see—girls large and small, young and old and some too big to be girls at all. Bar girls, street girls, go-go girls, go-go boys, go-go boys dressed as girls, either overly effeminate or sitting like men do, watching punters abound swimming in pussy or ladyboy cock. There were some like him just watching, others drunk and horny, grown men feeling like kids again on the pull and others alone or in small packs prowling the streets, hunting like sharks in a world full of neon and sin, their eyes scanning every nook and cranny as they looked for their prey. Those were the ones he'd like to nab, get the goods on. He'd fuck them up before they went home to the real world, just as they were intending to fuck up some poor girl making money so her children and parents could eat—not for crack or heroin as they usually did on the streets where he lived. But here they were selling their ass for what they could and for the chance the guy they were with may just fall in love.

Rann had found the Irishman a week later in a go-go bar, getting spanked by a girl leaning out from the stage bringing down her foam whip and slicing it across his ass while a woman who clearly must have been his girlfriend watched from the sidelines. Rann recognized both the accent and the arrogance right away, who didn't give a damn about him, or the supermodel-like figure of the woman who followed in his shadow for that matter, kissing him as he stretched his neck to her while he held another, his gut hanging out from under his shirt, his hands around the girl—or maybe-not's—pants, feeling what was there and not caring who could see or what they thought.

He waited, watching, and as the man got bored with himself, Rann moved over and sat beside him. The Irishman looked up and smiled saying, "You like the crack, does you?"

And Rann said, "Yeah!"

As the Irishman looked up at him surprised saying, "Well fock me if you're not one of those fucking London wankers disguised as a Paki."

Fuck you, you cunt, Rann thought, before he smiled and said, "Yeah I've got a corner store right up the street here. And I ain't a

Paki, I'm a Sikh."

"Whatever," The Irishman said as the lights from the club spun around for the moment, hitting him in the face, showing him as he was, a drunken fool. He carried on, his words steady, showing no sign of the amount of booze flowing through his system, "I'm sure you're a good man, who likes a crack don't you."

Rann was a good man, in his eyes at least, better than the fool who just sat kissing his girl with his hands down a ladyboy's pants for the world to see. He looked to the Irishman's girl sitting there with him, her hair long and straight.

"She's a fucking beauty, isn't she?" said Paddy.

"She is," Rann replied.

Then Paddy said out loud, "Sucks like a fucking baby calf she does. You wouldn't believe it."

No, I wouldn't, Rann thought, but what Rann really couldn't believe was this man telling a complete stranger shit like that about his girl. He asked, "She's your woman?"

"You want to fuck her?"

Rann didn't; in fact, not at all, to him the woman looked like a monkey with her high cheekbones and big lips—but fuck she had a nice body he thought as The Irishman carried on, "Well you can't 'cos she's my wife—four fucking years and she doesn't fuck anyone else but me—but I can tell you that's a one-sided deal!"

What a prick, Rann thought. Then he told him, "I'm a friend of Padu."

"Does he work with you at the store?" he asked back, knowing too well there was no store. Then said, "Never focking heard of him," as he stared at the twenty odd girls on the stage fighting for a spot, their tits out, dancing and prancing about in the dark with shoes they could barely walk in.

Rann sat back and looked over to the side of the bar at a girl there alone, in a shower booth built for two, with a sponge full of soap in both hands rubbing herself down and making huge hearts in the glass with the same sponge while staring him straight in the eye.

"You want to fock that, do you?" he heard the Irishman saying to him now.

He did, she was sexy, no doubts about that. "Take that hat off—get in the shower with her then, give us all a good focking laugh."

Not a good idea, Rann thought. Then he said to the Irishman, "Padu's gone down, he's doing time. If you want me to pick up where he left off, I'm happy to. I'll come find you again." And giving the girl in the shower one last look for the memory bank, he got up and left. The next day, the drunken Irishman with the bald head called Paddy found Rann. What else could he do? The man was a drunk, and drunks need their nectar. Money was money.

******

They sat in a booth. The Irishman drinking, doing all the talking. Rann hearing and seeing all. The wife doing nothing but looking sexy. People coming, and people going, girls at the bar leaning, their asses sticking out of their shorts, their shoes worn, cooing to the white men trying to pull. And Paddy saying, "You want the stuff they sell out there on the street? It ain't the right stooff I'm telling you?"

"What about at the pharmacy?"

"That's what I'm talking about. The focking pharmacy. They'll sell you the shite. I'll get you the stuff'll get you focking hard. What you want?"

Rann looked to the guy's wife, who apparently knows how to blow, seeing her in a different light now, thinking *she's hot but still kind of looks like a monkey*, deciding he wasn't imagining it, saying, "How much?"

"Five dollars a pack to you—and I'm not making much."

Not making much. After Padu had told him he was buying them at a dollar a pack. Rann spit right back at him saying, "Padu told me it was a dollar a pack, where the fuck you get five from?"

The Irishman, red now, looking at the girls at the bar trying to remember if he'd fucked one of them said, "He's in prison, you know and that's not where I wanna be so keep it in mind."

Rann stared at the man with his bald head and red nose, wishing he'd kept quiet about his predecessor's new abode. He said, "What's that got to do with it."

"Look I'm not in the mood to fock around, tell me how many of these little hard-on tablets you want?"

"About maybe 100,000."

Then Paddy stayed silent for the moment thinking, doing the maths, it was a number that Rann could see he was interested in just from the way his attention had gone completely away from the girls in the place. The Irishman asked, "I take it you'se talking boxes?"

"Tablets, but in boxes of 10."

"10,000 focking boxes of the shite—what the fock are you going to do, have a focking party?"

No, Rann thought, he was going to buy back the home back in

Kenya taken for a song from his grandfather by that shithead Malcolm Blou. And if it all went well, he'd still have a few dollars extra to play with after.

******

Two days later, they met again. This time away from the maddening crowds of the red-light district that Paddy liked to frequent. Now they sat in the coffee shop overlooking the river. It was a coffee shop, but the Irishman was still drinking whisky at eleven in the morning, listening to his wife talk to her friend she'd brought along for Rann to meet. The Irishman listened to them both chatting together in Thai, the prick nodding along with the conversation, looking as though he understood while Rann looked at the friend's long legs and nice shoes, enjoying it when she caught his eye.

There were more framed photos of the King on the wall in this place than usual, he thought, as he looked out across the river. The slim boats carrying tourists from around the world passing by with their rudders sticking out way behind, scooting them along in the sun through the dark murky river full of fish and filth.

They'd made their deal; as it stood, the Irishman would be the middle man, saying he'd have his man make it and package it all special, and Rann would buy through him. And now Rann wanted more, adding to the package, the tablet he took from Padu was just a tiny piece, only 25mg of a 100mg tablet. Butting in on the Irishman listening to his wife talk at five hundred miles an hour and still staring at her friend's legs, Rann said, "What I'm after is a special order. Think of me like I's one of them companies that come in, right, and I'm saying, give me a special order. What I want is this, 33,000 packets of six times 25 mg of this Sildenafil shit with a bit of sugar put in to make it taste nice and bulk it up a bit."

The Irishman stared at him, then said, "We can't focking do dat? Who'd you think you is, a fockin pharmaceutical company?"

And Rann replied, "No but you ain't paying, I am, so we can. So fuck off. You want kids damaging their dicks by taking too much, do you? Jesus—25 mg tablets will be fine, that's one 100mg tablet cut into a quarter—This is what I want and I won't keep up saying it over and over, so you'd better put that drink down and start listening."

And he said it again, "I want—33,000 packets containing six 25 or 30 mg tablets of Sildenafil mixed with sugar or orange or whatever other fruit the guy wants to compress, and on the package, I want printed the letters R.S."

And straight away, the Irishman asked, "And what the fock is that standing for?"

Rann smiling now as he replied, "It's me, my initials R.S., and it also stands for Rock Solid."

"That's ridiculous," said the Irishman.

"I'm paying, you're not," said Rann again straight back, and then said, "and I'm going to pay one dollar a packet which is thirty-three thousand dollars more than you would have had to play with. So, you can work out your commission and go sort it out and take your cut off the top or you can leave it and I'll go speak to another source I've got in Laos. So, I suggest you get on the blower quick and call him, or I'll be getting on the plane to Vientiane in the morning."

He liked that bit about Vientiane in Laos, having never heard of the place until he'd seen it on the map by accident that morning as he'd wandered about the hotel lobby looking at the pictures of the Thai King and Queen scattered all around his hotel, reminding him of his grandmother and his grandfather—but without the turban.

The Irishman's wife sat there listening to the two men bickering amongst themselves. She understood a bit—the odd words or numbers she'd learned working the bars, earning her keep, until the Irishman took her back to his room one night and she'd managed to get him to love her with her long sexy legs and tongue—enough to keep him as her own, to some extent. But the accents and the speed they were speaking made for an impossible translation. From her perspective, it was going to be worth his while. Her husband never left the part of town where he felt most at home. Just as she was about to smile and ask Rann if he liked her friend's dress, she heard her man snapping out, getting all red in the face, "I'm the man making it happen, I'm the guy with the focking connections. I'm setting it up, keep on treating me like a focking monkey, keep trying to be funny, ya focking gobshite and you'll be on your own!"

She got that—the monkey bit. She knew how funny they were, the monkeys, she knew Phetchaburi well, having grown up there and been back many times, picking up the packages for her husband while he slept with other women. There were monkeys everywhere around the pharmacist's building, coming off the mountain where the temples and palaces of the old king still stood but which now were unhoused and broken. Smiling and taking them both by surprise, she said, "The monkey families at the pharmacy are very funny."

They were. These monkeys, all living together at the edge of the city. Carrying on with cheek and audacity, living up to their name, acting as they were expected to, carrying on as they do, swinging from the telephone wires and scaling walls, unobstructed in the urban setting of a major city.

Rann stared at her, wondering if she was talking about herself or her family. Maybe the Irishman saw what he saw in her, he thought, and called her monkey woman or something like that in some strange but affectionate way. He said to her, "Your family, they live round there, near this guy?"

Paddy rolled his eyes. He'd had enough, the Paki with the turban was getting on his tits and he wanted to get this sorted. So, he said, "What she's got is a kid who lives round that way. But what's she's talking about is this, you get a shitload of monkeys live round the pharmacist's shop, the focking things are everywhere, pissing and shitting and fucking each other all over the place. Come in along the focking telephone wires they do, swinging on them 'an pulling 'em down, snapping them all the time, they are, that's why I can't call him just yet to make the focking deal. And once they get in his place and start reaching in the windows and eating this hard-on shit you want him to put together they'll be twice as many of the fockers."

Chapter Seventeen

Patrick arrived back in Vancouver, having taken a private jet that he knew was a waste of money. But he'd hoped to find some more celebrities going out of LAX in the executive bar, and he had; seeing Samson, a good looking young TV star, doing well from a series that was getting big, and his girl, Crazy Sue—who he'd never heard of. Both of them hiding away, being cool and elusive, and Patrick in there like a dirty shirt, letting it slip he was on his way up to Vancouver to have an evening meal sit-down with a couple of his clients—Marshaa, as she likes to be called, and the hot new kid doing the BlueBoy campaign, Dan, who wanted to talk to him. Catching their interest, he explained how he would chat with them for a bit, then pull them to one side and discreetly sort out this trouble that's giving them bad press. Because not all bad press is good press and they could do without it. It's a pain, but it's what he does and that's life. Saying also that Buffy was coming up. That she was taking her own executive jet once she's finished—she'd been so busy—and Marshaa was picking her up.

"Marsha's picking 'her' up?" they asked.

"Oh yeah, Buffy's great, she's so happy right now, but she's exhausted—just secured an incredible three picture deal with Tom Cruise, I honestly don't know how she does it. Soon I'm telling you, she's going to be taking over this town and we'll all be working for her," Patrick had said, and then, casually added, as though it was the norm, "Hey, come along. Marshaa's a big fan of you both, thinks you're fantastic and totally loves Crazy Sue, she'd go crazy herself if you turned up."

And she would, because the truth was Marsha hated her.

Patrick hit the plane running, still on form. Loving the Captain, the Captain loving him, laughing, joking, smiling. The hostess on the plane an actress herself, flirting with him as he told her how he'd just spent the afternoon with 'Marshaa' sorting out Marshaa's problems, it was a pain, but it's what he did. Her telling him he reminded her of that guy on the back of the bus she saw when she had a layover in Vancouver and visited her mother.

"A lot of people say that," he'd said, then carried on with a smile saying, "But I don't do public transport."

They should do lunch sometime, she'd said, just as he was thinking the same thing and wondering how kinky she could be, loving it, playing somebody and becoming that somebody in his mind with every breath he took.

He jumped into a limo and followed a bus on the road that ran away from the airport towards the city with its mountainous backdrop not too much further on from its center, standing there bold and strong, rising away from water into the sky above, covered in snow, sometimes mist or just pure sunshine.

Another bus took the first one's place, and Patrick was now smiling back at himself—the Indian driver doing the same to him in the rear-view mirror. Patrick waving his arm at the guy, dismissing himself and hating the man who he once was—the same guy who he used to be, whose smile had made him millions.

He sat back in his seat and stared at the mountains in the distance, wondering how Chendrill was doing with the maniac blackmailer he no longer cared about. People in the industry he was now in did that kind of shit, he thought, it's part of the package. They'd probably think there was something wrong if he didn't have some sort of perverted kinky itch he couldn't live without being scratched once in a while. I'm sure Marsha had one, he thought—liked it one way or the other. Maybe she got herself off with something whilst watching herself in the mirror, he thought. It had taken a lot of control to just play it cool and not say something cheesy to her all afternoon as he'd kept her beautiful firm titties just below frame.

Wanting to just say, "Why are you crying about this guy, when there's real men around."

Older men at that.

But he hadn't, he'd kept himself decent and worked it.

******

Mazzi Hegan was having a meltdown, just as he was about to tell Rann to fuck off, he'd got to him and all he'd had to say was— "Tax man."

Then he'd said, "I've got your file in front of me now and it looks like you're full of shit. You've been spending the money you sent back to Sweden paying off a credit card you use here."

And hung up.

He had, but how did this prick know, Mazzi thought, and was it wrong? Quickly he called his accountant and asked. It was, *fuck*. How did he know? The fucker had his file and was harassing him. He should call Chendrill, he thought, but if he did he'd never be able to call him an asshole again. And that could be a tough thing to live with.

He sat back on his chair and rubbed his fingers through his hair as he liked to do when he was stressed and shouted out loud, "Motherfucker!" so as everyone in their little cubicles could hear.

He liked to do that, get it off his chest. But normally it was stupid stuff like photos, or someone in the office wearing a pair of shoes that didn't go with an outfit, or Chendrill driving around in his car he wished he could park so he could look cool.

But this was different—a lot different.

Then just as Patrick had in a panic, Mazzi did the one thing he should never have done and called the man back.

******

Rann had a small bit of info to work on. But he was a professional and years of working his craft had taught him he could make a mountain out of any mole hill, and Mazzi Hegan's tax details were just that. He'd asked Malcolm Strong in a brief phone call to do him a favor, just like he'd been doing Malcolm, and give him some dirt on everyone at Slave, telling him it would be good for his soul and give him something to do whilst he waited for the box of hard-on drugs to come in from Asia.

Sebastian was a boy-scout and the government owed him money, but Mazzi Hegan had a bit of history that could be easily exploited, history in his creative use of expenses on his tax returns, history in his continual buying the whole bar drinks when he was bombed out of his skull and all sweaty on wine and poppers, history in waking up in a hired limo after it's taken him and a bunch of guys to Whistler to party and claiming it all as legitimate expenses. This was the kind of history Rann loved and thrived on. And it was just this and a whole load of other questionable filings the tax man was now considering which Rann now had his teeth into.

"I'm just trying to do you a favor that's all. It makes no difference to me," Rann said to Mazzi.

He wanted to tell him right there and then to fuck off, just like he had the last time, but something inside told him to keep talking and find out just what the prick was referring to, see what shit he had to say, that would be better, find out then straight after say 'Yeah well that's great, now why don't you just go back home and suck on Prince Charles's dick,' then when he realized he'd just insulted him and his precious royal family, Mazzi would say, 'and while you're down there, have a word with his friends about why you've no longer got a team that can play football, you English prick.' That would get him, the English hated that, knowing they were useless at the game they invented. So, he said, "Maybe I'll just put the phone down and send Chendrill back over to kick your ass."

"Tell that ape if he comes round here again, it won't be a lawn chair that drops onto his Ferrari."

He'd heard about Chendrill sorting it out for Patrick over dinner. Patrick telling them all what a superhero Chendrill was getting this parasite off his back, but he hadn't heard about the lawn chair hitting the Ferrari. What the fuck was that all about? He said, "Chendrill said the chair never hit the Ferrari, it missed."

"Really, is that right?" Rann said straight back, taking the bait. "The lying prick, if he comes here I'll put him out the window and as for you, you've got other issues."

"Which are?"

"Tax related."

"My taxes are fine."

"Then why did you call me back?"

"Because I like English guys, especially Sikhs. They turn me on. I like looking at the tops of their turbans when they're sucking me off."

Mazzi Hegan waited as he listened to the silence on the other end of the line. It was good. Hitting on him had thrown the prick and turned the tables for the moment at least. Then he heard the man say, "Tell that to the judge when the tax man's finished with you."

"I'll tell it to the judge when the police are finished with you—you blackmailing son of a bitch."

Then he hung up. A minute later, the phone rang again and he heard Rann say, "Forget the tax issue, forget the judge, no one speaks to me like that. All I wanted to do was help you. I'll be coming to see you and you'd better know how to fight."

Then he hung up.

Mazzi Hegan stared at the wall, this time, trying to be clever, he'd taken his crudeness to the wrong person. He'd been a smart ass once too often and now it was time to call Chendrill.

Chapter Eighteen

Chendrill paced up and down Mazzi Hegan's office, watching as Hegan nervously ran his fingers through his highlights as Hegan said, "Well how was I to know he was going to react like that?" His Swedish accent showing strong with the pressure.

"I wish you'd just called me."

"Well shoot me."

Chendrill stared at him saying, "This is the problem."

Hegan stood quickly, his silver belt buckle showing strong on top of his jeans. "You saying the guy's going to try and kill me?"

Chendrill took a deep breath. The Sikh was becoming more of a pain each day.

"Not at all."

Mazzi sat down again, took a deep breath, calming himself. Then, as the room drew quiet, suddenly screamed out, "Fuck!"

Then the door opened and Sebastian walked in, and looking to Chendrill said, "He does that, it's his thing, letting it all out. What's going on?"

And Chendrill said, "Our friend from your hometown has been harassing Mazzi."

"About what?" Then he said, "I'm sorry, it's none of my business."

Sebastian walked to the window. After thinking, he turned and said, "When I was a kid at school, I thought I had a friend and he was a true friend. I told him of my persuasion and he made me pay to keep it quiet. After that, I swore that I'd never do that again in my life, cowering down to such a beast of a person. Chuck darling, is there anything else we could do to get this retched person to leave us alone?"

And looking up at him, Chendrill simply said, "Yeah, don't pay."

Then Mazzi butted in, letting it all out saying, "Sebastian, I've got tax issues, he's found them somehow and that's why he's harassing me."

Sebastian walked over and placed his hand on his business partner's shoulder and said, "Mazzi, tax men are only human beings just like you and I—they'll strike a deal. I don't need to know what your issues are, but what I suggest is that you talk to my accountant. Tell him everything. Absolutely everything. And then let him sort it out and I'll cover his bill and whatever you owe. I want you to relax. Personal issues get in the way of your creativity, it's not healthy. My man will work it out and strike an anonymous deal for you and it will be done."

Fuck me, Chendrill thought, just like that, all the guy's tax issues sorted. But there was still the big issue of the lunatic East Indian still being out there. But as he glanced over to Mazzi, who looked as though he was going to cry, he decided that for now, he'd throw it out there again and see if Sebastian would take the bait.

"Yeah, I've got some tax issues of my own Mazzi, I know the feeling."

Then, completely ignoring him, he heard Sebastian say, "And Chuck I'll need your keys, I'm giving Mazzi back his Ferrari."

What? Dan the prick, Chendrill thought, stealing it and causing trouble, now he'd be back in a leased Buick or something. *Fuck. Fuck. Fuck.* If Sebastian was pissed at him, why couldn't he have just smashed his dinner plate?

"I've called the guys at Ferrari Mazzi, and they're putting a computerised radar system in that parks it for you—you can pretend you're still driving of course, go through the motions, no one will ever know."

Trying to hide his disappointment, Chendrill looked to Sebastian, feeling like a six foot four two-hundred-and-fifty-pound kid who'd just been told off by his dad, as Sebastian turned to him smiling and said, "Oh, and don't worry, Chuck. I'm getting you an Aston Martin."

Sebastian left Chendrill looking puzzled. And Mazzi, who couldn't help himself, had started to cry again. Leaving them both to it, Sebastian walked back to his huge office in the corner of the building with its big wooden beams and panelled windows and sat down.

He was a rich man, as rich as one can be if you looked at life knowing you have everything you need and want and could buy it all again a hundred times over with change. The advertising industry had been good to him. But all he really had now since his partner Alan had passed was Fluffy. They'd bought and enjoyed him as a pet when Alan was sick, and after he'd gone missing in the park, before Chendrill had found him, Sebastian had realized that if he didn't get him back, he would be completely alone.

Sebastian had money. And in the autumn of his years, with no children to pass it on to, he was happy to spend it, and spend it well, having fun and creating as much happiness with it as he could for the only family he now had left—his friends. And it felt good.

******

Rann Singh, on the other hand, was starting to get annoyed, and wished he hadn't paid out the five hundred bucks to the skinny white chick who needed her hair fixed and seen the photos of Patrick crying as one of the prettiest women he had ever seen slammed a huge dildo up his ass. Now he was in a right pickle. All he had to do was sit back and wait till his shipment of hard-on pills arrived and then he could say goodbye to all this blackmail shit. Say goodbye to it all once and for all and get on with his new life, make the necessary preparations for his grandfather's retirement. "But no!" he shouted out loud to himself as he stood in the shower with the jets combing his long black hair that reached down past his backside.

"You had to start trouble didn't you, you fucking idiot, you couldn't leave it be. You had to start a war."

And that's what he'd done, as he had done so many times. Same as he had in London and as he had in Thailand only a month before. It was his way, his nature.

Now he was in one again. This time with a guy who couldn't dress properly. He'd blown the deal with the realtor, gone to see Rasheed, crying to the man like a little baby, and caused more trouble with the guy's friends, making them come around so as he had to throw shit at them, trying to teach them a lesson. And now this shit with the PI, and this friend of Chendrill's, the gay guy with a filthy mouth. The prick insulting him like that, speaking about his future King, Charlie—disrespecting him same as the Irish cunt had with the King of Thailand, who looked like his grandfather.

He turned off the shower and, reaching for a towel, got out, rubbing himself down and wrapping his hair up.

Let it go, he thought, *let it go. Concentrate on the future, and let it go, take a break until the tablets come.* Turning, he looked at himself in the mirror, his hair all wrapped in a bun now on top of his head like a girl.

He'd let it go, he thought, he would forget it. *It's not worth the stress, just leave it be, put it to one side, put it to one side. Put it to one side, let it go Rann, he told himself again and again, let it go. Let it go Rann, let it fucking well go.*

But he knew he couldn't.

******

The first person he called was Malcolm Strong, sitting at home, not talking with his wife, when the phone rang. If there was anything good that had come out of him being blackmailed, then it was that he'd stopped getting his dick sucked by whores, for the moment anyhow, and he was trying to improve the relationship with his wife.

"Get me tax info on the PI Chendrill," Rann had said without saying 'hi'. Then he asked, "What're you doing now?"

What's it got to do with you, you piece of shit? Malcolm thought as he looked to his wife, wondering if she could hear and who she was texting.

"I'm at home."

"You're lucky you still got one mate, you can thank me for sorting that out, stopping you doing what you were doing."

Yeah, yeah, yeah. You piece of shit. Then he asked the guy who had been blackmailing him, "What do you want?"

"You fuckin deaf?"

"It's too hard to do; I could lose my job. Then where would you be?" Malcolm said quietly as he watched his wife walk through to the bedroom. Then he carried on, "There's only so much I can take, you know that." And he wasn't joking, he'd

already been pulled in and asked why he'd been looking into
Mazzi Hegan and had to talk his way quickly out of that one,
saying he'd heard stuff and wanted to waste his time first before
he sent it further up the line and wasted anyone else's. And he was
right too, as it was mostly nonsense. He said, "I can't do it."

"You can't afford not to."

"I'll lose my job."

"You'll lose your job if they see what you been doing and
you'll lose your wife. She'll be sucking someone else's dick."

Malcolm doubted that, he thought, that was what had gotten
him into all the trouble in the first place.

"If I do it, I'll lose my spot at the post office," he said,
knowing that would shut the piece of shit up, wondering for the
millionth time whether he should go straight to the police. But as
the guy who was trying to save him had said, if Malcolm did that,
then he won't be able to stop this born-again Christian from
unleashing his revenge.

He took a deep breath. *Fuck,* he was in a mess. This guy,
fucking with his life when all he wanted was to relax. He could
ask a friend, he thought, to look or just make it up, say he has and
this is what he's found. Fuck it, that's what he'd do. Make up some
shit about the guy and let him try to deny it, take some of the heat
off him. So, he said, "I'll look tomorrow." But he wouldn't he'd
do nothing of the sort, he thought, except lie.

Chapter Nineteen

Dan sat on the end of his bed and wondered who the guy in the linen suit was outside smiling and talking to his mum. Maybe she'd got pissy over Chendrill thumping him and this was the next one coming around. With any luck, the guy would own a burger franchise. Then he saw the man looking at him through the window from the road side smiling, giving him the thumbs up. Fuck he looked like that guy on the back of the buses, but different. Next thing, he was down in Dan's room with his arm around him with one of Dan's socks stuck to his foot, saying, "You are a good-looking young man, Daniel. I can tell you that."

So, they keep saying, Dan thought, wondering if the guy was gay.

"Hey, you been fighting, you a boxer, are you?" the man was saying now, the smile still there etched on, but not false.

Dan said, "Mum's guy thumped me out because I borrowed the car."

Then the guy said, "My name's Patrick."

Fuck, he is the guy on the buses, Dan thought, then said, "We selling our house? Is that what it is?"

And not missing a beat, Patrick said back with a smile, "No Dan, we're selling you. That's what we're doing."

******

They sat in the kitchen, Dan eating, his mother Tricia sitting at the table. Patrick sitting holding court working out how much he could make if he offered them 1.3 million for the place right now and then did a back-end deal on a rack of town homes he'd have his developer buddy step in and throw up a month later. Then he looked back to Tricia, as he sipped his tea and looked at her tight legs sticking out from under the table. She was hot. Putting down his tea, he said, "You don't know how big your son's become." She didn't, he was right, she'd seen the posters scattered about the place and it had taken her an hour to realize that it was Dan.

She said, "I saw the posters, yes. Chuck told me they were worldwide."

Chuck, Patrick thought, fucking Chendrill was already slipping in there, had to be, the way she'd said his name like they were an item. So, he said, "We talking about that big guy here, are we?"

"Yes, Chuck he makes sure Dan keeps out of trouble."

Patrick looked to her son, the big shiner on his eye right there for the world to see. Then heard his mother say, "Chuck did that."

Fuck me, Patrick thought, Chendrill coming round here, sleeping with mum and thumping out the talent. It wasn't good. Still smiling, he said, "Well it looks good on you buddy—makes you look like a brute, like a guy who knows how to stick up for himself, like a real man should."

Stick up for myself? Dan thought. *First worked over by a one-hundred-and-fifty-pound gay guy with his man bag, then sucker punched by my mum's boyfriend.*

"But you're not to go worrying about any of this," Patrick said. "This is all my problem now."

It is? How? How is it your problem that I got worked over because basically I was being a prick, Dan thought as he pulled out another four slices of pizza with smoked salmon and placed them on top of each other, making two sandwiches. And before he could speak, Patrick had answered his question.

"Because, young man, you need representation and Sebastian has asked me very nicely to do so. So, I am."

And Dan asked straight back, "Who else you look after then?"

And smiling, Patrick lied, "Marsha and Samson and Samson's girl Crazy Sue—she's so talented, they're clients, we were together yesterday down in L.A. talking about a movie deal with Tom Cruise—but Buffy takes care of them. You'll be my main concern."

Buffy, Dan thought as he stuffed so much of the first pizza sandwich into his mouth that it made his eye hurt. He remembered the big chick at the Sutton the night Marsha had kicked him out just because he was trying not to come and got her name wrong. He'd seen her in the lobby talking with some people and remembered her looking at him funny and realized he wasn't wearing his trousers. He said, "Yeah I met Buffy."

She'd taken him to the concierge who'd gotten him a dressing gown whilst she went up to Marsha's suite and retrieved Dan's clothes.

"She's really good. Looks after people."

And looking straight at Dan's mum, Patrick said, "She's the best out there, she really is, she works so hard, the only time she gets a good night's sleep these days is on one of those executive jet's bed when she's off to work in Europe."

******

Chendrill stood staring at the blue Aston Martin sitting pretty in the showroom off Burrard Street.

"It's second-hand, I got a good deal and you'll need a run around," Sebastian had said as though he was talking about a bicycle. He'd called just after Chendrill had left Slave.

"And like you said, Dan needs to look good; besides Mazzi needs his car back. I've teased him long enough."

He opened the door, feeling it's weight, the wood on the inside varnished and perfect, the leather still like new.

"It's just a year old," he heard the salesman say to him from behind.

Sebastian struck a good deal. Chendrill got in, gripping the wooden steering wheel, the seat hard but luxurious, feeling as though it had been custom built just for him. *Fuck*, he thought, *I give his top model a smack in the chops and he orders me an Aston.*

"I'll have it ready for you this afternoon, sir," said the guy leaning in, trying to sound English with his shoes perfectly shined and a smile.

Chendrill asked, "How much did he pay?"

"I'm not at liberty to comment, sir. But we sold a similar model some time back for around one hundred and eighty."

Jesus Christ, Chendrill thought, *one-hundred-and-eighty grand or there about on a run around.*

"Do you need a metal key to start it or has it got one of those electronic devices that are being used these days."

And the salesman replied, "Just the old-fashioned way with this model, sir, it has a very sophisticated alarm system though.

So did the Ferrari, Chendrill thought, but no key—just a sensor fitted because Mazzi kept getting the key stuck—so maybe Dan, the prick, will keep his hands off this one, unless he wants his other eye bruised.

He dropped the Ferrari off and walked back to the showroom and, shaking hands with the salesman, grabbed the car, adjusted the seat, and began to drive along the road. Ten minutes later, the phone rang. It was Sebastian with pure joy in his voice asking, "How does it feel?"

Different, he thought, less throaty than the Ferrari, but a little more refined.

"It's a nice car. Thank you, Sebastian. You should be the one driving it, not me."

"I've got my bicycle and Fluffy fits nicely in the little basket at the front," Sebastian replied without trying to be clever.

He did have it, it was all he needed around town, except when it was raining—it was a nice Peugeot three speed, the same as he used to have when he was a kid, until it got stolen from outside the chip shop. Now, though, he had another, exactly the same, custom made, and delivered all the way from France, with a soft saddle and a little basket up front made especially for the dog.

"Anyway, I'll need you to pick up a few plates for me. I don't know your source but I'm glad you've got one."

Then Chendrill asked, "Why, whose have you smashed now?" And the moment he said it, he knew it was his. And as stupid as Sebastian's little ways were, the feeling of total shame came over him. So, he said, "Maybe I shouldn't ask."

Sebastian stayed silent for a moment. Then said, "If I was angry with you I wouldn't have gotten you the Aston, would I, Chuck?"

He was right, he would have waited, which was probably what he did do. Then Sebastian asked, "Are you coming out tonight? Everyone's invited, Dan included, Marsha and Buffy are coming up and a couple of others Patrick's invited."

"Patrick?"

"Yes, he's been to Hollywood."

******

They all met at the Fish House in the center of Stanley park and sat around a huge table set aside from everyone else. Marsha making a late appearance with Buffy and a bodyguard following behind, picked up by Patrick from an agency in town. Dan sat on the other side of the table with a black eye, not giving a shit. Mazzi hating it all because of Chendrill's shirt. Patrick holding court, smiling and dazzling the place with his charm. Sebastian just happy sitting in amongst them all, his bicycle parked and locked up alongside the Ferrari that could park itself and the Aston Martin that just looked cool. Mazzi turned to him, saying, "It's never going to work."

Sebastian looked to Patrick oozing personality, "Give him time." Mazzi looked to Patrick with his arm around that big slut Marsha, who smelled of fish, and then turned back to Sebastian. "I'm not talking about him. As long as he still had a tongue, he could go anywhere and do anything. I'm talking about Chendrill and the Aston."

"What about him now?'

"You got it all wrong, Sebastian. Look at him—you had it right with the Ferrari, but you've got it wrong with the Aston, look at his shirt, he's not James Bond."

Sebastian looked over, noticing Chendrill staring at Marsha's breasts, and looked at his shirt for the fiftieth time. Mazzi was right, as always, he'd seen it as soon as he'd pulled up in the car—

his shirt a red Hawaiian, the car a deep navy blue.

"He should be wearing a tux," Mazzi said, and he wasn't wrong. Then Mazzi said, "we should have had this at your place, I knew it. People are going to talk."

Sebastian laughed, Mazzi getting it right, but now, as always, taking it too far. The next thing he'd be saying was that they should cancel the evening.

"Maybe one of us should go ill and blow this off," Mazzi said running both hands along his purple colored silk trousers that looked cool.

"Don't be silly Mazzi," Sebastian said as Mazzi carried on regardless.

"We've got that slut here, and Dan now, and you know the trouble he causes. There'll be Paps waiting at the end of the evening and if someone takes a shot of your big guy getting in the car, then where will we be?"

"They'll be here Mazzi. Don't think for a moment they won't. I'm quite sure that's why we're here. I wouldn't doubt it if Patrick hasn't called them himself."

Mazzi rubbed his hand through his highlights, took a swig of his white wine, and said quietly to himself, "Jesus!"

Sebastian laughed as Mazzi looked at him as serious as he could ever be.

"I've gone and got myself involved in a freak show," Mazzi said, as he felt Sebastian lean in and say, "Of your making, ultimately Mazzi. Sit back and enjoy the evening. Give Patrick the space he needs and in the end, we'll both reap the benefits. Believe me."

The night passed and as predicted, the paparazzi began to

gather outside. Dan sitting there not talking and eating, his eye still hurting. Marsha trying to look cool and staring at Dan. Mazzi forgetting about the shirt, drunk now on white wine and feeling playful, telling Patrick how he's seen the prints of him and that pretty girl and knows how he likes it. Chendrill listening and looking to Sebastian raising his eyebrows now and again, being a friend, and then through the window to the side as the small crowd that was gathering stood on tip toes trying to grab whatever glimpse they could of Marshaa and the new kid on the block with the swollen eye. Then in amongst them, he saw Rann standing there in his turban looking straight at him.

Fuck, that was all he needed, he thought. Getting a nice night out and now the chances were that he was going to have to deal with this idiot again. The guy was becoming a pain.

******

He stared at him through the window as Rann stared back, challenging him. The guy was a nut, he thought. What was it with him? He'd tried it on with blackmail and this time it hadn't worked, but that was life when you were self-employed, sometimes it did, sometimes it didn't. Slowly he got up, excused himself, and headed for the toilet. He made his way through the kitchen and let himself out the back door, down the steps, onto the paving slabs that lined the building, and then out of nowhere he felt the East Indian's foot slam itself hard into his throat, knocking him to the ground and sending another electric shock of pain through his body from the impact to his broken ribs.

Quickly, he got to his feet as the next blow came, this time to the other side of his throat. *Fuck me*, Chendrill thought, *this guy was fast*. Trying as hard as he could to breathe, knowing he was in trouble, he stood again. This time he could see where the guy was coming from, catching his silhouette in the light from the kitchen window as he came at him again, flying through the air for the third time. Standing straight this time and spinning, shielding his throat from the blow with his arm and bringing his other elbow in hard and fast into the man's crotch, Chendrill felt the East Indian's testicles crush themselves into his bony groin. He watched as Rann landed on one leg and backed away, the pain from the blow not quite hitting, but both of them knowing that in a few seconds it would.

Still finding it hard to breathe, Chendrill went for the man again, feigning a head shot and sweeping the East Indian off his feet. Rann landed, but flipped up again just as quick. Chendrill knew now the first two hits weren't cheap shots and hadn't landed by luck. The guy was a trained fighter and a good one at that.

He took a deep breath and prepared for the next assault, his left arm down protecting his broken ribs that now seemed to be causing more pain than when they were first broken. Then he said to the guy standing there in the darkness, all in black with his turban, "Why don't you let this be it and we'll call it quits." But he could see it wasn't going to be that easy.

Then he heard the guy say back, his London accent coming through strong now, "You think that just cause I ripped your shirt, that's going to be enough after you broke my computer over my head?"

And knocked you out twice, Chendrill thought. He looked down quick seeing his shirt in the light from the window. It was ripped, his favorite one at that as well, the prick. Then he said, "So, what do you want to do so as we can both walk away?"

"Tell that smarmy cunt in there he still owes me the $100,000 he promised. And tell the foul-mouthed fag he owes me an apology and the fucking Ferrari or he'll be dealing with me and the tax man—and once that starts, it'll ruin everyone's

Christmas."

Chendrill stood there wanting to get hold of him and end it, but he knew better. He'd been lucky the first couple of times catching him off guard, but not now, not here. The man was pumped up and ready for a fight, you could see that, his eyes looking vicious, the way he stood, ready to go. Not like the baker. This guy was good and fast and then suddenly, he wondered how the Gurkha would have dealt with him—that little fucker, as tough as nails, and deadly. It was an easy answer, the East Indian would be dead, no question. But Chendrill wasn't Bahadur, and Bahadur wasn't here to help as he had been previously, sorting out Chendrill's fight for him and probably saving his life in the process. Chendrill said, "The tax situation's sorted, so you can fuck off on that one and same goes for your apology as well. And Patrick no longer cares about the photos, so go fuck yourself on that one too."

Then he heard the East Indian say, "This ain't over." And he turned and walked away around to the front of the restaurant. Chendrill put his hand to his throat and felt the bruising from the kicks, both delivered with power and accuracy and designed no doubt to close the throat and leave him easy prey, gasping for breath. Had the third connected, it would have been lights out. But like he said, it ain't over, and it wasn't.

He looked at his shirt, ripped now completely. Fuck and it had been a good one, Chendrill saving it for something special, like tonight or a new ride, both of which had come on the same day and now look at it. He reached into his pocket, the keys to Aston Martin still there.

In under thirty minutes, he was back in the restaurant, the only clean shirt had been a white one with frills on the front given to him as a gift by his auntie years back; but in a strange way, it kind of fitted the car, so what the hell.

Pulling up outside the restaurant he got out, blasted by the Paparazzi as he did. Reaching the restaurant, he moved past Patrick, still holding court, and from behind he put his arms around Sebastian and Mazzi and said jokingly, "Sorry I was gone so long. I felt as though the shirt I was wearing didn't go with the car, so I went home and changed."

There *was* hope, Mazzi thought, as he watched Chendrill walk away, still in disbelief from what he'd said. The frilly top looked good on him for once, reminding him of one of those sexy flamenco dancers he liked to fuck whenever he got himself drunk down in the Baja. Turning, he said to Sebastian, "Your magic's working dear, it really is. Now just stop him from staring at that slut's tits and you're halfway there."

Putting his hand on Dan's shoulder, Chendrill sat down next to him, his ribs smarting again now as he sat and said, "You okay?"

Dan answered, "Why don't you ask my eye?"

Fucking baby, Chendrill thought, so he said, "It's simple, if you don't like it, don't steal."

He looked over to Marsha, playing with her hair, still being held captive in conversation by Patrick, making occasional glimpses towards Dan, who was still eating long after everyone else had stopped—apart from Marsha who had not even started. Then Dan said, "Who thumped you in the throat?"

Chendrill stared at him, wondering how he knew, and asked simply, "Why do you ask?"

"Because it's swollen and I saw you standing out back squaring off against some guy in a turban."

"And what else did you see?"

"He fucked up your shirt."

"Did anyone else here see?"

Dan shook his head. Then said, "How can they, it's impossible to get away from the guy off the back of the bus."

Chendrill looked over to Patrick, Buffy with him now, listening in great detail as he spoke. Marsha flipping her hair and looking good while she talked with Sebastian, who'd moved over to sit with her and was trying to hold her hand. Mazzi Hegan getting his camera out. Then he heard Dan say, "How come you keep getting beaten up all the time."

Chendrill shot him a look, saying, "Go look in the mirror and ask that question again to the guy staring back at you."

Then Dan said, "Yeah, you're right. You were lucky; sometimes those guys carry hockey sticks, I got one looking for me, they can get nasty. The only one I know who keeps calm is the guy who drives this lot about, he's cool and he keeps the lawn trim so he can sniff around mum."

Chendrill looked at him.

"What do you mean sniff around mum?"

Then Dan looked up, frowning, and changed the subject, "Something's going down; I can feel it." Chendrill looked around, hearing Dan say, "The gay guy's got his camera out, and he's got that look he gets when he's about to start taking his photos, same as he did that night in his apartment when he caught me in there eating his food."

Chendrill remembered it differently. Looking around, he could see that Marsha was starting to cry, her eyes tearing up.

"What's up with her?"

Dan leaned back in his chair saying, "It's because I'm not talking to her. She's getting pissed off. She's not used to that."

Then Chendrill asked him, "Yeah, what is it with you? Why are you sitting here like a dick and following me about when you've got her all gooey over you?"

"It's what Patrick told me to do. He's my new manager. He said just keep away from her all night and when the shit hits the fan, look cool."

And then she came at him, Marsha there crying, moving towards Dan, Dan sitting there leaning back looking cool one foot up on a chair. Patrick moved himself quickly between them, his linen shirt open, holding his arms up feigning concern as Marsha wound up by a couple of hours' worth of his subliminal messaging forgot herself and who she was, forgot to look good, forgot her supermodel status, which for the moment was broken down and gone. Then Patrick was grabbing her, holding her, comforting her as he moved himself and her towards Dan, who could care less. Patrick acting like a knight in shining armour holding off Dan with his free arm. And Dan going nowhere, as Patrick controlled the situation and let Mazzi get the candid photos he needed for Sebastian to put Patrick on the map.

Chapter Twenty

Rann was feeling good now, about himself at least, walking back along the seawall watching the girls pass by on English Bay, and wondering whether he'd be able to pick one up if he stopped. Getting the big fucker in the throat twice and ripping his nice shirt had settled the score a bit, but his nuts had paid the price; and although the intense pain had gone, the bruising was still there. But that would pass, physical pain always did with him, the torment from insults and slights though left deep scars that manifested quickly into such hatred that there was little he could do to control the thoughts of revenge that always came with it.

The Irishman had been the same, calling him a Paki straight off the bat, when he'd done nothing more than be polite. Ripping into him like he had for no reason other than that he was a racist married to a woman with the same colored skin as Rann himself had.

They'd met again in a hotel bar after the bickering on the river had settled down and reached a deal. A dollar twenty-five for a packet of six Sildenafil 25 mg mixed with sugar and a bit of caffeine to give a bit of energy to whoever thought their luck was in.

The Irishman was drinking whisky again, his wife with him dressed in a tight dress showing off her figure and legs. Rann wondered if her friend was going to show. The Irishman wasn't calling him a Paki now and said he needed his advance. Rann said, "I'll give you that tomorrow."

"Why not tonight?"

He could, Rann thought, he had enough now after pulling the max out of two credit cards for the last couple of weeks and storing it away in the hotel safe, but the Irishman was shifty, so he asked, "How much advance we talking then?"

"Fifty percent."

Fuck me, that's just over twenty grand, Rann thought. The guy was such a prick he could go on a bender and drink or gamble away the lot and all he'd have to show for it was a box of tabs that were full of talcum powder. So, he offered him two thousand US right there and said, "This should get you started."

The Irishman had said, "I'm not a focking charity. You want me to finance the operation and put me life on the line, then you need to pay for that focking privilege, because I telling you I don't deal with focking losers."

Here he goes again. Rann thought as the Irishman carried on saying.

"I'll set it all up for you'se, but I'll need the fucking money to do so, so stop focking with me and being a cunt. Or like I said before I'll be focking off, so don't waste me focking time."

Rann stared at the man, his bald head red now from the outburst, trying to work out if the guy was straight. Fifty percent was enough to buy a house out here. He asked, "Why'd you need twenty grand right now, you going to go buy the shit right off the bat? I'll give you five tonight." He added, "And after I see what comes back I'll start paying out more."

The first batch arrived four days later, the Irishman's wife going off with the cash to where the monkeys run riot to get the stuff as requested, while her husband ran riot himself. Rann keeping close tabs on the guy, watching him as they sat in the clubs, drinking whisky and getting his dick sucked in the back, calling him a Paki again as Rann watched the girl painting hearts with the soap suds in the shower booth at the side of the stage.

Then he saw the wife's friend, her hair dyed blonde, her legs long toned and sexy, walking through the place, coming up and talking to Paddy. Paddy smiling, as she looked at Rann sitting there in his white turban and white shirt feeling good. The Irishman leaning in now, telling him his wife's back and they should go and meet.

They took a corner booth at the sports bar in Rann's hotel, Rann sitting opposite the Irishman's wife who looked like a monkey, giving him the look, her silk dress tight pushing her boobs up, her friend the Thai blond sitting next to him, her knee touching his, making him feel special.

Digging into his pocket, the Irishman handed Rann a packet; he had two on him he said. Any more he'd get into grief if he was caught. Rann looked at them all sitting there in their little bubbles with the letters 'RS' printed across the top of each pill and the words 'ROCK SOLID' printed bold across the silver lined backing with 'Herbal Supplement' in small print along it's base.

"Try one," the Irishman said. Rann sat there staring at the packet. The Irishman was right, he'd have to try the goods—this packet, and selected ones from the boxes when they started to arrive for real. Paddy carried on as he took another hit off his whisky.

"Take a tablet, you cunt, you've paid for the focking things, haven't you just? So focking use them, take this focking blonde bitch back and give her a screwing be Jesus man. If not her, the bitch in the shower you can't keep your focking eyes off."

The Irishman said as he sat there, his eyes all glassy now. Listening to his new business partner saying, "I ain't paying for it, it ain't me."

The Irishman stared at him, surprised, saying, "Look at you all high and mighty, what makes you better than all the other people round here? I'll buy the focking bitch for you if that's what you want. You focking tight bastard."

Says the man drunk on the whisky I've been paying for all evening, Rann thought as he watched him nodding as he listened to his wife and her friend talking in Thai to each other as though he could understand what they were saying.

Then he asked the Irishman, "Why'd you do that, pretending to be following what they're saying in Thai, nodding your head and all that like you understand?"

Reaching out, the Irishman grabbed his arm and held it tight, and said, "It lets 'em think I know what the fuck they're saying so as they don't try to fuck me over, ya focking idiot."

Rann looked back at him, the man's eyes waterier than ever, celebrating his cut of the five grand he'd taken no doubt. Rann gave it some thought, staring at the girls, their long hair hanging straight down their slight backs. He said, "But if you knew what they were saying, you'd be talking with them, joining in, not sitting there like some guy who's had his tongue ripped out. How do you know they ain't calling you a dopey cunt for doing just that and you're sitting there agreeing with them as they do."

Rann was right, the Irishman knew it right there and then, the reality of it all sinking in. He could see it in his eyes and without a word, he got up and left.

Rann sat there and watched him go, then turning back to his wife, looked her straight in the eye and said, "What you doing wasting your life away hanging out with a cunt like that?"

But the wife didn't understand him and all she said back was, "Me—my friend like you. We like this." As they both reached out gently touching the top of his turban with her long fingers. Then she said, "We want know, how long your hair?"

And Rann said, "The only way you get to know that is if you sleep with me."

And that evening they'd come to him in his hotel room. The night long over with, the Irishman so drunk he could barely walk—saying to Rann as he'd walked out the hotel lobby how he was going to use his Rock Solid brand and fuck both the girls sideways, but he was a drunk and drunks just slept. And here they both were in his room, less than an hour later, as the drunken prick slept back at his place. Rann inquiring about where he was. Both saying, "He drunk!" Grinning and making sleeping gestures with their hands as they spoke and walked about the suite he now had that was bigger than his own place back home. The girls looking good in there, away from it all, parading about in their tight silk outfits and long legs, smiling at him calling him Mr. Rann and opening the mini bar without asking.

They took him to the bedroom and laid him down, gently pulling off his turban and releasing his hair so it flowed down his back when they sat him up to see it's length. Then they started to kiss him, both at the same time licking his face and eyes, taking it in turn to bite his lips as the other waited, both still fully clothed in their tight dresses kneeling on the king size bed.

The Irishman's wife let go of him, pulled her tongue from his mouth and reached into her purse, bringing out a packet of his pills, popped three through the silver backed lining and dropped one into his mouth and said, "One you, one me, one my friend."

They took him to the shower and stripped him bare then stripped each other bare, then left him there on the outside looking in as they climbed in, turning on the jets, feeling each other, rubbing each other, kissing each other hard as though they were alone and it was what they liked to do. Rann watched, standing there naked, his ass propped against the sink, their asses and backs and stomachs and breasts pressed against the glass of the shower stall as the water sprayed around them as they soaped each other down all over and drew soap hearts on the glass just for him. Then it was his turn, in there with them both, the water pulling his hair—longer than theirs—towards the ground as his hands ran soap all over the women's beautiful bodies, the blonde kissing him as the Irishman's wife, who looked like a monkey, sucked away on his solid cock just as her husband had told him she liked to.

They took him to the bed, laid him there still kissing him, taking it in turns to suck him. Then they turned and sat on him—one on his cock riding him as the other sat on his face. Rann felt himself solid inside each of them, his tongue digging deeper each time into them, feeling their juices flowing down into his mouth and across his cheeks as the other pressed down on him riding him hard, feeling his size within them as they bucked up and down on him, fucking him hard, feeling their tightness around his cock, hearing both each time he fucked them call out 'Hoy, Hoy, Hoy,' with every thrust. Then they made him fuck their asses, and that's when they really got going. It went on and on, back and front and every which way Rann could imagine, for hours and hours until the sun came up.

The new RS Rock Solid brand was working well.

The first thing the Irishman said to him the next day was, "Have you tried out those tablets yet because I focking have and they work focking fine I can tell you that."

Yeah, I did, on your wife and her best friend, Rann thought as he sat down and ordered a beer. Then he lied.

"Not yet no." Then he asked, "Where's your Missus?"

"She's focking tired, your tablets, I given it to her all focking night I has."

Yeah right.

Then he said to the East Indian in the turban, "I've the first box of your tablets in the back of the car. I'll meet you tonight and you can give me another five grand or you can give me the whole amount. Save us a lot of fucking about and get the job done."

******

But he couldn't give the Irishman anything like that anymore, Rann thought as he stopped and sat on a bench, giving his nuts a break from the hit this Chendrill guy in the shirt had just given him down there. The Irishman was dead now. He remembered him laying there at the bottom of the stairs—his wife, who he'd fucked the night before, long gone and the new price of the tablets the Irishman had asked for written across the forehead of the King and the Queen.

It had been too much, the Irishman taking him out again to another club that looked no different to all the others in Rann's eyes—the girls all up on stage with their scarred bellies and sad eyes, the wife in another league and knowing it, sitting with him giving Rann a knowing look whenever her husband fucked off to take a piss, and Rann wondering what was going to happen after Paddy fell asleep as he'd made them come so hard the night before.

Then the Irishman, coming back from the toilet with his phone to his ear, had said, "There's a problem we need to talk."

He'd taken them out back, bottles of beer in crates up the top of the stairs ready to fill up the foreigners with poison so as they could buy the girls out and take them home. The Irishman stood there with his wife saying, "The pharmacist says he can't make it work with the price he's getting; he needs more cash."

Rann looking at the guy now, telling him, "We had a deal."

The Irishman lit up a cigarette, blowing out the smoke, then saying, "Well the deals focking off, because the cunt can't make it work, he needs more money. He needs double, he says he has to pay off the cops."

"Well, pay him out of your share," Rann had said.

"That is not negotiable, I'm telling you this. I'm doing you a favor and you's trying to turn me over. You Paki cunt. You're not doing that."

They both stood silent for a moment, Rann wanting to thump the guy right there and make him chew on his words. Then the Irishman carried on, "He needs double, I told you at the start you need to pay $5 a pack and I'm getting you it for half that and that's what it is."

Rann tried to keep cool and doing some math in his head quickly said, "That was for 100mg of the Sildenafil, I broke it into quarters. That's why we did the deal at a dollar twenty-five US."

"The cops don't care a fock what percentage of focking shit is in it. What you could have a barrel load of the cum focking juice and they don't care. They want their cut and it's what you pay or you can fock off with your deal; it's simple. Look—this is how it works."

Quickly, the Irishman pulled out a pen and with his cigarette clasped firmly between his lips, began to look around for a piece of paper, and, not seeing one, he reached up to a picture of the royals on the wall and began to write numbers out on top of the King's forehead. Rann, shouted at him, saying, "Don't write on the King, show some respect."

But the Irishman hadn't any, not for anyone, not even for himself, and he'd carried on defacing the King and writing numbers across his forehead and the Queen's tits, saying, "You pay for focking—25mg of the chemical, you pay same price—25 mg for the cops—same cost as the 25 mg of the chemical—

pharmacist—I get half of the cost of a focking mg for me and I do all the work running about arranging and collecting, that's how it works, you stupid focking gobshite."

And then he'd seen him at the bottom of the stairs lying there twisted and broken, beer bottles all over the place, his wife who looked like a monkey and liked to suck cock nowhere to be seen— just him and the drunken Paddy, who was dead with his arm broken, wrapped around the backside of his head.

Rann looked up, staring at a gang of East Indian teenagers walking along the sea wall trying to look tough with the cops— just kids themselves, but in uniform—following right behind them trying to look tougher. Then he stood and adjusted his crotch, still hurting from Chendrill. Maybe the wife had pushed him, he thought, had enough of the drunken prick after getting fucked properly by a Sikh, a real man. *It'd had to be her who'd done it*, he thought. He'd worked it all out and done the math. She had twenty-six hundred packets containing now 30,000 odd tablets. If she split them up and sold them for ten bucks a pop on the street over the next year, she and her friend would be set up for life. They'd come over to see if the stuff worked, put on a show for him, and sat on his face, and as much as he'd liked it at the time —the thought of it all now made him want to puke.

The same thing though had happened with Rasheed, them talking, then Rasheed laying there dead. And Rann not remembering in between. Wondering if it was his temper, the one the school teachers back in Hounslow used to write about at the end of the year, telling his grandparents how he had to learn control.

Chapter Twenty-One

Sebastian wasn't happy. It seemed to him only he and Chendrill were not in on the plot. He felt sorry for the young girl getting all upset, and angry at Patrick for using her that way, and at Mazzi for knowing what was going on and not saying a word. But Mazzi knew him and how sensitive he could be, and Sebastian was just as annoyed at himself for not seeing the forest for the trees until the last second when he'd gone over to try and console the poor love.

But he'd settled things down in his own way, holding her hand and letting her know that she was just a girl and still special and boys can be like that. "And for goodness sake—I should know!" he'd said in a camp, exaggerated way to make her laugh, whilst Hegan still snapped off shots, which looked great, as always. Mazzi working his magic the way he did, capturing not only what was going on but the emotions that got them into the situation in the first place. He was a talent—that was one thing you could never take away from him, even if he couldn't drive.

Looking down he picked up Fluffy and placed him on his lap, the little dog who'd inherit millions if Sebastian died first, dropping from a heart attack or mysteriously falling down the stairs.

The first person to call when the pictures were leaked to the press was Gill Banton and Sebastian could tell she was still in bed—and not alone at that. She asked, "What are you up to, Sebastian?"

"Sorry?"

"You have a meal and don't invite me?"

"I'm sorry."

"I was thinking of coming up. How would you feel about me signing the BlueBoy guy?"

Wow, that was a big one, Sebastian thought. If he let that happen, Dan would hit superstar status for real within a year. But it was too early for the kid, so he said, "Sorry, he's signed with us."

"What about a buyout?"

"Sorry."

Gill was silent for a moment. Sebastian, certain he could hear the sheets moving, said, "Are you in bed?"

Gill carried on, "And who's this guy?"

"Which guy?"

"The one who came to my barbecue and spent the afternoon chatting up my clients and Buffy."

"Patrick, he's into real estate."

"Are you sure? He looks like an agent in the photos."

Good, Sebastian, thought that's exactly what he wanted to hear, and carried on, letting her know now she had problems.

"Well maybe he's taking up a new hobby, Gill."

Gill stayed silent for the moment. As much as Marsha was a pain, she was her pain, and it was not good to lose clients. She said, "Thank you darling," and hung up. If anything, Sebastian was honest. It was a tough world he'd grown rich in and he'd done so by never stabbing anyone in the back—in the front, yes, as he had just done with Gill Banton, but at least he'd been honest, and, for that matter, the bitch had threatened him with blackmail.

Sebastian stared at the photos—Patrick there holding Marsha back as she tried to reach Dan, who was sitting there nonchalantly just staring back. Patrick full of concern, never looking to camera, Buffy framed perfectly in the background, her hands out trying to help.

Where was Marsha's bodyguard? Sebastian thought, as he looked through the photos and remembered him standing discreetly by the door throughout the meal. *But where did he go? Paid off no doubt*, he thought—*Patrick not wanting anyone else to rain on his parade*. He shuffled through the pictures some more. Chendrill there but doing nothing, just sitting, watching, looking sexy with his hairy chest sticking out of the front of his new white frilly shirt, taken by Mazzi, no doubt, just for him. He'd keep that one, he thought—keep it for later when Fluffy was asleep.

******

Marsha was still in a tizz when she got up in her bed in the executive suite that Patrick had reserved for her at the Grand, which was twice as big as the one she usually stayed in and had a view across the water to the mountains on the other side.

How could Dan have ignored her like that? Her coming all the way up here to see him and all. Patrick doing all he could to help her when she got upset, as the other men in the place stared at her all night, especially the big flamenco guy; but not Mazzi though or Sebastian, for some reason they didn't seem interested, which was odd. Buffy, though, seemed more with it now since Patrick was looking after things—even lending her some tampons, which was a first. Normally she'd say something like 'use one of your sweaters, they're the same size,' or something bitchy like that, and by the time Marsha had understood what the girl had said, they'd be on another plane heading to some other place that made you sweat.

Patrick was good; she liked him. Dan was signing with him

soon, so he must be. And he said he was going to get him a three-picture deal as well. Dan was going to be a movie star and model on the weekends or between pictures. Patrick said Dan was Oscar bound and you couldn't beat that, he'd said. He'd also said he had some crazy young girls from Vesuvius who were going to set the world on fire and he hoped that Gill Banton had some aces up her sleeve, as he didn't want to see her left behind.

Later she'd asked Buffy where Vesuvius was and she'd said it was a volcano in Italy, and she'd said to Buffy, "no wonder then Patrick's girls are so hot, coming from there. No wonder they were going to set the world on fire." Patrick was going to do everything for all these people and what was her agent doing for her? Laying in bed, like everyone says she did. Patrick, though, he was making it happen. He'd said that, he said he was the best—he had the key to make the world turn, but she always thought they kept that in Fort Knox.

Picking up the phone, she looked for the number for her agent that Buffy had left next to the phone, as always, and as soon as Gill Banton had answered Marsha asked, "Patrick said he's got the key to make the world turn. Why haven't you got it?"

Gill Banton stayed quiet for the moment; she'd just had the biggest orgasm of her life courtesy of this hot young Cuban one of her scouts had found and could hardly get her breath.

"Marsha, who's Patrick?" she said.

"Dan's agent."

"I thought Dan was with Sebastian."

"Dan's not gay Gill, you know that."

"That's not what I meant, I thought he'd signed with 'Slave'."

"Dan's with Patrick, he's got some Italian talent coming in and he's worried I'm going to get left behind, and so am I."

Rock Solid

"It's hard to be left behind when you're sitting at the top, Marsha, and that's where you are, and I put you there. No hot bit of fluff from Italy is going to steal that from you as long as you are with me. So, don't worry, I've got you flying out to Milan in two days."

"But those girls come from inside a volcano, that's why they're so hot—Buffy told me that."

"Buffy told you that?"

"Yeah she's been really good since she's been working for Patrick. She even let me use her tampons."

******

Still wet, Gill Banton headed down the highway towards LAX and was on the next plane heading up to Vancouver—where the little people lived. If word got out that she'd lost her biggest client to one of them, then the rest would soon follow and she'd be back to square one. It happened—not to her yet—but it had to others. Vancouver was a small town, but it was the headquarters for Slave, and because of Sebastian, they were bigger than most.

She took a limo to the Sutton and asked for Marsha's room. She wasn't there.

Fuck. She took a suite, and called a guy she knew who'd moved back here over the summer because his visa had expired and lined him up for the night.

He'd looked good in his head shots and had what it took downstairs to make her smile, but every door she opened for him closed a little too quick, and in the end, she'd given up. For the moment, he'd do though—he knew what she liked.

She reached her suite, with its windows that didn't open, and

147

called Sebastian.

"I'm in town and I'm coming over," was all she said and then hung up. There was no fucking around in her world.

An hour later, she was in Slave's offices and walking up and down along the side of the boardroom table, saying to Sebastian and Mazzi Hegan, who had his feet up on the other side, "Sebastian, don't make me put a contract out on your dog. You need to tell me where you've got her hidden."

Mazzi Hegan smiled. He loved this shit, these agents who could do nothing but talk and manipulate. He was never surprised by the depths they could sink to—and the bit about killing Fluffy was about as low as he'd seen this one get.

Sebastian laughed, saying, "No one's kidnapped your client, Gill. She'd answer your calls if she wanted to speak to you."

"She's supposed to be preparing for Milan, she's due there in two days."

Preparing to do what, pout? Mazzi Hegan thought as he ran his fingers through his frosted tips and pulled his feet from the table. Then he said in his best Swedish accent, "The mirrors here are just as good as your ones down there you know."

"Fuck off, you Swedish cunt, and mind your own business," Gill Banton snapped back.

And then with a smile, Mazzi Hegan said back as calm as possible, "You're losing your cool, baby, and you're losing your star client."

"Like I said, mind your own business and be careful I don't go after your BlueBoy Dan. You know I can if I want. I'll take him with me in the jet back to L.A., along with Marshaa."

"If you can find her."

******

Patrick was still getting calls from the advertisements running through town, and estimated he had lost out on at least three hundred thousand over the last few weeks, but he didn't care. He had bigger fish to fry now and was enjoying playing games. The pictures he'd seen of himself on the front pages of the newspapers in town and on the internet had been sensational. He was going places, he could feel it.

Gill Banton was in town, wanting to see her star client, but thanks to the heads up from Sebastian, they were already on their way back to L.A.—Marsha sitting there looking cool in her big leather chair by the window drinking a cocktail that looked like something out of a comic. Buffy across the way watching a DVD on her computer. Patrick behind them both, laying it on thick to the flight attendant who he was certain was going to let him sleep with her as soon as they arrived in town. And for free, which would be a first for him in a long time; alright, the cost of the private jet had been $20,000, but who was counting? He had Marsha at his side, and with her around, the world was treating him differently. The only problem he had now was that Gill Banton was in Vancouver, and knowing agents of any breed, she'd try to grab Dan whilst she was there. Contracted to Slave or not, she had the clout to pull it off.

And that was exactly what she was going to do.

******

Dan had been looking at the outline of a huge carrot that was shaped like a dick that he'd found in the fridge when the doorbell rang. And now he had this woman in his kitchen who was hot like his mum, and wondered why she was coming on to him. Showing off her legs and tits and staring into his eyes, she told him he was going to be a star while he tried to explain to her, "Truth is, I'm more into electronics. Besides I don't want to be starved and hang around gay guys all day for the next two decades."

But whatever he said, the more she would stare at him. She wanted him to fuck her, he could feel that, his every bodily function he had as a young man was letting him know. And with Chendrill out to lunch with his mum, as they liked to do, the timing couldn't be better. He said taking a chance, "Why don't you stop pouting at me like you are and just come downstairs and talk to me about this in my room."

Gill Banton stared at the young man sitting there in the kitchen of this shit hole house just in his jeans, and from the bulge and outline of his cock it was obvious he was wearing no underwear, and she loved that. It had been making her wetter and wetter as she'd stood there looking at him with his hard stomach and broken nose and shiner. Now he was hitting on her. She should do it, she thought. Usually these guys did that because they wanted a contract with her and most of the time it never materialized. But this BlueBoy guy whose address she'd gotten from her paparazzi friend didn't seem bothered—he just wanted to fuck her. If she did, chances are she'd never get the contract with him and this prick Patrick would; after all, he was friends with Sebastian and he obviously had it in for her.

She stared at him, sitting there eating, a piece of toast still stuck to the side of his mouth—then he felt it there, making him itch and catching it out the corner of his eye. Sticking his tongue out, he tried to reach it, then with extra effort, he stretched out his tongue long and tight and caught the piece, and, still staring at her, slipped it into his mouth like a lizard.

Fuck, the guy was hot, she thought, smoking hot. No wonder Slave had picked him up like they had. That broken nose and chiselled looks and attitude, staying silent she stared at him as he looked back, chomping on the toast he was stuffing into his mouth and hadn't offered to her, but he was offering her something else and it would taste better than what he was eating. She moved her legs and could feel herself wet inside, her irrational thinking taking over like it always did whenever she got horny. She wanted him, who cared what happened after. All she wanted him to do was take her to his room downstairs or wherever it was in this cave of a home and for him to go Neanderthal on her—pin her down and make her come over and over. And as she did she could look up at him with his broken nose and black eye and scream and bite her top lip hard the way she did so that it made her pussy tingle even more.

And then, without regard for her career or consequences for the future, she said, "Yeah come on then, take me to your room and fuck me hard."

Fuck me, thought Dan, he hadn't been expecting that. Usually it was something more like his glass of Coca-Cola thrown in his face. What was he supposed to do now? This chick in her forties wanting him to plow it home, getting herself all hot and bothered because she keeps looking down at the carrot he'd found in the fridge and stuck down his jeans.

She was hot though and really did kind of look like his mum, which was a turn on in itself. Her tits hanging out and her skirt short enough to be sexy, her legs all tanned and smooth. He stared at her. She was toned, nice flat stomach, nice legs, sexy shoes everything, wow.

Now she was leaning in on him and he could feel her hand on his knee and, as she got closer, he smelled her perfume, her soft hair touching his face as she got closer and whispered into his ear, "Fuck me right now." Then she moved her head back and pushed her lips against his, feeling them on his, tasting her lipstick as he felt himself getting hard as she pushed her tongue inside his mouth, which still had remnants of the peanut butter and marmalade sandwich he'd just wolfed down. Pulling back, he looked at her face closely, seeing the minute soft womanly hairs around her cheeks, then she looked down to his crotch and said, "Oh my God. You've got two cocks."

And Dan, thinking quickly, said, "Yeah I was born like that."

Gill Banton began to breathe deeply, her heart beginning to race more than she'd felt it do in a long time. She'd heard about this phenomena in men, but had always thought it was a myth, and now she had one right here in front of her. No wonder Marsha was up here seeking him out and getting herself in such a mess in the papers like she had. Now it all made sense.

She leaned in again, this time trailing her hand along his leg, moving it slowly towards his crotch, savoring the moment. Saying to him as she did, "Fuck me with your two cocks, fuck me with your two cocks."

She reached the top, feeling the big one first, which was rock hard, and then the other which was now almost the same and jerking, almost pumping beneath his denim. Suddenly she needed this man to take her, needed to feel him above her, holding her, taking her. Pushing herself back, she pulled her skirt up around her waist, ripped her knickers down, and laid herself out across the kitchen table. She closed her eyes and felt her breasts, touching them uncontrollably, pulling them from her bra and squeezing her nipples beneath her slight and tender hands—feeling the shock waves run down to her groin as she did. She wanted him, wanted him to come to her with his two cocks and let him do to her something she'd never experienced before in her life.

Unable to resist herself, she moved her hand down and felt her own moistness and as soon as she did, she came, gasping as she felt her fingers rubbing slowly up and down, the sensation of her hardness stuck between her fingers, she called out, "Fuck me BlueBoy, come and fuck me with your two cocks."

And opening her eyes, she looked up to see Charles Chuck Chendrill and Dan's mum standing in the kitchen watching her and as quick as a flash, she was up off the table in one fluid motion, putting her tits away and pulling her skirt down, she stood and offering out her dry hand, said, "Hi, Mr. and Mrs. Treadle, I'm Gill Banton of Banton Talent, up from Los Angeles and looking to represent your son."

****

Dan sat in his room downstairs listening to the muffled voices upstairs in the kitchen. As soon as Gill Banton, his potential talent agent up from L.A., had touched his dick, he'd come in his pants again. And now he was wondering if he'd be able to sneak his other cock back into the fridge before his mother noticed it was gone and started asking more questions.

He'd heard the Aston Martin pull up outside at the same time as his body had betrayed him and he'd come in his pants for the second time that week. *Fuck, this was becoming a problem.* Not least because for the first time in his life, women were throwing themselves at him, especially this crazy bitch now talking to his mother up in the kitchen.

He leaned back on his bed and began to laugh to himself. God, he would have paid to see his Mum's face on that one, and Chendrill's. He could imagine him there in his fancy shirt trying to look cool. Her on the table with her legs spread, saying, '*fuck me BlueBoy.*' The stupid cow couldn't even remember his name. What the fuck was that all about? My God, if he was going to sign with anyone at the moment, Patrick seemed to be the best bet, at least he wouldn't have to be wary of being eaten by a cougar every minute of the day—even if she was hot.

Chapter Twenty-Two

Malcolm Strong was getting worse, his hands beginning to shake every time his phone rang, looking over his shoulder every minute while he was out, waiting for the guy with the English accent who wore a turban to appear. Things weren't getting any better at home either, his wife becoming more distant, more interested in her phone or the TV. Sex was now a thing of the past, not even a sniff. Lying there in their matrimonial bed, she'd play with her phone and go to sleep without a word.

He had it all worked out what he was going to say to the Indian next time he called. He'd give him the made-up info he wanted about the guy called Chendrill and he'd say, 'I've done this and I'll let your package through and if you come near me again after that then I'm going to the cops and fuck what happens next. I'd rather go to prison than live my life like this. So, go fuck yourself!'

He'd say it just like that as well, hard and firm, let the guy know it's time to fuck off and leave him be.

But he'd said that before and built himself up for the fight with the guy, but when it came down to it, the humiliation of it all scared him. The photos of him with his eyes closed getting blown in a shitty alley by the skanky whores he had been letting into his car and down into his pants, who let him into their panties—if they were wearing any—and touch their bruised, skinny legs and scabby faces and small dresses that turned him on like they did. He was in a mess, but he'd get out of it. This time he'd tell the guy to fuck off. He would. This time he really would. He'd say, 'here's enough on some other guy for you to work with, go work with this man Chendrill there's enough on him for you to leave me alone so do it and let me get on with my life,' and then once he was done, he'd move to the other side of the country and never come back to this place with its mountains and sea and its gay guys and girls and those people who dressed up their dogs. They could all go hang.

Rann got the package of info from his computer courtesy of an anonymous email account and looked at it for a while without getting up. His first instinct was to get straight on the phone and say, 'You cunt Chendrill, you think those two kicks to the throat were bad, then wait till your friends see this shit I've dug up on you.'

But there was something wrong. A guy who did the things that were written down in front of him didn't walk about dressed as a parrot. They lived in the darkness blending themselves into world and no one ever saw them. The two did not match up. But you couldn't write it off; some people were bold strutting about out there without fear. He picked up his mobile phone and dialed Chendrill. When he answered, he said, "Did you have a good holiday back in that prison in 1994?"

And Chendrill said nothing. Nothing, like Rann had been expecting anyway. What he did say, though, was, "If you don't fuck off and leave us all alone then you'll never get a chance to see or use any of them pills you're bringing in from Asia."

Now it was Rann's turn to go silent. Fuck, how did he know about that, no one here knew what he was up to—no one alive now that is, except Malcolm Strong. His mouth went dry now. This guy had turned it around on him. He was about to accuse the man for doing time for child offenses. He'd said nothing and not given a shit about 1994—he hadn't even balked like he himself did now. Not fucking about anymore, he said, "Stay away from that shit. Don't go near there if you know what's good for you."

"You want me to stay away like Rasheed didn't? You going to kill me too, Rann? Or was that what you were trying to do outside the restaurant, trying to close my throat? One kick on either side then the third straight in front, crush my Adams apple. How're your balls, though, still hurting?"

Rann stayed quiet. The guy was right; the third blow could have killed him had it hit home and connected like the first two had. He hadn't thought of that at the time, but when he'd seen him his rage took over for a second—the blow in the nuts snapping him out of it. Then he heard Chendrill say, "If you're interested in what I was doing in 1994, pop along to the Vancouver Police department because that's where I was back then, ask them what I was doing, I'm sure they'd be interested in talking to you."

Then he said, "Maybe though I'll call them for you and speak to the drug squad, give them your name and address, you can explain to them what you've been doing while you were hanging out in the Far East over the last few months."

And with that Chendrill hung up.

Rann stared at the small phone lying there in the palm of his hand, his thick silver Indian bangle the same color as its rim.

The fucker was turning it around on him now. Was he bluffing? He couldn't tell. Could he take a chance? How much did he know about Thailand? He hadn't mentioned the country—just said Asia. But he knew. He was holding the place back as another card to play later, same as he would.

The Irishman dying was a secret. No one knew he was there when the guy must have slipped and fell, except the wife, but where was she? Selling her ass and his hard-on pills some place in Bangkok now, no doubt, or in another brothel somewhere like it.

He had never seen her or the friend he'd fucked in the ass along with her again. He'd looked yeah, but not found. The main problem he'd had was he was back to square one, was five grand down to boot, and had two thousand odd packets of hard-on pills on the missing list.

The only lead he'd had was the pharmacist, but where was he? The Irishman's wife had gone down to pick them up, he'd said. 'Gone down,' that means southern Thailand, 'to see her family'— no hope there. 'The monkeys all over the place,' that was a lead and the only one he had. He asked around where could he see the monkeys, everywhere he was told, Chiang Mai, especially up north in the mountains.

"Naa not the mountains, in the city?"

It had taken a week of asking before he found the answer he was looking for. A group of German tourists staying at the hotel were upset about one of them getting a bite on the leg from a monkey when they were visiting the old temples at the edge of the city. Rann had heard the German man had come out of a shop and the monkey had come from behind and ripped the plastic bag open spilling the goods all over the road. He'd lashed out kicking it and as he did others came at him, jumping off the shop awnings and in a pack, all got around him snarling.

"Where's this place?" Rann had asked as he carried on about how he loved temples, especially old ones where monkeys sometimes lived.

"Phetchaburi City," the German had said. "You don't want to go there, they will bite you if you are on your own, they can be dangerous," the German had warned, standing there in his clean white shorts.

So can I, Rann thought, *so can I.*

******

He got off the train and was stared at by almost everyone as he did. His face darker now and his turban bright white in the sun. It had been a slow journey, passing through the mountains, moving from the city through the suburbs and out into the real Thailand—away from the whores and the packs of whites roaming the red-light districts hunting pussy.

He called over a Tuk-Tuk taxi and said to the driver, who didn't understand, "Show me the monkeys in the street." Half an hour later, he was there standing in a newly built square with its fountains flowing, its paving stones reflecting brilliant light into his eyes as the sun beat down. Fuck, it was hot here, he thought, his head itchy. Above him on the telephone wires monkeys roamed, crossing the roads with ease, balancing like trapeze artists without the net or the crowd to woo them on, just their tails straight and high in the air keeping them centered. He looked around. They were in the trees across the road, on top of the shops in amongst the people as though that's just how it was meant to be.

He walked around looking for a pharmacy on the edge of the town, wherever the little fuckers—as the Irishman had liked to call them—were. Crossing one street, then another, food markets on the edge of the road, motorbikes everywhere, the place full to the brim with people, but none of them white and only one guy in a turban.

He turned a corner and waited, looking up at the side of the buildings some four stories high. There were monkeys all along the eaves, living in groups or families, not harming anyone, just getting along eating fruit left out by locals and squabbling amongst themselves.

The German must have got it around here, he thought, got tough with a wild animal a third of his size and got his ass kicked by its mates. Then he saw him—a white guy staring at him from across the road. He watched as the guy stepped out into the road, moved casually through the passing motorbikes and cars, meeting him on the other side, and said in a strong Kiwi accent, "I've been wondering if you'd show up."

******

They sat down in a coffee shop along the way and watched the traffic pass by with three, four, even five people at a time squashed onto a scooter. The Kiwi, older than he looked, said, "I met him a few times and I was surprised to hear he'd died."

"Yeah tell me about it. It took me a few days to discover the same thing. Maybe you heard about it before I did. I thought the guy had done a runner with my money."

The Kiwi went by the name of John, John Smith, and from what Rann could work out with a name like that, he was in hiding. He was a pharmacist from New Zealand and that's about all Rann could gather from the questions he asked. The guy was cool and pleasant, accepting of others and cultures and about a million miles away from the piece of shit Irishman who they were both pretending to mourn.

From what he'd heard, the man had been found dead at the bottom of the stairs stinking of booze and within 24 hrs, he was in a box in the hull of the first plane back to Dublin.

"No enquiry?"

The Kiwi looked at him.

"Why, should there be?"

Rann shook his head and stared at the table for a moment, then said, "No, he was a drunk. I spent three days waiting for him at the place we'd been meeting until the barman told me he was dead. Usually there's an enquiry though, ain't there?"

The Kiwi shook his head. "Not here, not if a drunken idiot falls down the stairs there's not, if he's shot or hacked to death or has his dick cut off in the night and bleeds to death, then yes. But for him, no."

"His what cut off?"

"His dick. They'll do that here, the girls, if you fuck with them and they get jealous."

"Really?"

"Yep, be careful, my friend. I've seen it, they'll do it."

"I'm not here for that, I'm here for—" And the Kiwi, stopping him in his tracks, placed a packet of his tablets on the table. And said with a smile, "These?"

They went back to his place, a small house at the side of the road in amongst others in what looked to Rann like an alley. The place was nice, Monkeys along the walls and on the rooftops, but not pissing and shitting and fucking like the Irishman had said, just watching.

The man had a Thai wife and a small kid of mixed race and a machine out back that produced any form of pill you wanted, as long as you laid it all out correctly.

And staring at it the Kiwi said, "When I left Auckland, this is all I brought with me."

Stole it, Rann thought, when you got the hell out of dodge the same way he'd got the hell out of London a few years back when the police started to sniff around. He said, "If you know what you're doing, I'm sure it's great."

"Yeah that helps." Then the Kiwi said to him, "Listen Rann, I'm a straight shooter, I can't get back the tablets you've lost since Paddy passed on and I can deal direct with you if you want, but the money will have to stay the same."

"Which was?"

"Sixty cents US a packet of 6 x 2.5 mg Sildenafil mixed with caffeine and glucose and some herbs of my own all stamped accordingly, just as I showed you."

Rann looked at him confused. Then said, "Herbs?"

The Kiwi replied, "Yeah, just some local herbs I've found that do the trick thrown in."

Rann nodded, giving it some thought. What difference did it make, the product worked, he couldn't deny that. He said, "What about paying off the police?"

"Why?"

"You don't have to?"

The Kiwi nodded and said, "Yeah, of course, but that's all factored in and it's done bi-yearly. It doesn't affect the deal Paddy, yourself, and I made."

The fucking goddamn Irish cunt, Rann thought, *the greedy fucking bastard*. Getting himself in a state and falling down the stairs because he wanted him to pay out double when he was getting more than the fucking guy who was making them and sending his wife to pick them up to boot.

Fuck me, the guy was lucky he was dead. If he wasn't, he'd kill him, Rann thought—fucking with him like that, trying to take away his grandfather's old house in Kenya and ruin his retirement. He said to the Kiwi, who in his earlier days would have been a prime candidate to blackmail, "I heard it different, so what I'm going to do because the Irishman is no longer involved, I'm going to make it a dollar a pack for the first run and a dollar twenty-five for the second."

Rann sat and drank beer in the evening, having booked himself into a local hotel that was as old as the rundown temples that lay above it on the hillside, now covered by brush and trees. The Kiwi was delighted, having doubled his money, he relaxed, and said, "Why don't you get yourself a Thai wife? They'll love you forever."

Like Paddy's did, Rann thought, *loved him and everyone else it seemed*. He wondered if the Kiwi was perhaps on the list. Testing the guy out, he said, "The Irishman used to say his missus gave the best blowjob in the world, even introduced her to me that way."

The Kiwi silent for the moment, gave it some thought. He had, Rann thought, she'd been coming down here getting her husband's stuff and putting it out while she was in town. The guy said back, "He'd do that, he saw her as a status symbol you see, supermodel figure. The guy used to try to make himself feel good by making other people jealous—she certainly has a beautiful face."

Like a monkey, Rann thought as he listened to the Kiwi saying, "Lovely long legs, hair, yeah a real beautiful face."

Fuck, it was only him, why did no one else see it, but him. He carried on pushing it, "But there's something else about her isn't there, you know the way she looked, you know the high cheekbones and the way her eyes were."

"Oh, you mean because she's a guy?"

"Sorry?"

"She's a guy, that's what you're referring to?"

Rann stayed silent for a second holding his bottle of Chang about an inch from his lips and feeling the top of his head begin to heat up under his turban and looked around the place to see if anyone was listening.

"No, but, you're just kidding me, right?"

He wasn't. Rann leaned in, saying "She's all woman."

The Kiwi smiled, then said, "Now, yes, same as her friend the blonde one. She's a woman now too."

Then Rann remembered the Irishman saying she came here to see her kid. The guy was fucking with him.

"She's a kid here, she's got a kid here. That's why she comes down to collect the stuff from you."

"That's right she fathered a kid here, when she was a teenager at school."

"What?"

Then Rann remembered the two of them sitting on his face, their juices flowing into his mouth and down his cheeks and over his chin. Everything was normal, he knew it, with his appetite he'd seen enough. He said, "Tell me then if she's a guy how would a girl that had been a guy and had an operation stay moist below the same as a woman does?"

Answer that, Rann thought. He was fucking with him. They were too nice to be anything other than the beautiful women who'd come to him and fucked him the whole night through. And the Kiwi answered, "They have an op and if the surgeons are good, which they are here, then the glands still work the same when aroused, but just not as much. So, what the girls do is they keep themselves moist by keeping themselves full—if you know what I mean, with someone else's fluid, someone they can trust you know? Someone who's not got HIV or anything. It's what they do. I'm telling you, Rann, I know. I've lived here for nearly twenty years now and the girls with the most beautiful long legs and figures like supermodels used to be guys. Thai women as a race

163

just aren't built that way. Besides I know his wife; I've known her since she was a boy, she's the one who introduced me to Paddy in the first place."

Oh my God, Rann thought, and then thought he was going to throw up. Kept moist by the Irish cunt—both her and her mate too, he thought. And then the fucker sending them both over to sit on his face so as they could drip the man's spunk into his mouth.

He began to heave, took a swig of beer, and tried to quell it, then the Kiwi asked, "Why? You didn't sleep with her friend did you, the gorgeous blonde one—I knew him too."

And that was more than Rann and his masculine pride could handle.

Chapter Twenty-Three

After he'd just told Mazzi Hegan and Sebastian how he'd met Gill Banton, Chendrill had taken the call from the blackmailer and turned the tables on the guy. Coming back into Sebastian's office, he realized it was the only time Chendrill had ever seen Mazzi Hegan laugh, as he heard Sebastian saying, "Mazzi please, she's got a problem obviously."

But Mazzi couldn't stop and said to Chendrill, "Tell me again what she said."

And Chendrill smiled saying, "It went like, 'fuck me BlueBoy, fuck me.' Something like that."

"And then she got up and introduced herself like nothing happened?" Sebastian asked.

"Yep, got right up pulled down her dress, put her tits away and said, 'Hi I'm Gill Banton—and I'd like to represent your son.'"

Mazzi Hegan hit the floor and began crawling along in his silver pants towards the window. Sebastian watched him saying, "Please, Chuck no more. You're going to hurt Mazzi."

Chendrill began to laugh. He wasn't one to tell tales, but it was his job to tell them if some other outfit was treading on their toes. Then Sebastian said, "There's good reason her office is situated in her bedroom, you know. She's been trying to get help, you know, psychiatric help. She saw a guy from what I heard, and in the end got him a role on the soap 'Up and Away'."

"Who?" Mazzi asked.

"Dr. Hampton, the psychiatrist."

"He's hot; he's a real psychiatrist?"

"Yes," Sebastian replied, "Real. Of course, not being able to help herself, the poor love, she picked him to help her with her problem—didn't go to a granddad or someone sensible who didn't like girls. Word is she started fucking him in the office after a couple of weeks and then got him the role.'"

"I like that show," Chendrill said out of the blue.

"Sorry?"

"What's wrong with that?" Chendrill asked them both as they stared at him, Mazzi now standing by the window rubbing his eyes, wondering if Chendrill's revelation was possibly as funny as Gill Banton lying on the table in Dan's mother's kitchen. He said, "It's a little bit faggy for you to be watching, isn't it?"

"What's wrong with that? I like it," Chendrill carried on.

Sebastian opined, "What's 'wrong' with it, Chuck, is that it's mostly gay guys who like that show."

******

An hour later, Sebastian had Belinda pick up Dan and bring him to the office, wondering why Dan was wearing a jacket, but no shirt.

"Daniel dear, you are contracted to us, but there's a buyout. I suggest you don't go south just yet and stay here and let 'Slave' manage you. I'm going to hand you over, so to speak—Patrick's coming in as a freelancer to manage you and I'm going to keep an eye on things. So, don't worry, you're still in good hands."

And Dan said, "You brought me all the way in here to tell me that?"

Then, leaning in, Sebastian said, "No, I want you please to tell

Mazzi and myself everything that was said and went down with Gill Banton before Chuck arrived this afternoon. And I'm saying *everything!*"

And Dan did, telling them both the whole thing in its entirety—her asking him to sign with her, the carrot down his pants and Gill Banton losing it thinking he had two dicks. And once he'd finished, this time it was Sebastian who was crying.

And as the tears began to settle, he picked up the phone and called Patrick. It was time to sign Marsha.

Chapter Twenty-Four

Patrick hit L.A. with a bang, Marsha on one arm and Buffy on the other, him in the middle with a smile as long as Rodeo Drive. And that's just where they went. The stores closed their doors to others as Marsha spent thousands on clothes she'd never wear and Patrick spent thousands on clothes Buffy would. Then he sat in the store looking at Marsha trying on designer labels without realizing she'd already been offered them for free.

Then his phone rang. As he answered, he heard Sebastian say, "Marsha's agent Gill Banton has just made a fool of herself in Dan's home and she also made a play to sign him, so if that woman wants to play games, I'm going to speak with Marsha about coming over to us. And if she does, I'll need a few more on top, to keep her on her toes. We don't want to be dealing with a big fish in a small pond, but don't go signing more than ten or I'll go insane with all the dialogue. So, keep those beady eyes of yours peeled whilst you're on your travels."

Patrick looked back over to Marsha, she was stunning—way ahead of the other girls in the shop who were beautiful themselves. But Marsha, she was in another league. There was only one other girl he'd ever met who was prettier, but sadly she had troubles at the moment.

Then Sebastian said, "Oh, and also please thank Buffy for lending me those DVDs. Tell her Mazzi and I are watching an old Busby Berkley one right now in my office. Tell her I'd forgotten just how good the man was and ask her please if she's got any more."

Patrick hung up. That was a good call, he thought, things were looking up. Now he didn't have to lie when he would tell the next hostess who he met that he was looking for talent, not that he really cared either way.

He called over to the two girls and as many shop assistants as he could, telling them all as though they were soppy school kids to put the $10,000 dollar dresses down. He said, "Sebastian just called, Gill Banton was just round Dan's place trying to sign him with the company who represents you, Marshaa. She offered him the world, and made a fool of herself in the process because he said, 'Why would I go anywhere else when I'm already with the best.' Your agent Marshaa, she's frightened, you see. Slave's getting interested in movies now, Sebastian and Mazzi are looking at a Busby Berkley one right now as we speak and they've asked me to sign an incredibly beautiful model from the Ukraine to star in it once they sign Busby up—kind of a dual thing, great for her and great for Busby. He's onboard as soon as we sign a big name. So anyway, that's all the news for 'us' at Slave."

He pulled out his phone and flipped to a picture of Alla standing in a park he'd taken six months back, the sun in her hair, her face glowing with warmth, honesty, and truth, and showed it to them all.

"She and Dan are going to set the world on fire. And not only that, he's bringing in ten new models, ones who not only look fantastic, but can also act—but only the best. Newbies and ones established with other companies alike, and when they're all in and signed, the doors are closing: they're not signing another person and Slave's taking over."

Buffy stared at him. What the fuck was he talking about? Sebastian and Mazzi Hegan's company was good, but, take over the world? Not only that, Busby Berkley was dead, who was he kidding? She stared at him in complete amazement as Patrick said, "Buffy's so excited about it all." And she was just about to put him straight when she heard him follow it up with, "Sebastian's putting her in charge of research and development for the movie section. She's going to be running the whole thing! They're all geared up to do a movie as soon as the girl recovers from an operation she needed. And Mazzi Hegan's shooting it."

******

Alla Bragin lay in the hospital bed and tried with all her will and might to move her big toe. She'd done it once early in the morning and she was certain she could do it again. It wasn't the light changing or a breeze floating in from an open door that had moved the sheets, it was her, and if that was the case, she knew in time she would walk again.

Dennis, her husband, who'd once been a dentist, slept on the chair at the side of the bed in which his wife, half his age, lay crippled.

"It moved again," she said softly, waking her husband from his dream.

"Darling it moved again, my toe—I got it to move."

Dennis smiled, and hoped for her sake it wasn't just a dream.

"Good," he said, watching her, looking at her face, her eyes, her hands at the side of the bed laying above the sheet, her arms so slender, her fingers long and beautiful. "Keep trying," he said, "you'll get there," but deep down in the pit of his stomach, he knew the moment she did and could walk again the likelihood was that she would keep going and be gone forever. For he knew the sad reality: the injury was the only reason they were together again.

He knew the injury had come out of nowhere, his wife taking a blow to the spine by an unknown man while they'd been separated, her living downtown in a luxury apartment in Yaletown with a view across the creek and him in the basement suite. Now, though, he had her back and he would do all he could to stop her leaving him a second time.

She'd known Patrick well after she'd left her marital home and they had been lovers, him helping her on a financial level and her giving him what he needed, and once he fell in love, as had so many others, he began to pay in other ways. She said, "I've been watching you, Dennis love. You look beautiful when you sleep." The words touching his whole soul, hoping they were true as they melted him inside, the same as he felt when she touched him.

"You're the beautiful one," he said, knowing it was true and it was. Rann had felt the same way when he'd seen her in the photo and for all three, it was love at first sight because to them all and almost all men who set eyes on her, she was the most beautiful woman they had ever seen.

******

Charles Chuck Chendrill was still smiling when he arrived back in the Aston Martin and parked outside the front of Dan's home. The drive had been good, the car slightly larger than Hegan's Ferrari—which could now park itself—and it hurt his ribs less when he was getting in and out.

Maybe that was it, he thought, the only reason he'd been given a bigger car by Sebastian was because he knew his ribs were hurting every time he squeezed himself into the other one? He must have been watching him when he'd pull up and drive away from the allocated parking spaces just below his office at Slave. *Could be*, he thought, *probably was. Fuck me, the guy was a good man.*

He got out and looked about, no baker there with a baseball bat or ninja assassin turban-wearing Sikh. The coast was clear.

He walked up the steps and knocked on the door. Dan's mother Tricia answered. Leaning in, he kissed her on the lips, and she said, "Hello lover boy."

And when they reached the kitchen, Chendrill stared at the table and asked, "Have you spoken to Dan?"

She hadn't. He'd been in his room ever since they'd got back early from lunch and had been picked up in a limo, which she'd thought was the nymphomaniac again and discovered it was only the nice man who liked to keep the garden tidy. As he sat down briefly and watched as she put the kettle on, she said to Chendrill, "He was out, but he's back now."

Chendrill got up, walking back along the corridor, and went down the stairs to the basement. He knocked on Dan's door. Dan was asleep; and after hearing him wake and then unbolt the door, he was knocked back by the smell of a young man's room.

"You come down here to hit me in the other eye?" he heard Dan say.

He hadn't.

"Sebastian wants to see you."

"I was just there."

"Yeah and you were supposed to stay."

"Tell him I'll come over tomorrow."

"It doesn't work that way."

"What—you his gofer now, I thought you were a PI?"

Dan was right, Chendrill thought, a few months back if Sebastian had asked if he could go find Dan, he would have found him then told Sebastian to call a cab. But the man had a way about him. He could get you to do things for him you wouldn't normally do, and the grand a day and Aston Martin helped a bit with that.

"I am."

"Well go be one then and leave me alone, I'm tired."

"It's only three o'clock in the afternoon?"

"Tell him he kept me up past my bedtime last night at the fish place. So why don't you go fuck my mum for a bit and leave me be."

******

Mazzi and Sebastian had just finished another movie when Dan came through the door, his ass still sore and his throat hurting from where Chendrill had grabbed him by the scruff of the neck and kicked him up the backside as he threw him towards the stairs.

"What's wrong with your throat, Daniel?" Sebastian asked as Dan sat down on the sofa and put his feet up on the coffee table.

"Ask him," Dan replied as he saw Chendrill's big shape come past the smoked plate glass window and into the room.

"His throat's hurting him at the moment, because he's got a big mouth."

Sebastian looked to the both of them for a moment.

"Okay?"

The kid was obviously hard work and he could see the frustration in Chendrill's eyes. He said, "Dan, I can't help you here, you're the only person who can do that."

Then he carried on getting out a new contract for him to sign.

"As I mentioned earlier, before you decided to disappear on

us Daniel, in your old contract we had a clause that says we can extend and gain exclusivity to you, i.e., you can't go elsewhere."

Dan looked at him and said quite honestly, "What makes you think I want too?"

"Gill Banton."

Dan laughed to himself and stared at the floor. Then said, "What makes you think I want to do this stupid bullshit anyway?"

"Because you're good at it."

Dan looked to Chendrill, making friends now, saying sorry in his own way. Chendrill spoke for him, "Dan's more interested in electronics."

Sebastian's eyes lit up.

"Good for you. Maybe we can you put you through some kind of college course?"

Dan shook his head, he knew more than the lecturers.

"He's way beyond that," Chendrill said, answering for him again.

Mazzi Hegan, who'd been sitting in the chair quietly, piped up, "We do art here, Dan, not bullshit."

And quick as a flash, Dan replied, "Your art doesn't make it to the art galleries where the real art is—and if you don't like the truth, then you can suck my dick."

As soon as he'd said it, he realized this was the wrong thing to say to Mazzi Hegan, who simply said, "You couldn't handle the pleasure baby."

"Mazzi," Chendrill stepped in, "you shouldn't mock him. We've all got our talents. Dan's is electronics; some've said he's a genius."

Who gives a shit? Mazzi thought. He was here to make people look good and when he was distracted, Dan was just that. He said, "Dan's got a talent for looking good also, put the hobby on hold and grab the cash."

"What cash?" Dan asked.

Sebastian answered him, "You've a lot of cash, Dan—some now, but a huge amount coming. I want you to sign with us exclusive for the next 5 years."

"I could almost be a doctor by then if I wanted." And he could, as nutty and stupid as he was, he easily had the smarts, and he knew it.

Listening to what he said and giving it some thought, Sebastian reached to the floor and picked up Fluffy, placing him gently on his lap and said without looking up, "Daniel, I'm sure you could, but a second ago you were an electronics genius, love. What we want to do is not let you get ruined and left on the side of the road after signing up with a company that does just that."

"Marshaaa's doing all right with them," Dan replied, stretching out the end of her name for effect.

"Marshaa's a girl Daniel, and if Gill Banton was into girls, I'm sure that's where she'd be right now."

Dan sat there listening, watching Mazzi Hegan stroking his hair, Chendrill looking out the window at his new car and Sebastian stroking his dog and just being nice. Why would they think he'd ever want to go work with a crazy nut like this Banton woman anyway? He had no intention of going anywhere. The truth was he didn't even want to be here. But the money was there, he knew that, and the chicks that were giving him the eye now wherever he went was a bonus. Soon, if he played his cards right and didn't keep popping it out in his pants, he'd get some. So, he said, "Okay I want four things, though. First, I want an open account with the pizza delivery joint of my choosing. And second, I want Patrick to look after me because I like his style, but I don't want to have to listen to his bullshit. And the third is that I'd like a new computer and a decent soldering iron and bench with a vice for my room for the electronics I like to do."

Mazzi Hegan looked around, then with attitude said, "That's three things."

And Dan replied, "That's good you can count because the fourth thing I want is your Ferrari."

And he got it.

******

Rann Singh sat in his apartment, which no longer had a bucket, a china tea set, weights, or a deck chair for the balcony, and checked the internet on his new computer. Using his tracking number, he saw exactly where his shipment of pills were in the freight system. He had about three days to go now and they'd be here. Malcolm Strong was playing it up though, giving him ridiculous stuff about Chendrill that even his granny could spot as just plain nonsense. But like an idiot, he'd used it. He'd taken the bait and made himself look stupid—*real stupid*. Now Chendrill had turned it around on him, gone poking around in his affairs and found out about the shipment. How much did the guy know, though? Everything, like he was making out? Or just ten percent and bluffing the rest like Rann liked to do himself? At least he hoped, but what if it wasn't a bluff? What if Chendrill had called customs like he had said he would and told them there's a package coming in addressed to this guy, Rann Singh. But it wasn't addressed to Rann, it was addressed to Bill Moore, who'd rented the locker and handed the keys over to Rann so as his wife wouldn't find out about what he sometimes did on his way home late at night.

Rann had worked out the positioning and rented the storage locker at the back of the one where the package would be placed and when all was well and good and he'd seen no one was there to nab him, he'd cut the corrugated steel away in the back of the locker and grab it.

But first he needed it to clear customs and, with Malcolm being a pussy, he was getting worried. He took a deep breath, and called him, "You trying to make me look like a cunt? Giving me shit information like that, you trying to make a fool out of me?"

Malcolm stayed quiet on the end of the phone and for a moment, Rann thought he could hear the man crying. He said, "What you fucking doing? What you snivelling for?"

Malcolm stayed quiet, then he heard him say, "Leave me alone."

"What?"

"Leave me be."

"You should have thought about that when you fucked those whores, shouldn't you? Now it's time to pay for your sins, pay for your sins you cunt and do as I tell you."

The man was a monster. He carried on, "That's what this born-again Christian wants you to do, pay for your sins. So, you'd better start."

"There is no Christian man, a Christian wouldn't be like you. I know it's you and you can fuck off. I'm going to the police."

Now Rann was silent. He'd pushed the guy too far, same with this PI guy and that realtor who likes it up the ass. He needed to stop, leave it, let the man settle. The tablets would be here soon and they needed to be checked through. But as his temper burst, he said, "You do as you're told, you whimpering cunt of a man, or I'll post all those photos of you on the passport office's windows so as all your friends and work colleagues can see what a fucking nonce perverted cunt you really are. Then I'll do the same at your fucking house. Do you understand me. You asked for this shit. You did these things not me. You. You did this to you. Not me. So, fucking man up, you cunt, own it and do as I tell you, or you may as well go fucking hang yourself because when I'm done with you, your fucking life will be worth shit."

Malcolm Strong sat there on his own in his home, his wife out now. The phone in his hand was shaking, how long would this go on? It had to have been a year now of the abuse, the shouting, the name calling—muggers got less, murderers not a lot more. He could feel his heart pounding, it had been that way for a while now with him constantly on the verge of tears, putting on a brave face for the world to see, smiling on the outside, telling jokes, but crying within. The pain was incredible, this man on him unrelentingly, pushing him, destroying who he once was. And he wasn't giving up. Taking a deep breath so as he would not burst into tears again, as he just had when he'd seen the number on the phone, he said, "Go fuck yourself. I'm calling the police."

And that's exactly what he did.

Less than half an hour later, Williams arrived outside Malcolm's home and walked up and rang the doorbell. When no one answered, he went around the back and tried the back door. The lights were on, but nothing else; no TV, nothing, just lights. He tried the door again—still locked. The man had been crying on the phone the dispatcher had said, babbling, not making sense, saying he wouldn't leave him be.

Williams tried the door again, this time putting pressure on it with his foot. It gave way and he stepped inside, calling out as he did. He moved through the kitchen, then into the corridor of the house. Into the living room, the drink cabinet was open here, a bottle of wine and an empty bottle of scotch on the floor. Next to them, open packets of tablets, some still on the floor.

Shit.

He moved on, checking the dining room and headed upstairs through the bedroom and then opened the bathroom door, which was blocked slightly by Malcolm's leg. Malcolm was on the floor in his underpants, puke everywhere, blood everywhere, the bath full and still hot, the water red from the blood that had seeped out of his slashed wrists trailing over the dry porcelain and onto the floor where he'd gotten out and fallen, soaked, drugged, drunk, and bleeding onto the bathroom floor.

Quickly, Williams bent down and felt the man's pulse; he was barely alive. He slapped his face hard once, then twice, trying to bring him round. He lifted him slightly, slapped him again and then, as he saw the man's eyes open slightly, let him down again and called it in.

"Malcolm, Malcolm, do you know where you are?" were the words Malcolm had first heard as he opened his eyes to see the contained security camera looking down at him. He didn't.

The nurse moved toward him so he could see her and as he tried to move his arm, he found it was restrained, along with his leg.

"Do you know where you are?" she asked again, her voice kind and gentle.

He shook his head, not a clue. She said, "You're in a secure ward, Malcolm. You tried to hurt yourself." He looked to his free arm covered in cuts, some patched some still clear left alone to heal.

"You took an overdose, Malcolm."

He took a look around the room, the nurse still smiling. His head spinning with confusion.

"Do you remember?" the nurse asked, he didn't, he couldn't

179

remember a thing. He closed his eyes, and opened them again. Two hours had passed and Williams was still with him, standing in the room.

Chapter Twenty-Five

It wasn't long before Dan's wish came true and, having been dropped off at the showroom on Burrard by Belinda, he showed his licence to the salesman, who was doing well off of Slave this week, and who said to Dan in his best fake British accent, "You're going to love this one, sir."

Dan would, he couldn't believe that only a few weeks back he had one thing he could call his own, and now he had two, a Ferrari and an Xbox his mum bought him for Christmas that he was already getting bored with.

This would be more fun. He loved the way he could make Mazzi Hegan's rip away from the lights. Nothing had taken him yet and nothing was going to, not even Chendrill's Aston Martin. He looked around, the place looking at him now, Dan feeling like a million-dollar king with a contract worth more than that with Slave—if he stayed looking sexy, as Mazzi had told him as they walked out of Sebastian's office.

He looked over to a girl staring at his legs from behind her counter where she sat most of the day looking pretty. He gave her a wink. Then looked down to his feet. He had odd shoes on and they were both lace ups, both Converse—one red, one white. *How the fuck did that happen?* he thought. He didn't even know he had two pairs. Then he remembered he did. He liked the white ones, but had lost them when he'd been trying to walk around the garden on his hands and couldn't make it across the bit at the end which was gravelled and he'd taken down the neighbor's fence.

Fucking great, all he had to do was find the other and he was back on track.

The girl was still staring at him, looking like she wanted him, looking him right in the eyes. Him there in his jeans and odd shoes with his shirt not done up because he had it on back to front and he couldn't get the buttons in. It's the way he was.

He gave her a wink, she smiled, he gave her another, she smiled, he gave her another and she smiled more. *What do I do now?* he thought. *Go talk to her*, he told himself. *About what?* he wondered. *Doesn't matter. What if she wants to fuck like that woman had?* Not here, he thought, *she's at work. So what? they do that at these car showrooms.* He'd seen it on late night TV when he was younger after he opened up the cable box and switched the wires around to get the porn channel working—then his mum had found him with one of her new fluffy socks and she'd taken the box away.

But now he was being offered it for real. In the movie, the guy had looked like Chendrill, in a Hawaiian, and the girl had been blonde with curly hair and she was wearing leg warmers through the whole thing, even when he was fucking her on the hood of the car and she'd screamed and shook her head and made funny faces with her lips and then so did he, getting all serious with his eyes, staring into nowhere and saying shit like, 'fuck yeah, oh yeah fuck yeah, take it baby, take it' and then grunting. Dan hadn't got to see if he bought the car or not because his mum had come in getting all angry at exactly the same time that he'd come in his pants for the first time in his life.

The next day she took the box back to the cable company and they couldn't work out what the boy had done to the electronics inside.

The girl staring at him and smiling had the same hair, long and curly and permed, like they used to in the late eighties, he called out to her asking, "You wearing leg warmers?"

She shook her head, she wasn't. Shame.

He pulled the car out onto the main road and gunned it, listening to the engine purr and then watching as a guy in a Hyundai pulled past and disappeared into the distance. He pulled over, thinking *this isn't right* and gave the engine a rev. It all sounded great. Then he pulled away again with his foot to the floor and gave way for a bicycle.

What the fuck? This is ridiculous, he thought, pulling over again. He did a U-turn and gunned it slowly back to the dealer, where, in his precise voice, the guy said, "The car's fine sir. Sebastian's had it fitted with a governor, sir. Said you can remove it when your twenty-one, sir. He said he wanted you to feel good and look good, sir. But that's as far as it goes."

******

Patrick took a suite at the Wiltshire in Beverly Hills and booked another one for Buffy along the corridor. 'Marshaa', as she now liked to be called, had gone home to the little place she had in Malibu and was worrying whether Patrick was going to sign the beautiful girl in the photo and, if so, whether she would be left behind.

Patrick said, "Girls as beautiful as you, Marshaa, don't get left behind." But the seed was planted. In her eyes, Dan was going to be a movie star and he was going to have an affair with the girl from the Ukraine and they'd go run off there together because it sounded hot.

Patrick went down and hit the bar and within ten minutes, he was in love with the waitress and everyone there knew his name and that he'd just dropped off 'Marshaa' in Malibu, and that they'd had the weekend together working on a project, and that he was the guy who secured the contract for the incredible sexy kid in the BlueBoy campaign who was about to do a movie because he was

183

such a talent.

"Buffy's about to land him a three-picture deal that'll slide in nicely along with the next series of BlueBoy campaigns. The kid's going to be tied up for at least three years."

He sat down, then said, "Slave's just signed him for five years exclusive. Gill Banton was just up at his house trying to sign him, but he's with me."

"I know that kid," the executive at the bar had said.

"You can't not know him, he's worldwide. If I let him sign, those guys are looking at sellout distribution in theatres not just in North America, but all the Americas, Europe, Asia. He's incredibly hot in Japan."

Then the executive said, "We're going to camera on the 15th with ours, the director's Rupert Mikes—pure talent, did *Fallen Warriors.*"

"Oh yes," Patrick replied, not having a clue. "Fantastic—I loved that show. Wow that guy's talent. Who you got up front?"

"Dave Percell's the lead."

"Oh—Really?"

"He's so talented."

Patrick stayed silent. Then he said, "Great, oh totally, yeah well, good luck with that."

Within the hour, Patrick had skim read the script and Dave Percell, the up-and-coming new sensation, was out. Dan's three picture deal that did not exist was being pushed and he was in the running for the lead, along with 'Marshaa' who was yet to show off her incredible acting skills to the world. Buffy, who was still in her room watching DVD's and eating chocolate, was associate producer overseeing the 30% finance and worldwide distribution

Patrick had personally guaranteed for the show via Slave—as long as they were shooting in Vancouver and, of course, he had a back-end deal for himself and sole rights to distribution sales within three countries in Asia he could think of off the top of his head, one of which was Japan.

The only problem now was that Dan couldn't act, neither could Marsha, and he didn't have a clue about distribution, let alone guaranteeing it worldwide and not a word had been said to Sebastian about the 2.5 million he'd casually put them on the hook for.

But who cared about minor details, because he was having fun; and an hour after shaking hands on the deal, the waitress was up in his room to talk about her new modelling contract with 'Slave'. She would be his first signing and in the morning, the second was going to be 'Marshaa'.

He was unstoppable.

****

Megan Rawlis felt the early morning sun warming up the city as she made her way back to the apartment she shared with her friend. She had good news to tell her about what had just happened and how she'd met this guy and how within the week she'd be moving up to Vancouver to start her new life. The day before, she'd gone to work as a waitress and twenty-four hours later, she was a signed as a Slave model with a six-month extendable contract. This was what dreams were made of and it was a dream made true by a realtor who was still naked and laying on the big king size bed that smelled of sex, airing out his crotch because his balls were aching while he talked on the phone to the girl who had just been voted the most beautiful woman in the world, and who was in love with Dan because he couldn't care less about any of it.

"Marshaa, your going to love this, I just signed another beautiful girl to 'Slave', Sebastian's going crazy for her. They're setting up a shoot and taking her to Bali."

And Marsha said, "I'm sick of Bali—everyone goes there. I told my agent I didn't want to go there again."

Ignoring this he carried on, "Don't miss out on shit like this. You want to keep going to places where you can get malaria."

"I don't like Malaysia either, I'm sick of it over there."

"Dan's signing up on a picture—he's the lead. It's an incredible opportunity, the script's out of this world."

"What? Wow!"

"Yeah, you want me to talk to them about you?"

******

Charles Chuck Chendrill pulled out of Dan's mum and lay still on the bed, Tricia next to him, hot, breathing heavy, and happy.

"I think you're trying to kill me," he said.

She was, kill him with love. He was the best thing that had happened in her life, a guy who was a real man and took no shit from her son. The shirts, though, she wasn't sure about.

"I need to go to work," she said.

She was on an afternoon shift, starting at two. Nursing was a tough gig, but she liked it—dancing would have been better, but she was too old now. She still had the body, though. She got up and walked to the window. Outside of her house, with its stucco walls that needed painting, were two high performance cars and they didn't look right. She said, "The neighbors are going to think we've either won the lottery or we're dealing drugs."

Chendrill sat up. "Let them think what they want, they'll just be jealous."

He was right, *fuck 'em*, how many times had she come along the road off the bus with two arms full of shopping and they'd passed her in their cars, even in the rain. *Yeah let them think it.* Let them think what they will, it made no difference. By the looks of things, they'd be moving out and leaving here soon anyway. Dan would be buying a place for her. Somewhere nice, near her work so she could walk in and get some fresh air. It was early days yet, she knew, but if Chendrill wanted to join her, she'd say yes in a heartbeat. She'd been to his place downtown by the park with its view and its fancy lobby that made you feel special. His furniture was dark like most bachelor's places she'd been to. Not that she'd been to that many, the baker hadn't even taken her out—at least not that she could remember—and in retrospect he could very well have been married, even though he said he loved her—loved her but never took her to see his friends.

Chendrill's phone rang. It was Williams—they'd met and got along after he'd shown Chendrill he was a cop who cared, really cared, and didn't just drink coffee. He needed to talk with him.

Chendrill dropped off his girl and, making enough of a meal of it in the new car for her work friends to see, he pulled away slowly, turning left off the main drag, and heading over the bridge into town.

When Chendrill came in, Williams was out of uniform, sitting at the window of the coffee shop looking young. He shook his hand, smiling and before Chendrill could sit down and wipe the froth from his moustache Williams got straight to it.

"There's a guy, he called the emergency services, they said he was crying, struggling to get his words out, saying he needed to speak to the police, a man was harassing him, wanted him to do stuff, then he hung up. I went over and found him nearly dead from an overdose. He'd tried to do it all, you know, slashing his wrists in the bath, but he fucked it all up because he was so drunk from the bottle of scotch he'd used to get the courage to do it in the first place. Anyway, turns out he's one of us, a border agent. I spoke with him at the hospital and he's still not with it, but when I went back and listened to the recording of his initial call, your name was mentioned."

Chendrill put his coffee down and said, "In what way?"

"Like I say, the guy was crying, blubbing and all over the place and from what it sounds like, he'd already done the scotch by then, but he says, 'this guy keeps on and on and doesn't stop,' wants him to do shit and then says Chendrill."

Chendrill sat back and looked out the window to the cars passing and the couples walking by holding hands.

"What's his name?"

"Malcolm Strong."

"A border agent?"

"Yeah."

"Where's he posted, do you know?" Williams did, he came prepared knowing there'd be a hundred questions coming at him like a machine gun and wanted to be able to catch them all.

"He checks the overseas mail coming in downtown."

Chendrill nodded, smiled, and pulled out his phone.

Chapter Twenty-Six

Rann Singh paced up and down his apartment, kicking out at nothing as he went. He was worried now; the shipment was coming in within two days and Malcolm Strong had gone on the missing list. And now this prick of a private eye had just called and told him he was sitting right next to him.

Fuck me, he should have let it be, he thought, *should have let it be, always taking things too far and getting into wars, not letting it go,* letting his pride and his temper get the better of him instead of playing it cool and being the smart one. No, he was an idiot. He'd taken this guy on, started trouble, fucked with him, then with the people he worked for. He didn't check who he was fighting with, just thought he could take on the world like a British bulldog—and an Indian one at that—and now he'd gotten himself into a mess when he should have been just getting his dick sucked by some white slut while he waited.

Fuck. Fuck. Fuck.

Now it was all going down the drain—the shipment would be found because obviously Chendrill had found that fucking crack-whore-fucking wimp blabbing about all the cash he'd laid out to keep things quiet and about the parcel he was about to let through.

And he'd been stupid enough to blab when the fucker in the flashy shirt had said the border agent's name, even though he could have been bluffing—just blurting it out. What the fuck are you doing with him? Instead of thinking and playing it cool and saying, who the fuck is that, never heard of him—go call a psychic if you want to play mind games. But now the game was up. The fucker had Malcolm Strong's name and he was calling him with it. So, he knew what he was up to. Shit, shit and bollocks he'd made it worse by screaming down the phone—"Fuck you, you cunt!"—at Chendrill like he had, but was he really, was he really sitting with him? Rann carried on thinking, the guy played chess, he could see that.

He took a deep breath. He'd paid out a lot of cash, been sexually embarrassed along the way—but not in the same way they did to you when you were in prison, and he certainly wasn't there. No one had arrested him yet. He could walk right now. He could move on, recoup some cash in another city, and try again—after all, he had the source. The Kiwi was a cool dude. Just play it cool if Malcolm Strong is not there. It doesn't matter. He didn't know what was coming or when, a thousand items came in every day. *Wait*, he thought, wait and see and let it go through without having the backup plan in place. If it works, good; if they find it what have they found, heroin, crack? No, hard-on pills. Big deal.

Play it cool Rann, he said to himself over and over. Play it cool and wait. Just wait, calm down and wait. If it doesn't work, move on and try again elsewhere.

******

Chendrill was still laughing as he drove towards the hospital with Williams in the passenger seat, feeling the varnished wood of the steering wheel beneath his fingers. The hospital, big and white, was coming up in the distance, and his new girl was in there somewhere doing her thing.

The East Indian had lost it when he'd heard Malcolm Strong's name come out of Chendrill's mouth. He'd lost it, swearing down the phone, the guy was a hothead and hotheads always fell early on the fences and he'd just tripped—it's the way life went.

They took the elevator up to the secure wards and walked along the corridor until they reached the desk. A minute later,

Williams opened the door and entered Malcolm's room, leaving Chendrill outside briefly before bringing him in. The man was changed now, the border officer no longer a menace to himself.

Chendrill entered and, smiling, looked Malcolm in the eye and said, "Seems like you've been having a hard time I'd say. My name's Charles Chendrill and you've nothing to fear from me."

Malcolm closed his eyes for a moment and thought he was going to breakdown. This guy standing in front of him looked like a decent man in a loud shirt. He was smiling at him, even though he knew he'd put a dossier together turning him into a paedophile.

Fuck what had he become, he took a deep breath and simply said, "I'm sorry."

Chendrill looked at the man, covered in wires coming out from all over his body, his face gaunt, his skin white, and the cuts healing in their own way along the inside of his arm. What had that man been doing to him to push him that far?

"Like I mentioned before, you've nothing to fear from me," Chendrill said; then, with genuine concern in his eyes, he carried on, "why don't you tell my friend and I what's been going on."

And that's when Malcolm Strong began to cry again.

******

Megan Rawlis was still ecstatic, running around her small apartment like it was Christmas. Sleeping with the executive at Slave had paid off. He was old, yeah, but she liked daddy types and he'd been fun, even if he was a little bit kinky. She picked up her case and threw it onto the bed. What was the point in waiting, she thought, wait a couple of weeks for what? Get up there, she said to herself, get up there and strike while the iron's hot. And six hours after catching the first flight up from L.A., she was standing in the reception of Slave's offices waving her contract in her hand and saying she wanted to speak with either Mazzi Hegan or Sebastian.

"I've just been signed," she said to the receptionist sitting at her desk—who was prettier than her.

"My agent, Patrick, he just signed me to you guys. I'm on contract here now."

Then as quick as a flash, she was off and with her arms in the air and her head held back, she began to run along the corridor letting her long blonde hair flow behind her as she called out to everyone, "I'm here, I'm here!"

And reaching the end, she bumped straight into Mazzi Hegan, dressed entirely in cream, who simply said, "Who's here?"

"I'm here—I'm from L.A., Patrick just signed me. I'm the girl you've been looking for! He said that."

"Patrick just signed you?"

"Yes, I'm here."

And she was there, in all her long dressed, long haired, hippified glory. She was there and in her mind, she was there to stay, despite what the gay guy dressed like an ice cream thought.

"I'm not having it!" Mazzi Hegan said as he strutted around Sebastian's desk while Sebastian looked through the contract Patrick had hacked together and printed up whilst drunk at three in the morning. "I'm not."

Sebastian stared at him and knew his business partner was far from wrong. The girl was pretty for a girl, but when did Patrick get the right to just go signing girls up willy-nilly like that? Yeah, he'd said we need a stable of about ten so keep your eye out, but

Rock Solid

the guy should have at least called and checked. After all, there are procedures. He said, "There's two things we have to look at, Mazzi—the first is what did Patrick see in her that we did not see?"

"Her snatch, that's what he saw. Her fishy stinking snatch," Hegan snapped back.

Before he could carry on, Sebastian opened his eyes again and said, "And secondly, the young woman's feelings."

"Her feelings?"

"Yes."

"We do work in advertising, you know."

Sebastian took a deep breath, then said, "Yes but we don't have to be like animals, do we? It's a small six-month contract and from what I can see, Patrick's hashed it out of an old one he used to use to sell condos. If we cancel it, it could devastate the girl—completely change the course of her life."

"God forbid," said Mazzi as he walked to the window to look down at the street for any hot guys, hoping one would be wearing shorts as he passed so as he could for a moment take his mind off of things. Sebastian carried on, "No—we don't need that, do we? I'll call up Patrick and see what he's up to. Then we can go from there."

Mazzi Hegan took a deep breath and tried to calm himself down, ran his fingers through his blonde locks, and said, "And in the meantime, we all have to put up with listening to her singing Joni Mitchell?"

Megan leaned herself back into the large leather chair in the boardroom and let her hair fall into her face, feeling it blow away from her mouth as she bellowed out the rest of 'Big Yellow Taxi,' knowing everyone could hear her and how much they'd be

193

appreciating her voice right now—because everyone always had, especially the deaf man who used to live next door when she was a kid who loved to hear her sing in his ear. It was her thing, singing and poetry, which were pretty much the same thing in her eyes.

The days of taking orders from drunk businessmen in the hotel lounge were now a million miles away. Before long she'd be up there on the big screen and billboards all over the US, just like that skinny guy in his silver underpants. Then the world would see who she was, see the talent that was Megan, and all those men who'd pinched her ass could go kiss it as she was here and she was here to stay.

Suddenly in a burst of inspiration, she stood and, holding her bright purple shawl out above her head, moved along the long wood framed windows, spinning around and around as she began to sing louder and louder for the whole world to hear and about twenty minutes later, Charles Chuck Chendrill arrived and said, "What a lovely voice you have Megan. My name is Chuck."

******

They sat in the front of Chendrill's new Aston Martin as he drove through town with Megan listening to the big man as he spoke.

"Now it works two ways. You have a contract, but the man who can make or break you has sensitive ears and from what I can see, you can keep your singing voice locked away in the hotel room Sebastian's sorted out for you and never let it out again in Slaves offices or I can drive you to the airport."

And he'd heard her say, "But everyone loves my voice."

"Well sorry love, but they didn't."

"Patrick had me sing 'Unchained Melody' six times over and

over while he was having a bath."

Why? Chendrill thought as he saw the signs for the airport and wondered if he should just take Hegan's words to heart literally and head straight there—tell her they'd call her soon with a booking. From what he could see, the girl was pretty, but somewhere there was a screw loose. He said, "Patrick must like that song." Megan nodded and with a slight glance, Chendrill sensed she was about to cry. So, he said, "I know Mazzi could have been nicer. Sebastian told me what he'd said about you being in need of a new voice box, but if you're going to work there you need to know that he can be rude."

Megan took a deep breath and then another and then another and then another, each time letting her breath expel from her nostrils so precisely that Chendrill could almost count the seconds, four in six out, five in seven out, six in eight out as she reached ten he said, "You reach twelve you're going to go pop."

Then listening as she let out her final long long breath, he heard her say, "I've heard worse, it's not that. It's just been such a roller coaster of a day. I haven't even called the hotel restaurant to let them know I'm a model now."

Chendrill coasted the Aston to a stop and stared at the red lights in front of him and thought about his friend whose life had become swamped by the dramas of restaurant life after he'd bought one in the hope he could retire. How many of the girls there just didn't show up for a shift and disappeared off the face of the earth until he saw them working in a place around the corner. It went with the territory. Turning to her he said, "I'm sure they'll survive."

The lights turned green and they sat in silence for at least a minute as he drove before Megan eventually said, "I know everyone thinks I let Patrick fuck me to get this contract and that's why they aren't taking me seriously, but the truth is he didn't touch me—I'm the one who fucked him… And I enjoyed every minute of it, Chuck, you see it was empowering, you know, being the one in control and listening to the guy scream like a woman."

With his ears hurting and trying to remove the vision of what the girl had just planted in his mind, Chendrill dropped Megan off at the hotel. As wacky as the girl was, Sebastian would have still booked her a suite. She had a contract. She'd told him that as many times as she'd told him she loved his shirt, which was at least seven times since they'd left Slave's offices. She had a contract that was certain—even if it was written on the tissue paper Patrick had used to wipe his dick, Chendrill thought, but that was not his business. He pulled the car around in a huge U-turn and heard the polite beep the Vancouver drivers did when they saw someone make an illegal motoring manoeuver. Not too loud, not too soft, just enough of a beep to let you know 'I know you're wrong'. These people who would toot their horns for nothing then carry on and pass by the guys on the other side of town selling drugs or a teenage girl selling herself for these drugs and look straight ahead, pretending it wasn't happening.

He took a right at the lights and headed towards the highway, and forty minutes later, he pulled up outside Rann Singh's apartment building, parked along the way, and looked up at the balcony from which the lawn chair had dropped only days before. It was hot and most of the balcony doors were open to the suites, but Rann Singh's was closed.

Taking out his phone, he called his number again. The guy was up there at the moment—he was sure. No answer. He tried again, nothing. Then he sent a text,

> *I'm outside—if you want the shipment to go through, you'll need to come see me.*

Then he saw movement at the window, then at the balcony door. Then nothing. Chendrill looked again, trying to work out the launching capabilities the guy could have from up there. No chance with a lawn chair again, but smaller stuff yes. He picked up his phone again and this time wrote,

I'm off to the post office. If you want what you've been waiting for, then you'll need to come find me.

Chendrill looked up again, still no sign of the guy standing there—maybe this time with a howitzer rocket, not just a brick. He put the car into gear and moved on past the apartment's entrance and took a turn onto the main road. Laying there in the secure ward of the hospital, Malcolm Strong had said he was waiting for a package coming through addressed to a William Moore at a storage depot located on Vancouver's East Side and that he was supposed to just let it through. This guy was a blackmailer and blackmailers usually did just that and seldom drifted—it was easy money.

So what else did this guy with the vicious right foot have coming in apart from these hard-on pills, harder drugs? *Had to be*, Chendrill thought, if it was badly made suits or counterfeit shirts, why put Strong in the hospital in the process? It looked like the prick was off his clients' backs now anyway, so why put himself through it anymore with the idiot as long as he kept away? What was the point? All he had to do was keep an eye on Dan and stop the nutcase hippy from swinging by and belting songs from the seventies out in the boardroom and the rest of the day was his own; if he wanted, he could always slip over and see Dan's mother.

Chendrill reached the offices for the storage company and asked the little girl behind the desk if he could see one of the lockers—a ten by ten would be great. He walked along behind her as they found an empty one and watched as she bent down to lift up the shuttered door. Then he took a photo of the empty space and sent the picture to Rann's phone with a caption written underneath that simply read:

If you want what I have, then meet me on Denman Street at three this afternoon.

Then he called Williams and told him where he could find his blackmailer and at what time.

"How do you know he'll show?" Williams asked.

"Because he's stupid and I didn't give a specific location. Denman's a long road. He'll walk it or ride it in a cab, I guarantee. Just be there, sit in one of the cafes, and wait for an East Indian in a turban to walk past looking perplexed and then arrest him for blackmail. It's easy and you won't need to leave town and let the RCMP take the credit. It'll be all yours, gift wrapped."

******

Rann Singh sat on a bench at beach at the south side of Denman Street and looked to his watch. It was still 2:45 p.m. Fuck, he looked over his shoulder again towards the road. Why had the big prick in the loud shirt not given him an address, a corner or something. Denman had to be at least a mile long. What the fuck was he supposed to do, wander up and down until the big cunt jumped out and told him what he needed to do to get his pills?

If he had them that is.

He'd called the office of the storage depot and asked to speak with a Mr. Moore. He wasn't there or taking his calls either. "Has a package been dropped off for Mr. Moore by the postman?" he asked the girl. "Who is this please?" The girl had replied. But if there hadn't been, then why not just say no? Why the hesitation, why the suspicion? Chendrill had them—he'd worked it out, he had to have. He was a detective after all. And now he'd got so far down the road that Rann had designed it was ridiculous. Fuck he should have left if be. *Fuck—fuck—fuck*. Standing, he turned and looked through the crowd towards Denman Street just beyond the bronze statues of happy Chinese guys that he thought looked stupid and began to walk along the road.

It couldn't be a police trap. They'd have just come round his place if they wanted him. Come busting in with one of their big battering rams that they used, then come crashing in all jacked up on testosterone and adrenalin wearing masks and shit, wielding guns and stuff, then whisk him away so as he could sit in a room and say nothing.

It was Chendrill the big cunt, carrying on the feud. *That's all*, he told himself. The guy was playing with him now because he could. He'd let him get too deep because of his stupid ego and temper. He hit the road and stopped at the crossing, watching as the cars passed, and waited for the lights to change, wondering what side of the road to walk along. The shadow side was better, Rann thought, it was just as crowded, but easier to hide in case there was anyone else waiting for him. *But why the crowd*? *Fuck*. He couldn't work this guy out.

He crossed the road and carried along, passing tourists with ice creams, passing eateries and other businesses that were soon to fail. *Where was this prick*? he thought, as he made it halfway down and looked to his watch, which now read 2:55 p.m.

Turning, he headed back towards the beach as the sudden fear of a police sting sent a wave through his body. *Fuck*, it wasn't even three o'clock yet. *You should cruise it in a cab first, you fucking idiot*, he told himself, *cruise it at three, sit back in a cab, hide in the darkness, tour the back roads, look to see if there's a load of cops sitting around in their cars waiting for a bust to happen, work out how the land lays. See if you can see the prick in his bright fucking shirt or if there's a fucking bright red fucking Ferrari with a dent on the hood from a lawn chair. Play it cool, do the work, don't walk straight into a trap like an idiot*, he told himself as he paced up and down. *You be the cool guy, you be the one that sees them, then you be the one who calls the shots and tells that big prick when you're ready—not him. Say, 'So you have what I spent my savings on so I could buy back my grandad's farm in Kenya, now give the fucking pills back to me and let's make a deal so as we can walk away from each other and no one needs to know about me and no one needs to know about all that money you took as backhanders from the drug dealers when you were on the force.' That would do it,* he thought, throw some shit at him when he was off guard and see if it would stick.

Then, the old pay phone beside him began to ring. He stared at it until it stopped, and by the time it hit its second chime when it rang again, Rann picked it up to hear the man on the other end say, "Don't be frightened."

"I'm not frightened of you!" Rann Singh snapped back as he looked around trying to see where Chendrill was watching him from. Then he heard the man's voice say again, "I know you want me."

"Yeah I do and I want something else an all."

And he heard the man's voice say, "Good—look above you. I'm up here above you. Look to me up here."

Rann Singh looked up at all the windows above him, the glare from the sun beaming down back at him from their polished shine. Then he saw him standing there, the big man holding his phone in the huge plate glass window just in his cowboy boots and a red Hawaiian shirt as he heard the man say, "Yes it's me. Come up to my apartment—I'm here for you."

Chapter Twenty-Seven

Marsha paced up and down her Malibu home and stared at the peek-a-boo view of the ocean she'd paid $2.4 million for and wondered if she'd made a mistake telling Patrick she hated going to Bali. What if he took this new hot chick who was from that place with the funny name she couldn't remember and what if Dan went and fell in love with her? Then everyone would laugh at her and she'd be the one on the magazine who was sad and everyone would feel sorry for her, and not read about her meeting the Queen or being engaged to Dan like they were supposed to. It wasn't good, it really wasn't good at all. Quickly, she picked up her phone and called Gill Banton and said, "We need to talk."

"About what?"

"A movie, going to Bali."

"What movie? You don't like Bali, Marshaa, you told me that."

"I do, I love Bali. It's great."

"Why the change of heart?"

"Dan's going."

"Oh Dan, the condom guy yes—I met him."

Silence.

"I hear this."

"Heard this—Marsha, that's how you say it."

"I want to be an actress."

"Don't we all dear," said Gill as the words 'learn to speak

properly first' crossed her mind. Then, changing the subject, she said, "Bali's nice," and heard Marsha say back, "Yeah I like it there."

Gill Banton said, "You want to go, you want me to fix something up?"

And Marsha replied, "I want to be an actress." Then there was silence.

Gill Banton laid in her bed, listening to the shower run from the en-suite and looked out the window. How many times in her career had she dealt with this now, models at the top of their game getting bored with it all and wanting to take it further? They seldom had the chops for it. Some did, though, and did it well, but it was few and far between and there was a big difference between looking good and pouting and actually saying lines alongside of someone else who could. She said, "Well let's get you some professional help, try out a coach for a while and see how you like it. You won't be flying first class straight away when it comes to acting Marshaa, you'll need a coach, and that's the truth."

And that's when she heard Marsha cut her short and say back, "I'll call you back."

******

Rann Singh looked down at the incredible view of Denman Street that Samuel Meeken had from the window of his apartment and wondered how long the guy would be unconscious for.

It wasn't that he'd hit him that hard. It was that he'd hit him in the right place to knock some sense into the man. After all, if you are going to invite strangers up to your place, then you have to expect the odd one to be offended if you answer the door sporting nothing but a cowboy hat, boots, and a hard-on.

Especially when they're up there due to a case of mistaken identity, which now had turned out to be another turn of luck that had come his way. He could see the group of guys, who were obviously cops, through the side window, sitting in a café the next block up watching the road and not their mochas. His Sikh god Guru Nanak was looking out for him.

Leaning into the window, he looked further along the road to both sides, then back to the pay phone there below him. He had a good, almost unrestricted view of Denman Street from one end to the other. If Chendrill was there, he wasn't in the café with the police or anywhere to be seen. Rann looked around the room, the place almost as strange as the guy lying on the floor with his tongue hanging out. Hand-drawn pictures of mythical warriors were framed all over the walls and there were mirrors everywhere, binoculars on the bookshelf, and women's shoes lined up against the door that were, he figured, the same size as the cowboy's boots.

Leaning down, he picked up one of the high heeled shoes and measured it against the naked unconscious man's feet, realizing they were indeed his.

"What the fuck?" he said out loud.

He stood up straight again and walked into the bedroom, more mirrors and loose straps hanging off each corner of the mattress. Walking to the big wardrobe with its mirrored sliding doors that ran the length of the wall, he slid one side open and looked inside. Nothing out of the ordinary. He opened the other side, sliding the door so hard that it came to a stop with a *clunk* at the other end of the rail. Turning he looked to the bedroom door in case it had woken the guy on the floor; then looked back inside. *Plenty out of the ordinary here*, he thought—dresses, lingerie, huge dildos and lube in a drawer—and postal uniforms, some old, some new and not even worn yet, some with shorts, some with long pants with waterproof jackets. He stared at them and said out loud, "Why'd you dress up as a postman, you fucking weirdo?"

Almost a thousand people or more must have passed as Rann stood watching the café for the next hour, taking a moment here and there to check on the postman. And at just after four fifteen, he saw the Aston Martin pull up with the unmistakable figure of that prick Chendrill getting out, holding onto his ribs with one hand as he did, walking straight over, ordering a coffee; then, sitting himself down next to where Williams sat with two of his friends pretending not to be cops, he started to chat. Seconds later, Chendrill pulled out his phone, dialed it, and moments later Rann felt the buzz from his phone tingling in his pocket.

Pulling it out, he sat himself down on the back of Samuel Meeken's black leather sofa and, before Chendrill could speak, he said, "I'll be there at five like you said."

Then he watched as Chendrill shook his head, raised his eyes and looked to Williams sitting next to him, and watched his mouth move and heard Chendrill say through the earpiece, "I said three."

Rann smiled and shuffled his turban, catching his reflection in one of the many mirrors.

"No, mate you said five, I'll be there at five on Davie Street right?" and heard Chendrill say, "No—Denman."

Then he hung up and holding the binoculars to his eyes, watched as the others got up and stretched their legs, Chendrill telling the others what he'd just heard, mouthing the words, 'the dumb fuck' as he did.

Then Rann's phone rang again, but this time it was Bill Moore telling him his shipment had arrived and was waiting for him in his storage lock up.

"You sure?" Rann said, staring at the road at Chendrill now standing, stretching his arms in the air as he heard the man's voice nervous on the other end of the line saying, "Yes, it's there and once it's gone, if you come near me again... I'm going to kill you... And I don't care about what happens next."

Yeah yeah, Rann thought as he looked to the weirdo guy still out on the floor, then again to the big pair of platform high heels by the door. He'd heard it all before. 'Come near me again and I'll kill you,' death threats were as common to him as a plumber heard people tell them they never washed shit down the plug hole of the sink.

Knowing he'd just saved another soul and the man would one day realize this himself, he said, "If they're there as requested then send me a photo of the box in the locker I asked for and you'll get your wish."

And seconds later, the picture arrived on his phone, the box all sealed and professionally packaged just as the Kiwi pharmacist who had skipped out of Auckland decades before had put together for him, now sitting there on the concrete floor framed nicely in the middle of the orange storage locker with the number 1133 sitting right above the door frame.

Fuck me it's here, Rann thought as he closed his phone and stood. Now Chendrill was moving along the road, stretching his legs, coming right below the apartment, passing the telephone. Reaching out, Rann picked up the house phone, hit redial, and watched as the pay phone in the street below caught Chendrill's attention in amongst the traffic. Ignoring it for a second, Chendrill stood there below him, staring into nowhere in his big red flowery shirt, then he looked back towards the phone and walked over and picked it up just in time to hear Rann say, "You really are one big fucking dumb cunt!"

Then Rann hung up and, like a sniper hiding deep in the apartment, watched Chendrill standing there like a parrot looking up at the buildings and along the street with no clue.

Rann looked around the apartment again, then to Samuel Meeken, still laying there unconscious on the floor. He'd been out a long time. But that could happen if you took a big hit right on the chin. He stared at the door, then back to Meeken on the floor. Walking over, he felt the man's pulse. Still good. He wiped his prints from everything he'd touched, including the phone and dialed 911, listening for the answer before dropping it on the floor next to where the weirdo lay. Then he walked along the corridor past the oversized women's shoes all neatly lined up and out of the apartment. He took the staircase down to the emergency exit and, walking across the garden's newly cut grass, headed towards the park and away from Chendrill standing out there in the open on Denman Street with a pickle up his ass.

******

Rann made it to the outside of the storage lockers and watched the building from afar. The place was deserted. If anyone was waiting for him, there would be a police vehicle sitting there somewhere with its big tires and bumper and round black aerial transmitters sitting on the roof.

He walked to the back and let himself in with the passcode and entered the building, walking the long corridor of orange lockers and stopping at 1143. He opened it, stepped inside, and pulled the door down behind him. He opened the canvas bag sitting at the locker's rear, pulled out a small battery-operated drill, and started to make a tiny hole in the locker's rear wall.

Pushing his turban back a bit, Rann pushed his eye against the hole, looked through, and smiled. *Yes it was there*, he thought, sitting right in the center of the locker just as the picture sent to his phone an hour before had shown.

He put down the drill and pulled out a pair of tin-snips and worked the sharp end into the hole he'd just made. He began cutting out a hole big enough to reach through and pull back the box full of the hard-on pills that were going to make him rich.

He was there and he had done it.

Chapter Twenty-Eight

It was just after four the next day when Patrick arrived at the offices of Slave and within ten minutes had told Mazzi Hegan he didn't know a good thing when he saw it.

"Me?" Mazzi Hegan replied in complete astonishment and, without taking a breath, quickly reeled off his entire resume, which ended with Dan, the now international sensation who was fuck all before he lifted his lens to him.

And with both hands raised, Patrick had said to him, "Trust me."

"What?" asked Hegan as he rubbed his right hand through his already combed straight blonde locks.

"Trust me—the girl has talent, pure talent and that's the truth." And the truth was that at that precise moment Patrick was having trouble remembering what the girl looked like. So he said, "She's got a face you never forget."

"And that's the talent?" Mazzi Hegan asked.

"No—it's something beyond words, Mazzi. It's beauty, it's vulnerability, it's childlike innocence, it's honesty—she gives off more energy than any actress or model you'll ever meet."

Mazzi walked to the window and looked out. There was this guy working in the coffee shop across the road he'd seen earlier who was so hot and had the tightest shorts on. He turned back saying, "The girl just spent two years as a cocktail waitress at the one hotel in the world where every successful producer, agent, movie star, and director walks through and not one of them has picked up on this—but you did? You—the guy who only last week sold condominiums who's now a world authority on beauty and talent? You know there's this fit guy working across the road. Do you see me going over there and laying a six-month contract on him so I can see what's inside his shorts?"

To which Patrick simply said, "Trust me."

Anyway, it was beyond Mazzi now to get in a spat with the hired gun, even if he was part owner and had shares in Slave. Sebastian was the man to talk with and he had something he needed to get sorted out ASAP. So he said the words that had sold him over a thousand homes, "Mazzi, don't be the guy who got left behind—never turn your back on something that other people just haven't seen yet."

Then he said, "Sebastian's putting up the money for this picture Slave's making. Dan's got the lead, Marshaa's signing with me and moving here just so as she can be in it—it's that good. She wants to be a movie star."

"Excuse me?" Hegan asked, his mindset suddenly changing. As much as he totally hated her with her long hair and better nails than his own, she was money in the bank and huge kudos. But still not wanting to be beaten, said, "We don't need that slut around here."

And without missing a beat, Sebastian walked into the room and said, "Marshaa's had enough of Gill, said she's always in bed when she calls, and now she's told her she'll have to use the coach instead of flying first class, so she's coming here—she wants Patrick to represent her. Gill Banton's going crazy, blaming me, saying I poached her, says I'm the one who invited him along to her party."

Then Patrick piped up, "And the movie's only going to cost us five million."

"Us? You mean, me, Patrick. Me," Sebastian said as he picked up his dog Fluffy and sat down on his favorite chair. He said it again, "You mean, me, Patrick—you want me to foot the five million?"

And Patrick answered, "It's actually eight. Buffy's doing the numbers and you'll get the three back—off the government when it's done. You're going to love it."

Sebastian sat there stroking his dog and looked to Mazzi who was staying silent. He looked at Patrick. The guy had come to them for a life makeover and already, just from being in his presence, they were getting one. Then just as he heard Patrick say, "You can't put a price on quality."

Sebastian said, "I haven't even read the script, Patrick."

Neither had Patrick—at least not properly. He had skim read it, of course, in the bar at the Wiltshire with one eye on the type and his other on Megan's ass. He said, "It's incredible, absolutely out of this world."

"Why?"

Mazzi Hegan knew that, in Sebastian's mind, the money was already in Patrick's pocket for the piece of shit film he'd scraped off the floor in Hollywood—as Marsha's signature to Slave was worth double. So he said, "What's it about?"

"Oh it's incredible," Patrick piped up not even knowing the answer. "It's about love, relationships, honesty and space—outer space."

That's it, he was remembering now, the bit in the space ship where they are trapped and the capsule is going to crash into the moon. He held up his hands and said, "Outer space and Inner space—the turmoil and beauty of young love and the unconscious emotional state one finds oneself in when confronted with one's darkest fears."

Mazzi Hegan wasn't giving up. He walked back to the

window to take another look at the coffee shop. The guy was there now, and bending over to boot. He carried on, "What the fuck does that mean?"

And just as Patrick was about to say 'Trust me.' Sebastian answered for him, "It means, Mazzi, we get Marsha up here instead of Gill Banton having her down there. So it's a go."

That and the fact you'll have an excuse to chat with Chuck Chendrill every minute of the day for the next six months, Mazzi Hegan thought, but—for once—he kept his mouth shut. And he wasn't wrong, as the first thing Sebastian did when he got back to his office was call Chendrill, saying, "Chuck it's an emergency. We've just done a deal with Marshaa and I need to know Dan's not going to be upset."

And all he heard Chendrill say back was, "Dan's fine with it."

"You sure?"

"Yeah he's good, Sebastian—don't worry."

"Good, can you come over and pick up a script we need him to read?"

"When?"

"Now, is that okay? Why? Where are you? Where's Dan. Is he okay?"

Chendrill answered, "He's fine, he's in his room studying for his exams."

Sebastian smiled. It was the answer he wanted to hear, and Chendrill knew it. Then Sebastian asked again, "Where are you—are you at the house?"

He was.

"Good, can you come over to the office and pick up the

script?"

"You pay me to look after Dan, Sebastian, not run errands—you've got Belinda for that kind of stuff."

And without having missed a beat, he heard Sebastian say, "Great, I'll see you here in about half an hour then."

Chendrill drove the Aston Martin along the road and headed into downtown, wondering if it was worth it—a grand a day plus car. Not really, if truth be told, but he was getting to hang out with Dan's mother in the process—and had been doing just that in her bed when Sebastian had called. He did get the odd idiot to deal with, like the Punjabi warrior, even if the man did have the angle on him yesterday. And now Marsha was on the payroll, he thought, and that would bring to him paparazzi without a doubt, and stalkers, and the odd spat at a club and trips to and from the airport. He pulled the Aston up outside Slave's offices and looked up to see Mazzi Hegan looking out of the window.

He reached the offices upstairs and heard Mazzi call out as he passed by, "Red and royal blue will never do baby." And then heard Sebastian say as he entered his office, "He's got a thing about your shirts and the Aston Martin, Chuck, he says the colors don't blend."

Chendrill looked down at his shirt and then at himself in the mirror by the door. The shirt had red and blue in it and yellow and green as well, so what was the problem? He said, "Don't expect me to be picking Marshaa up at the airport. Life's too short for that kind of work Sebastian."

Sebastian stood and smiled, holding out his hand, "We've got Belinda on contract for that Chuck. You're the best PI in town—that's why we have you here, not to drive a taxi." He reached down to the desk and handed Chendrill a newly printed script and said, "Could you ask Dan to read this? Patrick's got him the lead and the director's coming into town tomorrow to meet him."

Chendrill nodded, "That's it?"

"And can you make sure he's here in the morning to meet him?"

"I thought I was a PI?"

"Oh you are Chuck, and a good one—we both know that. But could you just do me this little bitty favor, you see I'm having an early night tonight and if I know you're there for me, then I'm going to sleep. Belinda does a great job, but she's never the one who turns up to do the job—and I've heard the guy she sends has a thing about the garden."

They were the same person, Chendrill thought, *the same person*. He said, "Belinda and the guy are the same person. Belinda's a guy, not a girl."

Sebastian almost believed him. Then he burst out laughing and said, "Oh Chuck, stop it dear, you had me going then didn't you," and walked out of the office. Chendrill heard Sebastian call out to Mazzi in the office next door, "Mazzi, Chuck's getting me at it again, he is saying Belinda's a man!" Then he came back in and, picking up his dog and sitting down, said in his perfect English accent, "Would you like a biscuit?"

Chapter Twenty-Nine

Archall Diamond, as he liked to be called, stood at the back of his low-riding Mercedes with the dent in the roof and played with his gun. Rasheed was gone now and he was the man. He'd run the drugs now, he'd get that ecstasy shit from the guy who was putting himself through college making it and sell it in the clubs—except the commission rate was gonna get lower for them guys now 'cos he was in charge and if they didn't like it, they was gonna go float.

And since Rasheed's demise, he'd been around in his low rider with its duck pond roof and spoken to them all, telling them exactly this at every meeting in the back of a club or out in the street where they sold.

Rasheed took a third of what they made, and from now on, he was gonna take a fifth or they were gonna float and none had resisted. That's how much respect he commanded.

Math had never been Archall Diamond's strong point.

Now with his hands on the keys at Rasheed's rented home that was now his own—so long as he kept up the rent—with its triple garage that now fit his low rider Mercedes, his truck, and his boat with room to spare, and with the bag full of cash he'd found under the sink, that wasn't going to be a problem.

The bag full of money had been flowing well. His girlfriend was there with him now, as sexy as ever with her long legs and high heels, always looking to the sky and loving him more than ever now—and only him. All he needed to do was sort out that plastic Swahili-speaking wannabe Sikh to hand over those hard-on pills, which would be in by now, and the low-end narcotics in town would be sewn up.

He said to his girl Nina, "That guy, you remember his name,

you met him once. The one with the turban couldn't speak Punjabi, claimed he was English then said he was from Africa?"

And just to piss him off, Nina said, "The good looking one?"

Whatever, Archall Diamond thought, the guy couldn't even drive. Looking back at her while she kept looking at the sky, he said, "Is he still around?"

He was. A friend of hers who worked at the cinema was seeing him on occasions, liked it because he'd let his hair down and could go all night and then she'd call and tell Nina how many times she'd come—when Nina hadn't herself for a while unless she was on her own or with the guy who'd disappeared, who'd she been waiting for forever, but who had simply vanished. That guy, who had promised her the world, who she'd felt loving her, listening to his words—words she had been waiting for so long to hear—and then nothing. And now here she was, still with this prick, living in his old boss's house because Archall had grabbed the keys from his pocket as the guy lay there dying at the side of the road and had moved his boat into the garage on the same night.

She should have listened to Rasheed when he'd told her to go to Bollywood and start singing and get away from all this. She had the looks, she had those legs that went on for a mile that guys loved to look at when Archall took her to the hockey game.

She said, "He's probably loving some white chick, that's his thing."

Archall thought about it for a moment. He'd done that just once before and didn't like it. The girl's skin was too white and went red when he squeezed it, and her pussy smelled to boot. Not like his girls who kept themselves clean down there and tasted of saffron not salmon when they made him eat it. He said, "I need to speak with him. Call your friend and get his number."

"You don't have it?" Nina asked, not wanting to hear about

the guy anymore, jealous that her friend was getting it properly and her not.

Then he said, "He's got these pills that make your dick hard and I'm going to start selling them for him whether he likes it or not."

And hearing that, she made the call.

******

Rann Singh sat in the front room of his apartment and stared into the open box full of his own specialty hard-on pills he'd traveled halfway around the world to buy.

Reaching in, he opened a packet and stared at the contents, the pills slightly bigger now than the ones he'd tried out on the Irishman's girl and her friend—or whatever they were. *Fuck*, he was tempted to pop one right now and call that blonde bitch from the cinema he'd been taking to pound town ever since she'd given him the photos of that fuckhead realtor doing his thing.

He looked at the box and began to count the packets, which took a while—thirty-thousand packets in all with six in each. Five bucks a pill would make him a million bucks Canadian, enough to get the fuck out of here and to the other side of the world to buy back the ranch that looked out to the mountains for his grandad. And then he'd call him and say, 'you got it grandad, our Sikh god Guru Nanak has been looking out for us because I've got the farm back and you can come home now,' and they'd love him for it. And that's where he and his grandparents would live, speaking the Swahili he knew so well, away from the life he knew now with its back alleys and sad men who he was helping to see the light.

Then the phone rang and he said to the blonde girl with the almost pure white skin, "I need you to come over here so as I can try some stuff out."

But when he opened the door, it was Archall Diamond and his girl Nina. Archall standing out there in the corridor letting Rann see the diamond in his front tooth and his gun in his waist band. Rann saying to him, "You get that roof fixed on your car yet?"

******

They sat there in the living room with the box of hard-on pills in between them both and Nina standing out there on the balcony looking up again to the sky. Rann said, "You know who made these? Not some fucking prick with a how-to guide he got off the net like you've been using. These are made by a scientist from New Zealand with a degree in chemistry. They ain't full of shit like the stuff you sell on the street. There's just the right amount of Sildenafil to get you hard as a rock and some herbs mixed in to make you feel like a million dollars. Take one and your dick'll get so big you'll think you were one of those retro porn stars from the seventies."

Archall Diamond thought about the porn he'd watched from back then, the white guys with the huge hammers and the women with big teeth and bigger muffs. Then, keeping it real, he said, "You wanna sell them, I'm taking a sixth of what you make. Rasheed used to take a third off the top, but he's gone so now I'm in charge and the cost of business around here for you guys has just gone up. The rest of the dealers pay more than a third, they pay a fifth, but as you fucked up the roof on my ride, then you are going to pay me a sixth of what you make, that or I'll take the lot now and float ya."

"Float me, what like throw me out the window?"

Archall Diamond shook his head and said, "No I don't like

guys that fly. I'm talking about sticking you'se in an inner tube with some chains around ya feet and setting you'se loose on a rip that sends you out to sea so you can drop down somewhere and feed some of the crabs that your whitey girlfriends like to eat when some prick takes 'em to a fancy restaurant downtown. Just like I did to some guy the other night when he came sniffing around."

"You took him to dinner?"

"No, I made him the dinner. There's a difference."

Then he nodded to Nina out there on the balcony that used to have a recliner on it and carried on, "She's looking for this guy we used to know when we were kids. The fucker's supposed to be flying in unsuspected at the fireworks out on English bay, was gonna be wearing one of those special suits and come out the clouds, circle around for a bit like some fucking giant prehistoric eagle, then swoop in and buzz the crowd, scare the shit out of em all and let everyone know who he is, then retire. Everyone knows it and are waiting to see it happen, but then them is gonna be disappointed, 'cos that guy he got himself floated. So if he got floated and he a Punjabi, then don't think no wannabe Punjabi ain't gonna get floated also."

Rann nodded. He got the picture, kind of, and wondered if he should just punch the moron in the throat right now and be done with it or hear him out. He said, "Because these ain't no ordinary tablets. Rasheed and I had a deal set up before he passed control onto you by getting himself killed. It was ten dollars a pop. You still up for that? Or shall we go and try to see if either you or your girl out there can make me float like her boyfriend—or if I can make you fly right now out that window like her boyfriend."

And shaking his head, still trying to sound tough, Archall Diamond said, "I don't pay Rasheed's rates, I set my own. You take em or you float, your choice—you get five dollars less a tenth for setting it up and that's more than the crowd's paying, but like

I said, you fucked up the roof of the Mercedes, so that's the deal."

Then, trying it on, Rann said, "You saying I'm only getting eight a tablet now less a tenth when they'll sell for twenty dollars a pop and I already done a deal with Rasheed, only five dollars a tablet. You gotta be kidding?

And Archall said in his best gangster voice. "I got the cash in the Mercedes—take it or float."

So with the math working out to just under ten times what Rasheed had offered, Rann took the deal and in his mind was already on his way to Kenya with eight hundred thousand dollars in cash. And holding up his hand to shake on it, Archall Diamond raised his too and pulled a Taser out of nowhere with the other and stuck it into Rann's chest, sending 50,000 volts into him. Then, pulling his gun with the other, he looked down to Rann, momentarily paralyzed on the floor; as two more Punjabis dressed like cage fighters burst in, he followed up his offer by saying, "But 'cos you disrespected me like you did with smashing up the Mercedes, you not getting anything till I see you'se with ya head shaved."

With his right arm feeling as heavy as a rock, Rann Singh watched as the first of Archall Diamond's thugs came at him across the living room, jumping at Rann with a mistimed karate kick that hit Archall in the back, knocking the gun from his hand and the Taser from his other.

Rann managed to stand, and swung his right foot up and outwards in a spin—as he had thousands of times before in the gym—and caught the thug straight in the throat, putting him on his ass. Then he spun his left foot around and, feeling his balls squash in his jeans, brought his foot up into the remaining thug's chest and sent him off his feet and into the wall, breaking the off-white plasterboard as he hit.

Turning, he looked out to Nina, still texting outside on the balcony and then to Archall Diamond, who'd managed to retrieve his gun and was training it on Rann.

"Keep up the Bruce Lee shit and you'se getting shot and killed," he said.

And that's when Rann blacked out.

Chapter Thirty

Chendrill pulled the Aston Martin up behind the rear of Dan's new Ferrari, which he was too embarrassed to drive because it couldn't accelerate as fast as a Tour de France cyclist and would only go over ninety kilometers an hour if he was on going down a hill.

Lifting the script from the passenger seat, he opened it up on the first page and began to read. There was a lead guy called Marshall, a leading girl called Candy and they had to get to the moon with a huge deflector to send a fleet of alien space ships towards the sun so as they would burn up in the sun's rays. If they didn't make it, the aliens would come to earth and eat all the insects and that in turn would kill the planet. And only Candy knows they're coming because she can read minds and no one takes her seriously, except an astronaut who's just lost his job with NASA because he has flat feet, and they steal a space ship in the hope that they can save the world.

Fuck me, what a load of nonsense, Chendrill thought, as he lay on top off the bed and got to the last page. Then he looked up to see Dan's Mum, Tricia, standing there with no clothes on when he thought she was in the kitchen making him a cup of tea. He asked, "Where's Dan?"

"Asleep," Tricia answered and moved towards him, climbing inside the sheets. "Why don't you turn off your phone so that man doesn't interrupt us?"

"What if there's an emergency?" Chendrill answered with a smile and turned the phone off and began unbuttoning his nicely ironed yellow Hawaiian. She said, "I know I shouldn't say that. You know the way the man looks after you and Dan, giving you sports cars and stuff, but it's like he senses when we're making love and calls to interrupt."

221

"Maybe he does," Chendrill replied and thought it very well could be. He'd had an old girlfriend who did just that. He could be anywhere at any time and as soon as he was interested in another girl to any degree, she'd call. He said, "Some people are sensitive to that kind of thing."

"You think he likes you in that way?"

"You can't write it off," Chendrill replied. "The man's gay and I'm a heterosexual man and that's what most gay guys like, or so they say—you know real men, not over the top flowery ones like Mazzi Hegan. It's like expecting me to be attracted to some bull dyke because she's a woman, but looks like a guy and wants to thump me out because I've got a dick. It's the way the world turns."

"And what about Dan?"

"Girls love Dan."

"That's not what I asked?"

"Sorry?"

"Who does Dan like?"

******

Dan lay on his bed with his trousers around his knees and listened to the muffled sounds of Chendrill gabbing on to his mother upstairs and waited for them to get it on so he could also, turning on his computer watching porn that doesn't involve guys with big moustaches and knocking one out. Then after he was done he'd get the broom and start smashing it against the ceiling until they were done also. And so it went. Fifteen minutes after he'd banged the broom, they stopped. Thirty minutes after that, Chendrill was knocking on the door of Dan's basement room, wanting to give him something, and, taking the chance of getting another black eye, he replied, "Come back when you've got some style."

To which Chendrill said through the door, "Speak to me like that again and you'll be wearing that broom stick you keep by the bed as a hat."

Then he opened the door, which Dan thought was locked, and came uninvited in and heard Dan say, "How did you know about the broom?"

"There's no other way you could wrap on the ceiling without getting out of bed, unless you wear your high heels or stand on a chair."

Then he threw the script at him saying, "Here you go, movie star boy. Sebastian wants you to read this today, you're meeting the director tomorrow at the office."

"Can't he come here?"

Fuck me, Chendrill thought, the kid was either already a prima donna or completely bone idle, and settling on the latter he said, "Sebastian said I've got to make sure you read it or he won't sleep tonight."

"I will."

"Go on then, start."

Then he heard Dan say, "Who do you think you are, my dad?"

"No—just read the fucking thing, will you. You'll like it. It's a piece of shit all about space men and aliens that are going to destroy the planet by eating all the insects."

"What planet and what part of the solar system they from?"

It was a good question and one that wasn't answered in the screenplay. From what Chendrill could remember, they just came from outer space and even if it had been mentioned somewhere and they'd made the name up, he'd have been none the wiser. He said, "I don't know? Read it and find out."

And picking it up, Dan did, and taking about three to four seconds a page, skimmed the whole thing front to back then threw it to the corner on the floor, laid back on the bed, placed his arms behind his head and said to Chendrill, "There you go—done! You can go back upstairs—mum's waiting."

Letting the 'mum's waiting' go for now, Chendrill took a breath and said, "You're supposed to read the fucking thing."

"I just did. You saw me for fuck's sake, and now you can tell them all back at the office you watched me go through it front to back without lying."

And when he got back, he did just that and then heard Sebastian say, "Chuck, I've just heard on the hush-hush there's a parachutist guy who's going to fly in on the crowd at the fireworks tomorrow wearing a monkey suit."

"I know—and it's a squirrel suit. I was supposed to meet him the other night, but he didn't show. Probably got caught in a vortex somewhere as he was flying in."

"I've booked seats in the VIP box for everyone. Will you be able to be there?"

"Why don't you sit on the beach with everyone else?" It's what people did, the city would turn up every summer and sit on the beach for a week of international fireworks held in competition—unless you were stupid or rich enough to pay thousands to sit in an executive box, which Sebastian obviously had.

Chendrill asked, suddenly worried that he hadn't asked Dan's mother to go, "You asked Dan?"

Rock Solid

"Yes—I sent him a text."

"A text?"

"Yes, Chuck—it's the way you talk to the youth of today."

"What about his mother, you invite her?" and, true to form, Sebastian answered, "I wouldn't dream of not asking her."

Good, Chendrill thought, he'd go to see this guy fly in, tell everyone around him he was supposed to meet the guy—and would soon, even though Rasheed, who was supposed to introduce them, was dead. Then he'd sit next to Tricia and discreetly hold her hand and drink champagne all night while some corporate sponsor from some far-off land like China or Italy let off about a million dollars worth of gunpowder into the sky. It would've been nice, he thought, if he could still meet the guy in the squirrel suit before the show. Then he could invite him up to the executive box and steal some of the guy's glory as he introduced him to them all—but sadly, the man who had taught himself to fly like a bird was, like Rasheed, also dead.

It was about seven in the morning when Chendrill got out of Dan's mother's bed, took a shower, and walked down stairs to knock quietly on Dan's door to get him up for this important meeting for which he was already on the verge of being late. Belinda was already outside with the limo and Chendrill wondered if this time he was going to be either trimming the hedge or doing the lawn in the vain hope Dan's mother might see some future in the pair of them, and that she'd allow him to whisk her off to the Punjab to meet his family.

He said, "Dan—it's time to get up."

Nothing. Waiting, he knocked again.

"Dan!"

He tried again.

225

"Dan, get up, you need to go to work." Then he waited.

Nothing. He tried again.

"Dan—superstar, get up—you're working."

And not wanting to waste anymore time, he opened the door with his shoulder. The script still lay in the corner in exactly the same spot Dan had thrown it the evening before. And all pissed off as he looked up from the pillow, Chendrill heard Dan mumble, "You ever heard of knocking,"

"I've been doing that for five minutes. You need to get up or you'll be late."

"Late for what?"

"Meeting this director."

"Why?"

"I don't know why."

Putting his head back on the pillow, Dan closed his eyes and, dismissing him, said, "Tell him I'm not interested."

"You tell him you're not interested."

Then Dan opened his eyes again and this time even more pissy said, "Look, I'm tired alright so just lay off."

"I don't care," Chendrill said, wanting to just leave him where he lay and be done with this kid who wasn't his but who he had to act like a father to, and then carried on, "It's not my problem if you've been up all night wanking when you should have been reading that script and getting an early night because you had to meet this guy. So get up."

Dan sat himself up and looked Chendrill straight in the eye and said, "Tell 'em you'll be in it instead, it'll give you something else to do instead of hanging around here all day and sticking your dick in my mother."

And that was it.

******

No one was more surprised than Belinda when the door opened to
the back of his limo and Dan arrived on the plush leather back seat
with a thump, on time—wearing the pajamas his mother had
gotten for Christmas six years ago that he still liked to wear
because they were nice and soft, even if they were a bit tight and
the buttons had popped off.

Belinda looked to Chendrill and wondered if he was wearing
his pajamas also and said, "Hello Sir, I am happy Mr. Dan is on
time this morning. They are very happy this morning when I arrive
for this."

Belinda watched as Chendrill opened the front passenger seat
door and sat down. He said, "Stick the child locks on so the little
prick can't escape. He's tired."

They arrived an half hour later. Not having moved from the
position he'd landed in on the rear seat, Dan sat up, stared at
Chendrill, rubbed his face, then said, "There's no need to be so
rough."

"There's no need to be so rude," Chendrill replied, and heard
Dan say as he got out the car and began to walk across the road
without a word to Belinda, "I had every intention of coming in,
you know."

When, tomorrow? Chendrill thought, as he thanked Belinda
with a nod and tapped the roof top as he began to follow the new
international sensation across the road and through the doors to
Slave's offices.

They hit the lift together and rode it to the first floor without a word and saw that the whole crowd was there in the reception when the doors opened. Putting down Fluffy, Sebastian looked to Dan, and, seeing he was all pissed off and still in his pajamas, understood that getting the kid there hadn't been without incident. He walked straight to Chendrill, reached out, shook his hand, and said, "As always Chuck, you never let me down."

And with that, Chendrill knew all was forgiven for the black eye. He said to Sebastian, "Does this mean my plate's getting glued back together?"

And without letting go of Chendrill's hand, Sebastian replied, "You can rest assured Chuck, your plate will never be broken." Then he looked to Dan in his pajamas and said, "Stay young for as long as you can Daniel, but if you act like a baby, then you'll be dealing with Chuck."

Right on cue, Patrick took over the room. Although the closest he'd ever been to a movie in his life was the cinema, with his hands held high he still said to everyone, "Guys this is going to be easy—we're going to make history."

And he wasn't wrong.

******

Rupert Mikes was nervous as hell as he rode in the back of Belinda's limo and wondered where the dribble on the back seat had come from. He hadn't gotten much sleep the night before, worrying about his film, and was as happy as he was sad. First he'd gotten a call from the studio executive who'd told him they'd passed the movie over to Slave for a fee, and then one from his agent in L.A., who he hated, telling him that after four years of hard work the picture was being financed at last. He was happy for all this, but like all things in this world that fall from the tree of luck, he was also sad that the people now doing his film had, as far he could see, only made commercials. But what could he do? Leaning forward and looking for a glimmer of reassurance, he said to Belinda, "You work for these guys, do you?"

Belinda looked into the rear-view mirror and, happy he was being acknowledged as a human being, smiled at the man who was finding it hard to sit down and relax in the back.

"Yes sir, I have contract, sir."

"They're good then, are they? They're good, yes?"

"Yes, it is good. Very good contract, two owners—one rides bicycle and the other drive. I park car, you see, he cannot parallel park it on the road."

Taking it all in, Rupert sat there, closed his eyes, and shaking his head asked, "You saying they can't drive?"

"No sir, they drive, yes, very good, but cannot park."

Fuck me, he thought, and sat back in the seat and let out a deep breath—*fuck me, fuck me*. I'm in the hands of Canadians and if they don't even know how to drive properly, what the fuck's going to happen with my film? Then he said, "What about this other guy, this Patrick fellow? You know him?" And as he said it, a bus passed the car on the inside and stopped just in front of Belinda's limo with Patrick's face beaming his beautiful smile right back at them. Belinda said, "This is him sir, very nice man, sir."

He *was* a very nice man. He'd tipped him big time after Belinda dropped him at the airport and made him feel like a million dollars all the way there with his compliments. Belinda carried on, "He is very big movie producer and also agent."

"And realtor?" Rupert Mikes asked as the knot in his stomach grew twice the size that it was when he'd stepped out the shower only an hour earlier.

"Yes sir, he sells houses also."

Oh my God, oh my god, oh my God, Rupert thought as Belinda pulled away again, passing Patrick's pearly whites as he did.

That's it, he thought as Belinda took a right off the main drag into Yaletown and cruised slowly along the old wood-framed warehouse buildings converted into high-end shops and offices and pulled up out front of Slave Media. He was just going to go in and take the bull by the horns and get his film made. That's what he did—he got films made. He hadn't pulled out of the car park at UCLA with a degree in movie making and the students' favorite award for his film about the blind window cleaner and his best friend with no hands for nothing. He'd bring in a crew from L.A., kick some ass up here, and show these fuckers how it's done. He'd done it before in Jordan with the Arabs when he made *I'm a Christian so Stick Me on the Cross*, which had almost made it to Sundance and he'd do it again with these Canucks.

Without a word of thanks, Rupert Mikes was out the door of Belinda's limo, through the lobby, up the elevator, and straight into Slave's reception without barely taking a breath. With the briefest of 'hello's' he had Sebastian, Dan, Patrick, Buffy, and Chendrill lined up in the boardroom where he began to deliver his call to arms saying, "First I want you to know how much I love the work you do here at Slave. It's just fantastic and I appreciate your support for my film, which I know without a doubt is going to take the science fiction genre and turn it on its head. Forget Scott's *Alien* or even Cameron's *Aliens*—which was equally good—what I'm going to bring to you is something completely special and unique in its field. And starting with you Dan, whom I'd like to say firstly is doing sensational work taking everyone by storm in L.A. with his BlueBoy campaign and will continue to do so with *When the Shadows Form*. So getting right to it, I want you to tell me exactly how you feel about the script and if the elements within its subtext are right for you and your career right now."

And wondering if the man was ever going to stop, Dan stared at him with his feet up on a chair, still in his pajamas, and said, "Sorry, you're talking to me?"

Rupert Mikes nodded, took a deep breath, staying with it and still smiling, and said, "Yes, and I want you to be completely honest and open about how you feel about the script. You see, I find honesty is the best policy when it comes to making a movie, as we all know, it's not just me here who's going to be bringing this creation into existence—as I have brought many others to life—it's all of us, everyone, from the guy who's driving us in the mornings to the guy who's cleaning up the shit at the end of the night. We are all making this film together and once everyone's on board, I know then we're going to have a fantastic movie and something we can all be proud of. So Dan, right now, tell me what you think."

And nodding his appreciation to the man's openness, Dan answered, "Yeah sure—it's a complete and utter crock of shit."

Rupert Mikes stood there for a moment, not sure if he'd heard Dan right, then realizing he had. Looking at this male model sitting in his teddy bear pajama bottoms and top that didn't fit, he said, "I'm not joking here, have you actually read it?"

Dan nodded and looked to Chendrill. Then said, "Yeah, Chuck's seen me, he's read it and all."

Rupert Mikes stared at the group of Canadians, and not knowing what to say, went to speak again and began to choke, and two seconds later blurted out, "Well have you read it properly?"

Then without waiting for an answer, Rupert Mikes reached into his briefcase; quickly, he pulled out the script and said condescendingly, "Well please tell me where it needs work."

And without lifting a finger Dan replied, "You've got twenty-two characters in sixty-two scenes over one hundred and twenty-two pages with an average of ninety words per page. In it there are thirteen incidents where Marshall, your hero, is doing a spacewalk, all of which, in reality, can't be done, but when he gets back from the eighth space walk in particular on line five of scene fifty-two, just after he tells Candy he loves her, he looks through the window with a pair of binoculars she gave him that belonged to her grandfather. But that brand of binoculars came out five years after her grandfather was hit by the truck carrying fuel back in 1975. And besides that, how the fuck is he going to be able to see the bad guy alien driving his ship at what's got to be around 30,000 miles away with a pair of $200 binoculars bought at Canadian Tire back in the seventies."

Rupert took a deep breath and looked at the kid, wracking his brain. Then he said, "We don't have Canadian Tire in the States."

And Chendrill closed his eyes as he heard Dan say, "Well like I said, Chuck here's read it as well and thinks it's shit—and he didn't even pick up on the fact that you can't spit chewing gum to the floor in space, or have sex in the shower, because you can't take a shower as the water doesn't flow without gravity."

And with that, Rupert Mikes took a deep breath and said, "Well you're obviously missing the fundamentals of the story, really it's more character based than the films you're used too. Obviously you're too imature to understand the script's depth, let alone be in it. I'll call my agent and let him know you're not interested." And with those words, he left the room.

Watching the man go and the door closing behind him, Sebastian watched Patrick get up, adjust his shirt, and follow, looking at Dan and then Chuck as he left, trying his best not to smile. As always, he was well prepped and had read through the man's work of art twice and would have forked out another million to see the pretentious prick put in his place. He said, "Daniel darling, when Mr. Mikes said you need to be honest, what he really was saying was that he wanted you to tell him what he wanted to hear, which is that his script is fantastic."

Dan stared at him confused, shaking his head, "I thought Patrick said this was going to be easy?"

Then giving it some thought, Dan stared at the floor for a moment. *What the fuck was it with these people saying one thing then expecting the other and getting all pissed off when they got what they asked for in the first place?* So he said, "Why didn't he just say that then?"

"Because he's got an ego darling, all you have to do is feed it and then get yourself back home and let me worry about the binoculars."

Chapter Thirty-One

Rann Singh woke up on the floor. His whole body hurt and, from what he could see through two eyes that were swollen shut from bruising, the apartment was wrecked from fighting and his head was cold from the open balcony door that Nina had obviously neglected to close when she left.

He walked to the bathroom and turned on the taps, rubbed the dried blood from his face and eyes, looked in the mirror, and saw his hair was gone. Lifting his hand up, he rubbed it across his now terribly shaven head and felt the sting of the cuts across his knuckles. Clenching his fist in anger, he stood there in silence, looking at the new him.

Fuck, he thought, *that cunt*. He walked back into the wrecked living room and looked around again, the chairs everywhere, table on its side, his turban unravelled and his hair all around the floor where they must have held him down and cut it from his head.

Fuck, he hurt, he thought. He looked again to his knuckles, completely smashed, bloody and bruised, his trousers now split around his nuts and one sock left on his right foot, the other with a huge open gash to its side. Whatever they did to him, the way he felt with the bruising in all the right places, he must have inflicted as much damage on them.

Then he realized the pills were gone, and he felt the rage build within him again and that's when he saw the note. It had blood on it that could have only come from the person who'd written it. It read:

Yous damiged my Mercedis and Im taken the pills so now we's even. Next batch gits you same price plus less a tenf comishon like we's talk about.

Be fankfull yous not get floated

Fucking illiterate prick, but not a word about Rasheed, Rann thought, and he'd blacked out with that fucker as well. Then he felt the burns on his neck that could have only come from the Taser he'd blocked from connecting properly when Archall Diamond had tried to zap him the first time as he went to shake hands on a deal too good to be true.

He looked around again at his hair all over the floor, then rubbed his fingers through the few remaining tufts of hair sticking out of his scalp, like a punk rocker gone crazy. His hair would grow. It would take time to get it back to how it was, but it would grow nonetheless. The tablets, though, were another matter.

******

Chendrill was still laughing as he sat in the front of Belinda's limo and snagged a ride back to Dan's place to pick up his Aston Martin with Dan in the back half asleep.

What must the director, who thought he was a big shot, have thought as he stood there and listened while a kid in his jammies with teddy bears all over them ripped his script to pieces? The big shot was yet to return to the office and probably never would, he thought. From the boardroom, he had seen him disappear up the road and turn the corner, heading in the wrong direction from the hotel he was staying at. Chendrill said to Dan, "You up reading that script all night, is that why you were so grumpy?"

And without opening his eyes, Dan said, "No, you saw me

read it. I was up looking at porn like you said."

Chendrill laughed. At least the kid was honest. You couldn't accuse him of not being that, at least not today. Sebastian didn't seem to care and Hegan hadn't even bothered to turn up to meet the guy, that's how much Patrick's big movie meant to him. He carried on, "How did you know about those binoculars?"

"Read it in an old electronics magazine I found when I was eight, said they were new and had Porro prism design mirrored imagery."

"I thought you were just fucking with him."

And opening his eyes, Dan smiled, "Yeah I was completely bullshitting. Porro prism imagery's been around longer than you, but it was worth it though, don't you think—shut the fucker up?"

And Chendrill asked, "What about all the scene numbers and word counts you threw at him?"

"Total bullshit. I made it up, just happened to see the numbers when I was skimming through it."

But they both knew he was lying.

******

Archall Diamond was pissed. His front tooth that once sported his trademark diamond which had cost him five thousand dollars was gone now courtesy of Rann's right foot coming out of nowhere and catching him straight in the chops, giving him a fat lip and making him swallow his diamond. Now he was going to have to sift through his shit to get it back.

Moving his face from side to side, he tried to smile without opening his mouth. *Fuck*, he thought, now he'd have to go back to the dentist and bullshit the guy, say he tripped on his underpants after he was done fucking two chicks and fell and smashed it out on one of the girl's high heels or something like that. *Fucking Rann*, that plastic motherfucker and his Kung Fu shit that Sikhs weren't supposed to know—that kind of stuff was for the Chinese.

Well at least he no longer had a reason to wear those fancy turbans, he thought, as the picture of Rann laying there all tasered and knocked the fuck out with his head shaved whipped through his mind, making him smile and look in the mirror to see the tooth he loved that was no longer there. But he had the pills and he'd gotten them for free, and free was way less than Rasheed had worked out.

He walked out to the bedroom and looked at Nina still asleep with her long legs uncovered, then walked over to Rann's box of hard-on pills that he said had been designed by some Swedish scientist. He'd tried to make her come again the night before after they had been out drinking, and he was feeling good about being able to punch the plastic Paki hard in the gut, showing off while Nina watched from the balcony as his two heavies held Rann just like he'd seen the big gangster bosses do in the movies—even if both of them were bleeding from their noses and Rann had still managed to whip his foot up and kick him in the mouth as he'd gone in to hit him for a third time.

Yeah, he'd tried to fuck her when he got back, standing there in his silk shorts showing off his six pack as she lay looking to the window, but he couldn't. He'd gone soft like he did whenever he felt like the girl wasn't enjoying it, and then he'd heard her say that skydiving prick's name under her breath like she had that time before when he'd muffed her so hard he'd made his tongue bleed.

Walking to the box, he pulled out a packet and popped one out from its silver foiled wrapper, swallowed it whole, and then stared at his dick. Nothing was going on except that when he clenched his muscles down there, he could make it swell up a bit and see it move in his shorts. He waited, thirty seconds passing, then he pumped his muscles again and stared at his girl's long and sleek legs in the bed. A minute passed, then another, still nothing. Sticking his fingers into the packet, he popped another from its silver foil package and swallowed it whole, then popped another and then another, then the rest, and went downstairs to the kitchen to grab a bowl of cocoa pops—fuck it, if they worked as well as that prick said they would 'cos of the stuff that Swedish guy stuck in 'em, then he'd go up there and give it to her better than fly boy had before he'd fucked off to jump off bridges and shit.

And just as he finished his second bowl and looked at the back of the packet to the cartoons, he felt his dick begin to swell, and pulling his pants open watched it fill out sideways first and then begin to grow in length until it filled his silk shorts, pushing them tight like Geronimo's teepee.

Smiling, he walked through the kitchen, feeling the skin on his dick stretch and watching it wave from side to side as he went. He walked through the foyer and up the stairs along the landing into the master bedroom that used to be Rasheed's and said, as he saw the now empty bed, "Nina! Where the fuck are you?"

But Nina was gone and so were Rann's pills.

******

An hour later, Rann heard the buzzer to his entry phone go just after he had stepped out of the shower and was in the process of washing off the rest of hair he'd shaved from his now completely bald head down the drain hole. Wrapping the towel around his body and feeling the bruises to his stomach and kidneys, he walked to the entry phone and looked to see Nina standing there holding his box of tablets in her hands.

Rock Solid

His Sikh god Guru Nanak was looking out for him.

He opened the door and the first thing he heard Nina say as she passed him back his box of hard-on pills was, "It's a shame you don't like dusky maidens because from what I've heard, you don't need these."

And smiling, Rann replied in his perfect cockney accent, "Well sometimes I've been known to make the odd exception."

And placing the box on the floor in the corridor, Nina knelt down next to it, pulled the towel from around his waist, and took him in her mouth—a couple of seconds later, she knew she was right.

A minute later, she stood again, raising herself up to almost his head height in her long high heels, and kissing him softly on the lips. Then letting go, she rubbed her hand across the top of his now bald head and said, "You look even sexier with no hair."

Then she'd taken him, leading him to his bed and laying him on it, naked again now, as she pulled off her clothes slowly and sensually until she stood before him naked, her skin golden and perfectly toned, her long dark hair hanging loose, sweeping across her one shoulder, almost covering her breast. She said, "I want you to make love to me the same way you have been making love to my friend and when you're finished, I'm going to Europe so I never have to see that limped dicked cretin with his stupid diamond ever again."

And Rann had made love to her. Leaning forward and pulling her to him, laying her down and kissing her hard on the lips, feeling her soft skin beneath her hands as he caressed her body, his hands exploring her, holding her, touching her until she was ready for him. Moving his body above her and still holding her hands, his fingers clasped in her own, he held her down, pinning her arms into the soft feather pillows above her head and entered her. She felt him opening her as he moved inside, the solid bone

239

of his pelvis pushing hard against hers as he reached the top and began to move in and out, slowly at first, then faster and harder as she felt her body grow hotter, beads of sweat from her scalp moving through her hair, her forehead wet, his lips on hers pushing, biting as he moved inside her, instinctively lifting her legs up to feel him more as he began to pound harder and harder into her, his hands still clasping hers, pulling her arms lower down to her shoulders and holding her solid to the bed as he lifted himself above her, looking down into her eyes as she closed them with pleasure and opened them again so as she could look at him and the sweat on his head and his neck, the muscles on his chest hard and solid as only a man who is lean and trained to fight could be. Then she felt it build inside as she felt him slam against her hips, moving side to side, feeling his cock inside her filling every inch of her now engorged pussy. Then she came, suddenly hard, her hands slipping from his with ease as they ripped away and held him across his back, pushing herself against him, making him fill every inch of her until she could take it no more and lay there panting, staring up at him as he looked down on her until she felt her breath return, her hands long and slender, her beautifully manicured nails touching his face, his ears, his bruised eyes, the back of his head.

And then she kissed him.

Three hours later, Nina lay there in his bed looking up at the ceiling and ignoring the messages she knew were steadily mounting on her phone from Archall. Her body aching and her hair wet from sweat, she wondered how she would have been feeling now had she stayed home pretending to sleep, watching Archall Diamond pop six of Rann's hard-on tablets one after the other and go down to the kitchen to stuff his face with cocoa pops as he liked to do. She looked to Rann lying next to her staying silent, and said pensively, "I think Diamond killed my old boyfriend Paawan. I think he drowned him in the ocean."

Rann sat up and looked at her, knowing what Archall Diamond had already told him, but still wondering if it was bullshit or not. He said, "Why do you think this?"

"I saw him, you see—not do it, but I went with him in his speed boat. He kept throwing inner tubes with tiny holes in them in the ocean at the mouth of the river and attached anything heavy to them. He'd let whatever he found dangle in the water, then he'd let the tide take them way out and followed them till it went under. Kept saying it was a new way of doing things if he had to, that it was better than that guy had been doing, feeding the pigs like he had. Sometimes we crossed the border following them and watched them sink in US waters—I knew that because the border guards would always be on us soon after we went across it, not that we could tell where we were, 'cos there's no fence. But soon as we did, they were always on us, especially with Diamond looking the way he did with his tooth and all. I think this is what he did to Paawan."

Rann sat back, leaned against the headboard, and looked down at the shape of this beautiful woman and said, "But you don't know this for sure?"

Taking a deep breath, Nina said, "But I'm pretty certain. He was jealous of him, you see. He knew he was my man from before and knew Paawan was coming back soon. I was going to tell him we were done and move in with Paawan—Paawan said if he didn't like it, he was going to take him up in a plane and pretend to throw him out till he settled down. Said he was a chicken shit—but I think Archall turned the tables on him somehow because as brave as Paawan was, the one thing he couldn't do well was swim. Said it's because he saw his friend drown in a pond when they were kids, said his friend's feet got caught in a grate or something. And that's what I think he was doing the whole time when he had me out there, measuring the distance the tubes could carry a weighted body out into the ocean, doing it in front of me in a perverse fashion, knowing he was planning to kill my man that way if he ever came back."

******

Archall Diamond walked around and around his kitchen and dialed Nina's number for the forty-seventh time. Fuck, he was pissed off, but in a funny way he felt good at the same time. The reason was because he still had a hard-on that was so strong he'd spent the last hour pulling it down and letting himself go as he catapulted cocoa pops off the end of his dick and caught them in his mouth.

He had a problem now. His woman had run on him and taken his box of goods with her, and even if she came back begging him for forgiveness once she ran out of money or got bored, she'd still need to be disciplined somehow. After all, he was the boss.

Then his phone rang. It was Rann, who said, "I've got the next batch of pills here if you still want the deal, or should I go somewhere else."

Archall Diamond stayed silent, thinking for a moment, and stared at his dick standing up proud like a soldier. Then he said, "You seen Nina?"

And he heard Rann say, "Why, you sent her round to look for the front tooth I just found stuck inside my foot when I went to the bathroom a minute ago."

"How's your hair, you fucking cocksucker," Archall snapped back.

Wanting to say, 'It's your girlfriend who likes sucking dick my friend,' Rann said instead, "So I suppose we're even. You took my hair and I've got your tooth—you want to make a deal or what? And I tell you what, since I've got it here, I'll throw your front tooth in the mix for free."

And still staring at his dick, Archall Diamond said, "Sure."

Rann put down the phone. "I'll make a trade with you," Nina said as she walked to the front door and pulled out a packet of his pills from her pocket and gently squeezed them into his hand and wishing as she did she'd got it on with Rann the moment he'd set foot in town instead of listening to Archall going on about how much of a loser the man was—and believing him, when deep down she knew it was Archall flying that flag, but hiding well, living in the shadow of Rasheed.

"I've left all he stole from you with you, so promise me that when I'm gone, you'll call the cops on him as soon as you've got your money and tell them what he's done with Paawan. I'm going to do the same, it's the least I can do for the man. If they hear it from two different sources, then maybe they'll listen."

Chapter Thirty-Two

Patrick sat in the bar of the Sutton with Rupert Mikes listening to him ask him if he was a realtor and Patrick coming back at him as cool as a cucumber saying, "You're not up here to buy a house, Rupert, you're here to make a movie, and that's what we're going to do. But we're not going to make any movie—we're making your movie and it's going to be fantastic."

"Not according to the guy you're recommending as the lead. He just told me it was shit."

He did, Patrick couldn't deny that, he was right there when he said it. He said, "He's young, he's got spunk. That's what we're after, look at James Dean. What do you want, a yes man who gives you lip service and then delivers nothing? Or do you want a man in your movie who's not afraid to speak his mind, like Bruce Willis or Russel Crowe?"

And Rupert Mikes looked up from his beer and said, "I'd love them!"

To which Patrick replied, "And I'd like to cruise about in a Rolls Royce but I can't, so we need to start understanding that fresh talent is better than old talent when old talent isn't achievable."

The fact that Patrick could afford a Roller and in fact used to own one until it made him feel old was beside the point. It was a simple persuasive tact he'd used countless times before when he needed to move a condo and the buyer was more interested in the penthouse. Carrying on he said, "The kid's bright and intelligent. He's talent, it's that simple. Use him now, harness his talent, and trust me on the next one Bruce, Russell and Daniel will be knocking on your door."

"Yeah but like you said—he's a kid."

"A young man."

"How can a kid know how to fly a spaceship?"

Having enough of the guy's sulking because someone gave him a wakeup call, and wanting to get on with his day, Patrick decided to lay it all on the line, and exchanging the word Property for Project, he repeated an ultimatum he'd thrown down many times throughout the years to clinch a deal, "But if you're no longer interested in the project, the phone's ringing off the hook with people who are—so please let me know," and standing, shook Rupert's hand, then the hands of two others at the bar who he didn't know, but who looked important, and said for effect, "Hey good to see you, we still on for Saturday? Dan's really excited about meeting you."

And left.

Hitting the lobby, he looked around for any actors then, noticing the large breasts on the receptionist, he stopped, looked away, and then once she got busy again, looked back as they jumbled about beneath her blouse. *Fuck they were nice*, he thought, and wondered if he should pop over to see a new high-end hooker he'd found who was happy to work him.

He stepped through the door, trying to remember the woman's name. *Damn it*, he thought, thinking back to Alla and how not long ago he'd been able to make a call 24/7 and go straight over. He took a deep breath, trying to contain the urges that were starting to develop inside his underwear, and remembered he had someone else staying at the hotel. Just as his smile began to take him in the direction his dick was pointing, he saw a limo pull up; and when he saw who was getting out, he knew he had to have her in his movie. Walking straight up to her, he had her in his arms before her bodyguard could get close and said, "Adalia darling, how on earth are you? I can't believe it."

Adalia Seychan looked at Patrick, knowing his face well, but without a clue as to who he was—completely forgetting he was the realtor who'd sold her the waterfront property over in the salubrious part of town for five million some seven years back. It was during a period in her life she was going through, her leave-me-be phase with her third husband. They'd picked Dundarave in West Vancouver because of its wealth and quaint little shops and restaurants and for the fact that no one cared about who you were or what you did. And when no one cared about who she was or what she'd done, just as she had hoped for, she'd seen Patrick's smiling face roll by on the back of the number 250 bus one Sunday morning and called him up to sell the place again only two months to the day after she'd moved in—because after all, she hadn't just been in a movie or two, she had three Oscars lined up along her mantelpiece and deserved some recognition.

Then as she stood there outside the Sutton looking to its big wooden doors flanked by ushers in top hats, Patrick's name came popping out of the people-I-really-couldn't-give-a-fuck-about box in her head and she said, "Patrick, I was just thinking about you. Oh my God, you look fantastic!"

And Patrick said, "That's because I've bought Slave."

Adalia stared at Patrick for a moment, taking in what he'd said and with a gasp said, "Slave Media? Sebastian String's Slave Media?"

Patrick nodded, letting go a glimpse of his pearly whites and steering her away from the main road as a bus passed, and said, "The one and the same. Sebastian's retiring soon. Now listen, before you go anywhere, it's a sin for me to not let you come and meet Rupert Mikes. He's an incredible talent, Sebastian and I have been watching him grow since he was a kid and we're making his next movie. I've just been with him talking about you for the lead!"

******

Rupert Mikes sat in the bar and was still staring at his beer when he heard Patrick coming along the corridor and watched as he entered the bar again. This time he had Adalia Seychan on his arm and shook hands with almost everyone in the room before pulling a chair back and seating the three-time Oscar winner down in front of him and saying, "Adalia, I'd like you to meet Rupert Mikes. He's just here in town working on a project we've been developing about time travel, it's incredible. We've got the youth of Marshaa, who just signed with Slave—she's making her screen debut along with an unbelievable male actor by the name of Dan Treedle. He's the sensation fronting the 'BlueBoy' campaign you may have seen. But we were struggling to find a lead who is more beautiful than Marshaa and who can play her as a grown woman, and quite frankly the answer is there's only one person and we all agreed it's you—we had a meeting about it with Sebastian this morning in fact. He's about to call your agent."

Adalia stared at Patrick and smiled. She liked this. There was no doubt Marshaa was a beautiful woman and to be compared to her beauty even later in life was a wonderful compliment—and if it came from Sebastian String, then it was an endorsement worth its weight in gold. She said with an air of mystery in her voice, "Time travel?"

Which was exactly what Rupert Mikes had been thinking all along, but before he could utter a word, Patrick said, "Exactly—it's an incredible script. Dan Treedle loves it, he's so excited."

Adalia Seychan stared at Patrick, wondering how a man of his age could still have such perfect teeth. She'd seen this kid out there in his underwear looking so frightened and, putting aside his looks and the incredible body, she only had to look into the young man's eyes to see he could act. He had it, *God Sebastian String was good*, how the hell did he find that kind of talent, she thought?

"Him! That guy in the silver undies, this Dan Treedle—he's the lead? You're telling me Slave's behind that campaign?" she said.

And Patrick smiled and said, "Oh yes, we're so proud, 'BlueBoy' was a year in development—the guy's such a talent. Rupert here's been spending all his time with him—only this morning he was saying the guy's the next James Dean—and you know the best part about the movie? The next James Dean is the time traveler and he's only ever loved you and will be known throughout time as only ever loving you. In fact, that's the name of the movie."

What? Rupert Mikes thought, that isn't the name of his film! Then just as he was about to speak up in protest, Patrick stood and, holding up his hands and taking the perfect moment, said, "Trust me!"

And then carried straight on straight after saying, "It's a wonderful script, we had a read through this morning and Dan went crazy; told us exactly how he felt. I thought Rupert here was going to cry."

Not knowing what to think, Adalia Seychan was in a spin. Usually projects got weeded out by her people, but this one, it sounded good. Her being on the same screen with Marshaa could be risky, but Sebastian String was involved and the man's reputation was second to none. She said, "Patrick—I'd love to read it, and I'm sure Campbell Ewes would love to direct—he did such a great job with *Jumping Fire*, my third Oscar's down to him."

And with those words, Patrick, Adalia, and especially Rupert all knew that 'Rupert Mikes,' the new up-and-coming sensation writer/director had, without saying a single word, just lost his job.

******

"Adalia Seychan's a has been," were the first words out of Mazzi Hegan as he sat down on the sofa in the boardroom and listened to Patrick telling Sebastian about how Adalia's all over herself to be in a project he was involved in. Mazzi was especially interested now that he was realizing the whole thing was about time travel, as one of his greatest fantasies was to travel through time and fuck cavemen and gladiators. And with that in mind, he was also thinking it was about time he read the script. Then just as the vision of some Neanderthal hunk with a club evaporated from his mind, he piped up another reality, "And we can't afford her, or this Campbell Ewes, who I must say I've heard is in the closet and a prick."

And that's when Sebastian looked over to him and said, "You stick to the photography darling."

As Patrick said back, "Trust me!—You can't afford not to."

And he wasn't wrong. Sebastian knew that if Adalia Seychan's name was attached, it was money in the bank. How the hell Patrick had gotten close enough to her to pitch the project was beyond him. He walked over to Fluffy, picked him up, and sat the dog down on the sofa a little too close to Mazzi's new suede trousers for his liking. Sebastian said, "Now Patrick, it seems your make over here's going great, but I didn't ever imagine this. And I may be mistaken, but I don't remember reading anything about time travel in the script or seeing a position for an older female lead?"

And without missing a beat, Patrick said, "Oh that's not a problem, it's all sorted—I sent Mikes back to L.A. to cry in his soup. Megan's doing it, she's making the changes."

"Megan?" replied both Sebastian and Mazzi Hegan at exactly the same time.

Patrick said it again, "Megan's making the changes—I popped up to see her straight after the meeting with Adalia and talked to her about what was needed. It's another reason we signed her—she's not only an incredible actor, singer and model, she's a phenomenal writer too."

And she was—she'd told him so, right when he was on all fours with the hotel's complimentary apple in his mouth, while she was naked next to him, her right hand covered in body lotion from the bathroom and on his dick, stretching it down towards the bed so she could watch him cum all over the nice clean white sheets. Tugging it with every mention of her qualities, she'd said, "And you know I'm a writer too as well, Patrick. In fact, I'm an incredible singer... Actor... Model... Dancer... Writer..."

Chapter Thirty-Three

Rann Singh stood in the bathroom looking at himself in the mirror and wondered if he would be able to go out into the world with a bald head. Fuck, he looked odd with his big ears sticking out. He took a wash cloth, ran it under the cold tap, and placed it across both his swollen eyes. Archall Diamond would be back over soon, probably with his two goons who wore fighter clothes but couldn't fight and if anyone drew a Taser, he'd break their arm clean— same for a gun, he thought.

He walked back to the living room still holding the towel to his eye and sat down looking to the box that he'd wrapped so carefully with the Kiwi and so very nearly lost. It was still mostly full, bar a couple of packets that Archall Diamond must have snagged or his girlfriend had for that matter, not that she'd need them, he thought. Any guy who was having trouble around her already knew it and had been to the doctor.

He picked up the phone and dialed the estate agent in Kenya without a worry for the bill he knew he'd never pay. It would be early in the morning there now, but what the fuck—the guy either wanted to sell the ranch or he didn't. When he answered, Rann said in the tongue his family had elected to call their own but wasn't theirs, "You up, it's Rann Singh. You still want to sell that ranch?"

The guy did, very much so, so much so that Rann could hear the man's voice go from sleepy to wide awake in the matter of seconds it had taken him to say his first words.

"I am selling the house, yes." He heard the man reply.

Then, this time in English, he asked, "How much you want for it?"

And the voice on the other end said, "Everything is yours sir, home, land village, tractor, everything. The furniture too and you can keep on the staff sir, everything is the same, sir. My client will sell for $750,000 for the title."

Rann thought about it, remembering the name his grandfather had used as a curse word for so many years after the man who bought the property off him low-balled him in the deal at the last minute. He asked, "The guy selling the place, his name ain't Blou, is it?"

The estate agent, silent for a second, then answered, "Yes, I believe Mr. Blou is the current title holder of the aforementioned property."

Rann wondering why the man had to dress it up with fancy words when all he had to do was say 'yes'. The man Blou, the South African selling it now after low-balling his grandfather, dropping his bid to only two hundred thousand dollars just as they were about to sell, knowing Rann's grandfather had just lost his son and had to go look after Rann.

Fuck him, Rann thought, he'd low-ball him and if the guy was hungry enough, he'd take it and if the deal went through, there'd be enough in change to live off once he'd flown his grandfather and grandmother back first class. He said, "What about the zebra?"

"Zebra died sir."

Fuck, he wanted that. He remembered it as a kid when he'd visited and loved the stories his grandfather used to tell of being chased for no reason by the animal they'd saved after they'd watched its mother become lunch one afternoon out on the *Mara*. Then he heard the guy say, "But we can have one here for you—you'll have the zebra. I'll supply it myself if necessary."

Then Rann said, chancing his hand, "I'm going to turn up two days' time with two hundred thousand and one Canadian dollars. Call the guy now and wake him up—ask him if he'll take it or not." Then Rann followed it up with a slogan he'd read on a bench not long ago, put there by a guy with whom he'd lately had some dealings, "Tell him 'He can't afford not to'."

Then there was a silence that went on for so long that for a moment Rann thought the line had gone dead, then the estate agent came back on the line and said, "Well I'm very surprised, but my client wants to move to the coast. You see, he has another place there, so I suppose your slogan worked. The answer's 'yes'. Wire me a twenty percent deposit please to seal the deal and we'll see you in a couple of days."

And as he hung up the phone, the entry phone buzzer rang for the second time that day and this time it was Nina's ex.

******

Archall Diamond came in the front door and the first thing he asked for was his tooth. Rann answered, "You'll get it as soon as you've got the tablets and I've got my money. Then you can leave and I'll stick it in the post for you."

"Na," Archall Diamond said back and looked to both his goons, who were in worse shape than Rann.

"I heard, you see, if you lose a tooth and stick it back in quick enough, it latches on and grows back in."

How can it grow back in? Rann thought, feeling Archall's tooth in his pocket as they spoke and wondering if it was somehow attaching itself to his jeans or had been trying to attach itself to his foot, where he'd found it in the bathroom. He said, "Well we better be quick then ain't we, and when we're done, stand down by the road and I'll drop your tooth out the window." Then Archall saw the box sitting on the coffee table.

"Hey, these the same ones?" he said.

And Rann said, "How can that be when you got them?" Archall Diamond thought it through. Rann was right, how was he to know the ones he stole were missing, unless Nina had been over and given them to him. But why would she when he was such a moron. He said, "Well these ones better be from that Swedish scientist guy."

What the fuck was this idiot going on about now, coming in here all tough with two thugs he'd just beaten up so bad they'd had to Taser him to win. He said, "What Swedish guy?"

"You said they were done by a Swedish guy. A syintist and he put extra stuff in to make you happy, they better be them ones, right."

"Yeah they are," Rann said, "same Swedish guy. Came from Auckland, used to play rugby for the all-blacks."

"You said he was a white guy."

Fuck me.

Sitting down, Archall took a deep breath and felt the stiffness in his pants as he sucked air through the gap in his teeth. Pulling out his phone, he opened the calculator function, started doing math, and said, "You got 30,000 packets with six tabs in each at five dollars a tablet, less the tenth commission fee we spoke about, so that is, that is, that is—let's say four dollars and seventy-five a tab and there's six in the pack that makes it, eight hundred and fifty-five say thousand dollars for your box."

"And your tooth," Rann said.

"Yeah, that's a given."

Then out of nowhere, Rann said, knowing full well he was

never going to see the prick again, "Why don't you give me 50% upfront now for the next batch so as you can buy exclusivity with me and when the next batch comes through, as I know I've got a buyer and don't need to go through any bullshit, then you can have them for 30% less including your tenth commission."

Archall Diamond weighed it up. He'd got the fractional '-*ths*'s all worked out—that was easy, but percentages were still an issue, and 30% less sounded like he was on the losing side. And as straight as this plastic Punjabi turban-less cocksucker seemed now, there had to be an angle, and top of it all, he didn't know what exclusivity meant. Either way, even if the stuff here cost him $800,000 at $4.75 a pop, then he was going to double that and sell them at $24.00 and get back about three million. So, he said, "You can forget the 30% less shit and the exclusivity clause because from now on, you'se only gonna be dealing with the Diamond. And when the Diamond gives upfront money, the Diamond's gonna be cashing his money off coupons, so next time round you'se not getting the five dollars a tab less the tenth. You'se getting five dollars less a twentieth 'cos for that kind of deal Rasheed took a third straight off the top. But he ain't here and it's me your dealing with and you looking at taking a hit on the '-*ths*'s. If you don't like it, you can go cry me a river—tremble and shiver 'cos Archall Diamond's in charge now."

Math still wasn't Archall Diamond's strong point.

Rann's Sikh god Guru Nanak was definitely looking out for him.

******

Settling on a simple extra three hundred thousand upfront for the next batch of pills, Archall Diamond would never see Rann Singh again. Rann stood on his balcony, one million one hundred and fifty-five thousand dollars richer.

Writing 'keep on smiling' on the front of a sealed envelope and hoping it would get stuck in a tree, Rann dropped Archall Diamond's front tooth over the edge to him and his two goons, who were just as stupid as Archall was—if not more. Then carrying the cash in a blue sports bag, a small amount of clothes, and his Kenyan passport, Rann came out the front door and, with his head feeling like a boiled egg, jumped into a taxi, hit the first international bank with a branch in Nairobi, bought seven banker's drafts to the tune of one hundred grand each, and carried on to the airport where he proudly bought a business class seat all the way to Nairobi via Munich. At nine thirty in the evening, just as he was about to board the plane, he kept his promise to Nina and called Charles Chuck Chendrill, "Here superstar detective," he said, "if you're on the beach at English Bay waiting for the fireworks to happen, then you will've probably heard, there's supposed to be some skydiving lunatic going to come flying in and swoop the crowd, but I can tell you, save your neck for later, 'cos the guy's name is..."

"Paawan," Chendrill said for him, "I know, we're supposed to meet."

And without a breath, Rann carried on, "Well Paawan won't be coming 'cos he's dead. A man named Archall Diamond killed him—lives at Rasheed's place now—he floated him as he likes to call it. Put him in a truck inner tube, weighted him down, and kicked him off the pier as the tide was turning down there in that part of Surrey where the people live and pretend they from another district. Let him float out to sea. Archall Diamond did it because Paawan was fucking his sweet girl."

"And how do you know this?" asked Chendrill.

"'Cos Diamond told me, and so did his girl Nina, but she ain't gonna be around to say otherwise. She's leaving, same as me, as

Diamond just bought all those tablets you pretended you had and the guy's no good at math, so I'm out of your hair. If you don't believe me, see if he shows tonight. See if the man flies in like he's supposed to and when he does, buy him a beer from me. But if he don't, then you'll know where he is and apparently he weren't a good swimmer."

Then taking him by surprise, Chendrill said, "You know that postman's still in a coma, don't you?"

And Rann said, "Well he shouldn't answer the door wearing nothing but a hat, then should he?"

And with that, Rann Singh, the blackmailing Swahili-speaking Sikh with a *ten dan* black belt in karate and a blackout temper, was out of Chendrill's life for good.

******

Chendrill sat in the executive box up above the sands of English Bay, no longer looking to the sky. He put his phone back into his pocket. Leaning over, he said to Sebastian the same words Rann had just spoken, as deep down he knew they were true.

"Save your neck—he's not coming."

Rasheed had been looking out for the man over a week ago when they'd met the night before he'd died—maybe at the hands of his kung fu friend who outside the restaurant he remembered had given him the hardest kick to the throat he'd ever felt.

"How do you know, Chuck?" asked Sebastian, who'd only walked a couple of blocks to get to the bay and now sat in his section with an empty row of chairs and a view of the fireworks far worse than he had from his living room, with its luxurious penthouse view out across the bay. Patrick had called with some bullshit excuse, he'd thought. Dan hadn't called, but he wasn't expecting he would and Mazzi, he knew, liked to be with the people on the sand. But Chuck was there for him, there with his new girl holding her hand, hoping Sebastian wouldn't see, but he had and it was wonderful. Turning as he heard Chuck say to him, "Maybe I could be wrong though, so keep an eye open—but I doubt it."

Then he sat there and without thinking, he squeezed Tricia's hand for a moment. Looking at him, she said, "What's the matter?"

Chendrill shook his head, but deep down he wished he was a cop again. Intelligence like that used to come to him all the time when he was and it was simple enough after a while to sort the seed from the chaff, and this wasn't the latter. He said, "Just work." Or that's what it used to be, but now he was an overpaid babysitter who scared off blackmailers and tracked down the odd pimp cum psychopath in his spare time—but that one had been for Daltrey.

Slowly, the sun began to set and Paawan hadn't shown as he'd wanted to, coming in from the heavens as he spiralled down, leaving his trail of smoke high in the sky from the canister strapped to his ankle and letting his chute go at the last minute to drift down to the applause of hundreds of thousands on the beach.

He'd been planning it for months, Rasheed had said, letting everyone he could know it was a secret, telling all and sundry to keep it on the low down, knowing before long, everyone would know his name and would be waiting. But as the crowd waited for the man to fall from the sky, he didn't show, just as Rann Singh had said.

The first tester rocket ripped up from the barge as twilight set the stage for a million people to sit in awe. It was in amongst all these people that Sebastian felt more alone than he ever had.

Standing, he placed his hand upon Chendrill's shoulder, made his excuses, and thought of Patrick as he made his way against the flow of latecomers hopeful of finding a place to stand or sit and watch in silence as the night sky filled with its spectacle of color and light. The guy had come into his company looking for a makeover and turned the place upside down. It was quite funny really, even if he was getting himself on the hook for millions, but what the heck, he could make a hundred and still be comfortable— and he'd never made a movie, so it would pass the time.

He'd let everyone have some fun and watch the chaos, he thought, then bring in a heavy hitter producer he knew to straighten out the nonsense, pay for the thing himself, and keep final edit so nothing bad could tarnish his and Slave's already good name. It would be fun watching Patrick bullshit his way through it all and as long as Adalia Seychan behaved herself and the script was fine, which it would be in the end, all would be good.

He carried on up the street, weaving through the crowd and the youth—some already drunk on cheap booze—Fluffy was home alone, he thought, and would be all afraid—the duvet placed against the window hung with safety pins from the curtain rail of his bedroom doing little to dampen the explosions that would terrify the poor dog's mind. And as he opened the bedroom door, he reached down and held little Fluffy in his arms and stood looking from the living room window high above the city in his penthouse suite out across the bay at the night sky as the fireworks started racing and swirling high into the heavens, the thoughts came of Alan, who he missed so dearly. As the tears came, sending small streams of sadness and joy running down his soft skin, he held Fluffy tight to his chest as he had held Alan years before down there in amongst the crowds, when it was just the two of them in amongst a million other souls who all cared about nothing else for that moment bar an explosive sky.

Chendrill sat there alone with Dan's mother, the sole occupants of a ten-thousand-dollar box courtesy of Sebastian, and watched the sparkles rain down from the heavens. Tricia lay in his arms, her head resting softly on his chest as he leaned back in the chair, watching the red and gold, pink and blue sky that matched one of her boyfriend's shirts, thinking she was in love now as Chendrill watched the crowd thinking that somewhere out there amongst them all, Archall Diamond would be sitting there too— and he wanted to speak to him.

And he was right, only Archall wasn't sitting, he was laying, upside down, back to front with the crowd, with his head down in a hole in the sand and his face twisted up towards the sea like a patient in a dentist's chair, trying to stay still long enough for gravity to hold his tooth in place, so as it could grow back in.

He'd done his work for the day, bought the other batch of hard-on pills the flash Paki with the now bald head had hanging around. He'd handed them out to his dealers and anyone else who'd take them for free—just at first, of course, let them circulate for a bit. Keeping his tooth in with his tongue as he spoke, he'd told them as he distributed the tablets, "They were made in Scindinavian by a rugby syintist who's a black guy and cool 'cos I know him, lives in Auckland in Sweden, is a professor at a university there.'

And they work he'd said, "I'se had a boner all day and your dick gets so hard you can't believe the tricks you can do with it."

******

The next morning, like a dog looking for an old bone it had buried, Chendrill drove away from his apartment, dropped Tricia off at her home, and checked on Dan, who hadn't moved from the same spot, it seemed, he'd seen him in the evening before. He drove out of town and ripped the Aston Martin along the highway, heading east towards Surrey.

He reached the monster home painted bright pink that used to be Rasheed's, looked at the two terracotta lions that guarded the entranceway, and walked through, taking a peek in the garage as he did. Then the front door opened and he heard Archall Diamond say, "You looking for Rasheed? Well he's not here because he's dead."

Chendrill looked at the guy, standing there in his track suit and running shoes, but with a fat gut. He said, "Who gave you the fat lip?"

And Archall said again, "Rasheed ain't here, he died."

Chendrill stared at the man looking back at him touching around his front tooth with his tongue. He said, "You got any of them pills that make your dick grow?" And watched as Archall Diamond shook his head.

Then heard him say, "No, but I like your shirt."

Chendrill nodded appreciating the compliment and thinking the man did have taste after all. Then he said, "Thanks, you ever heard of a guy by the name of Paawan?" And watched as Archall Diamond opened his mouth and took a deep breath, showing his front tooth with a diamond in it, his tongue pushing hard up against its bottom.

"Who's looking?" And Chendrill offered out his hand.

"Chuck Chendrill, private investigator. We met before at the bar, just before Rasheed passed on but for some reason you kept to yourself."

As Archall nodded, trying to look cool, closing his mouth and turning his head from side to side, he said, "Yeah, it's the way I operate. You looking for Paawan? I don't know, he was a friend of Rasheed's, nothing to do with me."

"Was? Like he's dead?" Chendrill said straight back, knowing the man had already fucked up putting the skydiver in the past tense.

And Archall Diamond quickly came back, "No I mean he was Rasheed's friend and Rasheed's dead, that's what I meant."

"He's still alive then?"

And Archall shrugged, saying. "Could be, could be alive, but you know he liked to try to fly and you can't say one way or the other with those kind of people. When you walking, sometimes you see birds all squashed on the ground, feathers all over the place and shit. You know those people, they ain't easy to insure."

"Neither are gangsters," Chendrill said.

And Archall came straight back at him, "Yeah but gangsters don't need insurance because they rich."

"Till they fuck up and go to jail or die like Rasheed. Who killed him?"

"You looking for Paawan or you looking for what happened to Rasheed? If it's Rasheed, go ask the cops, they looking into that one. As for the prick who thinks he can fly, go ask someone who gives a shit."

Then, throwing it out there, Chendrill said, "I heard you took Paawan crabbing only it was him you used as bait."

And watched as Archall Diamond opened his mouth again and pushed up on his diamond studded front tooth. Then he said, "Well only fools listen to bullshit."

And only fools kept inner tubes, concrete breeze blocks, and chains in their garage after they'd used the same apparatus to drown someone, Chendrill thought as he said his thanks and left.

He reached the Aston, climbed in, and was about to leave when Archall Diamond appeared at his window and, pushing his front tooth up with his tongue as he spoke, asked, "So, you gonna let me know who's been going around saying I been killing people then?"

And putting the car into gear, Chendrill looked at him and said as he began to pull away, "You."

******

So Rann Singh was right, Chendrill thought, as he cruised away from the house looking to Archall Diamond getting smaller in his rear-view mirror, standing there with his finger in his mouth, he'd dig deeper, get to the bottom of it, then wait till he hit the downtown core and have Williams make the arrest.

And what was the deal with the guy trying to talk with either his finger in his mouth or his tongue sticking out?

******

Archall Diamond stood watching as the guy in the cool shirt and the Aston Martin disappeared up the road and turned the corner, and thought, *fuck him what did he know?* The guy coming here uninvited, getting smooth with him. He had nothing, had fuck all, wasn't even a real cop, then he said out loud, "Go look for the fucker in the ocean if you're that worried about him and take some scuba gear with you—it's a big place—you big fucking ape."

He took a deep breath and calmed himself down. Yeah, he thought, it's a big place and even he couldn't tell how far the riptide had taken him before the man dropped under—after all, there's no way he could have swam out, not after having the car squash him down like it had. "So, fuck him," he said again out loud and put his finger on the bottom of his diamond centered front tooth, pushing it hard back up into his gum. *Fuck it was getting sore*. That plastic prick wannabe Punjabi Rann doing his kung fu shit on him like that when all he was there for was to do a deal. Next time he saw him, he'd float him for what he did with his foot. Yeah, he'd float him—float the fucker like he had with Paawan 'cos he kicked his tooth out—that's what he'd do. *But what about the tablets?* he thought, as he walked up the steps to the big door of the house. He needed the fucker for the tablets, and the tablets made him feel good. Then he got it and smiled as he worked it out in his mind. All he'd need to do was go to Sweden himself like the plastic Punjabi had, find the guy at the university there, it shouldn't be hard, how many black guys were science professors in Auckland? It'd be easy—everyone was blonde over there anyway. That's what he'd do, go there, sort it out, cut out the middle man, come back, wack a few tabs back, and break open the cocoa pops. And *that*, he thought, as he reached the kitchen with a big grin on his face, was exactly what he was going to do right now.

******

Chendrill hit the highway and wondered how Dennis, the dentist with the beautiful wife, was doing and felt a tinge of guilt inside as he passed by the turnoff from the highway to where the man had lived. Was he still in the basement and was the high-end whore who could no longer walk sucking his dick now? He hoped so, he thought, hoped she'd seen the light and settled down with the good man, which Dennis no doubt was. But could the man stay with her knowing she was only there because she'd been hobbled? Truth was he probably could, and for as long as she was with him, hobbled or not, he would love her, cherish every moment they were together and hope that she would not ever leave him again.

Two hours later and with the family size packet of cocoa pops now empty, Archall Diamond was done, spent, exhausted, his dick so sore from propelling cereal into the air from its tip he could hardly move. This problem with his tooth though was becoming an issue. Three times he'd lost it under the fridge and it was obvious the thing wasn't growing back like it was supposed to, at least not in any hurry—so still naked and with the air of resignation falling upon him, he picked up his phone with its diamond studded case and called the new driver, Steven, who he'd replaced himself with, and said, "Listen, I need you to find me an underground dentist."

"An underground dentist?" the guy on the other end of the phone answered.

"Yeah—that's how we operate, keep everything off the system, ya know off grid, that's the way we work it."

And the voice on the other end of the phone said, "It's just a tooth."

And Archall said, "Yeah, but I don't need to be explaining how any of this happened okay or where it happened. You know what I's saying."

"Just say you did it playing ice hockey."

Then Archall said, "Just find me one and as we go along with things, I'll teach you how the system run, alright—I got to be careful, some private eye guy been sniffing around here, drives an Aston Martin."

"What's he want?"

"Not sure," Archall said, lying through his missing front tooth. "He's just been looking around; guy probably be working at the mall on the weekend."

"Why's he gonna be working at the mall if he's rides an Aston?"

"Might not be his?"

"What's his name?"

Archall thought about it but couldn't remember, so he said, "Didn't get it."

"How old was he?"

"Old?"

"How old, forties, fifties—sixty plus."

"Yeah, he was getting up there," Archall said, still not having a clue. Then carried on saying, "Older than me and you yeah."

Then Steven asked, "He have on a loud shirt?"

"Yeah a cool one."

"Was his name Chuck—Chuck Chendrill?"

"Yeah that's it, how'd you know?"

"The guy's a legend. Was driving about in a Ferrari, must have got an Aston now though—he ain't no mall cop for fuck's sake."

"You know him?" Archall asked again, now getting nervous.

"No, I know of him, like I say he's a legend, used to be a cop but now he's out there on his own in the corporate world, still likes to solve murders for fun though. You know that cop woman was burned to death last month downtown?"

Archall didn't know. "Yeah," he said.

"Well they said it was him who caught the guy and cut off his head."

Archall said, "Sounds like bullshit—was the woman cop hot?"

"So they say. Anyway you know that old saying, a Mountie always gets his man?"

"No."

"Well, they say that's true, but if Chendrill's involved, he gets him first."

"Oh yeah," Archall said, shitting himself, his mind racing now, and was about to carry on as his driver butted in, "But you got nothing to worry about? You ain't been killing anyone, have you? And why would he be interested in a small fry like you, ecstasy and shit ain't his thing." Then he laughed, saying, "You just need a dentist 'cos you got your tooth knocked out. But if you've been stupid and murdered someone—then you're fucked man."

And that's when Dennis got the call, which came a few hours after, just as Alla had called out from her bed again with a feeling of relief she, for some time now, would have never thought imaginable. She'd woke after dreaming she could move her feet and as she'd lifted the covers to look, she'd realized it was true.

"Oh my God, Oh my God." She screamed out to her husband who was halfway through the phone call from Archall, listening to him going on about his tooth and hearing his wife call out in the background about how she could move her feet, and, as he blanked out Archall, he knew it was the best news—and the worst news—he had ever heard.

******

Two hours later, he opened the door to his basement suite to see

Archall Diamond standing outside with two guys with black eyes in fighters' shirts and a low rider Mercedes with a dented roof parked in the neighbor's driveway. Dennis said, "You can't park there, that's the neighbor's driveway."

And Archall Diamond replied, "We can 'cos we gangsters."

They stepped in and looked around. Archall Diamond saying, "I thought you dentists were rich."

Dennis asking, "How can I help?"

They passed through the living room, all three of them staring at the beautiful girl sitting on the sofa watching TV and entered the surgery Dennis had set up in the back room, where he had a small recliner, some tools, an old dentist drill he'd kept from his student days, and a lamp he'd reappropriated from a movie set after everyone went home and left him to do the clean up. Backstreet dentistry paid well, but only half the price of front street. But it was better than humping sandbags in the movie business and would do until his licence came back again.

Sitting himself down on the recliner and half looking through the crack in the door to Alla watching the TV, then around to his two heavies who couldn't fight standing there trying to look cool, Archall said, "I was playing ice hockey and the bat, stick thing took my tooth out." And smiling, he showed Dennis what he'd seen as soon as he'd opened the front door. Washing his hands and putting on a pair of gloves, then pulling the tooth out with his fingers, Dennis said, "You'll be needing surgery to fix it."

And heard Archall say, "I's not growing back in then?"

Dennis looked at the guy, taking in what he'd just said, then looking to the heavies staring at the tooth, shook his head and answered, "No—you'll need a prosthetic built and since we've got the tooth, it'll be easy. I'll get the diamond set in it as well if you want to keep the look."

"Right bang in the center?" Archall Diamond replied and looked again to Alla sitting on the sofa. Then Dennis carried on saying, "I can do it for you right here if you'd like. Have the prosthetic made, the diamond set in it, and fit it back in right here and when I'm done, your smile will light up the room."

Archall looked around the room. It was pretty dark in there. He said. "In here?"

And Dennis told him, "You can go to some shopping mall practice with all the glitz and glam and chances are you'll have a smile that looks fake—with me you won't. It's not the chair you're sitting on or the fancy store front that fixes your teeth, it's the guy holding the tools." And he wasn't wrong.

******

Mazzi Hegan stood in the bedroom of his swishy penthouse suite and put on the tightest pair of shorts he could find so as there was no way he could hide his banana, and picking his loosest, shortest top, he grabbed his rollerblades, sunglasses, and headphones and headed out the door.

It was Sunday, it was sunny, and he was in Vancouver. Stanley Park would be beautiful and the seawall buzzing and he was going to just rock it all the way around the peninsular park, listening to eighties music as loud as he could and roller grooving all the way.

God, he was happy. The fireworks had been sensational and for once he'd put his camera down and spent the evening with the guy from the coffee shop who'd given him a couple of these pills made up by a Swedish doctor that were floating around. Apparently, the guy'd been a rugby player and spent almost five years studying herbs and the male reproductive system in Papua New Guinea and was onto something—because wow, were they great.

Lucking out, he parked the Ferrari right under a huge maple, slapped the blades on, and hit the path, tucking and floating and grooving as he sung out to the soundtrack to *Flashdance*. Wow, what a feeling it was, he thought. What was in those things? His bedroom was a mess, his living room was a mess, his hair was a mess. But who cared because he'd just had the best sex ever and still he had a chubby going that wouldn't go away, so why waste it and who cares if it scares someone's grandma because he was roller grooving baby and that's what roller groovers did.

He hit the pathway that led down the hill to the pool at Second Beach and tucked, reached the bottom, swirled round twice by the swings, and took a sharp right, then a left through the tunnel that took him under the road, shouting 'weeeeeeee' with his arms up as he went through; and as he came out the other side, he saw him coming towards him in the distance, crossing the small bridge at the end of Lost Lake, disappearing for a moment behind some long reeds and then reappearing, twirling on his blades in a perfect pirouette, the sun lighting up his blonde hair as he roller grooved, his top large and loose, his tight shorts squashing his banana beneath the spandex fabric.

Mazzi Hegan carried on towards him, their eyes meeting as they neared each other, the pair slowing and locking eyes as they passed, freewheeling Mazzi cruised to a stop, looking back at the guy as he did the very same, coming to a halt just before the tunnel entrance and staring back at him. *Wow! Sensational*, he thought, and feeling the sun on his back, he turned and set off again towards the guy who was now coming towards him for another pass, and as their eyes met again, for a second, it was electric.

With a quick double spin, Mazzi Hegan stopped and watched as the man did the same, spinning in around with the grace of a figure skater on ice, and stopping with both legs parted and waiting a moment before slowly cruising back along the path and coming to a halt, standing there in his blades and fluffy socks with what looked like a banana down his pants. Staring at Mazzi, a carbon copy of himself, he said, "You look familiar?"

And that's how Mazzi Hegan met Einer.

The next morning, with a sore ass and throat, Mazzi burst into the office with so much energy he may as well have still been in his rollerblades and announced to all and sundry, "I think I'm in love."

"You've said that before, I think," Sebastian said as he passed him in the corridor carrying a small water dish for Fluffy, and asked, "I take it it's the guy from the coffee shop?"

"No," Mazzi replied, "I was out blading in my shorts and bumped into this guy from Zurich. He's a photographer."

"Really?"

"Yeah and he looks great in shorts. He was blading. I was listening to *Flashdance* and he was listening to Donna Summers. We passed each other and it was just electric. We went straight back to my place and he fucked me all night because he'd taken these new pills that are floating about that make you look cool in shorts—some Danish rugby player/professor designed them after studying herbs and tribal mating rituals of male elders in Papua New Guinea. They are saying it's the guy's life's work."

"Really?" Sebastian said, as he carried on and wondered what the guy, who'd put his entire life to such good work, would think if he knew Mazzi Hegan was popping them like candy and whacking his sword around like Errol Flynn.

He said, "Well be careful if they're not legal Mazzi. Your body's a finely made tool and you don't want to do yourselves an injury with these things. You know, go too far."

You couldn't not go too far in Mazzi's book, Sebastian thought, that's why he had such a huge selection of oils and power jets in his shower; and he wanted to carry on, saying just that, but thought the better of it right as Mazzi said, "You know we have a great attraction to each other."

Sebastian nodded and understood exactly what Hegan was saying. The first time he and Alan had met in the corridors of the Royal College of Art in London it had been the same for the two of them, except they'd just gone for coffee. But this was Mazzi. Wondering how long this relationship would last, he said, "I'm glad you've met someone."

"Oh same—he's bi and so über cool, he's got blonde hair, cut just like mine. Dresses just like me, same height and build, but not down there though—he's bigger and loves sex."

If that's the case, stay in and stare in the mirror, Sebastian thought, and walked to his office and placed the dish down for Fluffy and wondered how long it would be before he heard his personal secretary tell him Patrick was here or on the phone. And before Fluffy had even began to get his ears wet, he had heard just that. By the time Patrick had reached his office, he had already heard all about Mazzi Hegan's new guy and, sitting down in his linen suit, said to Sebastian, "That must be the most Mazzi has ever said to me?"

"He's in love Patrick—don't worry, tomorrow he'll be bored with the guy and he'll go back to ignoring you again."

"He just hated seeing me every day on the back of the bus I think."

"It's not just you, Patrick. It's the way he is."

"It is, he's said as much, said he told me the other day, 'you'd never see me in a sweater my granny bought me for Christmas'."

Neither would I, Sebastian thought, not for all the tea in China. He wouldn't advertise himself on the back of a bus either for that matter, but to each their own. Somehow though it worked for Patrick and here he was now, trying to escape from the years of piling on the bullshit by doing just that—except now in fancier clothes. Wondering what the man's next move would be, he said, "So, what surprises have you got for me today?"

Patrick had plenty, but if the years of doing deals had taught him one thing, it was timing, so he simply said, "Everything's cool."

Everything's cool, Sebastian thought, cool; in the fact, you're sitting here smiling first thing in the morning in full knowledge you have a terrible script you're getting the flower child to repair, a director who's been sent packing by an aging lead, for whom we're going to have rent extra floor space to fit her ego into—and that was just for starters. God knows what would be coming their way for the main dish. He looked to the window and for a moment wondered what Chuck Chendrill was doing, then turned back and said, "Well that's good news. It's all getting exciting though, isn't it? Have you put any thought into how you're going to deal with the fact you've got new talent?"

He hadn't, despite the fact that the two people on whom he'd been selling the show had no actual acting experience—although he had no doubt some of Marshaa's tantrums were Oscar worthy. But this side of things were someone else's problem. After all, he didn't bake the cake—he just delivered the ingredients and someone else mixed them. Besides, they'd be at least a year before they'd get found out and by then, he'd have another project fired up and ready to go. Not lying for once, Patrick said, "Marshaa's going crazy about the film—she's so glad she's signed with Slave."

"I'm glad she did too, Patrick, that was a great coup. Tell her when you next speak to give me a call— there's a few projects I'd like her to take a look at and it's important she's happy."

Then Patrick asked, "What about Dan?"

"Dan's different, Dan needs nurturing. We don't want to foist him on the world or they'll get bored. What we should do though is put out a campaign with just Dan, Marsha, and Adalia Seychan's with nothing other than their pictures together, perhaps with them in a bed or something, get them doing something sexy together, give everyone a taster and get the gossips talking—you know as they say, less is more."

Patrick begged to differ. In his experience, he'd found the more photos he had of himself in a pressed shirt or a nice sweater with his teeth shinning, the more the phone rang—and it did ring. But for once, he kept quiet and stood and walked to the window and looked out to some young hotties finding their way to work in their nice clothes and sexy shoes. He said, "This guy Mazzi met isn't an actor, is he?"

Sebastian laughed, the guy who used to sell homes now not able to sit still—always thinking. He said bluntly, "Patrick, worry about the script darling please, or pretty soon you'll be standing there with a jar full of nothing and have a leading lady who's looking for the exit sign. And on that subject, you'll need to let Megan know never to put Adalia Seychan and Marshaa on the same page or they'll be a cat fight and both of them will have a breakdown."

Then Patrick said, "It's okay, they can't be. I've spoken to Megan and we're changing the script again. Adalia Seychan's now going to be a space traveler from another universe."

Chapter Thirty-Four

Despite the fact his girl had left him and he had a hot-shot private investigator on his tail, Archall Diamond was feeling good. He missed his girl yes, but that was just because he liked looking at her showing herself off when they went out to the hockey and the like. But that was about it. When it came to her, she smelled good yeah—but so did he with his coconut hair crème. This girl though, the one at the dentist, she was something else and there was a connection—he'd felt it, seen it as he'd kept his mouth wide open and caught her looking at him through the crack in the door in Dennis's back room surgery, sitting there with a blanket on her lap, looking like one of them women you see on TV hosting a dance show or something.

She'd looked at him, he'd seen it, her blue eyes meeting his as he tried not to dribble. *Who the fuck was she*, he thought, as he stuck his tongue up and into the groove where his missing front tooth used to be. Couldn't be the backstreet dentist's woman, he was too ugly and old to have a chick like that. Could be his daughter or niece or something. She'd be good, he thought, and I bet she'd like hockey. He'd have her stand there with him at the interval in a pair of high heels and tight jeans and a signed Pavel Bure jersey.

Standing up he walked up to the bedroom and opened the door to the wardrobe that still smelled of his girl. He picked up a Canucks jersey signed by one of the team's superstar twin brothers, and headed off towards Burnaby to see if she wanted to go.

It was just after four when he arrived, parking in the neighbor's drive like he did and covering his mouth with his hand. He rang the door to Dennis's place and, hearing Alla call out for him to come in, entered to find her sitting alone at the dinner table in a wheelchair eating a salad. With an accent that made his dick stir, she said, "Dennis is in the back with a patient. He'll be done soon."

And getting straight to the point, Archall Diamond said, "I was seeing this girl, but she's gone now. I got this hockey shirt and wondered if you'd like it."

Then he watched as the girl smiled at him and looked to the back of the basement suite towards the door where her husband was working. Then he heard her say, "I saw you here the other night?"

"Yeah—I got an ice hockey stick in the teeth, knocked out my diamond. That's why I'm here but I'm glad now 'cos I see you— that's why I came round to give you this hockey jersey, see if you want to go with me tomorrow so as you can wear it?"

Then he heard her soft voice say, "That's very kind. I'm sorry though, you see, my back's injured."

This was good, Archall thought, looking down and seeing the wheelchair for the first time. He'd asked her out and she hadn't said she was married to the dentist or anything, and fuck was she beautiful. He said, "You getting better though yeah?"

She was and smiling, she looked him straight in the eyes and said, "I am I think, yes."

Archall nodded, this was good. The girl needed to be able to at least stand if they went out, as hot as she was it wouldn't look cool, him pushing her around, even if she was the sexiest chick there. He said, "You like hockey?"

Alla nodded, the slightest of smiles coming from her gorgeous mouth, her eyes alight.

"You like the Canucks?"

"I do yes. Thank you for the shirt."

Then Archall asked, "The dentist guy, he's your father, is he?"

And without a hint of embarrassment Alla answered, "No, he's my husband."

Archall stood there for a moment not speaking, half looking at the back door to the bullshit surgery and then to Alla; then, pulling his tongue out of the gap in his teeth, he said, "Well I never knew that, so sorry. I asked 'cos you look younger than him, see."

Alla nodded and smiled this time right at him, her eyes holding his, her hair long and curly hanging loose across her shoulders, those high cheekbones. She said, "It's okay. I'm happy with what you say—and don't worry, I can keep a secret."

Then the door to the backroom surgery opened and Dennis came out, saw Archall, looked at Alla, then the shirt and, as Archall looked at the worn runners of the guy in the surgery's chair, heard Alla say, "Dennis, love, this gentleman's brought you a hockey shirt as a gift for you. He was wondering if while he was coming here maybe you could take a look at his wisdom teeth?"

******

Archall Diamond drove back towards his home and looked at his missing front tooth in the rear-view mirror. 'I can keep a secret,' she'd said and given him that look. Then the husband had gone and ruined it coming out like that as though he knew. But she wanted him, he could tell; he'd been saying he was busy pulling a guy's wisdom teeth out back, and her wanting him enough to suggest Archall have his wisdom teeth taken out as well the next day, so as she could see him again. Even if she was in a chair.

He was happy. The conversation had carried on after the dentist had thanked him for the shirt and gone back inside to dig around in some loser's mouth with a pair of pliers. The girl had told him about her back, how she'd damaged it slipping on the stairs and how they were saving for an operation so as she could walk again. All the time staring into his eyes like a school kid flattered he could be interested in her—her not knowing she was beautiful, him telling her and her blushing and looking to the door where her husband was pulling the guy with the shitty worn running shoes' teeth out.

Nina never looked at him like that. She just liked clothes, used him to get them and never said thank you after he'd pounded her for a good couple of minutes; giving it to her, making her come like he could, fast and furious.

'Alla', she'd said, Alla from Europe, sexy Alla, who'd told him she could keep a secret and then told him he'd made her feel like a woman again after he'd told her about this trick he could do with cocoa pops. He smiled at himself in the mirror, feeling like a million dollars, that plastic Paki Rann Singh out there now all smug thinking he'd done him up by kicking out his diamond tooth like he had, but he hadn't—he'd done him a favor. How else would he have met this girl, the one who looked at him the way she did and laughed at his jokes and said she felt comfortable with him, like they'd met before some other time in a previous life?

******

Rann Singh picked up his bag and walked through customs, wondering if anyone else had ever smuggled a shitload of money into Kenya in a turban he no longer needed. How long had it been since he'd last come through this airport? he thought. He'd been a boy, gone to the ranch to see his grandfather and been chased by the zebra that roamed free on their land.

He walked further into the arrivals—the army guards half asleep at the doorway, their Royal Enfield rifles hanging loosely in their arms. The air cool and the clouds in the distance low in the sky, black faces everywhere with cropped hair and their clothes worn thin, women in hugely colored gowns scraping the floor with their flip-flops.

He got a cab and headed along the Uhuru Highway into Nairobi, looking to the Acacia trees out there on the plains in amongst the low white clouds. He stopped at the first car lot he saw, got out and bought the best Land Rover there for twelve thousand dollars cash from a Kikuyu man in a brown suit, threw his small case in the back, and headed up north towards the mountains.

Two hours later, he was there rolling into the small town of Nyeri sitting at the edge of the Aberdare Mountains, driving around in his new ride with its spare tire bolted to the top of the hood and its tough plastic dashboard. One street, then the next, back around again through puddles and chunks of road worn thin, revealing soft red earth. Locals staring with their jet-black faces and cropped hair as they hung out under the shade of a tree or leaned against the front of a store in their trousers and shoes with no socks. The estate agent premises he'd used to seal the house deal there now, its windows clean, covered in pictures of people trying to move on. Getting out, he walked to the window and looked through them all, trying to find his grandfather's ranch, feeling the weight of the ceremonial spear he'd bought from a vendor when he'd stopped to take a piss. He moved his eyes from left to right, scanning the single dwellings, houses large and small, two shops, a small shithole of a hotel, and one ranch, which his grandfather once used to own and which was about to become his.

Smiling, he pulled out his phone, which still worked over here, and called to the shop, listening to the phone ring through the window pane and watching as a colonial came from the back still doing up his fly and answered.

He was at the right place, almost there, he said, "I'm here to buy the ranch."

He hung up the phone, walked inside still carrying the spear in his right hand, and said it again—but this time putting it different.

"I'm here to buy the ranch in cash— and don't worry, I'm just carrying this in case anyone tries to rip me off."

That'll do it, he thought, let them know he meant business. Then he turned to see a man looking at him through the storefront window, his hair cropped tight and his dinner jacket long in the sleeves; and before he could ask, he heard the agent say, "This is your man servant, Joseph, sir. He comes with the home."

******

They drove along the edge of the forest away from town, Joseph in the back of the Land Rover, the estate agent ahead driving his Peugeot, a lawyer sitting next to him now. Rann Singh driving, feeling the road underneath the machine as it ground along, the steering wheel with a life of its own.

It was just as he remembered it—green forest, bush, red earth along the roadside, sunny but not hot, with lower clouds than in Nairobi, and the terrain was flat, even though they were high above sea level. No one for miles, and then just a single figure standing at the side of the road, watching as they passed. *Where the fuck do they come from, these people out there standing doing nothing?* He thought, as they passed another, standing isolated from the world.

"You know that guy?"

Joseph shook his head and answering back in Swahili said, "No Bwana."

Then Rann Singh looked to Joseph saying, "He lives here?"

"No Bwana."

Rann Singh held onto the steering wheel and swung onto the other side of the road avoiding a dead animal. Then asked in English, "How'd you know that if you don't know him."

And Joseph replied, "It is because I know his brother."

Then he does know him. If he knows his brother, he knows him, Rann Singh thought—he couldn't not know him. He looked at this Joseph guy, his new 'man servant' as the real estate man had called him, the guy sitting in the back of his Land Rover like he belonged there and hadn't even been invited for the ride. He said, "If you know his brother how come you don't know him?"

And Joseph answered, "Yes, Bwana this is correct." Then he carried on, taking Rann by surprise, saying, "I know you also Bwana. You have grown but you look just like your father."

They drove for a while longer heading east, the road seeming to never end as it took him along twisting long curves dropping down to quickly rise again until they'd pass another brow of the hill where the forest grew thin, exposing the sharp jagged peaks of the Aberdare Mountains. He asked his new man servant, "You live in the town?"

"No, I live in the ranch, Bwana."

"You get the bus?"

"No bus, Bwana."

"You walked?"

"Yes, Bwana."

Then Joseph smiled, showing off a set of brilliant white teeth, and said, "I left the same day you called to say you were coming."

They reached a small path cut into the ground to the right at the bottom of a hill, a trail started by horses as their hooves ripped at the grasslands, slowly widening over the years once the horses died and the rubber of tires took over, its banks dug deep, smooth from when the rains came, the earth hard, baked and cracked by the sun, a deeper red than back in town.

Rann followed the Peugeot as it carefully wound its way along through the grasslands, the pathway lined by posted wire opening out into occasional gates. It must have been at least a couple of miles now, Rann thought, the forest small now in his rear-view mirror, the mountains high in the sky in the distance. He said, "Who owns this land?"

And Joseph smiled again and told him as he pointed all around, "You do Bwana, you own all this land, this land here, that land there. All the land from the ranch since we left the road."

And then it came back to him, the road and the lane, and how he'd passed along it years ago sleeping as a kid in the back of his grandfather's truck, warm in his mother's lap. Yeah this was it, the bumpy road where he'd smacked his head on the window looking out and after another mile passed, he saw in the distance the outline of the thatched roof of the ranch, its pillared front deck, its manicured garden, the small mud hut village to its right where he'd chased chickens with the local African kids and giggled as they'd hidden from the crazy zebra as it passed through.

They pulled up outside the front of a ranch that was smaller than Rann remembered but still big, the ground beneath them gravel now. The rocks around the flower beds painted white, the grass mown short and precise with a small light aircraft sitting on the lawn. Its owner standing there with a bodyguard on the deck in a safari suit not a lot whiter than his sun parched skin. Calling out to them as they got out, he said in an accent that was unmistakably South African, "So, you the one who's coming to take over the fort?"

They shook hands, the man in his late fifties not looking him straight in the eye and his suitcase ready at the door. The bodyguard ignored them all. The South African said, "Malcolm Blou, I knew your grandfather. How is he?"

"He's good thanks," Rann Singh answered still holding his spear in his right hand.

The South African saying, "You can leave that at the door, the only bandit here's Joseph. You'll have to watch him. You ask for two sugars in your tea, he'll keep one in his pocket for himself. You know what I'm saying?"

Just like you did when you took this place from Granddad, Rann thought as he smiled and walked around the deck looking in the windows, remembering the rooms inside. As the South African opened his brief case, pulling out some paperwork and looking to the agent, he heard Blou say, "Let's get it done so as I can get off."

Rann nodded and walked over and looked at the deeds now spread out ready on the coffee table, and heard Blou say, "I was thinking for another ten grand, you can keep the furniture."

The furniture which you stole from me in the first place, when you fucked over my grandfather, Rann thought.

And the man had—he knew it as much as Rann did. The man now pretending to do him a favor. Rann Singh saying, "Don't worry, grab what you can and stick it in the plane."

Then he looked at the paperwork, the deed of sale reading fifty thousand higher. Rann said, "And you can change that back to what we agreed."

Hearing the South African saying now, "The extras for the African's village, we never settled on that."

Rann took a deep breath. He'd had enough now and he hadn't been here more than five minutes, hadn't even stepped inside yet. He said, "You can fit that in the plane and all if you want." And watched as the Colonial real estate agent stepped away from them both in a bid to stay out of it, then, calmly, the lawyer stepped forward, speaking for the first time, and said, "Mr. Blou, the arrangement was for a quick sale, sir. There are many other properties available, please don't make our journey to yours ineffective."

And they signed the deal. Rann was there, he'd made it. His Sikh god Guru Nanak was looking out for him.

******

Megan sat at her desk in the suite Sebastian had rented for her, drinking herbal tea, and wondered how a script so bad had ever gotten this far. She remembered the face of the guy who'd written it and the night she'd waited his table listening to the bullshit, he and the producers spoke of its 'brilliance'. And now here she was somehow, free of her tight skirt and high heels, trying to make good out of something so bad when she was supposed to be modelling—but what the hell, at least she wasn't taking orders and smiling at assholes who were worth millions.

Patrick had given her carte blanche to do what she liked, so she was going to do just that—all the alien invasion nonsense would be out and time travel would be in, with emphasis on making an aging star look good by using the beauty of a young woman. She doubted 'Marshaa' could remember more than a couple of lines; but at least she looked similar to how Adalia had herself when her skin was tighter than whatever surgeon she was using these days could get it. As for the guy in the silver undies she saw everywhere she looked, time would tell. And as for the nonsense Patrick had last suggested—after he'd been over for another milking session the night before—about making Dan come from another universe, she'd have to lay back and see what the spirits brought to her once she'd breathed some of the scented candles she'd bought from the local herbal store.

Leaning back, she breathed a deep breath, taking in the scent of the candles burning by the window, and took another bite from the last of the special cookies she'd got at the same place. Feeling herself relax, she let her thoughts begin to tumble through her mind as if they were being left there by her own team of time travelers, whipping in and out of her life, dropping gems into a slot in her mind as a child would drop pennies into a piggy bank. And what came to her was just brilliant.

At least it was to her.

Patrick, you see, was beginning to be too much, coming over using her like a sex toy and getting her to use him like one also. Twice it had been now, her watching herself in the mirror, wondering what she was doing there as she milked him like a cow, before taking him as if she was some guy—or one of these butch women she'd seen floating around Vancouver giving her the eye. *Why didn't he go for one of them? But that wouldn't work*, she thought, *would it*? After all it was the feminine form they desired, and he was hardly that. And with that in mind, the story built and the words began to tumble, hitting her hard and fast. She knew now what the story needed, a new twist in the time traveler's tale. It wasn't about time travel—time travel was just the vehicle to carry the story. The story was ultimately all about love, but not just any love. This love was special, it was feminine love centered around girls who wanted to be boys and a lead who searched through time until she ultimately became the boy she always knew she was.

******

Sadly, Patrick still hadn't really read the script before he'd said it was simply brilliant after it landed at his door nearly two days later. He'd read it yes, skimming the pages, looking at the words people said and they said good stuff, really good stuff. They used phrases like, 'I love you, I always have' and 'I've changed for you so as we can have children together now—our children!'

It was brilliant, he'd seen the bit she'd added that he'd suggested with the beautiful girl who couldn't walk—fantastic, incredible, dazzling, the best script he'd ever read. Or not read—yet; or, properly that is, but he would when he got time.

He called Sebastian and said, "You read it? It's brilliant, absolutely amazing. The girls got incredible talent!"

And then listened as Sebastian's voice came through his telephone, which was laying on top of the script in the middle of the coffee shop at full volume for all and sundry to hear and know, without a doubt, that he, Patrick, was a movie producer.

"Has the guy who wrote the original draft got a copy?"

He hadn't. In fact, Patrick had completely forgotten about Rupert Mikes. He said, "He loves it—he's really excited." Then he threw out some names.

"Adalia Seychan's just got a copy, Marshaa's going crazy! And Buffy's just got off the phone with Tom Cruise."

"What?"

That was enough, he had their attention now, the whole café

was listening. Picking up the phone, Patrick took it off speaker, slapped it to his right ear and leaned back, stretching his left arm out above his head and said out loud, "Buffy's talking to Tom, he's all over it—can't wait to get started."

And heard Sebastian say back, bringing him down to earth, "All over what Patrick? We can't afford anymore names. Besides you're not proven yet. You won't get names till you're proven. You were lucky to get Adalia Seychan as it is."

And Patrick thought, *you're getting luck mixed up with bullshit*—and in his book, the two seldom went together. Everything was concocted, even if he was shooting from the hip and flying blind, which, of course, was how he'd made himself rich. He said, "Adalia's so excited."

"You said she just got the copy, so she probably hasn't read it yet," Sebastian said, then carried on, "you need to remember, Patrick, I'm having as much fun as you are just watching you have fun, but I know you Patrick—so don't get too carried away."

Sebastian put down the phone and, picking up Fluffy, walked to the window and looked outside to Mazzi Hegan's red Ferrari out in the parking lot. *Was it all getting too much*, this makeover he was allowing Patrick to indulge in at his expense? For the movie, no probably not, signing Marsha was still the hidden bonus to all this nonsense. He'd steer the ship in when the time came and all would come good. After all, look what had happened with the 'BlueBoy' campaign and you couldn't have gotten crazier than that. Besides, Fluffy was getting on, so he may as well have a bit of fun. Running his hand across the little dog's head, he gently squeezed Fluffy's ears just the way he liked it and looked back out to the carpark to see Chendrill arrive in his Aston, then waited and watched as the big guy and Dan got out.

They sat in Sebastian's office, Chendrill with his backside against the window ledge, Dan in the comfy chair with his feet up.

Sebastian back behind his desk. It was good to see them both. He said, "Dan's mother's not happy you're saying?"

She wasn't, she'd found the latest version of the script obviously thrown across the room and laying within inches of the previous version on the floor and decided to give it a go. Chendrill carried on, "Yeah, she's crying. I said I'd come down here and speak with you myself."

Dan's mother was crying? This wasn't good, Sebastian thought and stood and walked over, placing his hand on Dan's shoulder as if it was him who was upset and said to him, "Is she okay? What on earth could it be that has done this?"

And before Dan could say a word, Chendrill answered for him, "Dan's good, he doesn't care—he just came because I said I'd take him to McDonalds on the way back."

"Oh?"

"Yeah she was crying because she's worried about Dan getting into something that's going to stay with him all his life. You know with all these posters of him up everywhere—it's a mother thing."

Then Dan piped up, his voice as nonchalant as a kid in his late teens could get. He said, "She's worried about me playing it out as a girl who wants to be a guy who travels in time and comes back from a hundred years in the future with a mechanical dick and a big one at that."

Sebastian stared at him for a moment trying to take it all in. Then simply said, "What?"

And Dan said, "Yeah that's what I thought when I read it, but I'm getting used to being pointed at now since you got me plastered all over town in Mazzi's underpants. So what the hell. Besides, it ain't that bad to be honest, it could be cool."

Sebastian stared at them both. Chendrill shrugged his shoulders saying, "I haven't read this version."

Then Sebastian said, "Neither have I, but I will this evening."

Then Dan said, "Truth is, it's better now though than the other piece of shit. It's got this hot sexy chick in it and all who can't walk and gets taken through time by Patrick so as she can walk again."

"Patrick?" Sebastian asked, the surprise in his voice unmistakeable.

And Dan said, "Yeah, he's in it as well. He's got a guest role, he's in love with her and gives her his spine. At least it's original."

Chapter Thirty-Five

Archall Diamond sucked on the place where his trademark tooth used to be, then stared at his mouth in the mirror. His wisdom teeth were at the back. He knew that much because that was where your brain was and that's where his biology teacher had told him wisdom came from—telling him he needed to get some and stop putting the lab mice to death with the switchblade he carried so everyone at school would know he was cool.

The thought of having them out was worrying him. After all, there was nothing wrong with them and they weren't hurting like his new girl said they were. But she obviously needed an excuse to see him again and that's why she'd said it, but now it had escalated and the dentist was scheduling him in to pull them, saying it was best and that he needed to get them out or they'd cause problems for the others and he didn't need that with him having the new one put in at the front like he was. *What a fucking dilemma.*

He moved away from the mirror in the bathroom and opened another packet of tablets he'd bought off the plastic Paki made for him by the Swedish scientist professor guy and popped another tablet. He liked the way they made him feel happy and also liked the feel of his dick getting hard in his pants as it pushed against his jeans. She'd like that as well, Alla would, he could go in there to the dentist's basement and hang out, tell the guy his wisdom teeth were playing up and getting sore and she could see his dick in his jeans.

He'd do that, show it to her, turn her on.

Then he got the call from Steven, who said, "You're right. This guy Chendrill's been checking you out."

And he had been, Chendrill out there, making some calls, digging into stuff, poking his nose around. And now Steven on the end of the phone letting him know so. Archall Diamond said, "What's he been saying?"

"Wants to know if Paawan was fucking your girl."

"Well he weren't."

"He was also seen down looking around your boat."

Fuck me, Archall Diamond thought as he wandered around the kitchen feeling his dick swelling at the same rate as the lump in his stomach. He said, "Well it's a good boat."

And heard Steven say back down the phone, "Yeah but he wasn't trying to buy it. He wanted to know when you last used it. They keep records, you know?"

"Who does?"

"The guys at the marina, in and out and all that, they the ones who told me, said he's got a nice car."

He did, Archall thought. But if he had one, he'd change the wheels and get some LED rigged underneath. It was all good, he thought, yeah he'd drowned that flashy fucking birdman, yeah he had, but he hadn't used the boat. He'd just used that to work out the current flow of the riptide as it sucked everything out into the sound. He'd used his pickup, stuck him in that after he'd let the jack go on the motherfucker as he tried to skate under the car after he'd waited there in the garage listening to the guy fuck his girl upstairs, her pretending to come like she had, then after the pair of them laughing, giggling like school kids.

Then Paawan coming out the back way through the garage thinking Archall had gone on a run into the interior, dropping a package for another gang and scoring thirty grand like he did for doing nothing but keeping ten above the speed limit. Him standing there in the garage like he just got home, catching the birdman by surprise, then telling him how he just got the Merc lowered and the new LED's put in, wondering if he'd like him to jack it up so he could crawl under to have a look, see if the guy would do that and try to whip out the other side like a rat or try and get past Archall standing there big and strong with a wrench in his hand. He couldn't get over the top because Archall had blocked that up as well, hanging heavy metal objects from hooks drilled into the ceiling. The birdman played it cool like it was normal for him to be at Diamond's place with his girl at four in the morning, then taking a look, seeing the glow from the neon underneath the chassis as Archall turned it on, he said to Archall, "Yeah, they look good, how many you got?"

Archall had told him, "they'se all LED diodes, RGBW's, can give you's any color you's wants depending on ya mood." Archall jacked up the car a little more, giving the guy a taste of freedom under the vehicle, showing him the door, knowing he'd take it, remembering how fast the fucker was when they were kids and how the guy could whip himself under a moving freight train for fun—in one side, out the other, then back again as twenty tons of steel passed above him.

Then the birdman, quicker than he thought, bent down looking at the lights, and moved like a rocket. Archall Diamond's hand fumbled for the hydraulic trolley jack's release and twisted its lever around quickly, thinking the fucker had got away. But he hadn't. When Archall had walked around to look, the guy was there, stuck right at the edge like a rat in a trap who'd almost made it, the birdman right there on the garage floor unable to breathe as the weight of the Merc with its tinted windows and low-profile tyres and super sexy LED lights on the bottom crushed the air from his body until he went unconscious.

Then he'd been quick, just in case his girl came down. Jacking the car up again, he pulled the birdman from underneath and lifted him as he struggled to breathe into the back of his pickup truck—with its enclosed roof and inner tubes, pump and chains inside—sliding him in next to them, closing the back, and quietly driving off out towards the Fraser River.

The sun was nearly up when he arrived, Paawan in the back, out cold, but still breathing. The river flowing fast, pulling debris from along its banks as the ocean's riptide sucked the fresh water from its veins. He opened the back, putting the inner tube over the birdman's head and securing it tight under his arms, connected the electric pump, turned it on, and listened to the little motor whirring away, blowing it up tight around Paawan's chest as he secured the chain around the flying man's feet until the tube was right under the guy's arms—the tube now looking as though it would pop. He covered the birdman with camo netting, wrapped another tube around his feet, blew it up, then pulled out a pin he'd taped to the inside of the window and pricked three small holes in the tube below the birdman's face, then another six in the one around his feet. He dragged him out into the mud at the side of the bank, getting his feet wet, and pushed Paawan out into the water, let him go into the current, then watched as the water took him away.

Then Archall said to Steve on the other end of the phone, "I ain't drowned no one, right." And in his mind, he hadn't—he'd just floated the guy off and if he couldn't swim, it was his problem, even if he did have a punctured lung and a chain wrapped around his feet.

As Archall Diamond pulled on his dick through his jeans, he heard Steven say back, "You're the only one who's ever mentioned drowning."

"Yeah, well he probably thinks it if he's asking about my boat."

Then Steven went quiet and, starting to get really worried, said after the longest pause, "Like I said before, you're fucked if you think you been clever and gone and done something stupid."

******

Charles Chuck Chendrill had been snooping. He'd been digging around into Archall Diamond's past. So far, he'd been told Diamond had worked for Rasheed, which he already knew, but some were saying he'd been trying to carry on where Rasheed had left off. Somehow Archall Diamond had gotten hold of Rasheed's funds and was renegotiating deals; and at the same time, it seemed as though he was giving away what Chendrill could only surmise were the blackmailer's pills, which had somehow made it into the country despite Malcolm Strong's breakdown and subsequent confession. He'd heard nothing about a feud between Paawan and him though, and nothing about Diamond's girl Nina and Paawan. Although good sources had said she'd flown the coop just like Rann Singh the blackmailer—but that wasn't surprising.

He'd done something though, Chendrill knew it. He felt it in his bones when he'd met him and heard him talk. It was just a matter of time before all the pieces of the puzzle came together; had he still been on the force, he'd have already brought the guy in and let him talk his way into a life sentence behind bars. But times change.

He took the highway out of town and watched his speed over the bridge. There was another guy he'd heard about and wanted to chat to, someone who'd hung with them when they were kids, but got away from it all, gaining a scholarship and taking himself off to university. And now he worked as a pharmacist for a franchise in White Rock. Word had it that Steven was now Diamond's counsellor and the first thing he saw in the man's face as he looked up and spotted Chendrill walking through the sliding door and up the aisle towards him, was fear—fear first, then panic as he passed the toothpaste, resignation at the condoms, and finally just as Chendrill breezed by the hairbrushes and reached the counter, acceptance. Then before Chendrill managed to say a word, Steven blurted out, "It's not illegal to talk to someone, right?"

And Chendrill said, "Depends what you've been talking about." Steven told him Diamond had approached him, getting him to look at the pills, breakdown their medicinal quality; then, he asked if he could mix them with baby powder or laxative like he'd heard the big boys did so as he could double his yield.

Chendrill kept quiet, listening, Steven doing all the talking as they sat on a wall out front. Chendrill using up the man's break time.

"I said you can't mess with perfection. There's nothing bad in them, just herbs. There's not even any Sildenafil in them— although apparently even the guy who sold them to Archall thinks there is. Besides, they were already packaged. I said just sell them and get more, you know they work, whatever herbs this guy from Cape Town put in them work miracles."

Chendrill said, "I'd heard the guy who made them was from Stockholm?"

"Wherever, I think Archall's given almost all of them away. I haven't even seen the man more than three times and two of them were on the same day. He just keeps calling, said I'd be getting ten grand a month just for counsel."

"Counsel for what?"

"Stupid stuff like finding a dentist."

"Really—for that tooth?"

"You'd take that, wouldn't you? I'm no different than some smart mouthed lawyer saying 'yes', 'no', 'do this', 'do that'. I'm not the one doing anything illegal."

And Chendrill said it again, "Depends what else you've been talking about." Then he carried on and dropped the bomb right there and then to see what the man's face would do when he heard him say,

"What did you tell him to do after he dropped Paawan's body out at sea?"

Steven felt as though he was about to throw up. *Fuck*, what had he done getting involved with such a shithead as Archall Diamond? If he'd paid him ten grand a week instead, it wasn't enough to be feeling as frightened as he was now. And he hadn't even done anything. He said, "Diamond didn't like Paawan there was no secret there. We all thought he was cool when we were kids, you know the way he danced with death, cool and stupid at the same time, throwing himself under the freight trains like he did. Diamond tried it once, trying to keep up with the guy. Got under the first wheel and then froze, thought he'd have the courage, as Paawan made it look so easy. But Diamond couldn't move, his body wouldn't let him I suppose. He started crying and all Paawan kept saying was lie flat, you're cool, lie flat and let it pass; and when it did we see he was okay, and he'd just pissed himself with fear—that's all. We all laughed till we cried, but Paawan didn't. He felt sorry for him, put his arm round him. Diamond fucked him off though and has hated him ever since. Paawan was a good guy, wouldn't hurt a fly."

And all Chendrill said was, "Was?"

And then Steven went silent, staring at the floor. Then looking up said, "Yeah—was. I'm not certain, but something inside tells me you're not wrong."

******

Archall Diamond stood outside the front of his house and stared at his low rider Mercedes with its tinted windows and duck pond for a roof. It wasn't going to do, not with having a classy girl like he did now—even if she was married and couldn't walk at the moment. He needed to get it fixed if he was going to impress her once she got out from the surgery and left the loser backstreet dentist who was going to make him light up the room with his new front tooth. *Light up the room*, he thought. Light up Alla real good, as well, with his smile like the old days—one that could lift her out of that chair and carry her off to his new pink, terracotta-lion-guarded super mansion home he rented in Surrey.

He pulled the phone from his pocket and felt the tug on his dick. He dialed Steven and when he answered said, "I need to find a place that can sort out this roof on my Mercedes. I was thinking of going to one of those car wrecking places where they have those big magnets and strapping the car down to the ground, swinging the magnet over the top and let the magnet pull the dent out so as we don't chip the paint. You know, just like those miracle dent guys do who the dealers use to make their cars look cool again. What do you think?"

Steven sat there on the wall, with his phone in his hand on speaker phone for Chendrill to hear and looked at him. There was no doubt between the two that the guy was a moron. Steven said into the speaker, looking to Chendrill as he did, "Yeah that should do the trick."

They both heard Archall Diamond say back, "Yeah I thought so—so you going to find me one then? Make it a big one, tell the guy I'll pay it in cash."

"What about the place on Annacis Island called Joe's? They've got a big magnet on a crane there," Steven said, still looking at Chendrill like they were friends, and hearing Diamond say 'thanks' and hang up. He said, "See that's all I do, just answer stupid questions, that's all."

******

Rann Singh sat on the deck with his feet up and watched as the lawyer and estate agent and the South African stood by his two-seater plane and argued about commission, the bodyguard already on board waiting with his feet hanging out the small door, and Rann Singh sitting there proud, knowing he'd fulfilled his dreams and bought the ranch back—he'd done it, the ranch, the furniture, the village and all the land that came with it that ran for miles, stopping only at the road where the forest rested at the foot of the mountains.

Rann Singh's Sikh god Guru Nanak was looking out for him.

Malcolm Blou had been a prick. He'd tried to rip him off as he was now doing with the other guys, but he'd appreciated cash, the $200,001 Canadian in cash hidden away wrapped in the folds of a turban Rann Singh no longer needed to wear.

He had his grandfather's home now and the sawed-off shotgun the South African had given to him as a parting gift. Placing it by the door and mumbling to Joseph said, "Here give this to the *Choot*, tell him he'd better keep it close—he's going to need it."

Rann could see the relief in the man's eyes as he headed towards his plane, making his exit as quickly as possible with the other two following. The guy was getting the hell out. He looked at Joseph standing there now wearing an off-white coat.

"What's he running from?"

"The men come from the forest in the night-time, Bwana, and come to his room and tell him they kill him, Bwana, if he does not give money—it is nothing."

"Nothing?"

"Yes, Bwana."

"Like the Mau Mau?"

"No Bwana, before when the Mau Mau come here they kill—not talk about kill. They kill the family before your grandfather came, this is why he buy the ranch cheap."

Rann Singh let out a deep breath, the discovery of an unexpected truth making him laugh a little inside. His grandfather never mentioning the blood of the previous owners soaked in and staining the wooden flooring forever. But that was history, long before he was born, and every building holds a secret. He said, "Tell me more about these men."

"These men come in the night and wake him, stand round his bed with the *pangar* and tell him give them money. He give them money and next month they come back and ask him again. He'd say no and they slash him across his chest."

"Really?"

"Yes Bwana, they live in the forest, like the Mau Mau—but not the Mau Mau."

Then Rann Singh said, "Well you can tell these men who live in the forest that my doors are open and if they step inside, they'll be paying me not to kill them. And I ain't fucking kidding."

Then he said, "And what did he say to you just before, I got the bit about the gun but missed the other.

"He called you a *Choot*, Bwana, I hear this—same as women's vagina, Bwana."

Rann knew what a *Choot* was, didn't need the explanation. He was a Punjabi Indian after all. Standing there, he looked to the man climbing into the cab of the airplane and watched the other two walk away towards their cars all red in the face from arguing as the single engine aircraft started and began to immediately taxi along the garden, speed up, and lift off in a flash, disappearing into the sky. Without the faintest bit of a goodbye, it was gone.

Turning to Joseph as he sat back down, Rann said, "Well he's lucky he had that plane to escape in after calling me a cunt."

Seconds later, the agent and the lawyer were back on the deck, the noise of the Cessna faint in the distance, each holding their briefcases full of their cut tight to their thighs. With the smile of a man who'd just had a decent payout, the agent said, "Well he's always been a tricky one has Mr. Blou, but that's sorted now though then, isn't it. The place, my good man, is all yours."

Rann stood and smiled, it was, it was all his. He said, "I thought the ranch came with a zebra?"

Joseph standing there proud in place answered for them.

"Zebra died sir."

"You promised a zebra." And still smiling, the lawyer held out his hand in the sense that the deal was done regardless of the lack of any black and white animals. And as he shook Rann's hand he winked, and with a grin said again, "Zebra died, sir."

Turning, he walked to the car followed by the estate agent and opening the door called out, swatting a fly from his face as he spoke, "It's what happens here, things get eaten old chap!"

And with that, they were gone.

Chapter Thirty-Six

It was just after two thirty in the afternoon when Archall Diamond dropped the Mercedes off at the wreckers and asked the owner, who's name wasn't Joe, standing there with his unshaven face and greasy white muscle shirt, if he'd be able to lock the wheels to the ground and suck out the dent in the roof with the industrial electromagnet he had on his crane without damaging the paint.

The guy, who hadn't made it out of high school but was still rich, said, "Yeah no problem we can try—one hundred cash."

Archall, putting his hand in his pocket, gave him two for good measure. The man waved to his brother in the crane to swing the magnet above the Mercedes. Archall watched it come, asking if he should take his computer out of the trunk in case the magnet destroyed the hard drive and wondering how they were going to hold the wheels to the ground, and then watching as the magnet came down, landing hard on top of the car, carried it off through the air, and dropped it in the crusher in one smooth motion. The guy in his shirt waved his arms, running and shouting as Archall stood there with his mouth open in disbelief, listening as the crusher got to work.

That's when he got the call from Dennis that his front tooth was ready and there was no hurry, but he could fit him in this afternoon if he was free. Archall Diamond was happy and upset at the same time—he was going to see his girl, but he'd have to use the truck he used to deliver dope to the boonies—and to drop rivals-in-love in the river so they could be carried on the riptide out into the ocean to drown. Trying to sound cool, he said, "Yeah, I've got a problem with the car at the moment, but I think I can make it."

The problem being that all the money he had left in the world, some quarter of a million dollars after Rann Singh had fleeced him, was sitting in the back of his Mercedes, which had just dropped out the back of the crusher in the shape of a four-foot cube.

******

"Which bit do you think is the back?" Archall Diamond asked the guy in the greasy muscle shirt and a black eye as he lowered the now cubed Mercedes off the jib of his tow truck into Archall's two car garage. Archall stared at his ride, thinking he could make out the shape of his low profiles as he watched it land, and heard the guy say, "Why you got something in it you need?"

Thinking the guy was a moron, Archall said, "Yeah I got my sandwiches in the trunk and I'm hungry."

Then he told the guy to fuck off and got to work with the industrial metal grinder the man had given him, sending sparks across the ground everywhere, cutting out six inch chunks, working out in fine detail for the better part of an hour how he was going to float the stupid fuck in the crane who destroyed his ride until he found the bag.

Three hours later, he was there standing outside Dennis's basement suite all cleaned up with his hair combed back and covered in coconut oil. As the door opened he said, "I left the Mercedes up the road, you know, cause I know your neighbors got feelings."

"You got it fixed then?" Dennis asked as he let him in.

"Kind of," Archall said as he looked around the place for his new love, smiling as he saw her sitting there barefoot on the sofa with a blanket over her lap and the bottom of her long skinny legs showing—looking at him like they had a connection. Dennis was saying that his tooth was looking fantastic and, not hearing, Archall just said, "Yeah."

He lay on the recliner chair, the light in his face, Alla's feet visible in the corner of his eye through the crack in the door. *I could float the fucker*, he thought, as he felt the small pipe sucking away the spit and blood, smelling the latex gloves Dennis was wearing as he rooted around in Archall's mouth, trying to make him look cool again whilst he fucked around with his shiny tools.

He'd do it, he thought, let him finish, make sure he was looking good with his diamond back in, pick his moment, and float the fucker. Then he'd come back sparkling to get his wisdom teeth done all innocent like and let his girl cry on his shoulder about how the dentist with the bad breath hadn't come home. Then he'd say, 'Come with me, I'll look after you—live at my palace in Surrey and we can work on how we gonna find you the best back surgeon in the world, so as we can get you fixed up again and go to the hockey game.'

Two hours later, he was done, sitting there in the recliner smiling with his eyes at the man he was planning to drown and at the same time staring at his diamond studded front tooth planted firm and secure in his gum.

Fuck, he thought, it looked perfect—better than before. He said, "It looks like a million dollars."

Dennis smiled, knowing he'd done good work, looking at the man's gum line, seeing it had only slightly receded despite the trauma. He said, "Like I said, it's not the glossy surgery that works on your teeth. It's the guy holding the tools."

Yeah whatever, Archall thought, *you'll be feeling fishes' teeth soon enough*, as he held out his hand and shook Dennis' then turned, moving to get a better look at Alla's legs through the door. He said, lying, "I'm feeling a little faint. Do you mind if I sit in the living room for a moment whilst I come round? Then I'll sort

303

out your fee."

He sat down opposite Alla on a small wicker chair and stared at her eyes, my God she was beautiful—her long wavy hair, her shoulders, her beautiful thick and full lips. She'd look good in his car—if he had one, he thought. Then she spoke to him, saying, "Your tooth looks good. I like that diamond—it looks expensive."

It should, it was. It had cost him what he'd earned for two trips to Alberta in his pickup loaded with dope, the same as his Mercedes that was now sitting shaped like a cube in his garage. He said, "Yeah it cost a bit. But you got to look good, haven't you."

Alla smiled, pulling up her blanket to show off her legs which she wished she could move. This guy sitting there now, this wannabe gangster who couldn't take his eyes off her and was about to come on to her. She said, her voice almost in a whisper, "It suits you, you are very handsome." Archall Diamond heard her words and got a woody—even though he'd forgotten to take a pill like he'd wanted to. Then she said, "Maybe when I'm better, we can go out, like you said?"

Fuck me, Archall thought, his heart racing now. He wasn't wrong, he'd felt it, felt the connection between them, knew it right from the start when he'd flirted with her and told her about this trick he could do with the cocoa pops. She wanted to see him do it, just as much as he wanted to show her how he could also catch two. Then before he could speak, he heard her say in the softest of whispers, her eyes looking to the floor, "Once I have my operation that is."

Archall nodded. He got it, she was saying she was his once she was better. Then, looking back up at him, she said, "You'll come back to get your wisdom teeth done won't you, like you said?"

Maybe I'll bash the dentist over the head and float the fucker now, Archall thought, be done with it and save the toothache. It was a full moon right now and there was a high tide going out every seven hours.

He said, "Yeah, don't worry, I'll do that. It's important we see each other, right?"

And it was important, important at least to him.

******

Sebastian sat down on the large deck of his penthouse suite with a nice piece of cake and a cup of tea, reading the latest version of the movie Patrick had somehow convinced him to fund.

What on earth the man thought he was doing he didn't know and chances are he hadn't even read it himself, the whole thing being so absurd. A lesbian hippy finds a time machine and goes off into the future in search of an advanced sex change so good that she could father a child?

It could work, he thought—stranger things had happened. There was a long way to go still and if he was lucky, it would fizzle out as these things did sometimes. Patrick was good, though, he thought. Getting himself written in as the good guy for purposes of self-promotion so as he could hit the talk shows and everyone in Hollywood would know what he looked like. He was clever, he'd give him that.

Mazzi, though, was another issue, meeting this guy like he had—this clone. Coming into work late all black under the eyes, and his work suffering in the process.

He plopped the script down on the table and took a sip of his tea from a cup with the most delicate of handles from a set he'd found and picked up at a small market in Beijing.

He had an idea though for Adalia Seychan and it had only come to him after he'd taken his first bite of cake a few minutes prior. She was still gorgeous, after all; she still had that classic style that was almost gone and forgotten, as were so many antiquities these days. Not that she was old, because she wasn't, not by any means. But she had classic style and that's what he would use and tap into to sell business class seats on any airline who cared to listen and wanted to be stylish again. Just like in the old days when the world of travel was still a mystery, when propeller planes roared off into the sunset landing in a far-off land where the air was hot when the doors opened and you smelled the burned aviation fuel in your nostrils before the aromas of spice and flora floated in on the night air.

He'd send her around the world with Mazzi photographing her using sepia filters at sunset and dawn; traveling, as they once had with small umbrellas and white flowing gowns to keep out the heat, he would make her look glamourous and exotic. He would use her timeless beauty and capture her essence, and let the spirit of the far-off lands captivate her audience. The two of them would make it exotic to fly again—not like it had become these days in that bargain basement way; rather, it would be like how it was when journey was more luxurious than the trip itself, with incredible food served to you on fine china plates while you relaxed in chairs that were so soft you'd not want to get up. And Adalia Seychan would be the flagship lady, leading the way as she crossed mysterious lands in comfort and style.

He'd talk to her once Patrick had talked her into coming for some test shoots with Dan—have her looking and feeling sexy with a young man, he thought, pitch it to her then out of the blue in a way that she knew she couldn't refuse should someone else get the gig and steal the thunder that could have been hers. Then he'd draw up a promo on spec and let the airlines and ad agencies come running. And they would, for what he'd offer would be 'Timeless'.

******

Mazzi Hegan opened his second bottle of tequila of the night, stood on his coffee table, and, using the small little funnel he'd squeezed into the top, poured it all over his chest so as the guy that Einer had picked up at the bar—one inch taller than the classification of a midget and wearing leather chaps and a waist coat—could lick it off.

All three of them there in Mazzi's penthouse suite making a mess and getting hard and happy popping the pills Einer had scored for free from the East Indian guy he met at the beach on the night of the fireworks.

There was no doubt about it, Mazzi was a wreck and loving every minute of it. He called out, "Spank that midget's ass, spank his ass cowboy." And whooped and hollered as he watched Einer do just that.

And that's when the police came politely knocking at the door asking them to keep it down as it was ten in the evening and there were people who wanted to go to sleep. And Mazzi told them what he thought, standing up on the coffee table, "Well - tell - them - to - go - get - a - fucking - life!" And jumping down, he moved his hand across the front of his Bang and Olufsen stereo and turned the music up. At midnight, they called again, and then again at three a.m. Right in the middle of making love to Dan's mother, Charles Chuck Chendrill got a call to meet Samuel Gadot, Sebastian's lawyer, who was at the police station so he could bail Mazzi Hegan out. And when he got there, the first thing Gadot said to him was, "We need to tread carefully. Hegan's told one of the cops who booked him to suck his cock."

"Told him or asked him?" Chendrill replied. There was a difference.

"Good point," Samuel Gadot said, as they saw Mazzi coming through the door, looking worse for wear in just a pair of skin tight trousers and no shoes. Chendrill asked, "What about the other guy? And the midget Sebastian was telling me about?"

Gadot said, "Only Mazzi was arrested."

And he heard Mazzi Hegan say, "Yeah, I'm the only one there who was hot for a cop."

They drove back in silence, rain on the windshield. Hegan in the back like a pop star who's gone and embarrassed himself again. Chendrill thinking about how Sebastian had asked him ever so nicely if he could let Mazzi know his antics weren't reflecting well on the firm. It was above his pay scale, he'd said— he wasn't in human resources. And that's when he heard what he thought was a quiver in Sebastian's voice as he said, "But maybe he'll listen to you Chuck, he's not listening to me," and he could tell Sebastian was really getting worried.

So he said, "Mazzi, you know this doesn't look good on Sebastian or the firm."

Without even looking up, Mazzi snapped back, "Yeah and I'm part of the 'firm' and you're hired to drive, so fuck off."

And that's when Chendrill pulled up at the side of the road, got out of the car, opened the door, and, with his hands clasped firmly under Mazzi's sweaty armpits, dragged him out onto the pavement and left him lying there.

Chendrill drove back through the city and wondered if this time the incident would cost him more than a trip to the department store to get a new plate. He looked around as he stopped at a light, wondering what Hegan had done with himself.

Then he pulled away. If the guy was big enough to tell him to fuck off, he was big enough to deal with what came after, even if it was raining; and if it cost him the contract, so be it. At least he could look himself in the mirror. The guy was being an idiot, getting himself arrested, getting everyone out of bed, and then telling the guy who was taking him back home—to fall asleep long before Chendrill himself would—to fuck off. Yeah, he wasn't wrong, not at all.

He carried on through the night feeling his ribs and wondering about the turbaned karate kid and why he'd thrown Diamond under the bus the way he had. It wasn't a bad thing, but blackmailers would usually thrive on shit like that, then turn them in, making a buck first. The guy was gone, though—there was little doubt there, gone and out of his hair and all he'd cost him really was time, a new paint job for Hegan's ride, and a bruised throat from a couple of round house kicks straight out of a kung fu movie.

He reached Dan's place, let himself in through the back, and crept along the landing to Dan's mother's room. Dan's light was still on at four in the morning—either he was asleep, watching smut, or inventing circuitry. Moments later, he was back in bed feeling the warmth of Trish's back against his chest, feeling his moustache on her shoulder and the movement of her backside pushing up and against his crotch, asking him without words to take her.

He kissed her neck and held her stomach with his hands, feeling her move against him, making him grow below. She reached her hands down and grasped him, holding him for a moment before putting him inside herself. He lifted his hands, holding her shoulders, pushing her down onto him, her hair in his face as he kissed her neck. Pushing himself into her, thrusting into her, she moaned as he reached the top and felt her smoothness. Then she began to groan as he pushed harder, quickening with

309

every thrust, then the banging came from below, getting louder with every groan—bang, bang, bang, bang—Chendrill feeling her, Trish feeling him, and feeling the sensation of his mouth as he began to bite down into her shoulder and push her harder onto him. She groaned as he pounded harder—bang, bang, bang, bang went the floor as Dan smacked his broomstick against the ceiling above his bed, trying to shut them up.

******

Rann Singh sat on his deck of his new ranch and stared out at the women in the garden bending down with their brushes made of twigs sweeping the lawn. The endless fields beyond that were now his family's again stretched all the way to the forest at the foot of the mountains with their jagged peaks that cut a dark ragged line across a perfect sky.

The kids from the small village were there now playing barefoot as their parents had before with him—just as he remembered, throwing stones and chasing chickens. Joseph readily on hand with a tea or a Tusker, standing by not far away in his white top that could do with a wash. The breeze, fresh and clean, coming down from the jagged mountain through the forest and along the endless fields, blowing the long colorful skirts of the women from the village as they bent down to sweep the lawn with brushes made from twigs and fallen branches. Life was good.

He took a deep breath and looked around. The long endless unmoving fields that were now his, the forest beyond that stretched for miles reaching up to the jagged peaks etched in darkness across a perfect blue sky. He looked to them, watching them as the clouds skirted their peaks which ripped up into the heavens above. He closed his eyes taking it all in, waiting, relaxing, his feet up on the stool, head back, eyes opening to the mountains and their peaks, the forest below, the endless fields that were now proudly his, the wind playing with the colorful gowns of the women from the villages as they chatted, bending, looking to him with their small flirtatious smiles as they swept, their children still there and barefoot playing at the side of the village chasing chickens and throwing stones, Joseph waiting patiently for his next command.

Fuck he was bored, he thought as he looked back to the mountains for what seemed the hundredth time. Then he took another deep breath, spun his turban-less head around to Joseph and said, "You got any white women around here?"

"No Bwana. No white women."

"None."

Joseph shook his head and said again, "No Bwana."

"Really?"

"Yes Bwana, the coast Bwana."

"How far is that?"

"One day driving, Bwana. No good for you, the women there want us men, Bwana."

"Us men, you mean black men?"

"Yes Bwana. Your penis is too small."

Rann laughed, the cheeky bastard standing there on his deck telling him he had a small dick. He said, "You saying I got a small dick?"

"Yes Bwana."

"How'd you know that?" Rann asked, still dumbfounded at the man.

Then seeing Joseph nod to the women on the lawn and hearing him say as he showed off his teeth, "The women, they say, your grandfather had a small penis, so you have a small penis also, Bwana. It is called heredity. I say this to you with knowledge as it is a fact of nature, Indian men are not big, Bwana. African men are big, Bwana, it is a fact. To say this is the truth."

Ignoring this, Rann sat watching the women in the garden for a while longer. It didn't matter to him how big anyone thought his dick was, he had plenty of satisfied customers. Besides, he had done what he had set out to do—he had his grandfather's ranch back—the one he'd spent the last ten or so years wanting to return to and now he had. His grandfather, his grandmother, him and whoever else from the family wanted to come and live or stay could because he'd done it, the family ranch was theirs again and with an excited smile and tears welling up in his eyes, Rann pulled out his phone, looked at the time, did the math and, smiling, said to Joseph, "Well I'm calling Grandad now and when he gets here in a few days' time, we can have this conversation again."

Then feeling his heart beating hard in his chest and waiting patiently for him to answer, Rann listened to the sound of his grandfather's phone ringing in the U.K. in his ear, and burst into tears as he heard his grandfather's voice on the other end of the phone.

It had been a really long journey. He said, "Grandad, it's Rann."

And heard his grandfather's voice rise as he heard him say back, "Rann? Is this you?"

"Yes Grandad, it's me. How are you?"

"I am good, I am good. How are you? Where are you now?"

And then Rann took a deep breath and heard himself say the words he'd longed to say for so many years.

"Grandad, I am in Kenya, in Nyrie by the Aberdare Mountains, on the edge of the forest, at your ranch."

"What—you are at the ranch?"

"Yes, I'm the owner now, I've bought it back for you. You can come home!"

There was silence for a moment and then he heard his grandfather say, "Rann, are you playing with me?"

Rann shook his head and stood, beginning to walk back and forth along the deck, feeling the wooden planks give as he moved, saying, "No, No I'm not joking. I've got it, I bought it this morning from Blou! He's gone in his plane and it's ours again, I'm with Joseph—you can come home!"

Then he waited and heard his grandfather say, "How much you pay Rann?"

Rann replied, "It doesn't matter. All that matters is that you call the movers and I'll book you and Grandmother two first class tickets one way to Nairobi, because Grandad, you're coming home."

And then his Grandfather said, "Rann, your Grandmother and I are old now and our lives are here in Hounslow, in England, Rann."

Rann heard himself say, "But I've got it, I've your ranch back, Grandad. I've got it, it's yours again."

His grandfather said, "Our lives are here, Rann."

"But I bought it for you."

"You be happy there, Rann."

"But I bought it for you," Rann said again and heard his grandfather's voice say, "You should have asked, Rann."

"It's all you ever talked about though—it's all you ever said."

Rann's Grandfather saying now, "You should have asked Rann. You have always been this way, jumping the gun—it is a lesson one must learn. Thank you, call again. I have to go, I want to watch the TV."

And with that he was gone, along with all of Rann's dreams.

Chapter Thirty-Seven

Archall Diamond stood in the bathroom of his monster home in Surrey and looked at his new front tooth in the mirror. *Fuck it looked good*, sparkling in the light like it was. Slapping a little coconut gel on, he fucked with his hair and, closing his mouth, he turned to the side, looking away, then spun his head back again, opening his mouth with a smile. Bam! He was back, Archall Diamond—Gangster.

Walking out, he looked at his large king size bed with Rasheed's black sheets and the last of his money, some two hundred and fifty thousand odd dollars, all spread above the covers and a few hundred packets of hard-on pills he had yet to give away. Putting on his sunglasses, he lifted his gun, which he couldn't shoot straight, and started taking selfies with his phone— him with his piece, his money on the bed, and his new front tooth. He was Gangsta, Gang-sta man, Archall Di a Mond—Gang, Gang, Gang -Staaa.

He walked back, sweeping stale cocoa pops onto the floor, and propped his phone up on his dresser mirror, getting a good shot of it all, then he hit the video button and leaning down into the lens showing off his new tooth and gun and stash of money and drugs, he started to rap:

"I is Archall Di Mond – Man wit his mind on – got what the people need on – 'cos I am Arch – All – Di - mon – Gotta big house - Ya – De Mecedes 4 by 4 in de garage - Ya – girls on me arm ya – got what I need – Ma – And I ain't stopping yet - Na – going to the top – Sistaa – with me pills dat make you strong – Ya – But you get in me way – Bra – I saaaa gonna float – Yaaaa."

Archall the gangster showing off, setting himself up for the world to see—with Rasheed's money, giving away thousands of pills he could never source again, a girl leading him on for the price of removing his four back teeth and a scrap metal 4 x 4 cube for a ride. He picked up the phone and played back the video of himself looking and sounding like a prick with a new diamond studded front tooth and said out loud to himself, "You's cool Bro."

Then he dialed Steven, who picked up right away like he did, but this time saying, "The deal's off Archall, forget the money you owe, it's on me. That big fucker Chendrill's been around here and I ain't playing no more."

Archall Diamond listen to what was being said and took it in, then saying, "But I just got my tooth done man—done a rap video an all, gonna put it on YouTube and I need a new ride man."

Steven asked, "You try out that magnet trick you were thinking about?"

Archall nodded, "Yeah, it's all cool, but it's having trouble starting now, so I'm selling it."

Steven explained why, "Yeah, I should have said those high-end vehicles are sensitive—you need to keep the computer systems away from magnets. That'll be the problem. You'll need it re-chipped."

"Yeah."

"Use one of those guys from the gym you had go with you to see Rann, they're sharp, they can help you out from now on."

Archall nodded. *Yeah*, he thought, they were sharp, couldn't fight for toffee but one of them had a Rolex. He said, "Yeah you're right, what was the name of the guy with the Rolex who got half his ear ripped off?"

"Rolex?"

"Yeah that's him."

Then he heard Steven say, "That Rolex is not real though. Anyway, I'm out of town man, maybe a year. You call Rolex right, he's cool."

But Steven wasn't going anywhere. Nonetheless, though, Archall Diamond—Gangsta—was going to have to find new counsel as that was the last he ever heard from Steven.

Archall got in his truck and kept his shades on so no one would see him driving it and pulled out of the driveway, passing the terracotta lions and keeping an eye out for Chendrill as he went. The guy was out there now looking for him, hunting him down, but what could the fucker prove? Go find the birdman or someone who saw something—he had nothing to go on, he had nothing to worry about—he hoped.

"Forget about it," he said to himself out loud and looked once in his mirror and then a second time in case it was the big ape on his tail. You can't have a rap video out there on the internet if you ain't got people out there trying to put you jail. It went with the territory, what kind of Gangsta would he be if all he had to worry about were parking tickets?

"Be cool Bro, be cool," he said to himself, looking in the mirror at his tooth. He'd go see his girl, take his mind off things, tell her about a chiropractor he knew who he used to take Rasheed to see. He was good. He'd fix her up. Then he'd drive down to the martial arts gym and see Rolex watching other guys train. He'd make him a cash offer for some work, see if he's interested. Then he'd go find the plastic Paki Rann and work out where he's getting this stuff from so as he can remove him from the equation like he was going to. Then he'd check the tide times and get the truck ready so he could float the dentist before the guy had a chance to get hold of his back teeth with his pliers.

******

Patrick strolled down the sidewalk in the trendy district of Vancouver's Yaletown as though he owned it. There were only a few things he had to do now—one was to read the script, another was to find the whereabouts of the beautiful Russian girl he used to be in love with, and the other was to somehow get all the photos of him off the back of every other bus running around before Adalia Seychan came back into town.

He stopped off in a coffee shop and bought enough for the whole office and then some, plus cakes, and walked into Slave Media like Santa Clause on a summer's day. As Sebastian dug into an éclair, he asked, "What day did you have in mind to do a test with Adalia Seychan?"

Sebastian looked at him confused, telling him he thought he was driving the ship. Patrick opened up saying, "It's the ads on the buses. I don't want her seeing them."

"We've all got pasts, Patrick," Sebastian replied. Besides, he had his own problems with Mazzi Hegan at the moment—going off the rails with this new guy he'd been seeing, hoping it would fizzle out before he got into serious trouble.

"Tell them to pull them," Patrick said.

"I have. They said it takes at least a month for them to clear."

It was nonsense, Sebastian knew that much. They had a schedule which Patrick had already firmly paid into. Bottom line, it was overtime pay to call the crews in to strip them overnight while the buses and their drivers were sleeping. So he said simply, "You're going to have to pay."

"How much?" Sebastian knew, he'd done it before when a star who was fronting a project got caught with his trousers down with a prostitute and the agency wanted to pull the campaign they'd spent millions on. And, overnight, they had, right across North America. Patrick was just one city, and mainly in the downtown core; which would be enough, as he didn't see Adalia Seychan popping out to the suburbs to see her aunt or go shopping. He said,

"A hundred grand tops." Patrick let out a sigh. He'd just seen the bill on his platinum card for the private jets and now even the cakes and coffee were looking steep.

"A hundred grand?"

Sebastian nodded, for God's sake the guy was rich, but sometimes a tight ass.

"That or you blindfold her on the way to and from the airport, then keep her in her room."

It was an option, Patrick thought, make it a game. Then he said, "Why not take the mountain to Mohamed, you know—shoot the whole thing in Hollywood?"

Sebastian stared at him for a moment, then asked, "You read the script yet?"

Patrick lied saying, "It's fantastic."

Then Sebastian said in a quiet tone that let anyone listening know he was in charge, "This is our town Patrick. You go south, you're the guest and when you're the guest, they have the power. We shoot here or we don't shoot anything."

As Sebastian walked away, Patrick asked, "You don't have an account with the transit company do you so we can get this sorted?"

And just before Sebastian's door shut in Patrick's face as he followed him along the corridor to Sebastian's office, he heard Sebastian say, "Sort out your own problems, Patrick."

The prick, Sebastian thought as he sat down, taking off the lid to his caramel mocha Patrick had just tried to butter him up with before hitting him up for a hundred grand less than a minute after.

He picked up the phone and dialed Mazzi. There was still no answer.

He'll be in tomorrow with his head up high, pretending nothing was wrong, then he'd speak to him, ask him how this new relationship was going. Patrick was still standing outside the door pretending to talk to one of the office staff who wanted advice on the housing market. Butting in, Sebastian called out saying, "And Patrick, I take it since you've had yourself written into this movie, you've also got someone else in mind to play alongside you?"

And as soon as the door opened, Sebastian saw the glint in Patrick's eye as he said, "Yeah, I want it to be the most beautiful woman I have ever seen, only there's one—no, sorry, two things that may be an issue. The first is that I don't know where she is and the second is she may not be able to walk."

******

Chendrill waited along the road to see if Archall Diamond was going to come back and after some minutes, decided the guy was long gone. Why he'd decided to ditch the Mercedes with the low profiles, though, he didn't know. Maybe he was doing another dope run and wouldn't be back till the weekend—it was hard to say.

He walked to the garage, picked the lock to the side door, went in and stared at one half of the crushed up cubed car that had been hacked to pieces by the grinder still plugged in sitting at its side.

It was the Merc, he thought, peeling off a piece of paint from the side of the hacked-up square.

Fuck me it was. But why on earth would he do that, he thought, unless the birdman was inside somehow? He pulled out his flashlight and took a closer look. It was possible. Maybe that's what he was up to. He looked around, the inner tubes and chains still to one side, tools on the wall, other trucker stuff from when Archall was a hired gun trucking eighteen wheelers down to the states for his cousin. Till he'd lipped off to a cop early in the morning on the wrong side of the border and still had booze in him from sitting in a tittie bar and wasn't allowed back.

That's when he started hauling dope in his pickup until he had enough cash floating around to buy the Mercedes, not long after that, he took to driving Rasheed. There was a lot he'd found out about Diamond, but having talked to maybe a dozen people, the only common denominator Chendrill could find from them all was that the guy was thick.

But thick people still killed people—prisons were full of them and from what Chendrill could make out, Archall Diamond was soon to be in good company.

He moved to the door that connected the garage to the kitchen and gave it a try—open, good work Archall, nice security. He walked in though the kitchen, cocoa pops crunching under his feet, nothing to report. He went upstairs, looked in one bedroom, pictures on the wall of a pretty East Indian posing, leaning against a wall with her head tilted back. Then one of Archall showing off his tooth trying to look cool holding a rubber chicken.

He moved into the next room and saw the bed with its black sheets covered in money and maybe two hundred odd packets of pills. Chendrill picked a packet up and read the label that simply said, 'Rock Solid' saying out loud, "So, these are what all the fuss has been about."

He slipped a pack in his pocket, then stared at the cash. He could do the same, take a couple of years off and see the world— him and Dan's mother, pull her out of her nursing shoes for a bit and romance her. But thieving wasn't his style—though if it was, he'd have done well. Pulling out a twenty from his pocket he dropped it down, adding it to the rest.

"There you go Diamond, go get your teeth fixed."

And that's exactly what Archall was trying to organise at that very same moment, standing in Dennis' living room telling him his wisdom teeth were becoming troublesome. Dennis wondered what the fuck was going on, because the guy didn't have any.

Archall saying, "Yeah I can't concentrate when I got to do the math from the cash I bring in every night from my business." Trying to sound cool.

Dennis wondered if he should scam the guy for a few grand and send him on his way, but instead told him the truth, "I don't think the problem is with your wisdom teeth because, in fact, you don't have any."

Feeling stupid now but relieved the pliers could stay in the drawer, Archall instead said, "Yeah well I was really young when I had them out. You know, like when I was about six." Dennis thinking the guy must be the only human to have teeth that grow in reverse, as at that age his babies were still planted firm, remembering the scar tissue at the back of his mouth and estimating that it could only have been sometime last year he'd had them removed.

He said, "Maybe there's some other issue you need to deal with?"

There was, Archall thought; and in fact, it's you. Alla wasn't there for him to look at and give her the eye. As he made a mental note of the guy's chest size so as he could get the right fitting inner tube to float him with, he said, "Yeah maybe I'll see how it goes, if the wisdom teeth are out, I'll see if they start getting better."

Dennis said. "Your tooth is looking great."

Archall grinned now loving it, saying, "Yeah, it already on YouTube."

******

Dan laid in his bed and stared at the ceiling where the plaster was beginning to come away due to his mother's new love interest. It was beginning to drive him crazy; he was, after all, a sex symbol, but it seemed his mum was still getting more than he ever would—even if he was still getting texts every hour from the most beautiful women in the world. *Fuck it*, he thought, he'll take the car out and pretend he'd just been going fast and had to slow down because of the cops.

That'll do it, maybe this time he could get laid—maybe.

Putting his t-shirt on back to front, he walked to the front door, slipped on a pair of his mother's flip-flops, which were too small for him, and walked to the new Ferrari that Sebastian had kindly leased—and governed—for him.

It was almost eight in the evening now. He could cruise for a bit, see if that worked, give some chicks the eye, take them for a spin in the car and get stuck in traffic for a bit whilst he tried to get it on.

He hit Hastings, looking to the open road ahead, passing posters of himself looking like a fool; then, he checked his rearview mirror to see the line-up of traffic beginning to build behind him, as cars that may very well have been driven by old ladies passed him on the inside. Seeing some girls, he slowed, pushed in the clutch and gave the engine a rev, the engine roaring like a true sports car—but going nowhere.

Looking at him, the girls began to stare, then point, covering their mouths in astonishment and then screaming. *My God, it was beginning to work*, he thought, *it was indeed more fun than the bus*. He carried on, saw other girls, two this time, and threw the clutch down, roaring the engine, girls staring, girls doing nothing.

He moved on, seeing no one for a bit except for a few women who looked like hookers. Then he kept his head down through the rough part, ignoring the chants and the cat calls from the crack heads on Main and carried on into town.

He hit the downtown core, revving it up as he had with Melissa when the car had run fine and he could tear off up the road, oblivious to the fact that no one cared. But now he knew it, could see it firsthand. Pulling over, he sat there in the car and turned on the radio, the sound system fantastic, the smell of the new leather still stinging in his nostrils.

And then he saw her walking along the street in her lovely dress and her perfect shoes, the way she walked, swaying her arms in time with her little backside—and not for a second looking at him or the Ferrari—as though she didn't have a care in the world.

Getting out, he followed her, keeping a good distance back as she switched back and forth along the roads around Yaletown, passing Slave, stopping, coming back, looking at signs, then spotting the bar, quiet and reserved in amongst so many that were not. She walked on in.

Seconds later, Dan was inside also, sitting alone on a leather chair at a table opposite the girl who'd just found her friend, hearing her giggling about how she'd just been walking up and down for half an hour, her friend covering her mouth and holding the girl's arm as she laughed. Dan watched the Canadian football on the TV screen above them, pretending to care about what was going on.

Then he ordered a beer, the girls noticing him now as he showed his ID, both of them laughing at his mum's flip-flops. Dan smiling, not giving a shit. Then the girls, really laughing, still holding onto each other's arms the way young women do in an innocent way, burying their heads into the upright of the leather seat, covering their eyes and peeking out at Dan. Dan stared back grinning. Then the friend asked him, "You that guy who wears the silver pants?"

Dan was about to say, 'yes,' as the girl carried on saying, "We hate that guy." And laughing as she pretended to make herself vomit.

Dan smiled, not knowing what to do now, then trying to instigate a relationship with a lie and denying who he was, laughed and said, "Yeah—same here, I get that a lot. Imagine being me, walking around town seeing that guy up there all day, having people pointing and shit."

They laughed again, this time through embarrassment though. The girl he'd followed said sorry, then carried on, "You do look like him though, your nose is broken in the same way."

Dan smiled, saying, "Yeah thanks—lucky me."

They laughed again, really happy girly laughter, the type young girls can have until life slowly begins to beat it out of them. Looking to the one he'd stalked, Dan said, "Sorry."

Then she leaned over and held out her hand and said, "You're a really handsome guy though, even if you do look like Pantie Man."

"Pantie Man!" Dan replied pointing to himself and staring at the girl's legs. *God she was nice*, he thought, young and innocent, around his age and a million miles away from 'Marshaa' with all her glam and hair and entourage.

They carried on chatting as the night went on, Dan moving to their table, buying drinks and food with the small amount Sebastian allowed him from his newfound wealth, digging himself in deeper with the lies, telling them how he'd never eat McDonalds because it made him throw up. The girls unable to keep their eyes off him, staring at his feet, him at their tits.

They were from Victoria, on the Island, both studying history at Simon Fraser University in their first year, one with her own room on campus, the other in digs with friends. Dan was sharing his knowledge of Inuit tribal history on Baffin Island and on which Subway sandwiches give you heartburn, keeping quiet about the Ferrari parked outside and offering them a cab ride home when they said it was time to go.

They jumped in the cab, an East Indian in the driver's seat, staring at the two brunettes in the back as they headed east, the girls still giggling, calling out 'Pantie Man' each time they passed a poster of Dan in his undies looking terrified. The driver joining in, trying to be part of the fun saying, "I hate him, I hate him." Every time. The girl Dan had followed sitting next to him now with her head on his shoulder getting cozy.

They dropped off the other girl at her apartment, waved goodbye, and carried on up the hill towards campus. The night air was still and cool, wafting in from the front passenger side window. The girl silent, comfortable, breathing slowly, her finger unconsciously rubbing Dan's knee, passing 'Pantie Man' and saying nothing now. Then after letting the driver know which block was hers, the cab pulled up outside and they sat there quietly, not wanting to move for a moment as she kept her head on Dan's shoulder and said quietly, "I've never done this before, but I like you Dan and if—" she said, thinking out loud, weighing up the night and taking a breath. "If—you can remember my name, then you can come upstairs with me—okay?"

They sat in silence, the three of them, there in the cab, the driver with his turban in the front motionless now waiting, the girl with her head on Dan's shoulder, Dan sitting there having heard her every word with his mind whipping back, recalling every bit of the conversation they'd had that evening and coming back a complete blank. One second passed, then two, then four, then six, and at ten she was off his shoulder, out the door, up a short flight of concrete steps, through another door, and gone. Then the cab driver spoke up, "You fucking idiot!"

Dan moved to the center of the cab's rear bench as though that was going to bring her back as the cab driver looked at him in the rear-view mirror. He put the battery powered taxi in gear and pulled away, and said it again, "You fucking idiot!"

They turned a corner, Dan in silence watching the cab driver's head shake from side to side as he glanced back at him in the darkness, saying, "She was beautiful—beautiful!"

Fuck, Dan thought as they drove back down the hill. *Fuck!* he thought, *what the hell happened?* He could read a book in fifteen minutes glancing at a page and recite it three years later, but he couldn't remember one fucking name?

"You ask her her name?" the cabbie asked, staring at him now in the rear-view mirror as they pulled up at the bottom of the hill. He hadn't, he thought, that was why—what an idiot he was. Then the taxi driver said to him, still mad as he shouted out and into his front screen as the orange campus lights bled through, lighting his off-white turban, "Always ask a girl her name—always ask a girl her name."

Dan nodded his head, looking back at the cabbie as he pulled away from the lights. The guy looked familiar. He said, "Yeah I'm an idiot."

Then he saw the field hockey stick propped up against the door in the front seat as he shifted positions in the back. *No. It couldn't be?* he thought. The cab cruised along the main road heading back into town and the cabbie shouted at another forty-foot poster of Dan in Mazzi Hegan's underpants as they went, "I hate that guy!"

He paused, and then said again, "I fucking hate that guy."

It was him, Dan thought, the same cabbie he'd run from on the night he got busted at Mazzi Hegan's pad. But that guy was older, much older, he thought, as he sank back more to the side of the cab, keeping out of the man's line of sight. The guy trying to talk to him, adjusting his mirror as he went. Still saying, "That fucking guy, he run from me—he not pay. I kill him."

Fuck, it was him, Dan thought. Jesus, he was having shitty luck. He hadn't taken a cab since he'd run from this guy and the first one he steps into is his—and he was wearing his mum's flip-flops.

They carried on along the empty dual carriage way, the man leaving him be for a moment, the engine off, the vehicle running on batteries. Then ahead Dan saw it, a green stoplight which was about to turn red, directly next to it at a bus stop a picture of Dan beautifully back lit with LEDs. Slowly the driver braked as the lights changed and the electric motor whirred to a stop.

The driver sat there staring at the poster six feet from his face, Dan sitting in the back, the driver adjusting his mirror, Dan scratching his forehead, the driver looking back at the poster, Dan's picture in the poster looking back at him with his nose bleeding.

Suddenly, finally realizing just who he had in the back, the driver whipped his head around to see an empty seat and, through an open rear door, saw Dan running off across the road, jumping the central reservation in his mum's flip-flops. Running as fast as they would take him, Dan headed along the road in the opposite direction, watching over his shoulder to see if the crazy hockey stick wielding cab driver had left his vehicle. Then he saw the cab moving, its reversing lights on and its yellow top shining brilliant under the street lights as it reversed up silently on battery power following him backwards, going the wrong way on the other side of the street—the cabbie alongside him and leaning out of his open window banging his field hockey stick on the door with only the concrete bollard there to stop him from cutting across and running him down. Dan looked up at the sky train tracks running above him and then to the station. The steps leading up to it were just some three hundred feet ahead, and a train in the distance was coming towards the station along the tracks held almost fifty feet in the air by monolithic concrete pillars.

He reached the steps, hearing the other motorists' horns as they approached the out of control cab, forcing the crazed man to the side of the road. Dan raced up the steps and made it, hot and panting, to the platform just as the train pulled into the station and looked back to see the cabbie, in his turban, field hockey stick in hand, appear at the bottom of the steps and begin to climb, screaming, "Fuck you!—Fuck you!" as he did, stopping only once he reached the top and then speeding across the platform and jumping on the train—just making it as the doors shut.

Only Dan wasn't on the train.

******

Dan watched from the alcove he'd snuck into as the train pulled out of sight, stepped out onto the platform, and took a deep breath. *Fuck me, what a night.* He knew from experience the next station was about a mile or so away and that Gandhi, realizing he'd been duped, would get off there and either be running back or on the next train. He had about five minutes.

He walked down the stairs and looked at the cab half on and half off the road with its lights still on. He walked across the road and looked in through the open driver's window at the keys still in the ignition. He could steal it, he thought, drive it all the way back into town. But what was the point? It would only get worse; and in the end, Chendrill would get involved because somehow he'd find out and he'd get another black eye on top of the one he already had, and then on and on the trouble would go.

But his legs were aching and so were his feet. It was getting late and he was all sweaty now and couldn't be bothered to play hide and seek. Anyway, he didn't ask for the guy to suddenly go nuts on him, so he opened the door and got in, pushed the seat back, started the cab up, slapped it into drive, and pulled back onto the Lougheed Highway heading back into town, ignoring anyone trying to flag him down as he went until he'd reached the city. When the coast was clear, he parked the Punjabi field hockey playing warrior's cab right under a 'Pantie Boy' poster just for good measure.

He moved along the street, his mum's flip-flops flapping with every step, and reached his Ferrari, pulled a parking ticket off the windscreen, balled it up and threw it onto the ground, beep bop beeped the doors unlocked and was about to get in when he heard a woman's voice from behind say, "You always do that with your tickets, do you?"

As a matter of fact, he did, but what did she care. He turned around, a woman there now in a tight dress and heels, sexy as hell with short blonde hair. She said, handing him back the ticket, "If I was a cop, I'd ticket you."

Dan replied quickly, "Lucky you're not then."

She said, "You're that 'BlueBoy' guy, aren't you?"

"Yeah, but the girls are calling me 'Pantie boy' now."

"Really?" the woman said, then carried on asking, "I hear you've got a penthouse?"

Dan replied, "Who from?"

"Magazines."

Dan said back, "Really?"

He looked at her titties, big and firm, bursting out of her dress. Watching him look, she smiled and said, "You like them, do you? I saw you pull up here earlier in your car before you shot off after that girl. You should have waited a moment because I've been fantasizing about you for weeks and you could have been having a sexy time with me all evening instead."

Fuck me, Dan thought, *just like that*. The woman offering herself up to him on a plate. Then she said, "Well, you're not going to have made me wait around here all night for you for nothing, are you?"

And Dan said, "No."

He took it easy as he cruised along through the downtown core, the woman telling him her name was Jane, Dan not forgetting to ask this time. Jane there with him now letting her skirt ride up so as he could see her stockings. She said, "Nice car. Why don't you put your foot down and let it pull me back into the seat ?"

Dan, taking it easy, playing it cool, said, "That's not me."

She said, "I've got family staying—you taking me back to the penthouse?"

Still looking at her titties and getting hard at the same time, Dan said, "I live lower."

Jane smiled, saying, "I like lower."

Dan said, "Quite a lot lower actually."

Jane told him with her hand on his leg she didn't care how low or where he took her as long as he took her. Dan wished the car would go faster so he could get her home.

"My pussy's so wet," was all Jane said when he pulled the Ferrari up outside his mother's place and turned off the engine—

happy, for once, to see Chendrill's Aston not parked in his spot.

Then wrapping her hand around the back of his head, she pulled him towards her, kissed him, opening her legs slightly as her lips left his, saying, "Feel me down there, feel what you're doing to me." And he did, twisting himself around and slowly slipping his left hand up her short skirt, feeling her stocking tops and the wetness beneath the silk of her knickers. Pulling him into her, she said, "You see." Just before she kissed him again and gasped as she felt him slide his fingers inside her.

They got out, Dan telling her they need to be quiet as he walked up the path, Jane on her tip toes in her high heel slip-ons, Dan telling her he's looking after his aunt's cat for the week because she's in hospital and staying in the basement because he can't stand the crochet doilies. Jane crept down the stairs into his room, having him leave the side light on so she could see his body as he undressed, her dropping out of her dress, keeping her stockings on just for him and laying on his unmade bed, not caring about the mess.

Dan undressed, his dick almost popping itself out the front of his Y fronts, Jane laying back watching, wishing he had the silver ones on. She said, "I'm so horny, Dan. I want to suck your cock so bad, I want to suck it, lick it up and down your shaft, lick your balls, lick your ass. I want to lick it, stick my tongue right inside. Then I want you to fuck my throat, fuck it deep, then fuck my pussy—fuck it real hard, Dan, fuck my pussy till I come and fuck me deep in the ass too until I come again."

And as he heard the filth pour from her mouth as she lay back waiting for him to come to her, Dan's body began to shudder as the now familiar feeling of panic overwhelmed him and right there and then in his underpants, he came, as he had many times before.

Jane looked at him understanding right away what had just happened and, opening her legs to him, said, "I don't care, come

here lick my pussy while I lick all the come from around your crotch."

And that's what she did, leaning forward and pulling his Y fronts down, stuck his now spent semi-hard cock in her mouth, sucking it, wanking it with her hand and licking and pulling up as much of his come as she could from around his balls and wherever she could find it. Then when she could find no more, she pulled him onto the bed and kissed him hard, sticking her tongue into his mouth, licking all around his teeth and as far into the back of his throat as she could get as she grabbed his hand, forcing it between her legs, pushing his fingers inside her, making him fingerbang her as her pussy got more and more wet until she began to tense up, shudder, and groan as her juices began to run from inside, soaking the sides of her legs and gushing out onto Dan's hands and legs. Then she said to Dan as she pulled her tongue from his mouth, "You like that do you, feeling me come like that? You want me to fuck your face, don't you? You want me to squirt come like that on your face, don't you?"

He didn't, in fact he wanted her to leave.

Then before he could get a word in, she spun around, taking his still semi-hard cock in her mouth and licking it, swirling her tongue around and around its end with the softest of touches, making him groan with pleasure. Then suddenly in an instant, he felt himself getting hard again as she took him deep down into her throat, caressing the top of his penis with the back of her throat and sucking both of his balls into her mouth and licking them and playing with them with her tongue. Dan began to call out with pleasure. He'd never felt anything like it in his life—not even the vacuum cleaner or a jar of liver from the fridge heated in the microwave came close. He called out loud, "Ahh—Ahhh—Ahhh!"

As he felt himself coming uncontrollably again, he heard the strange banging from above. Then Jane took him out of her mouth and burying her face into his backside, licked his ass, crazily prodding and poking inside him as she pushed and forced her tongue inside him as he groaned more, her hand wanking his cock, still soaked with her slippery saliva.

Then she pulled her mouth out of his ass and spun around and kissed him again all over his face, licking and dribbling all around his eyes and nose and his mouth. Then she pulled back and said, "Now it's my turn."

And she pushed him back onto the bed and, back to front, straddled his face with his nostrils in direct line with her ass, she began to ride and fuck his face, twisting around to him so as she could look at him as she forced herself on him, leaning over, giving him instructions, saying, "Use your tongue, get it inside me."

She rubbed her juices into his face, pushing herself onto him, calling out and groaning as she said, "Work it, yeah, work it, work it." Dan felt the stubble from her shaved pussy digging into his skin like something his mother used to clean the bath with. She carried on pushing herself onto him harder, rubbing her clitoris on the bottom of his chin and her ass on his broken nose that now hurt as he felt her tense and build again, then she pushed harder, rubbing herself onto him with twice the force, her pussy juices running over his face as he tried to lift her off him but couldn't. Then suddenly she lifted herself up and, ignoring the banging from above and screaming with pleasure, ejaculated her fluids, squirting them hard and fast all over his face, mouth, neck, and chest.

Then Dan heard his mother from upstairs calling through the ceiling saying, "Dan, Dan! What on earth are you doing down there?"

And getting up, Dan said, "Oh, shit it's my mum."

Then he heard her coming down the stairs and banging on his basement room door. The woman saying, "Your mum?"

Trish asked, "Daniel, who have you got in there?"

Then with a thump, Trish forced the door open, breaking the little lock Dan put in for when he was wanking, and the ugly fluorescent lights came on—harsh and bluey green coming down from the ceiling lighting the room up bright for the world to see. Trish looked straight to the woman seeing her hair all wet and her makeup smeared and said, "Who the fuck are you?"

Then she looked to Dan, his face rubbed raw and his bottom lip bleeding and screamed, "What have you just done to my child."

Dan said, "It's okay, this is Jane, she's my girlfriend."

His mother screamed back, "She's older than me, Dan! I'm surprised there's not a set of dentures sitting in a glass by the bed!"

And from the way Dan's dick had been feeling a few minutes earlier, so was he. Then he saw his mother open the door wide and say to his new girlfriend Jane, "Get out of here you fucking hag, and stay away from my child!"

As Dan had always said so far throughout his short life, 'my mother has a temper.' And that was that.

Chapter Thirty-Eight

They'd all been sitting together around the boardroom table at Slave looking like a Neapolitan cake, Patrick wearing brown, Buffy in crème, and Mazzi in complete denial in pink—and it was making Sebastian hungry. There were three things to discuss—the script first, which was being sorted. Adalia Seychan was coming up today on short notice for a photo shoot the following morning with Dan to get people's taste buds moistened—Mazzi was in charge—and while they had her here, Sebastian would pitch her about a six-week commercial that would take them all around the world after the movie was finished—or before, if it all fell through. And lastly Dan, who'd they'd just been told was about to be charged with stealing a taxi.

Chendrill was late, having been up all night, he'd said, doing God knows what, when he was supposed to be keeping his eye on their latest hot star—which in a way was the fourth topic, but rather than side bar it for later, Sebastian had decided to let it go. "After all," he'd said, "we don't own the man."

Half an hour later, he was in, along with Dan, with his face all red and scratched and his lips swollen. Sebastian said, "Daniel darling, what on earth has happened? Have you been in another fight?"

In some ways, yes he had, Dan thought. Then answered, "No," and, sitting down, he put his feet up on a chair as he liked to do there, and carried on, "'Cos you've made me a model, I had one of them facial scrubs, you know, trying to look young."

Sebastian knew all about youth-enhancing cleansing scrubs, having had a few acid peel sessions himself; and for that matter, so had Mazzi—because God knows how many times over the years he had seen him come to work looking like Dan. He said,

Rock Solid

"You are young Daniel dear—don't become obsessive."

Then Dan said, "What do you want anyway? I was asleep." As he proceeded to stare out the window.

Sebastian carried on, "Daniel, there's a rumour spreading around that you're about to be arrested for car theft."

Dan looked over to Sebastian, then at Mazzi Hegan, and wondered how many times he'd stolen his car—and Chuck Chendrill's—for that matter and said, "Yeah, what happened was that I'd been out on a date, took this girl home in a cab and on the way back, the cabbie had a nervous breakdown and said he couldn't drive anymore. Said he'd been driving all day every day like they do, and he wanted to take the train back. So I did him a favor and parked it up for him in a safe place, just like he asked. You see, it was parked badly on the road and he didn't want anyone to have an accident."

Sebastian looked to Chendrill, who couldn't believe he'd just heard what may have been the dumbest excuse ever come out of Dan's mouth. Smiling, Chendrill said, "Sounds like Dan did the right thing! You know these cabbies work 24/7. It's inevitable things like this happen."

Sebastian stared at him for a moment thinking. There was more to this, obviously, than Chendrill was letting on—and there was, as Dan had been back in his basement making tender love to a woman twice his age and then some, Chendrill had been at the station putting out the fire Dan had started by stealing the cab. If it hadn't been for a heads-up from Williams, it wouldn't have been Dan's mother who'd come crashing down into the basement, pounding on the door while he was having his face sat on.

Sebastian said, "Well that's great then." He stood up, looked to Patrick, and then turned to Chendrill and said, "Also, we've got a shoot in the morning at Iron Works Studio with Adalia Seychan. It's all last minute and I've got people all over it—they're driving

337

her personal trailer as we speak. Dan's involved and I need you to absolutely guarantee he'll be there at seven a.m., Chuck. Adalia's a sweetie, but she's still got Hollywood written all over her, so we don't need to be embarrassed by you being late Dan, do we? Oh, and Patrick needs you to put your missing persons hat on and find an old sweetheart, because he'd like to get a few shots of her while we're there if she's interested. I know it's all a bit rushed, but Adalia's a busy girl."

Busy doing nothing, Chendrill thought and he had absolutely no doubts who he was about to be asked to find.

******

They sat in the boardroom after everyone else had gone, Dan looking out the window, Patrick at the table with Chendrill, who was leaning in and talking quietly to him, "Let it go, Patrick. The girl can't walk. She's in a fucking wheelchair and the marriage is struggling as it is. They don't need you poking your nose about."

Patrick said, "I'm just trying to get Alla working, you know, back on her feet." He looked over and caught a grin spreading across Dan's face at the last comment. Calling out, he said to him with a smile, "Hey Pantie Boy—could you go get us both a coffee?."

Fuck, Dan thought, that's twice in two days now he'd been called that—the girls weren't kidding. He got up and turned to head for the door so as back-of-the-bus-lover-boy could spout bullshit in private, remembering the photos he'd found hidden in the trunk of Chendrill's Ferrari just after he'd stolen it. As he passed, he said, "Don't forget to remind her to bring the toys."

Feeling Patrick's eyes digging into his back as he closed the soundproof glass door behind him, Dan left. Patrick wondered how on earth the kid knew about the pictures. He said to Chendrill in a soft tone, "Fucking prick, here I am trying to make him a movie star and all I get is grief."

Chendrill also wondered how Dan knew about the photos; looking at Patrick and thinking the same thing, he said, "I thought you'd had enough of that girl, with all that blackmail shit that went down?"

Patrick feigned frustration, and answered clearly and precisely, holding his hands out, so that right away Chendrill knew before he spoke that it was all going to be bullshit, "Look—Trust me—there was something with me and Anna before, we both know that. But—I can assure you my actions right now are nothing more than professional."

Chendrill stared at him for a moment, giving him the look, then said, "If there's one thing we both know, this world's not short of beautiful actresses who need a job."

And Patrick said, "No one's as beautiful as Anna, Chuck, and we know each other well and trust each other. And that's what you need—trust and loyalty."

Chendrill said, "The girl used to be a hooker and you don't even know her real name. It's Alla, not fucking Anna."

Patrick came straight back at him with, "We all wear different hats and have different names Chuck. Look at you, you've got three."

Chendrill shrugged and leaned back in his chair—the realtor pretending to be a producer wasn't wrong. *Look at me*, he thought, *I'm a cop trying to be a private eye, pretending to be a babysitter*. He said, without lying, "I'll go see how she is." And he would see how she was, but not see if she wanted to be a movie star so he could fuck up Dennis's life before he'd got a chance to straighten himself out. After all, he owed them a visit.

******

Chendrill had stood and discreetly looked down at his crotch to see if he was bulging at all. He wasn't. He'd worn the tightest underpants he could find, the loosest trousers, and his bright red Hawaiian. He'd gone home; or, he should say, he went back to Dan's mother's house just as Dan had left the previous evening in search of adventure, and had thought, *great we have the evening to ourselves*. And that's exactly what Dan's mother had thought the moment she saw him parking exactly where Dan's new Ferrari had just sat for the last week.

She'd kissed him the moment he'd entered the door, a kiss born of growing love and tenderness—her lips on his, her fingers gently combing his hair, one foot unconsciously off the floor. She said lightly as she pulled back away from him, "Sorry my son's gone out for the evening, but you can come in and wait if you'd like?"

And Chendrill had waited, waited naked in her bed, while they kissed each other, touched each other and made love all evening, slow beautiful love with him on top of her, gently pushing himself into her, feeling the sweat run from his brow, her hands on his back, her wetness inside until they'd finished and he'd rolled off and they'd laid together on the bed listening to the silence. Then he'd remembered Archall Diamond's tablets and how Steven the pharmacist had said they were nothing more than herbs and had said, "I picked up these pills today that have been floating about and I've been wondering what all the fuss was about."

"Pills for what?"

"Make you're dick hard and bigger."

Trish leaned over, putting her hand up to prop up her head and said, "And you want to try them out?"

Grinning, Chendrill said, "I already have."

Trish stared at him, not believing his words for a moment, then slipped her hand down under the sheets and felt him, clasping her hand around his dick, feeling it still hard against his stomach when normally things would have eased off. She said, her eyes lighting up, "Oh my God, I thought you felt a bit bigger."

Chendrill replied, "Yeah, and I feel incredibly happy."

It was just after midnight after an entire evening had passed without hearing Dan whack the broom into his bedroom ceiling when Chendrill's phone had rung and he'd learned about Dan's latest move. Despite it all, he was strangely still happy—and hard—and he'd made his excuses and again barely missed Dan coming home with the older woman.

Half an hour later, he'd met Williams, who was standing next to the two other police cars. A tall Asian police woman was dealing with a very irate taxi driver standing and looking up at the poster of Dan, shouting, "Fucking man steal my car!"

Within an hour, they were all at the police station looking at all the footage wired over from the transit police from the CCTV cameras strategically placed around the station Dan had been chased into. They saw Dan running scared along the road being chased by the wild man driving in reverse on the other side of the concrete buffers, waving his field hockey stick in a threatening manner at him out the window. Chendrill looked at the police woman who was tall and skinny enough to be a model and wondered what Dan had said to the guy in the first place to make him that mad. He said to the police woman, "Looks like he had little other choice than to use the taxi as a means to get away from this lunatic. He did the right thing in the circumstances, taking himself away from the situation and to safety by any means possible."

She looked at him, frowned and said, "Took himself all the

way downtown and parked under a picture of himself instead of driving to the police station or even perhaps calling them on his cell phone?"

They were both right and she knew it, even if Chendrill was stretching things a bit. The police woman, who liked riding shotgun on the night shifts because more things went down, was also wondering what the guy had said to piss off the cabbie that bad. Loving the fact she'd got the chance, at last, to meet the legend that was Charles Chuck Chendrill she said, "People are saying it was you who'd worked out who killed Daltrey, you know that don't you?"

Chendrill smiled. He liked her and could see she was not a by-the-book type of person and used her brain. Normally he would have skirted around it, but he answered truthfully, and nodded to the screen, 'You're not wrong and the truth is I'm lucky to be here."

The police woman answered him and pushed the envelope a little further, "And you know what happened to the Russian?" Chendrill smiled. He did, then giving her a look and pointing again to the computer monitor, the picture of the cabbie there half out the window with his field hockey stick, he said, "Yeah and he had nothing to do with it."

******

The sun was just breaking, filling the city with fresh new light as Chendrill drove back towards Dan's. The crazed cabbie had been told off and sent home with his tail between his legs. Chendrill had the police woman's number in his back pocket—though he knew he'd never call. The woman saying before he'd left, "All's good with Dan, as long as it's the first and last time it happens." Then she'd given him the slightest of looks that sent instantaneous blood flowing south to a place where, due to the pills, there was already plenty of activity, and handed him her card. "But if there's anything else you might like to talk to me about, then you'll find me here."

But he wouldn't call—even if she was super fine, he thought as he drove, heading into the rising morning sun. He wouldn't call, no he wouldn't, no not at all, he wouldn't—no, no, he wasn't going to call.

He reached Dan's home, parked up behind the Ferrari, and opened the front door; and although he had done nothing wrong, he felt a small wave of guilt wash over him as he saw Trish standing in the hallway in her dressing gown with her eyes all red from crying. He asked, "What's wrong?"

She came to him and held him tight, saying, "This monster had hold of Dan in his room and I burst in and stopped her."

"What?"

"This woman came back with Dan and attacked him and I threw her out."

Chendrill asked, "Where's Dan?"

"He's asleep, he just came upstairs, drank a pint of milk and ate all the cheese, then went to sleep. He didn't even take a shower."

But Chendrill did. And as he stood there tired and naked with the water running down his body, he wondered what on earth Dan had gotten into this time to upset his mother so badly. He got out and stood naked in the bathroom with a towel against his chest and looked in the mirror, his dick still like a drooping rocket halfway from lift off. Reaching down, he picked up his jeans and pulled the Asian police woman's card from his pocket, looked at it once and then ripped it to shreds, throwing it into the toilet and flushing it out of harm's way. Then, with his dick still at half mast, he walked naked into Trish's bedroom, got in next to her, and fell asleep holding her in his arms.

Two hours later, the phone rang, and he answered to an irate Sebastian saying, "Chuck there's an emergency—Dan's stolen a car." Chendrill's first thought was *what's new there?* Then he wondered how the hell Sebastian had heard about it, as he believed he'd already put the incident to bed.

He said, "How did you find out about that?"

Sebastian said, "It's on the news, Chuck."

And then they came in, Chendrill driving the Aston back downtown, Dan sitting there still in his mum's flip-flops and a creased shirt, not speaking with Chendrill saying, "Your mum was crying, told me you'd been attacked.

He had, he thought, but kind of in a good way, except for the fact his face was sore as hell. But what the woman had done with her mouth, he wouldn't mind that again, even if his balls did hurt. He was right, he thought, about what he'd thought earlier—no doubt about it—it was better than the jar of liver or that pound of Brie his mum won in the raffle at work that time. Dan said, "Yeah."

Chendrill waited for more, but it did not come. So, he said, "And?"

"And what?"

"And is there anything else you want to tell me."

"About what?"

"About the fact your mother was crying?"

"What, are you my fucking dad now?"

Chendrill waited, wondering if this was what being a father to a teenage boy was like, then said, throwing it out there, "I think your mother, maybe, would like me to be."

Dan said, "That was quick—she was with the baker longer."

Chendrill took the hit from the kid, who was worried about his mother, then said, "Thanks, next time you steal a car, you better know this—I won't claw you out of every bucket of shit you get yourself into, even if I'm with your mum or if that's what Sebastian's paying me to do."

Dan looked at him, thinking, *shit*. Then he said, "I never stole nothing."

Chendrill slowed the Aston to a stop, pulling up along Hastings next to a second-hand car dealership that Chendrill knew had a history of being no better than Dan and said, "Why was that guy chasing you with the field hockey stick?"

"Because he didn't like me," Dan said.

Chendrill closed his eyes and took a deep breath thinking, *well thanks for clearing that up*. Then he said, "Maybe you'd like to elaborate?"

Dan stayed quiet, looking at the cars, wondering if they were any good. Knowing Chendrill was not going anywhere till he started talking, he said, "The guy doesn't like me 'cos he drives around all day and night round town seeing me naked, it rubs him up the wrong way, it's a religious thing."

Chendrill got it—sometimes over the last week, he'd been feeling the same way. It was nonsense though. He said, "Maybe this is the same guy you spoke of earlier, and the reason he's been looking for you is that in the past you'd run on him and he recognized you, how about that?"

Dan said, "How'd you know that?"

Chendrill replied, "Because I was also young once—and you just told me."

Chapter Thirty-Nine

Archall Diamond had it all worked out. There was a tide that turned at midnight and he'd decided the dentist was going to be on it. It was risky because people were still out at that time along the river fishing and fucking in their cars, so he'd have to pick his moment. Also, there was the issue with this Chendrill—the ape who drove the Aston.

What he thought he'd do is get the truck loaded with what he needed beforehand and attach a small winch, then he'd put two wooden planks in so he could drag the fucker up if the dentist was too heavy. Getting him on his own was going to be the hard part. The last thing he needed to do was Taser him in the backroom surgery of the basement suite and take a chance that Alla was going to find out and have it cause problems in the relationship, which he knew it could. This is why he'd given up that idea. What he needed to do was be slick and shrewd, which he knew he was—after all, he'd done the birdman and got away with it. But if it got out he'd done the dentist, then people would be putting two and two together and he'd be getting a rep with the ladies he didn't need, especially if things didn't work out with Alla, which happens—he knew that.

There was a lot to think about. The caveman days of bashing a love rival over the head with a rock were long past. Man had evolved and the consequences involving a woman's feelings needed to be taken into consideration—he was, after all, a ladies' man.

******

Rann Singh walked around his new ranch home that was once his grandfather's for what seemed now the hundredth time. But now he'd gotten off his ass and found the money to buy it back; only no one was coming and he was alone. All the work he'd done, all the nights of following those sad fuckers around the East Side, helping them convert their ways to the good—all via cash transactions—was worthless. Yes, he had the ranch with the view he was already bored of, yes, he had the African village and the fields that stretched out to the forest, but he didn't have his granddaddy to come and enjoy it with him, and he was bitter.

Yes, he'd been around the village talking to his workers he'd be paying a pittance to, and he'd played with their children as they hung on his arms and legs as he walked through smiling and enjoying them, but it couldn't break the heartache. He walked back out to the deck, kicking out at nothing, and stared at the mountains, looking at his Land Rover, considering taking another trip into town to see the estate agent with his limp wristed handshake to ask him when he'd be delivering his zebra like he'd promised. He'd been their twice earlier, thrashing the Land Rover through the gears and thinking it was going to roll on the corners, telling Joseph he couldn't come because it was going to get nasty.

Standing there outside the agent's window and spitting on the ground, waiting for him to come in even though it was a Sunday. Wondering where he lived and leaving heavy messages on the guy's answering service in English and Swahili. He'd promised it and he could take it out that fucking fat commission he'd earned off the South African asshole who'd called him a *Choot* and given him a shotgun but no cartridges to go with it.

But the South African was another issue—the first was the zebra, and he wanted it.

He walked back into the ranch and into the main bedroom. It was a huge room with log walls and a king size bed in the center. Overhead, a fan wafted the mosquito net he'd so often dreamed of sleeping under, dreaming of laying with the windows open listening to the night and feeling the breeze coming off the mountain on his face until he slept, dreaming of waking to the call of morning birds as dawn broke. But not now. He looked under the bed and saw Joseph hiding there, sleeping, just as his grandfather told him he would often do, but even this wasn't funny now. He kicked the bed, waking Joseph, and followed him back out onto the deck as he scurried off, disappearing out the back.

He stood there for the longest time, thinking about it all without moving anything except his tongue and lips as he spat, not caring anymore if his phlegm hit the wooden deck or the whitewashed rocks of the garden below. The lawyer with the big mouth would be getting a visit soon. He'd tell him, he's going to die—that's what happens here in Africa, or whatever the prick had said, standing there with his briefcase and soft suede beige desert boots like these Brit colonials all like to wear, like they were the fucking elite. Yeah, he'd get a fucking visit too, he'd tell him to cough in for the zebra and to stop being a fucking prick mouth piece.

Soon it was dark, the birds going to bed, the village children not long after, some fires still burning, lighting up the side of the huts as the women finished cooking. Rann's dinner was still on the table, half eaten where Joseph had left it along with the Tusker beer that was long drank. It would be sorted tomorrow, he thought, by this time tomorrow it would be done. He'd be up early with the birds in the morning and head straight into town to catch the estate agent before he'd put the key in the lock of the front door, and whisper in his ear that he had till the end of the week to get a zebra on his lawn as promised—and it had better be a young one, he didn't want something on its last legs that couldn't outrun the kids, or he'd be coming back to stick the Land Rover through the shop window.

Then he'd see the lawyer, and tell him what he thought of his boots and his smart mouth. But the real issue was that South

African cunt who'd been stupid enough to call him a *Choot* and leave his forwarding address in the living room. *Bad move, you fucking Nazi fuck.* Rann was coming after him right after he'd been to see the lawyer. He'd better have the engine running on that plane, Rann thought, because it was going to be a long old ride to the coast; and by the time Rann was there, he wasn't going to be in a good mood whilst he'd be standing on the doorstep of his waterfront mansion in Mombasa asking that fuck to repeat the exact words he'd said to him as he'd left the house the day before. He'd see if the man had the guts to do it, to look him in the eye and call the guy who'd just given him $200,001 cash for his house a *Choot*.

And that's exactly what he was going to do.

He didn't know how long he'd been standing out there in the darkness staring into nothing, oblivious to the mosquitos and the sounds of the village as it finally settled, the fires dying, their warmth and golden light fading as just the ambers glowed.

He went into the bedroom's *en suite* bathroom and got ready for bed. He took a shower and tried to calm down. The water was still warm from the fire Joseph lit just before dusk under the forty-five-gallon drum that contained water out back. He finished and dried himself with a towel so old he wondered if it went back all the way to his grandfather's time there before that Nazi with the big mouth had cheated the place from him.

Rann walked to the bed and lay down. He looked up at the mosquito net knotted above him hanging from an ornate hook dug into a thick wooden rafter above. He could stand on his tip toes and get it down, stretch it out around the bed, protect himself from the mosquitos hiding in the shadows waiting for him to sleep so they could swoop down and take his blood. But what was the point? What was the point of any of it, being here laying on the bed his grandfather no longer wanted and that had been home to a guy who'd just called him a cunt?

He closed his eyes and listened to the darkness as the crickets sang their night song. The breeze gently blew the leaves in the trees. Tomorrow, he thought, tomorrow he'd sort out these people who had mocked him, reneging on a deal that was nothing to them but everything to him. He thought of that guy with the plane, laying there five hundred miles away on a mattress loaded with money. *Tomorrow*, tomorrow he'd extinguish the rage that roared within him. If he was lucky, the bodyguard would be there with the South African, and he would get tough and come at him, so Rann could show him how to fight.

And closing his eyes, he listened to the night, breathing the mountain air that swept through the forest and across the fields that he owned deep into his lungs. He let it out slowly, over and over, just as his Sensei had taught him during his training days, until his body had unconsciously taken over—breathing until he relaxed, allowing him control enough to permit sleep, despite the rage that surged within. But when sleep eventually did come, it was a sleep fitful and turbulent, filled with angry dreams of conflict that shook him into semi-consciousness hour by hour until at last, at four a.m., he awoke from a dream in which the world was shaking and opened his eyes to find five Africans who'd come in off the mountains holding *pangar* machetes in their hands standing there around his bed in the darkness.

Rann Singh's Sikh god Guru Nanak was looking out for him.

******

Charles Chuck Chendrill stopped the Aston outside of the house in Burnaby with its basement suite where he'd first met the dentist named Dennis who'd lost his licence because he'd married a woman who was a whore and she'd destroyed him. The last time they'd spoken, things were good again between them, and there had been talk of a new future in the remote Northern Territories, where some of the inhabitants wanted to keep hold of their remaining teeth. "It would pay well," he'd said to Chendrill, and Chendrill had felt happy for him.

Closing the door quietly, he walked down the driveway and knocked on the suite's side entrance and waited, the lights on but no TV. Stepping back, he stood in the darkness watching the light on the curtains, the basement suite apartment appearing still within. Then he saw movement, someone at the window, then another, a figure coming from the back room moving towards the window that looked out towards the front road. The curtain moved slightly and then the figure crossed, casting a huge shadow through the front door as it opened. Chendrill stepped forward out of the shadow, "Dennis, who are you hiding from?"

But he wasn't hiding from anyone—the idiot who was sniffing around his wife was already sitting inside.

Archall Diamond sat in the living room with a pair of Ray-Bans on as though any second the sun may come out, even though it was night-time. The 'gangsta' sitting there gawking at Alla while Dennis messed about in his bullshit surgery. Moments before he'd just been about to lean in and ask her to leave her husband for him so he wouldn't have to kill him, giving her the option before things went too far, when he'd heard the door and felt irritated at the interruption, sneaking a look and shitting his pants when he saw it was Chendrill's Aston Martin.

Seeing Chendrill, Dennis smiled. "Chuck, just the man I wanted to see. How are you?"

Dennis let him in and Chendrill looked at Archall as though he knew he was there all along.

"I was about to call you about a problem that is developing," said Dennis.

And he had been, the gangster guy with the stupid tooth was becoming a pest. Chendrill smiled at Alla and sat himself down at the kitchen table where he always sat, guessing Archall Diamond was the problem. "Well I'm here now, what's up?" Dennis just stood there, not knowing what to say.

Already knowing the answer from putting two and two together, Chendrill asked, loud enough for everyone to hear, if it was Dennis who'd fixed Diamond's front tooth.

"Yes, it looks really good."

Chendrill looked at Dennis, unsurprised that the man was doing backstreet work now that he had his mind in gear and imagined he had a set up out back. Looking past him, he saw Alla, who still managed to look gorgeous, despite living through her own hell. Archall sat opposite her in his sunglasses, mesmerized by the beautiful woman sitting politely with a blanket across her lap. *Archall and Patrick are the same, though,* Chendrill thought—both men were transfixed by the woman and neither was half the man her husband was.

He said quietly, "How's Alla doing?"

Dennis smiled. It wasn't often anyone asked him about his wife, not these days.

"She's getting better I think. She's managing to move her toes. Apparently, we were lucky—the guy who worked on her that night was a top surgeon. She's been to see him and had x-rays done. The man's saying a couple more operations and things may improve tenfold. He's even suggesting she may be able to walk again."

Chendrill said, "But?"

And Dennis nodded, "Yeah, you're right, there's always a 'but', and it's a big one, it's going to cost money to do it now or we can wait and let it go through the healthcare system. But there's another problem there, which I'm ashamed to say is mine, because, you see, when I lost everything, I let the healthcare insurance slip too. Luckily someone—and I don't even want to think about who—but someone luckily put up the money for the accident, and I'm hoping whoever did was from the past and stays there."

Chendrill stared at him, then down at the table cloth, and thought about Patrick, knowing deep down it was him—the guy living his life without any real responsibility, treating hookers the same way others would treat a girl with whom they were in a serious relationship. Looking up again, he said, "Many 'buts' hey?"

Dennis nodded again, "Yeah too many."

Chendrill sat there staring at Archall Diamond, wondering why the guy was sitting in their living room at eight-thirty in the evening wearing sunglasses. What he'd do, he thought, was speak to Sebastian about Alla and see if he could help and then have Sebastian tell Patrick to lay off and stay away. After all, Sebastian was the only person the sexed-up ex-condo salesman would listen to, for the moment anyhow. "How much for the operation if you go private?" said Chendrill.

"About a hundred grand for them both," Dennis answered.

Then Chendrill nodded towards Archall Diamond, "And can I ask you why that asshole is here?"

And from Dennis's face, he could see the man was a pain. Coming straight out with it, Dennis said, "I haven't got my licence back yet—as you've probably guessed—and one of the problems with operating outside the system is that first of all, you may not get paid and second of all, some of the people aren't nice, but they do pay, and pay well. And Archall pays well. He just got here actually and has told me about a friend of his who also wants a diamond in his tooth. Apparently, he liked Archall's so much he'd like me to go see him out in Richmond—at some house on the river."

Chendrill said, "I don't recommend you go anywhere with him," and watched Dennis shrug.

"Obviously I need the money Chuck, it's not what I'd prefer to do, but I can't afford to turn anything down right now, even if it costs me my licence for good, which to be frank I may never get back anyway."

Chendrill nodded. The man was so honest with his friends, but not with himself. Or maybe he was? At least he was trying to make it work again with the woman he loved when so many would have given up. Chendrill said, "When you go, call me. I want to come along with you—I'm serious. If this guy gives you a problem about it, you call me okay. Do not go alone."

Chendrill stood. "I can't promise anything, I'm going to speak with someone about Alla and—he may be able to help financially."

Then changing the subject, Chendrill called out loudly to Alla, "Alla, I'm glad to see you're looking well." Then nodding towards Archall Diamond, he followed it up jokingly with, "And keep away from him, he's trouble."

Then he turned and said quietly to Dennis, "Don't forget what I said."

Chendrill left the basement, but not before crossing the open suite to hug Alla and kiss her cheek, smelling her perfect skin and getting a closer look at Diamond as he tried to read what the guy was up to.

He pulled the Aston away from the curb and drove up the street, then went around the block and stopped in the shadows a distance away, looking at the lights in the windows of the basement suite that now doubled as Dennis' surgery. Archall Diamond was sitting in his friend's home, he thought, more interested in some friend's tooth than in his Mercedes, which for some reason was sitting crushed to a cube in the garage.

"A friend of his also wants a diamond in his tooth," Dennis had said.

Guys like Diamond don't arrange for other people to fuck up their perfectly good front teeth like that, thought Chendrill, they want to be unique—even if they were as dumb as that fuckhead. There was more to it. The guy had removed one love rival, of that much he was certain, but there was nothing going on between those two. From what Chendrill could tell, all Archall Diamond was doing was gawking at a beautiful woman who was being polite.

An hour later, Chendrill was still there watching the front of Dennis's when he saw Diamond come out, still with his sunglasses on, even though it was night-time, smiling to himself and, stopping in the driveway for a moment, he stared at the windows, then walked to the rear of a truck and opened it.

Quietly, Chendrill opened the Aston's driver side door, slipped out, closed it again, and moved in the shadows along the other side of the street towards where Diamond was standing with the back of the truck down and both hands in a tool bag sifting through it until he pulled out a pair of long nose pliers.

Coming up from behind at an angle and catching him on his blind side, Chendrill said, "You going back in there with those to help him pull some teeth?" Archall turned, quickly pulling the Taser from his bag and firing the unit's two small darts with their thin wires trailing behind and catching Chendrill right in the shoulder as he tried to twist away, sending fifty thousand volts into him and throwing him helplessly to the ground.

Rock Solid

******

Rann Singh sat up in bed and looked to the five Africans surrounding him as they stood, *pangars* in hand, with ragged clothes and unkempt dreadlocked matted hair and said in Swahili, "I'll give you about thirty seconds to leave peacefully right now or I'm going to leave you all for dead and if you live you live."

Rann watched as the one in the center held up Blou's empty shotgun then threw it on the floor. Rann stared at him summing them all up. He was the biggest, and in the moonlight Rann could see his eyes were watery and yellow, but he looked strong. The others were smaller with the same blotchy bearded look of the same age; another, looking nervous, was younger, just a kid, maybe in his early twenties. Rann said, "The other guy needed that, I don't."

And the African replied simply, "Money or we kill you."

Then Rann smiled and said as he raised his hands, speaking Swahili, the language he loved so much, "Okay, okay. You win—you win. You can have the money. It's behind the door." And asking with his eyes if it was okay to move, he slowly slid out of bed, shuffling his way toward the door as the Africans kept their distance, but blocked his path as Rann stood and leaned forward, placing his hands out in front of himself, touching the wood of the beamed wall, and feeling its varnish beneath his palms. He said again, "I'm going to get your money, it's right here by the door."

And slowly Rann began to move towards the door along the wall. Passing his grandfather's coat hook, he saw the small nail he'd watched him hammer in for him when he was a child, remembering how he had stood holding a huge hammer in both hands as his grandfather held the nail and Rann tried to knock it into one of the beams.

He moved on slowly, step by step along the wall until he was out and away from the bed. He reached the door, large and solid and open wide, just as he'd left it before he'd slept, its inner face hidden from view flat against the wooden wall beams. The Africans in the open doorway watched him cautiously as he slowly pulled it away from the wall and gently brought them inside, respecting their superiority with his eyes as he squeezed it past them, feeling the weight of the mahogany bite down tight against the door jam as he closed the solid door and gently turned the key, feeling the bronze of the deadbolt fall into place as he locked them all in the room with him.

Slowly he turned to them, dropping the key into his trouser pocket for them all to see, and said in the language he knew they'd all understand, "Don't say I didn't warn you."

He brought his right foot up hard and fast, catching the African who'd thrown the shotgun on the floor perfectly in the throat, crushing his windpipe and knocking him into the wall as a younger second man came at him, instinctively hacking down blindly with his *pangar*. Rann felt the young man's arm break at the elbow as he stepped to the side, holding the man's wrist with his left hand and snapping the elbow with his other as he took the man's knee out with his left foot, all in one swift move, and then let go.

Taking a quick step forward, he smashed the flat of his foot into the third African's chest, sending him off his feet and into the wall; then ducking, feeling the swish of a *pangar* blade skimming his head right before feeling the weight of the fifth African as he grabbed him from the side and ran him into the wall. He felt the sting in his back as he landed hard next to his grandfather's coat hook, and then the other African who'd taken the kick to the chest was on him, holding him fast along with the other, both clinging desperately to their *pangars* as they pushed against him holding him there. Rann felt their strong hands and arms pressing against him and smelled their breath, sweat, and hair as they tried to tire him with their strength, rubbing their heads and elbows into his face. Then he felt one release the hand he was holding the *pangar* in as he worked the butt of the weapon into his neck, the man pulling back and swinging in for the kill, Rann waiting till the last second as the blade came down, pulling away from the other, spinning inside and using the man's momentum to roll him around, smashing him into the wall, crushing the man's nose with the back of his head and hearing the metal from his grandfather's coat hook pierce through the man's skull as he hit the wall. Then like lightning, he was away, coming again back at the other African, moving inside him as the man came at him hitting as hard as he had ever hit another man with an eight punch combo, crashing his fists with incredible speed and precision into the African's solar plexus, stomach, and heart and hearing the man's *pangar* hit the ground as he felt the muscles and ribs break down as his fists flew in and out like whips, one after the other, sending him momentarily to the floor.

Then he backed off, bouncing around the floor at the foot of his grandfather's bed, like a boxer catching his breath and surveying the damage. One was dead, hanging limp from his grandfather's hook, another on the floor not breathing from the kick to the throat that crushed his windpipe, the kid down with a broken arm looking terrified, another was moving quickly from the side swinging his *pangar* like Zorro, hacking and slashing the air from side to side as he came. Rann moved to the corner by the door as he approached, letting the African pin him there, using each wall as a shield, waiting for the angle to change as the man switched the swinging from side to side and tried to throw down a thrust from another angle that he'd hope would be the last, then it came at him like lightning from above, the man raising the *pangar* and bringing it down with both hands, hoping to smash through Rann's forearms as he lifted them to protect himself from the blow. As soon as the African committed to the swipe, like a whip, Rann was on him grabbing both the man's wrists as he twisted himself down to the side, using the man's momentum to pull him downward and smash him face-first to the floor.

Rann backed off again, bouncing like a fighter, keeping on his toes, getting his air and looking around him, the Africans in shock from what had happened to them in nothing more than a matter of seconds. He looked around feeling air rush in and out of his lungs as he felt his heart race in his chest. No one was coming at him yet. One dead, maybe two by now, as he'd felt the power of his foot hit the man's throat. Another, the young one unmoving, crouching down with a broken arm and busted knee, was still terrified. The African Zorro was playing dead. The one who'd suffered the punch combo to the stomach and chest was on his hands and knees and now just getting his wind. He'd be next and would be coming at him again.

He waited, knowing he could finish them all, but he waited, breathing, skipping in the center of the room as he regained his strength and kicked any *pangars* he could see under the bed. Then the African who thought he was Zorro stood and looked at Rann, his face covered in blood, his lip and nose split open; the other African was staring at Rann now too. Rann, who was trained to fight, still keeping on his toes and wiping the sweat from his eyes and his now bald head, only too happy to have no hair for any of them to grab and hold.

The remaining two men looked at each other, then to the kid on the floor who'd given up, motioning with their eyes, signalling him to stand. Rann said in Swahili, "If you think you can just say sorry and leave you can't. You had your chance."

But these men who lived in the forest at the foot of the mountain weren't going anywhere. Slowly the kid with the broken arm got to his feet. Still bobbing, Rann said to him, "Sit back down and stay out of it and I'll not break the other one and maybe you'll live."

But he didn't listen. Suddenly the one by the door came at

him, running full force as the other came at the same time. Rann moved to the side at the last second, lifting his left leg and tripping one, sending him headfirst into the dresser and smashing face first into the mirror as he landed. The other dove on him, pinning Rann to the floor, grabbing him by his neck in a choke hold as he began to shout at the kid with the broken arm.

"Pangar, Pangar."

The kid moved towards the collection of *pangars* under the bed, reaching under and picking one up and slowly moving back towards them as the African struggled to hold onto Rann as he wriggled and wriggled, trying to break free. The African shouted at the kid desperately, "Hit him in the head—Hit him in the head."

As the kid moved forward, trying to hold his broken arm at the same time as the *pangar*, reaching them at the foot of the bed and looking down at Rann's head, Rann wriggling like crazy, tasting the man's blood from his arm, smelling his breath, feeling the African's face against the side of his head, the man wrapping his legs around him, clasping him with his whole body, still screaming at the kid, "Kill him—Kill him!" The kid drew nearer, trying to summon the courage to slay a man. Then he was right there above them, letting his broken arm dangle as he raised the *pangar* wiping the tears from his eyes from the fear and pain with the back of his hand. Rann watched as he lined up on him with his eyes for a hit that would land right above his forehead, and waited, listening to the African screaming in his ear as he did. Then he went still, allowing the kid to gain focus for a split second to take the hit that would put him out of his misery. Just then, the African who hit the dresser came around, stirring and lifting himself from the glass, distracting the kid as he swung the *pangar* down at the same time that Rann, who was waiting for the very last second, shifted his weight with all his might, swung the African holding him around to take the blow right above his ear.

Before the kid could realize what had just happened, Rann

quickly shook the dead man off him, stood, and with a spinning back kick into the kid's chest, sent him flying across his grandfather's bed and onto the floor on the other side. Then Rann was up again bobbing on his feet, arms up at his chest getting his breath, surveying the damage, saying to himself "Three dead, two to go." He spat the dead man's blood from his mouth and watched the African who hit the dresser look around the room at his three dead comrades.

"Like I said, it's too late, if you want to say sorry."

The African was looking for a *pangar* now, and saw them in the darkness in a pile under the bed—and saw too the one stuck in his friend's head on the other side of Rann—still bobbing on his toes like he'd been trained, watching him and watching the side of the bed where he'd sent the kid with his broken arm and *pangar* flying, keeping them both in his line of site. The African stood with his tough bare feet in the broken glass mirror looking for a weapon. Then he saw the shotgun on the floor next to his friend with the crushed windpipe, and ran over to it and picked it up and held it at Rann, getting ready to fire. Rann looked at the two large barrels aiming straight at him and wished the South African had never left it for him as a parting gift, then remembered the guy had given him the shotgun but no cartridges. Rann said in Swahili, "If that was loaded, you'd have already shot me."

The African smiled back at him with the gun saying, "Maybe it is and I want to shoot you twice, once to bring you down and then next to kill you."

Rann watched him, trying to work out which end the man was going to use as a club—the barrel or the stock? He knew if it was loaded, there was little he could do at this range. But it wasn't, there wasn't any ammo—besides, the guy would have fired by now. The African was still coming at him slowly, laughing and smiling.

"We been here before and we know where the man keep the ammunition *Bwana choot* and I'm going to shoot you *Bwana choot*, first in the legs then in the face. I going to blow your legs off first then shoot you in the face, yeah in the face *choot* boy, in the face."

And that's when he raised the gun aimed at Rann's legs and pulled the trigger. Hearing the trigger but not the hammer releasing, in that split second, Rann was on him, knocking the gun to one side with the palm of his hand and bringing his foot up hard into the African's chin, knocking his head back and taking him clean off his feet, landing back in the mirror glass behind him. Leaning over as he landed to pick up the gun, Rann held it in his hand as he walked carefully towards the side of the bed where he'd sent the kid flying to see him lying there on the ground, still holding the *pangar* with which he'd missed Rann and killed his friend—its blade now stuck deep in his side.

******

Archall Diamond stood above Charles Chuck Chendrill and pulled the trigger, sending another pulse of incapacitating electricity down the gun's wires and into the dart electrodes that had pierced his clothing and attached themselves to his skin and thought, *that'll do it.*

The big ape was now out cold on the ground. Quickly, he slid the two heavy wooden planks out of the back of the truck, attached them, and reached into the back, pulling the hook and wire from the winch and attaching it to Chendrill's thick leather belt. He hit the switch at the end of the control cord and dragged the big man off the road and up the planks into the rear of his canopied truck, with its big fuck-you wheels, picked up the priest he carried for fishing— so he could administer their last rights—and cracked Chendrill across the back of the head before closing the hatch down.

Taking it easy as he pulled away from the curb, Archall drove for a minute through Burnaby, passing houses and cops and people on their way home from nights out or whatever it was they were doing, getting on with their lives. Archall Diamond was getting on with his. He reached a quiet strip mall and parked up with the rear of his truck against the wall and got out. From what he could tell, it had only been about three minutes since he'd given the big ape a blast and a smack around the head to keep him quiet.

Walking around the back, he looked in, putting his face against the blacked out rear window. Chendrill was still out—at least he hoped. Opening the back slightly, he snuck his hand in and pulled the trigger to the Taser gun he'd left by the door again and watched Chendrill's body spasm as the current shot down the gun's thin electrical cables and into his body.

He was out now for certain. Opening up the hatch, he jumped up and climbed in and sat on the wheel well looking at the big guy laying there all fucked up, saying to no one but himself, "You used to be a big man, didn't you?"

Then he got to work with the first inner tube, pulling its thick rubber over Chendrill's head, threading his arms through and tucking it up under his armpits. Then he grabbed a chain he'd bought at the store and wrapped it around his ankles tight, fastened it all with tape, added the second inner tube to his feet to stop the chain snagging in the shallows and pulled out an electric battery powered pump. He hit the switch and blew them both up nice and tight, one after the other.

The big ape was ready to go swimming in the swimsuit he'd bought for the dentist to wear, Archall thought as he drove his way out to a quiet spot he knew in the Fraser River. The big man, who'd been going around town asking personal questions about the Diamond, checking him out to see if he was a killer—well guess what, he was. *Yeah, he was a killer, a fucking badass motherfucking killer, Archall Di – A – Mond. The man wit his mind on, gonna take you down, make you drown, if you mess with the man in his town.* Yeah, he liked that one, he thought, wishing he had a piece of paper to write the words on. But he'd leave out the words drown—didn't need to leave any clues as to how the Diamond operated, even though he went around telling anyone who cared to listen how they were gonna get floated, but what did that mean? Could be he put them in a balloon, sent them off into the sky. But still, 'drown' was no good for a rap, it needed to be something else—maybe to 'frown'. Maybe.

He stopped at the lights and opened the rear window that connected the driver's cab to the back of the truck and looked at Chendrill all trussed up like a pig on the way to market with a camo net on its head. Archall stretched his arm through giving him another wallop with the Taser. How many had that been now, he thought. Too many, but what the fuck difference did that make?

He reached the river and crossed it on the Alex Fraser Bridge, swinging north again towards River Road and wondering about the time. He could see the river lit up by the lights from the bridge now—its surface looking calm. The tide out there on the Strait of Georgia was beginning to turn, just around midnight. He looked at the clock on his dashboard illuminated in green—11:50 p.m.

Not yet, he thought, give it half hour to let the rip build at the river's mouth, then it can drag him south for a while until the air's all gone from the tube.

He kept on going, heading west along the riverbank, the water to his right, passing the occasional car driving the other way before he snuck into one of the sidings he'd researched a year or so back when he had been thinking of seeing if Rasheed could swim. Checking his mirrors, he turned off the truck's lights and reversed right to the edge of the river bank and looked at his clock. It was just after midnight. The water was passing him now, fast and strong, heading out towards the ocean.

The funniest thing, he thought, as he sat there reaching into the back to give Chendrill one last long electrical taser blast before he got out, was that after the big ape had left the dentist's, while her husband was in his surgery he'd asked Alla if she'd consider leaving him so as they could be together and she'd looked him in the eye and said, "I can't make plans until my surgery and that's a long way now."

And Diamond had asked, "Why?"

And taking a deep breath and fighting back tears that were real, Alla had said, lying, "Dennis won't pay for the operation. But yes, when I've had it and I can walk again, I'll be looking to the future."

And that was all Archall Diamond needed to hear. She was his for certain and all it was going to take was a quick run upstairs to pick up an easy hundred grand off the bed. And all he needed to do then was get a hold of Rann, sell those tablets for… whatever he needed to make and re-coup the loss he'd incurred giving away the first batch as a promotion and then he'd be sorted. He wouldn't even notice it, and she'd be up on her feet in time for the hockey season to start.

And that's why he left his Ray-Bans on when he left the house, because the future was looking so God damn bright. Then he saw Chendrill's Aston, recognizing it because he liked the wheels and that's all he could see, and he'd waited there for him to come over to say something smart like he had and then zapped the fucker.

He walked to the back of the truck and picked up a stick and threw it in the water and *whoosh* it was gone—perfect. Turning around, he looked again through the tinted black windows and opened the back, dropping down the short tailgate, and climbed in, staring at Chendrill all ready to set sail, still in his blue Hawaiian. It was a shame to waste a nice shirt like that, but there you go. The fucker had to go, had to get himself floated, *get himself demoted,* 'cos he couldn't keep his nose out of the Diamond's life. Showing up at his girl's and trying to look cool and being a pain. Then as he reached for the pin and the gaffer tape he knew the ocean would eventually pull off, he ripped off three pieces and poked the three holes in the tube in front of Chendrill's face, sealed them up along with one across his mouth and moustache for good measure, then he punctured another six at the top of the tube around his feet and covered them with tape before saying out loud, "I hope you'se took them swimming lessons as a kid Mr. Snooper Dooper Super PI man."

He sat himself with his back to the bulkhead of the truck's cab, put his feet on top of the camo netting on Chendrill's head and shoulders, and began to push Chendill out over the tailgate, dropping him—still unconscious—straight down into the fast-flowing water.

******

Dan sat in his bedroom and thought back to the woman who his mother had said was older than her and wondered how long it had taken for the lady to learn to do a trick like that with her mouth. Marsha hadn't gone near it with hers, and neither had Melisa. The blind girl in the park was about to try—just before her dog attacked him.

He picked up his phone and looked to it—another text from Marsha, 'wondering how you are?' to which he replied, 'absolutely no different.' And he wasn't lying, as nothing had happened over the last twenty minutes, apart from him staining one of Chendrill's socks. Then he got another one. This time from Sebastian. It read:

Daniel, get some sleep. Tomorrow's seven am call is

really important. Be up and running in the morning first thing—don't forget. Sebastian.'

Completely ignoring it, he thought, *Yeah whatever*, and then wondered if maybe older women were the way to go? After all, look at the way the crazy agent from L.A. had reacted in his kitchen, before his mother had kicked her out as well. Maybe it's just the way they were? No wonder Chuck Chendrill spends so much time here and the baker for that matter, who used to come around at 6:00 a.m. with his tray.

He got up and looked out the window to see if the woman across the road was in her bedroom getting undressed with the curtains open as she often did. No. Then he turned on his computer and typed in Adalia Seychan's name and watched as a host of information flooded forward. An Oscar, big deal, Golden Globe, another two Oscars, yeah yeah, big deal. He opened the images of her and flipped through Adalia standing there in her gown, statue in hand smiling, then another photo—*wow she was hot in the 80s.* He recognized her now and remembered his mother crying over some soppy movie she was in when he was a kid, remembering her saying with tears in her eyes as the sun was setting in the sky behind her, 'You'll be mine, always be mine.'

So this was the woman he was doing the photo shoot with tomorrow, *but what the fuck for*? He didn't know, and didn't care. This one Sebastian was getting so hot under the collar about and making such a fuss about him being there real early so as he could sit around again for three hours doing nothing and wait for Adalia Seychan to strut out onto that green stage and lick the sweat off his chest just like Marsha had?

******

Chuck Chendrill came around just as the inner tubes took him floating out into the open water and the larger waves started hitting his face. What the fuck was happening? He was freezing, wet, in complete darkness and barely able to breathe with his whole-body stiff with cramps.

He looked around in blind panic, as another wave hit him in the face, the riptide taking him quickly out to sea. He was in the ocean, floating. With his hands left free, he felt around him as he started to spin in the water, the lights from the shore small and orange, now almost half a mile away, barely visible as he bobbed up and down in the swell.

Reaching up, he began to pull at the camo net around his head, feeling its thin nylon string digging into his eyes—its bottom fastened loosely around the tube. Something was also on his mouth, loosening now from the sea water. He opened his mouth, breaking the tape's adhesive seal, as another wave hit him hard, stinging his eyes and washing up his nose. Lifting his hand up, he ripped the netting away from his head, and still holding it in his right hand, he looked around properly as he rose up, peaking in the swell.

Nothing was around, no fishing boats, no yachts making a night sail across to the islands, no ferries, just fast-moving water that was taking him south—and he was cold. He looked at his feet lit up by the full moon as they bobbed up and down, the fresh new chain he'd seen hanging up in Archall Diamond's garage was now wrapped around his ankles holding the other tube just under the water at an upright angle. Something was on top, silver in color, another strip of tape, then he saw a similar strip on the inner tube under his arms keeping his body up.

He moved along in the water, pushing the chain with his legs, trying to free it from his ankles. The rip tide was pulling him down the coast. His body felt solid, hurting and in pain from the tasering and freezing cold. As he spun slowly in the water, he said to himself, "You're still breathing, you're still breathing."

He remembered coming up behind Archall and almost dodging the Taser gun, cussing himself for underestimating the man and thinking he was a fool. He took a deep breath and let the sea air fill his lungs, feeling the drips of salt water pull up inside his nostrils, stinging as they went. *Let it out, breathe,* he thought as he said to himself again, trying to keep his lips closed as he spoke.

"You're still alive, you're still alive."

He looked to the land, the mouth of the river was nowhere to be seen now, the lights of the mainland distant. He looked to his watch—it was still there, Diamond had not thought to steal it, or just didn't care. Either way, it was on his wrist and still working despite the salt water.

It was just coming up to twelve thirty now. He'd left Dennis' before ten and waited till Diamond came out at around eleven—and that was in Burnaby. It was a half hour trip to the coast from there and he still had to prep this shit and get him in the water. Half hour, half hour tops, he'd been in the water, floating.

"I'm still here, still breathing."

He was out a long way, but it wasn't the first time he'd been out this far floating, not swimming. It had been about the same time of year, out there with his friends swimming in English Bay when he was a kid, taking it easy with them, cruising out slowly to the freight ships way out there on a hot summer's day, taking an hour or two to get there floating on their backs in their shorts chatting as the water lapped around them, feeling the warmth of the sun on their faces and chests and the cold of the water the deeper their legs went.

Back then, they would reach the ships, looking up at them from below, painted monoliths of rust-stained steel rising up from the water, and swim to the rudder, hanging on its back with their feet on the propeller tops, climbing and diving from the ship's coned nose, lounging on it in the sun as they listened to the crew talking above in a foreign tongue as they worked on deck—unseen people from some distant land oblivious to Chendrill and his friends trespassing below.

But that was twenty-five years ago, Chendrill thought, though the water's temperature was the same give or take a couple of degrees. He hurt, yes, his body was tight and in pain, but he could still move his hands and arms and feet. And he was still alive.

And then as a wave hit him, slapping the tubes and stinging his face, he looked to his feet to see the tape loose now, flapping in the cold sea breeze. He stared at it, then at the one in front of his face with its adhesive beginning to give. Reaching in, he lifted a corner of the tape, peeling it back and instantly heard the hissing of air as he uncovered the first pin prick. *Shit,* he thought, *bad move, bad move.* He tried to smooth the tape back down with his fingers then smother it, holding it flat with his palm as he felt the cold of the water splash up across the top of his hand.

He looked to the tube at his feet, getting smaller now as he felt the weight of his legs and the chains begin to shift his position in the water until he could no longer see his legs and felt the colder, deeper water at his feet.

Shit.

He looked to the tape on the tube now only inches from his face and could hear the faint hissing as the air escaped from beneath his palm and he felt the weight of the chain around his legs trying to pull him under. Then another wave hit him fast, sucker punching him from the side, catching him unaware, feeling its stinging cold in his eyes, ears, nose, and mouth, forcing its way through his tightly pursed lips into his mouth and down his throat, choking him.

Coughing and wheezing, Chendrill gathered himself, fighting

for breath, spitting out sea water, and then finding his breath again. He breathed in a deep lungful of air, smelled rubber and looked to the tape which was now gone. Quickly, he slapped his hand on it and for the first time called out for no one to hear. He kicked as hard as his body could on the chain around his ankles, pulling up and pushing down, feeling the flesh rip from his skin with the force, up down, up down, forward backward, up down, up down. The water lapping around his ears, going up his nose. The air from the tube bubbling around his feet as he slammed his feet up and down and around and around like a cyclist, feeling the tension of the chain differ with every kick, the links shifting with every movement, the inner tube getting softer.

Then watching the air escape under his hands, Chendrill pushed his head forward, covering the holes with his mouth, sealing the pin holed area with his lips, pushing down on the tubes, feeling the salt water in his eyes and running directly up his nose as he kicked and kicked with his feet. His mind racing, as he said to himself over and over, 'You're still alive, you're still alive, you're not dead yet.' Locking his mouth around the tube as it got softer, the chain pulling on the remaining air in the tube, Chendrill bit hard on the tube's rubber, trying to seal the holes off with his teeth as the riptide carried him along in the water.

He continued to kick as the waves splashing above him covered his head, dipping his face completely under the water, then he stopped kicking, shifted his weight, arched his back and neck, forcing the inner tube up into the crook of his neck, trying to lay on his back with his face against the night sky as he bit into the rubber and held the soft tube against his face. He gripped and squeezed the tube with either side of his mouth, sealing it as best he could with each hand forcing whatever air was left behind him as he hung there in the moving current, feeling its water cold on his face as each swell hit.

Reaching down with one hand, he tried to reach the laces on

his boots, pulling his knees up to him as he did, feeling the chain tightening around his legs then his cold fingertips touching the top of his boots, the laces double knotted tight as he always liked to do. Then in frustration he started to kick again with incredible fury, irrespective of pain, he pushed and pulled harder than he thought possible, feeling as though any moment his legs would snap off and drop down to the seabed.

Then just as Chendrill managed to get a full breath of air through his nose, the chain pulled him under, dropping him slowly deeper into the water. He felt the temperature change around his body as he slowly sank down towards the seabed, holding his breath the best he could, the water pressure squeezing his ears as he dropped. Sucking and biting into the rubber with his teeth, opening up a small hole with his incisors and releasing what little air he could through one clasped hand as he reached down with the other, lifting his body, rotating it in the cold dark water, grabbing the chain with his free hand and shaking it as he spun himself around and around, pulling and pulling, trying to feel for the chain's end as he sucked on the foul-tasting, life-giving air from within the tube. Then he found it with a finger, the chain's end attached to another piece with a small plastic cable tie already stretched from his determination.

Taking a deep breath from the tube, Chendrill dug his fingers in, wrapped his free hand around the chain, and pulled it as hard as he could, jerking it and jerking it as he slowly floated downward. Then with a snap he felt the tension give and the chain loosen as he kicked and pulled and spun his body around in the water until he felt it drop away. He continued to kick and his body began to rise back up towards the surface. The pressure loosened from his ears, the temperature changed as he rose through the water, the remaining air in the tube clasped firmly in his teeth pulling him up and up until he burst through the surface back into the swell.

Chendrill lay there on his back in the swell looking up to the sky, his heart racing as he felt the water splash on his face again, but he did not care. Trying to relax with as little effort as possible he stayed still, swirling one hand at his sides enough to keep him afloat as he moved along with the current, drifting up and down on the swell. He was tired and cold and hurt all over. The water was cold on his feet, his boots now gone—squeezed and shaken off despite their laced double knots—but he was still alive, just.

He lifted his arm from the water and looked at his watch, which was still there and working just fine. *Just like me*, he thought, *just like me*. From what he could tell, he was still only about two miles from shore, the lights faint in the distance as the riptide eased. It was almost one a.m. Twenty years prior, he'd spend a good four hours out on the ocean, in the bay. This experience wasn't new to him, and as long as he cruised with the current instead of against it, taking it as slow as he needed to, edging bit by bit towards the shore, letting the current do the work, he'd make it—unless his heart gave out.

So, he lay there on his back, resting, relaxing, drifting with the current, and once he began to get his wind and felt whatever strength he had left begin to return, he let go of the inner tube that had saved his life; and flipping onto his stomach, as he had as a young man so many years ago, he began to swim calmly and surely away from the current and back towards land.

It was almost three in the morning when he first felt the seabed beneath his feet and stood for a moment in a shallow with the water at his chest, staring at the land now only some three hundred feet away with its rocky shale beach covered with logs pushed high by the tide and further still by storms.

He leaned forward and pushed himself into the now calm water and, exhausted, gently cruised quietly towards the shore, finally reaching land and pulling himself from the water. He stepped up twelve feet onto the beach, lay between two huge cedars and, smiling to himself, slept in the warm night air.

An hour later he woke, feeling his body ache all over. He crouched between the logs, finding the strength to carry on, then eventually stood. There were houses there beyond the beach safe from the rising tide, long gardens with cut grass and swing sets and chairs ready for the sun, which would be along soon. Chendrill looked to one with its big cedar shakes, painted dark green and flying the stars and stripes proudly from its rooftop. He was in the United States, he thought, and wondered why he hadn't seen the flag as he'd come ashore.

Anyone in their right mind would go and knock on the door and ask for help, have the police and ambulance come take him away to a warm bed with about five hundred questions and news crews. He'd sit there like a chump in a private room and watch his story unfold on KOMO News—with pictures of Archall Diamond being arrested, showing off his fucking front tooth to the cameras. But that wasn't his style. He needed to cross the border, get back into Canada—besides it was almost 4:15 a.m. and he needed to pick up Dan in a couple of hours.

He took a deep breath and felt his clothing, his Hawaiian still damp but not too bad, his jeans damper. Crouching down, he took off his socks, then doing the same with his jeans he saw the heavy bruising around his ankles and shins from the chain.

He rung out his socks and felt the swelling along his shins and ankles. It was bad, but it could have been worse, he thought. He looked to the house, whoever was in there asleep now. Then he remembered his phone and pulled it out and looked at it as he sat back down behind the log in his underpants and looked out to the sea that had nearly taken him. Hitting the button, he gave it a try, nothing—not surprising though. Digging back into his pocket, he pulled out the keys to the Aston and his wallet. Diamond hadn't taken anything, he thought, just trussed him up and thrown him in the drink.

He placed the wallet and phone to one side and wrung out his jeans and shirt, feeling his hands shake as he did. Then, putting everything back on, he grabbed his keys and wallet and felt his shoulder ache as he threw the phone back into the ocean and said, "That's all you get of me, Archall Diamond."

He walked north feeling the rocks beneath his feet along the beach for fifteen minutes until he could see the first border camera and a black SUV patrol car passing in the distance. He knew the border well, hanging out there on the other side often as a kid and then as a young man. 'The Border'—at Zero Avenue in Canada, was little less than a two-foot ditch separating two countries and their different attitudes. Patrolled by land and air and watched by camera diligently on the south side from the Pacific to the Atlantic, the north was patrolled by air sometimes and by land occasionally—it's the way it was.

Staying away from the cameras, Chendrill cut inland, feeling the ground beneath his feet slide in his still damp socks. He reached the road and stood in the darkness at the side of a tree and stared at the open border a good thousand feet away in the distance. Then he saw the black SUV coming back his way from the south and sinking back into the trees, he let it pass, following it with his eyes as it cruised along and settled in a siding some five hundred feet ahead.

The driver sat there with his engine running and all his lights off so as no one could see him hidden in his huge black vehicle, looking north—Chendrill wanting to go north. Waiting and watching, Chendrill looked to his watch. It was coming up to a quarter to five. He could do it, he thought, jump the border as he had as a kid, running across and running back again for a dare. Watching the border patrol come screaming along from the south and then hiding from the RCMP on his side in the north.

The guy was still sitting there five minutes later, his silhouette unmoved in the vehicle's cab. If he was lucky, the guy would be asleep, taking an unscheduled work nap in a spot where the cameras couldn't see him and Chendrill could sneak past in the trees, then make the quick dash and jump the huge two-foot ditch. But he was no longer a kid, and the world had been a different place back then.

Slowly he moved forward from the rear, the silence of the night broken by the SUV's idling engine, the border patrol officer's balding head unmoving, visible through the rear window. He stopped by a tree and waited, the guy had to be asleep. Then suddenly he moved, his duck pond head turning around and looking out to the side, then the door opened and he got out.

Chendrill stayed still and watched as the man wandered around the vehicle. There was still time to approach the man, he thought, tell him his tall story that it would take him a day to prove after he'd come clean.

Then with the engine still running, the man walked away from the vehicle into the woods, stopping some hundred feet away out of sight of any cameras to unzip his fly, and, with his back to his vehicle, he started to pee. Chendrill moved closer, listening to the engine running. The big man in his Hawaiian and socks made his way through the darkness along the side of the SUV and opened the door and quietly sat, feeling the warmth inside. Quickly, he slammed the thing into drive and sped off as fast as the vehicle could travel—the sound of gunshots ringing in the air. He hit the border barrier, and slammed the patrol officer's vehicle across the ditch with a crash and a thump and bounced his way back into Canada.

He had less than five minutes before the whole international incident fully hit the grid, Chendrill thought, as he pulled the SUV to its left and made his way away from the officer, who he could only assume was still shooting at him. Seeing a right turn heading north, he took it and carried on up as far as he could, then took another right and a left, hit a main road, and screamed it along for almost half a mile until he was in the heart of Tsawwassen and saw a bus terminal. He slowed and snuck into a side road, parked the SUV in the driveway of an abandoned house that was due to be demolished, wiping everything down with the border patrol's napkin. He grabbed the guy's water bottle and sandwiches wrapped up in silver foil, and headed barefoot for the bus station.

It was 5:00 a.m.

It was two minutes past 5:00 a.m. when he heard and saw the RCMP cars go screaming past, heading south to the border and a minute after that, he heard the helicopter fly overhead as he sat on the bus, waiting for it to move and taking the first bite out of the patrol officer's cheese and ham sandwich.

It was bad, he knew it. This guy who's snack he was now eating was in a lot of trouble, he thought as he felt the engine of the first bus into Vancouver that morning start up and pull away, but there you go, as the old saying goes—you snooze you lose, or better still, always take your keys with you when you leave the vehicle for a piss. The poor guy, Chendrill thought as the bus took a turn onto the highway. He looked at the people all around him on a journey they probably took every day, just as the guy whose career he'd just put a dent in had probably taken a piss at the same tree every time he was on duty.

By 5:45 a.m., the bus was in Vancouver and Chendrill got out, feeling his whole body stiffen as he tried to move. Hurting badly, he raised his right arm and hailed a cab and with bleary eyes saw the turbaned driver and wondered if it was Dan's friend as he sat in the back. He gave the driver the address to Dan's mother's place and thirty minutes later when he opened his eyes, he was there. It was ten minutes after 6:00 a.m. and Dan was still asleep.

He opened the door with the key he kept on the same ring as the Aston's and shouted down the stairs to Dan to wake up as he passed through. He opened the door to Trish's room as she turned the bedside light on and sat up saying, "Chuck, I've been worried sick, I've been trying to call."

Chendrill said as he came in and sat on the bed, "Sorry, my phone got wet; it's not working."

Then she looked at him closely, kissed him on the cheek, and said, "Oh my God! You look awful!"

"Thanks."

"No Chuck, what on earth happened? Something's terrible has been going on, I had a really bad feeling that something had happened to you. I thought you were dead and now you're here, thank God, but you're covered in salt; it's all over your face and in your hair."

Chendrill thought, *you thought I was dead, so did I love*. His woman wasn't wrong, she'd felt it whatever it was, out there in the ether. Then Chendrill looked at his watch, took a deep breath and said, "I'm fine, don't worry. Dan needs to get ready. He has to be there in forty-five minutes."

He walked to the top of the stairs and called down, "Dan get up, we're leaving."

He heard Dan reply, saying, "Tell them I'm not coming in. I'm tired and I feel sick."

He's sick, Chendrill thought as he stood at the top of the stairs, feeling the bump on the back of his head for the first time. *Not feeling well—fuck me* after what he'd just gone through and he's still on time, then he felt a temper rush through him borne of tiredness and frustration as he shouted down, "Be ready outside with the keys to your car in fifteen minutes or I'll be down there and I'll drag you out by your fucking hair."

Then he turned and walked back to the bedroom and as soon as he saw Trish, he apologized.

She said, "It's okay." Then, she said, "Do you want to take a shower? I've got some of your clothes you left here clean in the cupboard." Chendrill looked to her and noticed her hands were shaking. But the truth was, so were his. He got up and walked into the bathroom and stripped down, and saw the salt lines in his dark denim trousers lying on the floor, his lower legs bruised to the bone, a mix of red and blue. Then Trish came in seeing them immediately and burst into tears.

Chendrill said, "It's okay, I just had an accident, it's okay."

"I knew it," Trish said as she bent down to look at his legs, "I knew it."

Then as he turned on the shower, Chendrill said, "Could you make sure he's ready. I'm feeling a little tired and I don't want to embarrass myself again shouting at him."

He looked to his watch—it was now twenty after. He'd forget shaving and be out in five minutes. He stepped in and put his head under the warm water, immediately tasting the sea salt as it ran down his face from his hair and skin as it all came rushing back to him as the words, 'I'm still alive, I'm still alive,' whirled through his mind.

By 6:30 a.m. he stepped outside in clean clothes. Dan stood there looking pissed off. Trish was holding the Ferrari's keys and asking if he'd like her to drive him and continued with, "You haven't got long."

Chendrill grabbed them, saying, "Don't worry, I'm driving a Ferrari. I'll be there in no time."

They pulled out onto the main road and headed towards Iron Works Studio, Chendrill feeling every muscle in his body hurt as he turned the wheel, especially his left leg and ankle as he used the clutch. Moving out into the inside lane, he put his foot down and listened to the Ferrari roar and go nowhere fast. Dan looked at him smirking. Then said, "Yeah, frustrating init." Then Dan said, "The way this sex machine drives, we'll be lucky if we get there tomorrow."

They arrived at three minutes past 7:00 a.m. and pulled up next to Sebastian, who was waiting in the carpark with the face of a man who's been forced to work a long weekend. He said, "You're late, Chuck."

Chendrill looked to his watch as he struggled to get out of the car. Sebastian wasn't wrong; he couldn't deny it. He said, "Yeah sorry, I had some problems."

And totally out of character, Sebastian said, "I've got problems too, Chuck. You're not the only one—I've got a sore back, but I made it in on time."

Then Dan piped up, passing them as he walked towards the caterers, "That's what happens when you stick governors on Ferraris."

******

Rann Singh pulled the key from his pocket and opened the door. He left the bedroom without looking back and locked it again from the hallway. Carrying the shotgun along, he walked out onto the deck and sat down on his grandfather's chair and stared at the mountains, now backlit by the sun as it began to light the morning sky to the east.

His back hurt in and around his kidneys. Those fucking pricks coming into his home with their *pangar* swords like they owned it. But they were dead and gone now, four of them at least, the big one that hit the dresser, maybe not. But there you go, he did warn them. He took a deep breath, the mountain air cooling his lungs, the sweat from the fight drying now on his back and brow, the taste of another man's blood still in his mouth.

That had been a fight, he thought, a good one. Those guys were strong, really strong and tough as old boots. Except the young one, poor guy going with them trying to be dangerous when he wasn't. Dead now, when he should have stayed down with a busted knee and arm like he'd told him. There you go, sometimes you don't know who you're fucking with. He felt calm now, incredibly calm. The shit with the zebra all forgotten, the South African off the hook—for now at least, unless Rann had a trip to the coast and saw him and the guy wasn't in any hurry to offer up an apology on account of having called him a *choot*, or for having given him the gift of a shotgun he knew no longer fired.

He closed his eyes and thought about what had just happened when less than ten minutes ago he'd been asleep in his bed. And for once, he remembered everything. No blacking out this time as he had so many times before when he'd lost his temper in the street or at the final of a martial arts tournament, when he'd come around on the mat, pinned down by coaches and officials with bloody noses, seeing carnage and his opponent knocked out on the floor as he looked around.

Then they'd banned him, barred him for life for winning a fight and awarded the trophy to the guy he'd left unconscious on the mat. A week after, the call had come asking him if he wanted to earn some money by getting into a cage with an animal—except the animal was a human who'd told his managers to go find someone who knows how to fight, telling them straight, "I don't want to fight no chump."

And in Rann went, entering the packed arena with a hanky covering his hair tied up on the center of his head, listening to the crowd roar with laughter, seeing the tough guy who didn't want to fight no chump standing around shaking his arms with his tattooed muscles and sweat and plastic girlfriends with their big fake titties stretching their T-shirts tight. Rann listened to the guy once the cage door closed as he called Rann a black, Paki, Indian cunt, and, as he posed for the cameras, told him how he was going to rip that hanky from his head and kill him. Then he came at him, swinging and charging and missing as Rann bobbed and weaved—the guy using up his strength trying to catch him, trying to put him down on the mat so as he could choke Rann out, then stand there triumphant with his hands in the air like a gladiator who'd killed another lion. But this time it was different. Rann moved fast, punishing the man's knees every time he came close with a lunge or a kick or a swipe—the bull of a man almost getting there but getting nowhere, full of sweat, getting frustrated and too full of steroids to move fast, using his mouth as a weapon, calling Rann a Paki cunt over and over until Rann had had enough of the animal's mouth and put his foot in it and then put another in his throat as he went down on his back and swallowed his tongue. Then Rann stood there watching as the officials and ambulance men tried to bring him round as the crowd screamed and yelled at him, telling him how they were now going to kill him if he'd killed their tattooed hero. And he had.

Then the next morning, the metropolitan police came to his grandfather's home to chat, only to find Rann gone along with his prize money.

He leaned back looking at the silent sky as the orange grew, remembering his grandfather's words, he wasn't wrong in not wanting to come here, and now he saw why. What if it had been him lying there in his bed with his grandmother when the men from the mountains came? What if Rann was out of town? What if his granddad were there slowly being carved up until he gave them the cash he'd been hiding away for a rainy day. The man was right—his life was there in the England now, living near the airport, watching soaps and listening to Radio 2 as the airplanes landed.

Then, as he leaned his head back, breathed deep and closed

his eyes, a calmness deeper than he'd ever known enveloped him as the now clear, once blacked out memories unfolded. Girls on his bed with their blonde hair, the dog he loved as a kid laying asleep with its head on his lap as it died, then seeing it running as fast as it could through the park. His parents holding each other and him before they took that ill-fated journey along the Great West Road and passed on. The kids at school bullying him all the time until he took himself off to the gym to learn how to defend himself and kept training night by night until they stopped.

Then he thought of Chendrill, laughing as he remembered the big fucker hitting him in the street, harder than he'd ever been hit, catching him unaware when he was thinking about pussy and knocking him to the ground. Then getting him back outside the fish restaurant and better still telling him he was a dumb fuck on the phone at the kinky guy's place who liked to dress up as a postman. And Rasheed, standing at the side of the busy road and pissing him off, the guy there getting all gangster with him and Rann getting mad when it didn't really matter now. He thought of Rasheed seeing his face and the anger in his eyes, the gangster looking scared and stepping back too close to the traffic and getting clipped by the passing truck that didn't stop. He remembered holding the man, seeing the light go from his eyes and seeing the smile on the idiot with the diamond in his tooth's face when he realized he had.

Then the Irishman was there in his mind, drunk and stinking of whisky at the top off those stairs with his girl who'd just been around with her friend and fucked his brains out. The Irishman getting greedy, trying to rip him off and writing on the picture of the King, then his girl there with him, shouting at him in a fury to stop in English and then in Thai—and he wasn't listening, telling her to fuck off and her getting angry, whipping her leg up fast hitting him in the chest twice like one of the prize fighting kickboxers he'd seen touring the bars of Bangkok, making the Irishman drop the pen and stumble back, his legs buckling under him as he tried to get air into his winded body, then one foot catching the edge of the stair slipping down, his body following, rolling over and over head to toe, his eyes looking up at Rann at the bottom and the man's girlfriend—or whatever she was, he or she—it didn't matter now—gone. At least he hadn't killed the man like he thought he had—or Rasheed for that matter; in fact, he hadn't killed anyone except the cage fighter and the guys in his bedroom he'd asked to leave after they'd just told him they were about to kill him.

Then he felt the pain in his back grow and wondered where Joseph was. He was thirsty and now remembered the African slamming him against the wall and feeling his small coat hook he'd used as a kid break off as it punctured his skin, leaving itself inside like a huge splinter to rip up his insides as he fought like he'd never fought before.

He looked to the mountains feeling his insides go numb as they bled and listened to the first people in the village wake, knowing Joseph would be along soon with his tea and he could tell him what had happened and ask him to call the police.

Then he looked back to the mountain, with its jagged range clawing at the sunrise as the sun began to rake its slopes, laying its rays across the treetops of the forest, catching the morning dew on the fields that were now his, fields that stretched all the way from the forest to the garden that the women from the village who his grandfather knew so well swept in the afternoon—and where his mother and father now stood, waiting for their only son to come join them.

Chapter Forty

Dan stepped inside Iron Works and wondered where the big green field was that he'd stood against before on the day Mazzi Hegan had starved him and nailed his feet to the floor, the day he'd met Marsha and punched out Philipe Tu La Monde for getting too familiar. Then he saw Mazzi Hegan standing on the other side of the open space around a movie type set talking with another guy who looked just like him.

Dan walked over as Mazzi saw him and, all flustered, said, "Oh my God, you're here. Sebastian's been going crazy since six!"

"Why? He said be here by seven and I was," Dan said as he watched Mazzi run his fingers through his hair and then the guy who looked just like him do exactly the same.

Mazzi said, "It's how he is, Dan. He gets all worked up on something and can't let it go." Then he said, "This is my friend Einer. He's over from Germany." And Einer said, sounding English, "Hey, glad to meet you, I thought you'd be bigger?"

Fuck you, Dan thought, then said, "Yeah and from over there I thought you were a girl."

Mazzi said, "Speaking of that, we need to get you sorted."

Then Dan saw her coming through the door with five people hanging all around her as she walked, eating a breakfast wrap and heading towards her personal Airstream trailer covered in chrome and positioned inside. Dan asked, "Who's that?"

And Einer replied, "It's Adalia Seychan. She's going to eat you for breakfast."

Looking for food, Dan walked about a bit hearing his mum's

flip-flops slap against the bottom of his feet as he wandered around on the concrete floor. He found a tray of pastries, in the craft service truck, took two, stuffed them down his throat and then another one before he felt the soft touch of Buffy holding his elbow. She said, "Dan, you're not supposed to eat."

Dan said, "I'm doing a photoshoot, not going for an operation."

"Mazzi says, we need to keep your stomach flat."

For fuck's sake, Dan thought. He said, "I just saw Adalia Seychan and she was eating."

Buffy said, "She's not taking her top off, Dan."

Dan said, "Well leave mine on as well then."

"That's not why you're here." Then she said quietly, holding his arm again as though she was doing him a favor, "Dan, get the shoot done then eat as much as you want, okay."

Thanks for fuck all, Dan thought, and wondered if the big girl had a boyfriend. Throwing her, he said, "I need to increase my body mass index—it's against the law to starve models these days."

Which was only half true, and was something he'd glimpsed from a newspaper Chendrill had left in the kitchen and the article was referring to a law recently passed in France, not Canada. And all Buffy said was, "Go call your lawyer."

They took him to makeup, where they washed his hair in a basin and faffed with him for twenty minutes until, in his eyes, he looked no different to how he'd looked when he'd went in. Then they escorted him to wardrobe where a guy who Mazzi used to know put him in a pair of tight shorts and said, "You look fabulous!" And giving him a bathrobe, aimed him out the door.

He spotted Sebastian sitting on a chair by the monitors and wondered what TV show the man could be watching at 7:30 a.m. in the morning and walked over to see the screen was blank. Sebastian looked at him and asked, "Did you get the shorts?"

He did, and they were too tight. Dan said, "Yeah but I can't feel my feet."

Sebastian smiled, that was perfect, he thought. If it all went well, he was going to use the footage for another pitch and had flown in a corporate representative of Mammoth Clothing to give them a taster of Dan in their shorts and hopefully of things to come. All things being equal, he was on for laying the foundations down for two campaigns that would cover the costs of Patrick's new ever-changing venture. He said, "I don't think it's a good thing you're talking with Mazzi's new friend."

Dan said, "Too late, I've already told him he looks like a girl."

Sebastian replied, "I know, Mazzi's upset."

Dan said, "Well Mazzi can fuck off, and tell him to tell his friend not to wear pink."

Then Sebastian asked, "Has Gill Banton been in touch?"

Dan stared at him. Then said, "Yeah, she said if I come work for her, she'd never have me in before eleven."

Sebastian replied, saying, "I doubt that darling." The woman was starting to concern him now, as the rumours were beginning to fly that she was so pissed off about losing out on Dan and about Marsha being poached that she was going to open offices along the road from Sebastian and flood it with talent. He asked again, "She's been in touch—yes or no?"

Dan thought about it, smiling at the memory of the last time he'd seen her and said, "No."

Sebastian said, "If she contacts you, you let me know okay?" Dan nodded, knowing that the last thing he was going to do was go running to phone Slave if anyone called him—and it wasn't because he would be looking for a better offer to advance his career. It was simply because he wouldn't be assed.

Then Sebastian said, "Have you read the script I sent? It's really short, but I thought it would be good to see if there's any chemistry between you and Adalia."

Dan thought about the chemistry between him and the woman he had in his bedroom a couple of nights back. He also hadn't read anything. He said, "No."

"What do you mean—No? You're saying you haven't read it?" Sebastian scoffed.

Dan stared at him a moment confused and then said, "What do you think I meant?"

"You're supposed to read it."

"Well I haven't." Sebastian stared at him in complete amazement. Dan said to him, "What you looking at me like that for? You're the one wanting me here. I didn't come banging on your door on the way home from acting school wanting to be a star."

Sebastian thought about it and frowned. The kid was right, they were leaning on him as though he was one of these driven go-getting cool boys that bludgeoned Slave's offices with their portfolio's full of pictures taken by parasite photographers who didn't have what it takes to get a real job and preyed on the hopeful. Dan didn't want to be there—and that's exactly why he was there. It was also why Mazzi had cancelled the trailer which had been ordered for him to relax in so he could stand all day and get pissed off and frustrated in his shorts that were too tight—it was the look he was after. Pulling some sides from his briefcase,

Sebastian said, "Well, read it for me now, please?"

Dan took them, skimming in a matter of seconds the three little pages pulled from Megan's script that amounted to a scene and handed them back, and said, "You changed it a bit?"

Sebastian had, but God knows how Dan could have known as he hardly looked at it; yes, he'd tinkered so to speak. It was a hobby he had that had started back in university in London when he and Alan had put on shows in the art house pub theatres over in trendy Camden town. Although the only thing he'd done in this one was have Dan in less clothing. He said, "Are you going to read it or not?"

Dan stared at him confused, "I did! You just saw me?"

******

Two hours later, Dan was still wandering around in his bathrobe looking for food and only being given water. Why the fuck he'd been gotten up so early and had to suffer Chendrill getting pissy at him, he didn't know. Finding an apple box, he sat down and stared across the building's vast interior at Adalia Seychan's personal Airstream trailer with its blacked-out windows and thought about the woman inside, probably sleeping on a huge bed with silk pillows and one of those night masks on her eyes. He looked around at some people doing stuff, but almost everyone else was just chatting and eating. Then Einer with his hair bleached blonde pulled up an apple box next to him and sat down. He said, "Had enough yet?"

You're kidding, Dan thought, and said, "What the fuck's going on."

As he looked at Hegan, futzing around a light with a guy in shorts. Einer saying, "It takes time to get it looking good."

Dan looked at the man, a little younger than Mazzi Hegan, with the same haircut, but rougher around the edges. He said, "All looks the same to me, I've been watching him switch things around—here there, up down." Mimicking Hegan in his best camp Mazzi Hegan voice, "Little something there, little something here."

Einer looked to the kid sitting there in his bathrobe and his mum's flip-flops. He wanted to give him a quick lesson in photography, but what was the point? In his eyes, the kid was probably as dumb as a plank but just looked good on film with his tight body and busted up face. He looked to Adalia Seychan's trailer and said, "I bet you'd like to be in there sorting her out? I know I would."

Dan looked to him confused, this Einer in a pink shirt who was 'friends' with Mazzi but had the hots for the Oscar-winning superstar? Einer said, without taking his eyes off the trailer, "Oh yeah, I could throw that bitch around the room."

And Dan said, "I thought you were a faggot."

Surprised, Einer looked at him, staring for a moment.

"Why'd you think that?"

Fucking hell, Dan thought, *try the pink shirt for one and the tight trousers and the hair like Hegan's*. He said, "Just did—maybe 'cos you're hanging with Mazzi Hegan staying over at his place." *And he's got that painting on the ceiling of his bedroom of a guy sucking another guy's dick.*

Einer nodding now, getting it, saying, "Yeah—well, you only see that if you lay down. Mazzi showed it to me, but no I'm not into guys. We're friends, he likes to party yeah, but no, I eat fish."

Dan looked at him and smiled and after the woman the other night giving him a face scrub, he understood exactly what he was saying. He said, "Oh?"

Einer nodding, looking at Dan then to the trailer, saying, "You ever been with an older woman?"

And as a matter of fact, he had—kind of.

******

They sat for an hour talking about women, Dan realizing the man was as far as he could tell a straight guy who hung with gay guys. It was the way he liked it, he said, "Gay guys have girlfriends— and I prey on them. Let them think I'm safe then next thing you know, they're digging me because I'm not."

Dan saying, "Why don't you just go to the bar and be normal?" Einer didn't have an answer.

Then Einer looked to the Airstream trailer again and after a moment said, "You know she wants you, don't you?"

"Who?" Dan asked.

"This chick, this superstar up from Hollywood for a test." Einer saying 'test' like it was the stupidest thing he'd ever heard. He carried on, "I'd say she's been looking at those posters of you Slave's put out there and when the chance came to be in the same building with you, then she jumped on it."

Dan said, "She walked right past me this morning and didn't even know I existed."

"Did Marshaa acknowledge you straight away?" Dan thought about it, remembering how she looked at him, the first time she'd ever laid eyes on him as she'd walked up on that stupid green stage, licked the sweat from his chest, and asked him to fuck her.

He said, "Yeah she did."

Einer said, "Yeah and look, you had the most beautiful woman in the world who could work anywhere and with anyone come here to work with you just because Sebastian showed her the photos they had of you in the elevator. You think this horny bitch in her trailer's not seen those posters out there? Got herself all wet and gooey downstairs and wondered what it would be like to feel you all over and have you slip it to her. She's not married, you know. She divorced her third husband last month; she's hot and primed and here for you."

Dan said, "Yeah, I had some woman come onto me the other night, said a similar thing. Except she kind off roughed me over and then my mum kicked her out."

Einer started to laugh and it was genuine, this 'straight' guy in a gay guy's clothes having fun. He said, "What, you're mum kicked her out?"

Dan said, "Yeah, she got me going just by saying dirty stuff, then I came in my pants and so she sat on my face and that's when my mum came in."

Einer nodded, still laughing quietly as he looked around, wondering and hoping no one else had heard Dan as the tears began to run down his cheeks. He said, "You got to take control Dan. It's got to be you that says, 'sit on my face, or, get on down there and start sucking'."

Dan said, "Yeah she did that an all."

Einer then stood and said, "You're a good kid Dan, I can see why they've got you here, you're honest." Then he said as he pulled a packet of Archall Diamond's pills he'd picked up for free on the beach from his pocket, "Take a couple of these now; then if she comes onto you, you won't have to worry about any unexpected accidents in your shorts, because regardless of what happens down there, these'll keep you as hard as a rock."

******

Sebastian wasn't happy. This man who'd been hanging out with Mazzi and disrupting him had been talking to Daniel for over an hour, chumming up with him, laughing and looking at Adalia's Seychan's trailer. Knowing that Dan hadn't read the script yet, Sebastian was thinking the worst.

Patrick arrived late, as producers often do, carrying on as though the shoot day was the last thing on their list. The guy coming in and taking over the studio with his grandiose hand gestures and laughter, sitting around the monitors, asking where Sebastian's dog Fluffy was and wondering why Mazzi was taking so long to get things up and running. It was his new friend, Sebastian had wanted to say, keeping him up all night clubbing— and he knew what time they'd been getting home. Belinda's driver, who worked the night shift, had been keeping him up to speed on that front, telling him where they'd been and the types of people they'd been with and how, strangely, there had been girls involved, which wasn't usually Mazzi's thing.

Then the corporate guy from Mammoth Clothing arrived. Sebastian smiled at him, playing the game, and wondered if he should introduce him to Dan, whom he'd been watching as he wandered around adjusting the bathrobe while he tried to scam food before going to the toilet every fifteen minutes. He said to the corporate guy, "I think you're going to like this a lot," putting the seed in the man's head before he had a chance to make up his own mind himself, "We're following on from the 'BlueBoy' campaign—maybe just going to have Daniel in only his shorts or shorts and a shirt, just that, keep it open. I'm glad you were able to make it up here—you know BlueBoy sales have tripled since the campaign started." The corporate guy looked around, being polite and keeping quiet, looking at the kid in the white bathrobe wandering about adjusting his crotch and wondering when he was going to meet Adalia Seychan so as he could call his wife and tell her.

Eventually they were ready, Sebastian giving Mazzi a look that told him he'd been taking too long, then telling him the set looked amazing, "Amazing absolutely amazing, Mazzi." Playing the game, when deep down he knew it was flat and the man's work was usually a lot better.

They all met at the monitor, Adalia in a beautiful silk wedding dress, Dan in his bathrobe, Sebastian hugging Adalia, telling her how beautiful she was looking and her taking it all on board, Patrick taking over before the corporate guy had a chance to chat, Adalia looking to Dan with his broken nose and eyes that were just healing now from being thumped out by Chendrill. She said to him with a smile, "Hello young man."

Dan nodded, "Hi," and hoped no one could see the erection in his pants through the robe, wondering what the hell the straight guy who pretended to be gay had just given him and why Sebastian was still fussing because he hadn't learned his lines.

They cleared out the workers and the important people walked to the set Mazzi had just lit, ready for the shoot, with its aisle and columns and the altar at the top—backlit through a fake stain glass window. Dan, wondering who the priest was; Adalia, taking over when Mazzi was supposed to be directing, said, "Let's get going then. Dan, I'll be here at the altar and you come rushing in and grab me from behind." And after they'd gone through the motions enough, they got down to it for a first take as they stood and sat around the monitors and watched Dan come in, crashing through the door of the set in his shorts and running down the aisle, grabbing Adalia, who was, surprisingly, crying on cue. Then he held her by the arms and twisted her around to face him, telling her with the maturity and depth of a grown man, "I wasn't ever not going to not be here, I'll never not be here. Never, ever not."

Then he grabbed her, holding her just as it had been described in the small cheesy script he'd glanced at and cast aside, and then let her go as he heard Adalia say through the tears in her eyes, "Henry?"

Then he kissed her again, holding her to him, Adalia holding him back, feeling his bare skin tight beneath her hands and his dick rock solid beneath his shorts against her leg.

She held him there and looked him in the eye and then glanced down as she pulled away, looking at his penis squashed to the side underneath the tight fabric of his Mammoth shorts as though it was indicating that he was about to turn right.

Adalia stared into his eyes and still in character said, "You got to be kidding me, right?"

That's not in the script, Dan thought, but went with it, skipping the next line and improvising, remembering a slushy movie his mother had made him watch as a kid and repeating the lines and the man's actions verbatim, holding her by the wrists, making her look him in the eye as he spoke, "No, I'm here because I love you and can't ever stop loving you."

Adalia, holding his stare, looking into his eyes as she tried not to look at his crotch, not knowing what to do as he carried on, "You are mine, no one else's, I'll never let you go." Then remembering another line he'd heard as he looked up to the television one day when he was six as he'd sat on the floor playing with his toys—his mother home after finishing a night shift at the hospital, sleeping on the sofa, not getting to the end of the movie she'd been looking forward to seeing, as the guy on the screen held the woman, looking into her eyes just as Dan was holding Adalia and repeating what he'd seen and heard as a young boy with exactly the same passion.

"You marry this man, I'll disappear and never come back,

you'll never know I existed. But if you don't and marry me, I'll give up everything, everything I've ever had and worked for and in doing so it'll mean I have everything—because I'll have you."

This kid there before her with his broken nose talking to her in character, her, thirty years his senior, him, a boy on the outside, but inside a man.

Still feeling his erection pressed against her leg, Adalia gave in to temptation and looked to Dan's dick and then to Sebastian and said, "I can't work like this."

And stormed off towards her trailer with her wedding dress tail dragging behind her. Dan watched her leave, then, looking to Sebastian, said, "Can I go home now?"

As far as Mazzi Hegan was concerned, he could, because he and Einer had had their cameras out and you were never going to get anything better than what they'd just shot.

An older woman in a wedding dress almost at the altar and a handsome young man holding her back as she struggled, trying not to look at the erection in his tight shorts as he fought to make her hear his words, trying to make her listen, as she turned away unable to look any longer, then storming off without looking back in a beautiful silk gown, leaving him there at the altar naked in a pair off Mammoth shorts. Perfect.

With a little help from his friend, this time Mazzi had struck again—and what he had was golden.

An hour later, Sebastian wasn't sure what to do. He had Adalia in her trailer, refusing to talk, Mazzi happy as pie, Patrick oblivious to it all, and the corporate guy from Mammoth wondering when he was going to get a chance to talk to the superstar.

He looked at Dan back in his bathrobe, sitting back on the

apple box, and wondered where Chuck Chendrill was when he needed him? The friend had given him something to make the kid's penis that big he was sure, he'd seen something going on, the guy pulling something from his pocket then Dan going off and swigging down some water. He walked over, wondering if he should get the young boy some ice to put on his penis. Putting his arm on his shoulder he said, "Daniel, can I speak?" Dan nodded as Sebastian bent down and Mazzi started shooting again, seeing a young man sitting while the older crouched next to him. Sebastian said, "Daniel, I heard you deliver those lines, you were teasing me when you said you hadn't read the scene weren't you?" He wasn't.

Dan said, "I got lucky."

Sebastian carried on adjusting his feet, "You delivered them well. I think you surprised us all."

And Dan said, surprising Sebastian, "So did she, she's really good."

And then the door to Adalia's trailer opened and her personal assistant came out and spoke to Buffy first before pulling Sebastian aside as Buffy said, "Adalia doesn't feel like she should do any more today with Dan, but she was very impressed with his performance. She understands he is young and that she's a beautiful woman and these things happen, and she'd like to speak with him to clear the air and spend the rest of the day with the pair of them running through the script together as she feels he has a lot of potential."

Dan was almost at the food truck and about to grab a huge piece of cake, hoping he was finished and about to see Chendrill or Belinda come around the corner to take him home safely, when Buffy grabbed him and told him about Adalia's request. "You got to be kidding" he said.

Buffy said, "Dan it's not even lunch yet, we've only been here five hours?"

And off he went, still in his bathrobe. Buffy knocked on the trailer door and handed Dan her script as Dan stepped inside and Adalia's assistant stepped out.

Adalia sat alone at a desk as though she was at home, out of costume. Dan looked at her, then at the windows to the crew outside, as usual, doing nothing but eating, wondering how it was he could see out and no one could see in. Adalia said, "You read well, Daniel."

Thinking all he needed was another one calling him by his given name, Dan said, "You ain't so bad yourself."

She replied, "I know I didn't say much but after a while you don't need to, you can convey as much as you need with just a look." Then taking a deep breath, she looked to the floor for a moment and then back to Dan as her eyes began to smile as though she was just seventeen all over again and she said, "And Daniel, I want you to know that it's not often a woman in her fifties has a young man like you as attracted to her as you were earlier, even if I am famous. I know I took off like some crazy diva, but the truth is I'm flattered."

Dan stayed quiet, waiting for a 'But' to come as he looked at her bare feet sneaking out from the bottom of her casual wear designer dress. Then she said, "Like I said before, you read well, Dan very well. It was brief, but I've been around the block long enough to spot talent. Have you been to acting school?"

Dan smiled and said, "No it comes naturally, when you eat as much as me you need to be able to bullshit when the fridge is empty."

Adalia smiled, walking over to him, and said, "Dan can I ask you something personal?" Dan nodded and, from the way she was looking at him, could feel his already swollen penis get another influx of blood, as she said, "Are you a virgin, Dan?"

And stumbling for words Dan said, "Well there's been some—you know girls—and there was this blind girl in the park, but her dog bit me…" Adalia came closer and placed her hands on his shoulders and said, "Do you do drugs, Dan?"

And taking a deep breath Dan shook his head and, for once, not lying said, "Never."

Then Adalia kissed him above his eyes and said, "Daniel earlier today, you made me feel young again. You made me feel sexy." And she also wasn't lying, showing off his huge boner on set and not worrying or being self-conscious when ninety-nine percent of men would have run and hid. The boy was innocence in its simplest form. He obviously liked her, she liked him and it had been a long time since a young man had shown such honesty.

And holding him by the hand, she led him to the bed nestled in to the side of the million-dollar trailer and laid herself down in a place as familiar to her as her own home, pulling him to her as she whispered, "I'm going to teach you all I know Daniel. I'm going to show you how—and make you a man."

And Dan said, "Well don't sit on my face because if you do my mum's going to get angry."

But Adalia wasn't listening to much, just snippets of his words reaching her mind as she took off his bathrobe and ran her hands up and down his stomach, whispering into his ear as she went, "Our secret, Daniel our secret, let me show you the way." Then he watched as she slipped off her dress and felt her hand on the outside of his shorts, stroking him with her hand as her other held his back. Feeling his body begin to tremble, his arms and shoulders shaking as he held himself above her, smelling the perfume in her hair as she took him out with her hand and, opening her legs, slipped him inside of her as he instinctively began to jerk his pelvis back and forth slowly at first then pounding fast and faster as he heard her gasp seconds later as he came so fast even he couldn't believe it was over.

But it wasn't because Adalia held him there feeling him still hard inside her, she leaned up and kissed him on the cheek and said, "You've made love to me as a boy, but in the future. I'm going to show you how to make love to me the way a man would."

And after feeling her ex-husband's fat gut squash her as they made love for so many years, she knew this would be her last chance in life to feel young again, so she would show him and she would show him well, but that wasn't the only guidance Adalia Seychan had planned for the young man who'd just delivered a flawless performance without direction off the back of a ramshackle blocking with no rehearsal, unwavered by the fact that he was unable to hide his natural bodily functions. And as she'd sat back in her personal Airstream trailer brought up all the way from Hollywood for the day, pretending to be miffed she had decided to make him a star.

Chapter Forty-One

Archall Diamond was king of the hill. At least his hill. He had his hard-on tablets that worked just fine, he had his tooth that made him look fine, he'd floated the ape, and he had his mate. *Yeah—That was a good one,* he thought as he sat in the cab of his truck, looking out and dreaming of the future.

He'd been at the dentist's house at first light after not sleeping well, worrying about how he could still look cool and lift Alla into the cab of his semi-monster truck at the same time. The Gangster/Rapper knowing he'd be struggling to curl eighty pounds at the gym and the girl had to be a hundred pounds plus even if she was thin. If he still had the Mercedes, he'd be cool.

Archall Diamond waiting now for the dentist to go out so he could steal the man's girl. Getting ready as he did, looking at his new tooth sparkle in the mirror and doing his hair as he played with the two hundred thousand in the sports bag sitting on the passenger seat he was going to show Alla he'd put aside just for her, so as she could walk again.

He finished preening and sat there staring at the house—the dentist would leave soon. Alla telling him earlier her husband would be going out in the morning after he'd called and told her he had the cash and he'd pay for the operation—Alla not believing him, but hoping it would be true.

His wisdom teeth were hurting now though, even if the dentist said they were already out—what did he know though? Yeah, he'd had some teeth out a while ago, but they were at the back. Besides all that could wait, after today he'd be needing to find a new dentist anyway. A real one.

Half an hour passed as Archall Diamond waited until eventually he saw the side door open and the dentist leave carrying a small rucksack. He waited, making sure the guy wasn't coming back. Then, taking his bag, he walked along the road, knocked on the door and waited again. After a few minutes, he called out his new girl's name, following it up with, "I've got the money for your operation!"

And then he saw her through the window looking frustrated as she wheeled herself along through the basement looking up at him as he held the bag full of money up for her to see through window of the door. As she opened it up, she said, "God has sent you to me."

They went back to his house, Archall Diamond driving, feeling embarrassed that he'd not been able to lift his new girl out of the chair and into the cab like they do in the movies. Alla holding his hand looking at its size with the money on her lap and wondering if he had a family as they passed the terracotta lions guarding the gate. Feigning delight and smiling as he struggled once again to lift her from the cab and carefully place her in her wheelchair. Pushing her up the same scaffold boards he'd used to drag Chendrill into the trucks rear the night before, utilizing them again quickly to make an improvised ramp up to the front door. Archall saying to her as he wheeled her inside,

"Welcome to your new home."

Alla looked around at the mess with the cereal all over the floor, hearing the cocoa pops crunching under the wheels of her chair as she went, wondering what the hell she was doing, the guy was a moron, but she'd seen worse and he had what she needed right now. As soon as she was in the hospital with his money in their bank, she could forget his name and maybe call Dennis— maybe. For now though, this Archall Diamond was king of the hill, with his new girl and he'd sat quietly with her on the way over after stopping in the same parking lot of the shopping mall as he'd used to prepare Chendrill for his voyage. Archall Diamond listening and looking out the window as she'd called the private hospital to speak to the back surgeon who her husband had taken her to see—the guy with the slick hair only interested in money. The man at the top of his game, limiting now his *pro bono* freebies down to children and teens, the goodwill beaten out of him by ex-wives and years of charity work in remote villages that stunk of faeces, doing surgery on children only to be stoned as the convoy left.

"Two hundred thousand will get you on your feet" he'd said as he leaned forward and held her by the hand, ignoring her beautiful eyes, the guy was no fool—not like Archall Diamond, who thought he was her soulmate. And all she needed to do now was hand over the bag of cash and book herself in.

She moved herself around the downstairs of the monster home and, picking up his house phone, called the hospital for a second time and waited on hold as she looked about at the bad, harsh-colored décor and wondered if she'd ever been inside a Sikh's home before—not that she cared, as in her mind she'd only be in this one for as long as it took her to convince him to take her into town and check her into the hospital, even if it meant she'd have to give the guy a blow job first.

Spinning her chair, she looked at a picture of Rasheed on the wall, sporting a turban and holding his girl in a beautiful sari wondering if the guy was Archall's brother as she listened to Archall as he began to sing in the kitchen, hearing him bellow out, "Archall Diamond the man with his mind on—standing in the kitchen—man's got nothing missen—girl in the back room gonna get her fixed soon—people gonna see her beau-I-tee when she out in the street wit me—passing through the neighborhoods people staring like they should—'cos she with Archall Diamond, the man wit his mind on."

✶✶✶✶✶✶

Alla put down the phone as she heard the guy singing to himself like he had for the last hour, wishing she was back at home with Dennis—at least he looked after her. It was all arranged. All she needed to do was tell them when and a private ambulance would be there to pick her up. Dr. Dawson was away in the States performing surgery, but as soon as he was back and free, he had said he would perform the first operation. The second would need to be a later depending on x-rays.

Then she'd ditch this fool before the hockey season even started up again—this guy wanting her for her looks and not even knowing her birthday. She called to Archall, still rapping in the other room, looking at himself in the mirror. And when he arrived she said, "Could you help me into the bathroom please."

As she felt him come up behind her and begin to push, she continued, "I just spoke with the hospital. They said if I get there today, then I'll be out and walking again in time for the start of the hockey season."

Cool, thought Archall, wondering what her ass would look like standing up—hoping she'd be able to wear high heels with jeans and, getting so turned on by the thought of it, pulled out a packet of his hard-on tablets and wacked a whole six straight back whilst Alla watched, looking up at him smiling, hoping he comes through and hands over the cash in advance like the private hospital had stipulated when she'd called.

He helped her off the chair and onto his downstairs toilet, and left her on the seat closing the door and giving her the room she needed to pull down the track pants Dennis had bought her to keep her legs warm. Then walked back down the corridor, calling out as he did saying, "While you on the shitter, I gonna get the cocoa pops and show you that trick I told you about. You'se gonna love it!"

Archall Diamond the man with his mind on, multitasking, putting another rap song together in his head as he walked away and spoke, singing out some lines and half humming the rest as the lyrics came together.

"Archall Diamond—de man with his mind on—they gonna get to see me soon. Got the girl in the bathroom—going in the main room—gonna get her fixing—then I get a mixing—gonna get the new car—don't wanna have her bitchin—Chendrill in da kitchin."

Chendrill in the kitchen, pulling his fist back and punching Archall Diamond straight in the face, knocking him out cold on the floor.

******

Chendrill had dropped off Dan without getting out and headed back to Trish's house as promised, surprised that no one had yet noticed he didn't have any shoes on his feet. Getting out, he let himself in, smelled the freshly cooked bacon as soon as he opened the door, pulled off his trousers as instructed by Trish, and sat there in the kitchen at the table in just a clean pair of underpants as Trish looked at the heavy bruising on his legs and ankles, the skin rubbed through still bloody as she dabbed it with a hot flannel. She said, "You need to go to the hospital with this."

Chendrill agreed, but knew he never would as he felt her dress his wounds and bind him up. Trish looked up at him, knowing from his eyes and fatigue that something bad had gone down; and later, as she watched him in her bed twitch in his sleep, she thanked God silently that he was alive.

He'd woken up around five, finding it hard to stand, and thanked his girl, telling her he'd be back later. He took a cab to Dennis', grabbed another pair of boots, gloves, and a screwdriver from the trunk of the Aston, and drove out to the airport where he bought a ticket for the long stay carpark. There he found himself a van and, hitting the screwdriver hard into the door and ignition locks, headed straight out to Surrey to look for Archall Diamond. He slipped in past Archall's truck and crushed Mercedes and through the back door, just as he heard him walking back along the corridor rapping after leaving Alla; then, giving the man with the diamond in his tooth that had floated him enough time to register that he was back, he punched the fucker in the jaw so hard he wondered if the man would ever wake up. Feeling the pain in his legs burn, he picked the gangsta off the floor, slung him over his shoulder, marched him outside, and threw him hard into the back of the van.

******

Alla sat there on the toilet feeling helpless with a huge knot in her stomach. She'd listened to Archall as he walked along the corridor singing and humming out the tunes to whatever dumb rap song he was concocting and had heard the cold hard snap of the hit, then his groan as he hit the floor, and then the movement of Archall being picked up and taken away as the door slammed behind him. She'd been around violence enough to know the sounds. It was always fast and vicious and seldom as swift as the way Archall had been taken or the man who had hit her and broken her spine.

She sat there listening to the sound of a vehicle starting up outside and driving away and then all she could hear was herself. *Oh my God no*, she thought, *don't take him just yet please wait, just wait till she was at the hospital with that bag of cash he'd promised her*. But no, he was gone. Leaning over, Alla reached her wheelchair and pulled it to her, locked the wheels and lifted herself in. Pulling the door open with her right hand, she wheeled herself out into the hall.

She reached the kitchen and looked around, there was no sign of a struggle—but there hadn't really been one. She carried on, her wheels crunching cocoa pops as she went, and reached the living room and began searching around for the bag—it wasn't in there. She hit the study and looked around, just a bag on the shelf of a book cabinet standing tall against the wall.

Shifting herself to one side and leaving herself room to get out, Alla placed both hands behind the side of the cabinet and gripping its light plywood rear, sent it crashing to the ground spilling Rasheed's books and papers everywhere across the room. She wheeled forward, pushing herself up on one side as she bumped up on top of some books, reached down, and grabbed the bag. Empty.

Alla moved on back out into the hallway and, reaching the staircase, looked up at the two flights that led to the bedrooms. She'd seen him go up there with that bag, she thought. Archall Diamond, calling out like a little kid to her to wait there as he ran up to the bedroom, as though she could go anywhere else.

Alla spun the chair around, positioning it as close to the bottom of the staircase as she could and, using the handrail, pulled herself out onto the stairs. One step at a time, she began to pull herself up with her arms as her soft toned legs dragged behind her.

In incredible pain, covered in sweat and with tears in her eyes, she reached the top and began to drag herself along the carpeted hallway. Reaching the bathroom, she looked inside at the towels and cocoa pops on the floor. Then she carried on, dragging her body to the next bedroom and, stretching herself up, opening the door. Nothing, empty. She hit the next room, the same, then she reached the master bedroom with its door open and the light still on. And there was Archall's bag sitting on the center of the bed, clothes everywhere, and more cocoa pops on the floor around the mirror.

Alla pulled herself up and peered over the top of the bed and although still in great pain, began to smile as she saw one half of the bed was slept in and the other along with the bag was covered in small packets of tablets and cash.

It was almost ten minutes later before she'd got back down the stairs, throwing the bag into which she'd stuffed all the money and packets of tablets down to the bottom and surfing down after it like a kid whose mum wasn't watching. She reached the bottom and pulled herself back up and into her wheelchair.

Clutching the bag to her chest, Alla opened the front door and steadily maneuvered herself down the scaffold plank ramp and out and along the darkness of the street until she reached its end. Stopping on a corner and waving her arms, she flagged down the first car she saw with a woman driving. She looked up at the lady who had stopped as she got out and hurried around to see if she was okay, and then, with her eyes full of tears and clutching the bag with over two hundred and fifty thousand dollars in it that she'd just stolen from Archall Diamond, she cried like a wounded deer and said, "My husband just left me here—I'm so sorry, I'm so sorry—I'm pregnant and I need to get to the hospital."

******

Chendrill stuck the electrodes of Archall Diamond's Taser gun into Archall's thigh and woke the man up. Then watching him as he came around, he said, "Archall Diamond—the man with his mind on?"

Archall looked around, wondering where he was and how he'd managed to end up handcuffed to the steering wheel of a family van. Then he saw Chendrill and the car inner tube pumped up and stuck between his knees. Chendrill carried on saying, "Tell me about the birdman—Paawan Gill."

"Never fucking heard of him," Archall Diamond said, rubbing his face with his free hand and showing off his front tooth and then realizing it wasn't there anymore.

Chendrill said, "He's the guy who you went to school with and used to throw himself under freight trains for a hobby to show off in front of you and your friends, except when you tried to copy him, you pissed your pants with fear. He's also the guy who was fucking your girl and the same guy you stuck in an inner tube and threw into the Fraser as the tide was going out with a chain around his legs. That Paawan Gill in case you forgot. And if you're wondering where that stupid tooth is, it's in the ashtray."

Archall Diamond stared at the big man, wondering how the fuck he'd survived as he looked around outside to see they were parked at the front of a small docking pier on a thin tributary of the Fraser River. Then he turned back to see Chendrill open the ashtray, pull his tooth out, show him, and then throw it on the dash. He said, "It fell out when I punched you in the mouth."

As he felt the gap in his teeth again with his tongue, Archall said back, "I'se never put you in the river."

Chendrill smiling and saying back, "I never said I'd been in the water, so how did you know I had? But we haven't even gotten to me yet."

"I never did nothing."

Chendrill sat there looking at the man who had nearly drowned him, the guy handcuffed to the steering wheel of the family van he'd stolen, neither of them going anywhere fast. Chendrill said, "It's pretty quiet around here. We could sit here till dawn if you want and wait till someone walking his dog sees you crying for help and calls the police."

Archall looked out the window to the small dock and then to the inner tube. He didn't need the police involved. *Fuck that, no way*. Then he said, "You gonna throw me in there?"

"No, you are going to tell me what you did to the birdman and then you are going to throw you in there," Chendrill said as he sat there now himself talking like the Diamond, then he said, "Or like I said we can wait till the sun comes up."

He stared at Archall, sitting there keeping as far from Chendrill as he could with his arm stretched out.

"So, what did you do to Paawan Gill?"

Archall stayed quiet. Chendrill leaned over and gave the Diamond another wallop with the Taser set on stun and heard the man scream out in pain, then waited for him to stop. He held the Taser up for him to see.

"It's a long time till sun up. If you think this hurts, you try it when it's on the other incapacitation setting, that really fucks you up, you should give it a go, see how it feels. Or you can start telling me about your girlfriend's lover. And once you tell me, I'll let you go and you can walk straight to the end of that dock, jump in and swim to the other side and we can call it quits. Or you can try and run and I'll catch you and bring you in for trying to murder me. I've got witnesses that saw you shoot me with this Taser and then take me away in your truck and dump me in the water."

Archall Diamond sat there taking it all in, thinking that there hadn't been anyone around, not a soul—no one had seen. The man was full of shit. Wishing he had killed him properly like a real gangster would have instead of being a chicken shit and letting the ocean do it, he said, "What witnesses you got?"

Chendrill said, "Well, for a start, there's you and there's me and the guy in the house opposite your friend the dentist and there's your girlfriend, Alla. The pretty one you can't keep your eyes off."

Archall started to worry now shifting in his seat, wondering if it was true, and wondering too if Alla was still stuck on the toilet where he'd left her. He said, "Alla not seen nothing."

And Chendrill said, "But, like I say, it's not about you and me—that's not important, that's—'Water under the bridge.' It's like I say, about Paawan Gill, the birdman. I'm not a cop you know that, I just want to know what happened. Then you can go swim across the river and I'll let you take your chances the same way you let me, except I won't wrap your legs in chains and put holes in the tubes the way you did."

Archall looked at the water. The river bank on the other side was only three hundred feet away at the most, he could do it easy, he was a good swimmer, he'd fallen off the back of his boat enough to know that. The Ape here, trying to get tough like The Diamond but not having the guts to get the chains out and go the whole nine yards. He could run the dock, dive in keep hold of the tube, and if he got pulled out he'd sit out there with just his ass in its center and wait, the tide was changing soon, he knew the times and when it did it'd bring him back home, he could treat it as a holiday. Getting all gangster, he said, "Yeah birds like the sky so the Diamond floated the birdman, I squashed him under de Mercedes and then I see if he could swim."

Chendrill smiled, and said, "Who, Paawan Gill?"

Archall nodded now, liking the feeling of showing he wasn't afraid, he said, "Yeah Paawan Gill the guy who could fly but couldn't swim, didn't like to get wet. I'se floated the fucker. Now let me out of this family van before I's get broody, so as I can get to the other side of this river."

Then Chendrill leaned forward and, taking Archall's phone off the dash, handed it to him along with his tooth. He said,"You can keep this, but you'll see it's been recording our chat. If you try to run and throw it in, I'll catch you and find it and hand it in along with everything else I know. You dive in and the water will erase it all if you're lucky."

Archall looked back towards the water and the bank on the other side lit up by the full moon, yeah, he could do it he thought, this clown got out of it and he was unconscious and trussed up like a stuck pig. Then he heard the loud click of the family van's central locking system open as Chendrill opened the door for him. Archall looked to the door then to the phone to see it was still recording. It was. He switched it off as he felt the cuff release as Chendrill unlocked it. He said, "You's keeping your'se word— you letting me go?"

Chendrill shrugged saying, "You let me go."

Suspicious, Archall Diamond opened the door and looked around, expecting to see a SWAT team of RCMP officers and a helicopter come swooping in with its search light, and to hear some guy with a megaphone shouting, "Diamond, put your hands in the air and step away from the family van with the kid's seat in the back." But there was nothing out there other than a dock that ran away from the door and water and moonlight. Chendrill had positioned the van well, Archall thought, as he looked further around, the only way to get to land was through him or to jump from the dock into the water and try to climb out along the bank to where the big fucking ape would be waiting.

He stepped out, put his phone and tooth in his pocket, and, reaching in, pulled out the inner tube as he heard Chendrill say with real concern in his voice, "Archall, it looks easy but you're going to drown. Get back in the van and let me take you to the police station and if you tell them everything you've done, you'll get off lightly and be back out telling everyone how you dumped me in the drink and looking cool by the time you're in your thirties. They'll even fix your tooth for free."

Archall stared at him, looking at the man in his Aerostar,

trying to make it look as though he's doing him a favor, putting the Diamond in jail when all he has to do is swim.

Archall said, "You think you better than me—you don't think I can swim?"

Chendrill shaking his head saying, "Not like me, no." And wishing he'd taken him in straight to the nearest police station and dealt with it properly instead of playing games, he lifted the Taser quickly and tried to shoot him as Archall slammed the door shut and ran along the dock as fast as he could with the inner tube in his arms and jumped out and into the river, the water's cold chill enveloping him as he went under. He felt the current pull him away with his arms above him still clinging as tightly as he could to the inner tube.

Then he surfaced and looked around, seeing Chendrill there standing at the end of the dock now in the distance watching as he floated away. Spinning his body around, Archall Diamond looked to the bank on the other side, now only a hundred feet away or so, keeping his head above water with his right arm around the tube he began to scramble towards it, kicking and lashing out with his free arm and then letting go of the tube he went for it, swimming like a crazy man kicking and splashing both arms into the water in front of him heading against the current as it pulled him along towards the shore now only some twenty feet in front of him. Powering on, he thrashed his arms and legs, seeing the bank in front of him now only feet away as he reached out still kicking, trying to grab hold of the grass and rocks on the bank, then suddenly there was no shore.

Archall stopped swimming and looked around him feeling the cold water hitting his face, it's salt stinging his eyes as he bobbed up and down, treading water in the swell. He was moving fast in the riptide, the land way off now, too far to swim against the current that was taking him further away by the second. Chendrill was way away now somewhere back down the river. He felt himself rise again in the water and saw the inner tube floating further out in the distance. That's it, he thought, get the tube and wait just as he had planned. Thrusting forward, he began to swim with the riptide out to sea, lifting one arm after the other over and over, kicking his feet in a regular motion feeling his body work with the tide, his cupped hands slapping the cold dark water and pulling him forward with every stroke as he thought about reaching the inner tube where he could climb in and wait for the tide to turn, his head lifting to the side reaching out of the sea for air as his left hand swooped above pulling him up, his body moving in sequence as his mouth opened drawing in a deep breath of salty air past his missing tooth and into his lungs as he stretched out his feet behind him. His legs powering him forward towards the tube and out to sea as he thought about Alla, his new girl and what she'd look like with him in his car and how sexy she'd look at a hockey game with everyone looking at her tits and her beautiful face and her eyes and her sexy legs, and how they'd both laugh as he played cocoa pop games with his dick in the kitchen. Then in the cold of the water as his mind whirled around with thoughts of his new girl, who was so beautiful he felt his dick, still half hard in his pants from the packet of tablets he'd popped earlier in the kitchen, start to rise. And there it sat, sticking out and pointing downward towards the ocean bed in his loose basketball shorts, like a rudder, engorged with blood, keeping him nice and steady as he powered on out to sea, Rock Solid.

The end.

With many thanks to Justin Gouin.

Paul Slatter grew up in London, England and now lives in both Canada and Thailand.

He is married and has four children.

CPSIA information can be obtained
at www.ICGtesting.com
Printed in the USA
LVHW112202020919
629734LV00001B/22/P